PENGUIN BOOKS

The Library of War and Peace

Louise Morrish is a librarian whose debut novel won the 2019 Penguin Random House First Novel Competition. She finds inspiration for her stories in the real-life adventures of women in the past, whom history has forgotten. She lives in Hampshire with her family.

By the same author

Operation Moonlight
Women of War

The Library of War and Peace

LOUISE MORRISH

PENGUIN BOOKS

PENGUIN BOOKS

UK | USA | Canada | Ireland | Australia
India | New Zealand | South Africa

Penguin Books is part of the Penguin Random House group of companies
whose addresses can be found at global.penguinrandomhouse.com

First published 2026

001

Copyright © Louise Morrish, 2026

The moral right of the author has been asserted

Penguin Random House values and supports copyright.
Copyright fuels creativity, encourages diverse voices, promotes freedom
of expression and supports a vibrant culture. Thank you for purchasing
an authorized edition of this book and for respecting intellectual property
laws by not reproducing, scanning or distributing any part of it by any
means without permission. You are supporting authors and enabling
Penguin Random House to continue to publish books for everyone.
No part of this book may be used or reproduced in any manner for the
purpose of training artificial intelligence technologies or systems. In accordance
with Article 4(3) of the DSM Directive 2019/790, Penguin Random House
expressly reserves this work from the text and data mining exception.

Set in 12.5/14.75pt Garamond MT
Typeset by Falcon Oast Graphic Art Ltd
Printed in Great Britain by Clays Ltd, Elcograf S.p.A.

The authorized representative in the EEA is Penguin Random House Ireland,
Morrison Chambers, 32 Nassau Street, Dublin D02 YH68

A CIP catalogue record for this book is available from the British Library

ISBN: 978–1–405–96776–1

Penguin Random House is committed to a sustainable future
for our business, our readers and our planet. This book is made from
Forest Stewardship Council® certified paper

For my sons, Andrew and William,
and for all my fellow librarians, past, present
and future.

CUNARD LINE

The Quadruple-Screw Turbine Steamers
LUSITANIA and MAURETANIA
the Fastest Steamers in the World.

✦ ATLANTIC SERVICES ✦

NEW YORK ⚓ LIVERPOOL

LUSITANIA and MAURETANIA call at
Queenstown *Westbound*, and Fishguard *Eastbound*.

1ST MAY 1915

NOTICE!

Travellers intending to embark on the Atlantic voyage are reminded that a state of war exists between Germany and her allies and Great Britain and her allies; that the zone of war includes the waters adjacent to the British Isles; that in accordance with formal notice given by the Imperial German Government, vessels flying the flag of Great Britain, or of any of her allies are liable to destruction in those waters and that travellers sailing in the war zone on ships of Great Britain or her allies do so at their own risk.

Imperial German Embassy

I

Josie – Atlantic Ocean

The RMS *Lusitania*'s first-class library is a precious sanctuary. While the passengers are finishing their four-course lunch in the dining saloon, Josie Everley, the sole library stewardess on board, has the place briefly to herself. She ought to be tackling a heinous list of chores, but instead she's perched on a velvet armchair, half hidden behind a fake marble Corinthian column, head in her hands. Ever since the ship left New York this morning, she's struggled to hold herself together. But now, for a brief moment, she can let her guard down. Her body trembles with the effort not to scream.

Nico's abandonment feels like a kick in the guts. The absence of her sweetheart on this particular crossing, of all the crossings they've worked on together, hurts even more. How could he leave her when she was still reeling from the loss of her mother?

In her mind's eye, she relives the departure from New York earlier that morning. Some unknown crisis had delayed the *Lusitania*'s sailing by a couple of hours, resulting in more than usually chaotic docks teeming with passengers and porters, cabs, carriages and crew. By the time the ship was ready to sail, Pier 54 had become crowded with overwrought people, weeping and embracing and waving handkerchiefs.

Josie had waited for Nico in their usual spot, at the bottom of the gangway that led to the crew entrance. They always boarded together, to register with the chief steward. Then, a quick, surreptitious kiss before they went their separate ways, Nico to the men's quarters, then on to his post in baggage, Josie to her shared cabin to deposit her small suitcase, and then on to the library. Josie's brother Jem had already signed on and disappeared into the ship to begin his shift. She'd given him a last brief hug, praying that this, Jem's first voyage, would go smoothly and the other baggage stewards would look out for him. She'd heard nightmare rumours of the crew down below playing cruel pranks on the new hands, even locking them into the hold.

Nico should have been with Jem, showing him the ropes, but the minutes had ticked by and still he hadn't appeared. Josie had grown more and more worried. The final call for boarding came, and she was about to give up, when at last Nico had appeared, pushing through the crowd. He wasn't wearing his steward's uniform, and had no luggage with him.

'Josie . . .' Nico was breathing hard, face flushed. 'You waited . . . thank God . . .'

'Where've you been?' Josie had snapped. 'Where's your stuff? Hyde's going to skin us if we don't board right now.'

'We can't.' Nico had taken hold of her arm, tugging her away from the gangway.

'What?' Josie had pulled free. 'What're you talking about?'

'Where's Jem?'

'On board,' Josie said, through gritted teeth. 'Where we should be.'

'It's not safe, Jo. We can't ignore the warnings no more.' He'd brandished a newspaper clipping, a missive from the German Embassy that Josie had seen before.

'It's just war games,' she'd replied, with more confidence than she truly felt. 'Scare tactics.'

'It's serious, Jo! It's getting really dangerous out there with the U-boat threat. Cunard shouldn't be ignoring the signs.'

'We've no choice, Nico.'

'There's always a choice.'

Josie had swallowed a curse, barely holding her anger in check. 'You might have a choice, Nico,' she'd managed, 'but some of us don't. If I lose this job, I won't get another on the ships, and then what'll happen to me and Jem?'

'We've talked about this,' Nico had argued. 'If you won't listen to me, then . . .' His voice had been eclipsed by the ship's whistle, mustering all crew aboard. They had seconds left.

'Then what?' Josie had pressed.

Nico had met her gaze, and Josie's heart had stuttered. 'Then it's the end, Jo.'

She took a breath. 'The end of us?' How could he leave her? Apart from Jem, he was all she had. They'd sailed together on the liners for six years now, and she couldn't imagine a voyage without him. For the last few months they'd been talking about marriage, growing a family one day. But for now all they had was this seaborne life.

Nico shook his head, eyes glistening. 'I can't do this no more, Jo.'

He'd tried to take her hand, but she'd resisted as into her mind had come a faint internal whisper: *He doesn't love you.*

She'd looked into Nico's warm hazel eyes, waiting for him to tell her he was joking, that of course he'd never leave her.

'Good luck, Jo.'

Nico's words had cut her heart to shreds.

It had taken everything she had to walk away.

As the *Lusitania* had left New York harbour, the ship's orchestra had played 'Tipperary' on the boat deck, and the mood among the passengers was buoyant.

Less so among the crew.

Several other stewards had failed to report for duty, Josie had soon discovered. She and her colleagues on the crossing to Liverpool were under greater pressure than ever, especially as a number of the crew, like her brother, had never sailed before.

Wiping the tears from her eyes, she contemplates the opulently furnished library, her sole kingdom on this vast liner. Her gaze slides from the capacious wood and glass bookcases, over the half-dozen mahogany writing desks, each with its own mercury gilt lamp, on to the velvet-upholstered chairs artfully scattered throughout the space. A library of affluence and luxury, and Josie is fortunate to work here.

But if she's caught shirking by the chief steward she'll be on a charge, her wages docked, and she can't afford that. Her stomach churns queasily at the thought.

The clock above the hearth ticks towards two. She must prepare herself before the clientele begin drifting back in, sated after their lunch, ready to make their demands on her again – tea, coffee, writing paper, ink for their pens.

Yet she can't get Nico out of her head, his auburn curls and beautiful eyes, the way he made her laugh until her ribs hurt.

She needed this moment alone to gather herself.

You can't help who you fall in love with, honey. Her late mother's words come to Josie now, and fresh tears threaten.

Pull yourself together, she counsels herself.

Sunshine burns through the sheets of brown paper covering the skylights. They had been put up on the ship's previous voyage, on Captain Turner's orders. No lights must show at night – a safety precaution against U-boat attack, though the captain has expressly forbidden any mention of war in front of the passengers. The muted light lends the library a subterranean feel, and Josie fleetingly imagines herself out on deck, beneath the achingly blue sky, feeling the warmth of the sun on her face.

It's been a calm crossing so far, weather-wise, she

thinks, apart from the fog this morning. Through the windows, the Atlantic Ocean stretches away towards the horizon, like an endless silver carpet. Nico's talk of hidden danger and threats from German attack is hard to reconcile with such a breathtaking vista.

Not that Josie's seen much of it, confined to the library, waiting on the first-class passengers, such as Mrs Cavendish and her cronies.

Movement snags her eye from out on the boat deck. The daily lifeboat drill is under way. The activity always centres around the same lifeboat, No. 7, Josie's lucky number. She can hear the staff captain's whistle, and now six crewmen, all wearing badges bearing the number of the lifeboat, are scrambling up the davits, leaping into the wooden tender. Josie watches as each crewman dons a cork life vest, the staff captain counting down the minutes before ordering the men out of the lifeboat again. The drill lasts less than five minutes, and none of the handling gear is operated. But Josie knows the crew can't very well swing a heavy wooden lifeboat filled with men over the side of the ship, then lower it, all while travelling at twenty knots. The liner can't be stopped: it would cause too much of a delay.

Usually the drill is observed by a gathering of passengers, most finding the training exercise amusing, a few of the more anxious watching with expressions of concern. Today, the crew have only wheeling gulls as their audience. And a heartbroken stewardess.

Josie drags her attention back to the library, and her long list of chores. First she must find vases for the many bouquets of flowers that have been left there, a nuisance task she always puts off for as long as possible. Heaps of blooms were sent on board by heartsick friends and relatives to remind the departing passengers of home, and it fell to Josie and the other stewardesses to arrange them in the staterooms and cabins. But there were never enough vases, and Josie often fought the urge to send the surplus bouquets sailing through an open porthole. It never ceased to amaze her that people considered fresh flowers a good send-off gift. She would much prefer a book. What use were flowers after a few days? Their wilting petals served only to depress.

As well as flowers to be dealt with, those writing desks littered with discarded papers and half-empty cups need tidying. But first she really ought to give the shelves a quick dust before the passengers return. She moves to the nearest glass-fronted bookcase, neatly stocked with several hundred volumes. Most are in English, with a small number of Italian, Spanish and French texts. Josie's eyes graze over the *Encyclopaedia Britannica*, a long block of glossy blue that to her knowledge has never been touched by any of the rich patrons who use this room. Her gaze moves along the shelves, drifting over more current popular literature: works by E. M. Forster, Frances Hodgson Burnett, L. M. Montgomery. Like the reference volumes, these pristine novels have barely been read, their lustrous calfskin jackets largely untouched by human hands apart from hers. Such an expensive resource is wasted on the first-class passengers, in Josie's opinion.

She slides open a casement, can't resist pulling her favourite novel from its nest: her wounded soul is in need of soothing. Turning to the first page, she reads a sentence she knows by heart.

'Christmas won't be Christmas without presents,' grumbled Jo, lying on the rug.

She thinks of her aunt Pearl, who'd introduced her to *Little Women* when Josie was a child. Over the years, the tale of the March sisters has never failed to lift her spirits, transporting her from whatever worries or troubles she's facing.

This voyage was supposed to be the start of a new chapter for her, Nico and Jem, all of them working for Cunard. Six months on from the darkness of her mother's death, life had been slowly returning to normal, and Josie had begun to dream of a future again.

Until Nico had destroyed that dream.

'Hey . . .'

A voice from the doorway startles her, and she whips round, almost dropping the book.

She's been caught.

In the freefall between heartbeats, recognition dawns. 'Jem . . .' She exhales, as her brother weaves towards her through the desks and scattered armchairs, tall and smart in his white steward's uniform and cap. Despite his height, he looks younger than his seventeen years, Josie thinks, with a pang of tenderness. He's more precious to her than ever, now it's just the two of them.

She notes his pallor as she moves to meet him, the plush rose carpet gently undulating beneath her feet.

Jem removes his cap, his russet hair springing up, thick as a squirrel's tail, the constellation of cinnamon freckles across his nose and cheeks stark in his pale face. They both share their late mother's colouring, but there the familial resemblance ends. Josie had cut her brother's hair only last week, in readiness for the voyage, but already it looks messy.

'You nearly gave me a heart attack.' She sighs. 'Thought you were Hyde.' To be caught shirking by the chief steward guaranteed punishment.

Jem collapses into a chair, groaning. 'I feel so damn sick.'

Josie winces inwardly at her brother's language. Good thing they're alone, but for how much longer? 'You just haven't found your sea legs yet,' she tells him.

'I'm dying here, Jo.'

'You're going to be fine.' Josie shoves *Little Women* into her apron pocket, and crouches before her brother. She takes one of his clammy hands in her own. 'The sickness will pass. You just have to give it time.'

'I don't want to go back in the hold, Jo. What if I hurl down there?' He blinks at her, moist puppy eyes.

'You won't, Jem.' Out of his sight, Josie crosses her fingers. 'Are you on a break?' She refrains from adding that he shouldn't be up here in the first-class library, even in his free time. This area was exclusively for first-class passengers, not lowly baggage stewards.

'Yeah.' Jem leans his head back against the chair. 'Got ten minutes. But it's taken me that long to find you.'

'All right, just sit here for a minute.' The best cure for

seasickness, Josie knows from experience, is to stand out on deck, breathe fresh air and fix your gaze on the far horizon. But, of course, her brother can't do that if he's working in the bowels of the ship.

From across the library, the chimes of the mantel clock alert Josie that lunch is over. Any minute now Mrs Cavendish and the other first-class passengers will invade her sanctuary once more.

'Where's Nico?' Jem asks. 'Was he fired? That's what they're saying.'

Josie swallows. 'Not fired.'

'So where is he?'

'He chose not to come.' There. She's said it.

'Why?'

'I don't know, Jem.' A lie.

Jem looks at her. 'Is it true we'll be entering the war zone soon?'

'Who told you that? Listen, don't worry about it, all right?'

'The captain's said no one's to shine lights or smoke on deck,' Jem goes on, as though Josie hasn't spoken. 'In case U-boats spot us.'

'Don't think about it, Jem.'

'And all the windows have got to be curtained at night . . .'

Josie's mind flashes back to the previous August soon after war had been declared. The *Lusitania*'s funnels had been painted grey, and her interior salons were kept dimly lit at night. Josie and the rest of the crew had spent their evening shifts stumbling along gloomy corridors, colliding with passengers and each other, cursing in whispers. The fear of attack by the German Navy had loomed over that voyage back in August, yet they'd reached Liverpool intact. Over the following eight months the fear has gradually faded, with the German Navy contained in the North Sea. At least, that's what they've been told.

Surely the Germans wouldn't dare to sink the legendary RMS *Lusitania*? Not when she's filled with innocent civilians. Were it not that they were afloat, Josie could believe she was in some ritzy hotel on land. Meals were served at regular intervals, flowers adorned every available surface, passengers played deck games, smoked in the lounges or read newspapers in the library. It hardly seems possible that elsewhere a war is raging.

'Captain Turner said we have to be vigilant for submarines.' Jem's eyes are wide, frightened.

'Don't worry about them,' Josie says, feigning confidence. 'Turner has to say stuff like that. It's his job. There are lookouts on the bridge, and if there's anything out there they'll spot it.'

Jem gives her a dubious look. He doesn't wholly believe her, and she can't blame him, really. No one with half a brain can be dismissive of the very real risks they face on this journey across the notoriously fickle Atlantic. And, of course, everyone remembers the tragedy of the supposedly unsinkable *Titanic* only three years ago.

But the chance of being targeted by the Germans, out here in the vast ocean, must be truly tiny. At least, Josie hopes this is true.

'In a few days we'll be in sight of Ireland, anyway,' she adds. She thinks of the previous voyage, when she and Nico had snatched a few minutes together on the saloon promenade, and a distant smudge of land had come into view on the port side. Nico had taken her hand, and they'd gazed out over the sea. For a moment Josie had felt such love in her heart it hurt.

'Wait till you see the Kinsale lighthouse,' she says. 'Its stack is painted with black and white horizontal bands, and you can see it from miles out at sea.'

Approaching Old Head always raises Josie's spirits, signifying as it does that the worst of the crossing is behind her, and she's on the home stretch.

She chews her lip as a thought occurs. Will they be joined by any British sea patrols, the cruisers and destroyers that usually escorted the liners when they were nearing their destination? So far on this voyage, they've been entirely alone on the wide, wild ocean, but that was normal at this early stage of the journey.

She won't mention this to Jem. He doesn't need to know about naval patrols: it would only scare him more. 'The captain knows what he's doing,' she says, rising to her feet. 'Think about it. He's done this journey many, many times, and nothing bad has happened. Are you feeling a bit better?'

Jem shakes his head slowly. 'I heard one of the firemen say that Turner's ordered the watertight doors on the lower decks to be closed.'

'Just a precaution,' Josie replies. 'The doors are always closed at some point,' she fibs.

'And he said the ship's running too slow. Are we really a sitting duck, Jo?'

'We're going slow because of the coal rationing,' Josie counters. 'And there's a shortage of stokers, isn't there?'

It's no secret there's a shortfall of manpower on the ship, and as a result the *Lusitania* is running significantly slower than her regular speed. Josie has done her best not to worry about something so out of her control.

'And even travelling at only twenty knots,' she adds, 'the ship can outrun most things.'

'Even German submarines?'

'I reckon.'

At least the ship's foghorn has ceased its sinister, booming call since the earlier sea mist lifted.

'Wish Nico was here,' Jem mutters.

Her brother's words twist Josie's heart anew. If Jem found out why Nico had never got on to the ship . . . She shuts off the thought. 'I do too,' she replies. 'You'd better get back to work.' She gently pulls her brother to his feet, shunting him towards the door. 'Mrs Cavendish will be back any minute.'

Sometimes she feels as though she's nothing but prey, awaiting somebody's pleasure.

They briefly hug, and from somewhere on the saloon promenade Josie hears the orchestra tuning up. Soon the strains of a waltz drift through the partly open windows: 'The Blue Danube'. The orchestra play the same set each day, 'Danube' signalling the end of lunch and the beginning of the afternoon's entertainment.

'See you soon, Jo.' Jem gives her a watery smile, and heads back towards the baggage hold.

'I'll come find you later,' Josie calls after him. She'd vowed on their mother's deathbed that she'd look after her kid brother. How Mom would smile to know they were working the ships together.

As the next few days slide past, Nico's absence continues to haunt Josie. She's reminded of him at every turn, and finds herself avoiding certain areas of the ship for fear of running into crew members who would want to talk about him.

She can't get him out of her mind, especially at night, alone in her bunk. Memory is like an anchor, she thinks. It can hold you fast in a storm, stop you drifting, but it can also weigh you down.

Somehow she has to cut Nico free or be dragged down into the depths.

During lunch on the sixth and penultimate day of the voyage, Josie is hiding in a corner of the empty library, illicitly reading *Little Women*, when Mrs Cavendish sweeps through the doorway. The elderly widow, bedecked in her usual ensemble of black bombazine and lace, trails with her the aroma of cooked meat. Josie's stomach growls as she jumps to her feet, shoving the book into her apron pocket. Breakfast was a long time ago, and her shift has another hour to go before she can take a refreshment break.

Mrs Cavendish spies Josie and, galleon-like, alters her

course. 'Tea, girl,' the widow orders, before settling her bulk in an armchair.

Josie bites her lip. She isn't a *girl*, or Mrs Cavendish's skivvy: she's a library stewardess. With an internal sigh, she fixes a well-practised impassive expression on her face. 'Of course, ma'am.'

Two older English gentlemen have followed Mrs Cavendish into the library, and they too demand tea. Josie wonders if these pampered people even know there's a war on. Their days are a never-ending round of meals, socializing and more meals. The passengers on this crossing are a mix of American, British and other nationalities. Many are young and gregarious, others older, some generous with their tips, others demanding. A few, like Mrs Cavendish, are holy terrors, in Josie's opinion. She's had the misfortune to encounter the American widow on a few previous crossings, as the heiress regularly visits family in England. The woman is forever complaining that the chairs in the library are uncomfortable, and while it's clear Mrs Cavendish's generous dimensions don't quite coincide with Cunard's seating, Josie doesn't know what she can do to help.

What Josie *must never* do is forget that Mrs Cavendish is very good friends with the president of Cunard, and one word from her could get Josie struck off the ship's register. Over time, she has learned to maintain her composure, no matter what demands are made of her. After all, she and Jem wouldn't have a job if it wasn't for the likes of these rich passengers.

Josie is heading to the door when, without warning,

there comes a huge, bone-shuddering bang from somewhere outside. The floor vibrates, sending her staggering, and she grabs the back of a chair to stop herself falling.

'Great heavens!' Mrs Cavendish cries. 'What on earth was that?'

Josie's heart hammers in her chest. She's about to say she'll go and find out, when a second explosion rocks the ship, the impact so powerful it sends her to her knees. She scrambles to her feet, her eye caught by movement through the starboard window. Beyond lifeboat No. 7, a giant column of water and debris shoots skywards.

What the hell's happening?

Josie's heart slams. Are they under attack? No, she can't go there. Maybe one of the ship's boilers has blown. Nico had once told her that the engines work at unbelievable pressure, and only careful handling by the engineers and stokers keeps the whole vessel from exploding.

A sense of dread is growing, a knot of panic forming in Josie's throat. Something tells her this isn't an engine malfunction.

The elderly gentlemen are on their feet, one clutching his newspaper, the other a cup of tea, and now the sound of people shouting emanates from the entrance foyer and the saloon promenade.

'What on earth . . .' Mrs Cavendish hauls herself up and staggers the few steps to Josie, seizing her wrist as the floor dips. Josie braces her legs, supporting much of the widow's weight, as the shouting outside intensifies.

'I'll go and see what's happening.' Josie twists free of Mrs Cavendish's grasp, hurrying to the door.

A single thought blares through her mind: *Find Jem.*

2

Edie – London

She surfaces from a nightmare, soaked in cold sweat, limbs tangled in the sheets. In the dream she'd been a crow on the wing, flying low over battlefields littered with the broken bodies of men and horses, shell craters brimming with blood. Somehow, at the same time, she'd been on the ground, crawling through the mud, labouring across a vast, desolate landscape. The familiar reek of death clagged the back of Edie's throat, making it hard to breathe, but she had to keep searching, searching . . .

Every time, she wakes before she finds him.

Edie sinks back against her damp pillow, taking long, slow breaths, the dream haunting the dark nooks of her mind. When will these night terrors end? Her inability to control them is terrifying, and her deepest dread is that she'll spend every night for the rest of her life dreaming herself back to the hell of the battlefield, yet never find Stanley.

Although six months have passed, it's as though time has stood still for her, marked by that fateful trench raid in France. Occasionally, on good days, she can almost forget she'd risked her life in a stunt to make her name as a journalist. It hardly seems real that she'd falsely enlisted with the British Army, fought alongside her platoon, and lost her dear friend Stanley.

Except it is real, and these regular night terrors serve to remind her of it almost every time she closes her eyes.

At least she hasn't woken to find herself cowering under the bed like last time, convinced the German soldier she'd impaled on her bayonet had come back to life to bludgeon her. That time, her cries had woken the whole house. Mary had discovered her on the bedroom floor, and it had taken the best part of an hour before Edie had stopped shaking, held tenderly in Mary's arms.

Edie wipes sweat from her eyes with the sleeve of her nightgown. Where would she be without her friends Harry and Mary Levinson? The war correspondent she'd met in France and his dear wife have shown nothing but kindness to Edie, taking her in, letting her stay in their attic room. Harry, immersed in his war reporting, treats Edie as an unofficial junior assistant, but his wife fusses over her as if she's one of their own children. She's forever pushing extra portions on Edie at mealtimes to 'feed her up', or altering her grown daughters' spare slips, blouses and skirts to fit Edie's meagre frame. Mary has even taken to wearing slippers around the house so that the sudden clip of her heels on the floorboards doesn't startle her.

If it wasn't for the Levinsons, Edie fears she might have done something drastic by now, like throw herself into the Thames. Anything to stop the relentless night terrors that destroy her sleep, often leaving her weakened and foggy-headed, hands trembling, flinching at every slammed door or raised voice in the street. Living with the Levinsons is a blessing, she knows, but even so it's a busy household with rarely a moment of peace. Daily tradesmen and visitors must be endured, and Harry and Mary's two married daughters often return home, bringing with them their husbands and children, and sometimes other family members.

Whenever Edie feels overwhelmed by it all, she retreats to her garret room at the top of the house until she's able to face people again. Her frayed nerves frustrate her, but worse than that, she feels ashamed when there are far more desperate folk who have suffered far worse than her, struggling to survive beneath the dark shadow of war.

She sits on the edge of the bed, gathering her strength. Her right leg, stiff and slow to respond on waking, is an aching reminder of the injury she sustained almost six months ago. She hitches up the voluminous nightgown borrowed from Mary, which swamps her, and examines her upper thigh. The skin is puckered and livid, the flesh tight and ridged where Dr Garland had stitched her back together. She was lucky, Edie knows. An inch higher, and the shrapnel could have severed an artery. She'd have bled to death in that trench, long before she ended up on Dr Garland's operating table.

The ache eases after a minute or two, and she's able to plant her bare feet on the cool wooden boards and stand.

Above her, the tiny skylight glows pale gold, heralding another warm spring day. She limps the few steps to the dresser, washing her face and hands in the fresh bowl of water Susan must have left earlier. The maid moves silently about the house, instructed by Mary not to disturb Edie. The mottled glass of the mirror reflects Edie's pale face, her shadow-ringed eyes large in their sockets.

She roughly drags a comb through her short dark hair. It's growing out slowly, and no doubt she'll need the rough ends trimmed soon. But for now, the prospect of sitting trapped in a chair while someone comes at her with sharp implements is more than she can bear. At least she can hide her unconventional hair beneath the blue crocheted beret Mary has lent her.

She pulls on a skirt and fumbles at the buttons of her blouse. In a strange way she would never admit to anyone, not even Mary, that she misses wearing her army uniform. She misses the feel of her legs encased in trousers, the freedom they gave her to stride everywhere, the way the khaki tunic had broadened her shoulders. She'd felt stronger in male clothing somehow, although her body beneath was the same.

Dressed at last, she takes a moment to collect herself. Fear simmers just beneath her breastbone, a constant tightness, like a band around her chest. Only the act of writing ever seems to ease this. When she's in Harry's study downstairs, curled up in the deep leather armchair, penning thoughts in her notebook, or reading one of Harry's novels, she can forget herself for a short while. Lately, Harry has been urging her to write about her experiences in France. It's time to publish her 'stunt' in the newspapers, he says. People will love to read of the plucky girl-soldier who fought the Hun and survived to tell the tale.

But although Edie wants to share her story, she finds she can't yet return to the horror, if only on the page. She much prefers to edit Harry's pieces, giving voice to the refugees and soldiers who can't speak for themselves. Today, she's due to begin helping Harry with his latest project, documenting the work of London's military hospitals. But the prospect of writing about wounded men only makes her think of Stanley.

She makes her way carefully downstairs to find Harry in the dining room tucking into a plate of kippers. The smell of smoked fish turns Edie's stomach as she greets her friend and takes her place at the table.

'Good morning, little scribe.' Harry gives Edie a warm smile. 'Sleep well?'

'Better, thank you,' Edie fibs.

'Marvellous.' Harry wipes his moustache with a napkin, as Mary bustles into the room, her footsteps soft. She touches Edie's shoulder tenderly as she passes her chair, before settling opposite her husband.

'Are you ready for today, Edie?' Mary's gaze is steady and keen.

'I think so,' Edie lies again, willing her hand not to tremble as she pours a cup of tea. Why is she so nervous? She's only meeting Dr Garland, she reminds herself. The doctor who saved her life in France. The doctor who's been good friends with Harry and Mary for years.

It's the task she faces that's daunting. A month ago, Dr Garland and her partner Dr Maberry opened their new trailblazing, all-female-run military hospital in Endell Street. Harry has given Edie the task of writing about the women's incredible achievements, with a view to getting the pieces published. To be trusted with this is a privilege and an honour, Edie knows, and yet it is also terrifying.

She can't let Harry down.

'Mind you don't get mistaken for a Tommy patient,' Harry says, winking at Edie. 'They'll have you tucked up in bed before you know it.'

'Harold!' Mary scolds. 'Don't tease the girl.' She turns to Edie. 'You look lovely, dear.'

Edie manages a weak smile, as she spreads blackberry jam on a slice of bread. Mary only means to be kind, but there's little that's lovely about Edie's appearance. With her short hair and spare build, not to mention her crooked nose, which has never quite healed properly, Edie wonders if she could indeed pass for an Endell Street patient. She nibbles the bread and jam, forcing it down her dry throat.

Harry passes Edie a newspaper, one of several piled next to his plate. 'There's a piece on Endell Street in *The Times* today.' He points at an article. 'Read it. I know you'll do better, little scribe.'

The article is brief, focusing on the hospital's previous history as a workhouse, and more recently a home for refugees from the Continent. Edie reaches the end and glances up to find Harry and Mary regarding her. Mary looks as though she wants to say something, but it's Harry who breaks the silence.

'I wish I could come with you today,' he says, 'but I know you'll be fine. You're the bravest young journalist

I know, and Lucinda and Florence will be thrilled to see you again.'

Edie pictures Dr Garland, the handsome doctor with the kind eyes, and a part of her is looking forward to seeing her, but another part is hesitant. Will she be able to control her nerves enough? Will being back among wounded soldiers bring all her fearful memories to the fore?

The dining-room door creaks, and Edie stiffens, but it's only Susan bringing more tea.

Mary reaches across the table, giving Edie's hand a brief squeeze. 'You'll be all right.'

Edie wishes she could believe her.

'Good luck, little scribe,' Harry says, pushing back his chair and rising. 'You'll do us all proud, I know.'

A taciturn RAMC guard stops Edie at Endell Street Hospital's main gate, refusing her entry without a letter of admittance.

'I'm here to see Dr Garland,' Edie stammers. 'She's expecting me.'

'Your name, miss?'

'Edie Lawrence.'

To her surprise and relief, the guard recognizes her name, and grants her entry with a respectful nod. Edie finds herself in a large courtyard bordered on three sides by tall, sooty brick buildings. Rows and rows of sash windows, some covered with blinds, others open to the warm breeze, stare down at her. Bisecting the courtyard is a long, glass-covered walkway, beneath which patients are sheltering, some parked in wheelchairs, others sitting on benches, a few leaning on crutches. All are male, Edie notes, almost all of them wearing the distinctive hospital garb of blue flannelette suit and maroon tie.

Scattered throughout the rest of the courtyard are several bistro tables, each shaded by a colourful umbrella, around which are seated more patients, smoking, playing cards or enjoying refreshments. Wooden tubs and horse troughs, planted with fragrant herbs, flowers and small fruit trees, border the yard.

If it weren't for the bustling presence of nurses and orderlies, it could almost be a holiday scene, Edie thinks, as she follows the guard's directions towards the hospital's entrance. She passes a black metal post, then notices others set at regular intervals across the yard. A shudder ripples through her, as she recognizes the outlines of exercise pens, a reminder of the workhouse this place had once been.

She limps on, reaching a set of double doors, and asks a passing orderly for directions to Dr Garland's office.

'You bin to Endell before, miss?' the orderly asks.

'No,' Edie admits, holding her satchel close as a quartet of nurses hurries past.

'We get lots of visitors,' the orderly remarks brightly, as she leads Edie further into the building. 'Royals, gents, ladies, everyone.'

Edie follows the orderly along freshly painted corridors, polished white tiles underfoot. She notes veins of black and red wire tacked along the skirting boards, presumably for the electric lights, or perhaps telephones.

When Edie asks, the orderly confirms that they do indeed have telephones. Medical staff dash past, and Edie breathes in the distinctive harsh smell of carbolic, her heart beating a tattoo in her chest.

'D'you know Dr Garland, then?' the young orderly chatters on, as they navigate another corridor, this one quieter with only a nurse assisting a shuffling patient. To her relief, no one pays Edie any attention: her appearance must not look out of place here.

Before Edie can reply, the orderly makes a sharp left at a T-junction, heading towards another set of doors, and Edie realizes she's lost her bearings. She doubts she could find her way back to the courtyard on her own.

'Here we are.' The orderly finally stops before a dark green door, a sign above it declaring: *Dr Garland (chief surgeon) and Dr Maberry (doctor-in-charge)*.

The orderly dashes away, and Edie takes a steadying breath. She knocks, and hears a dog's high bark. Then the door is opening, and there is Dr Garland.

'Edie!' the doctor greets her warmly. 'Come in, come in.'

Edie hopes her face doesn't betray her shock. Dr Garland has changed in the few months since Edie last saw her when she came to tea at the Levinsons'. She's grown thinner, her eyes bruised with tiredness. But Os, her wiry little black and white terrier, is the same bundle of energy, jumping up at Edie, trying to lick her hands.

'Down, Os, naughty boy!' Dr Garland gently bats the dog away, as she ushers Edie into her office. The room is comfortably furnished, shelves crammed with texts filling one wall, open windows overlooking the courtyard. Most of the space is taken up by two large matching desks, facing each other from opposite sides of the room. The nearest desk is covered with a mini avalanche of folders, loose papers and books, and what looks to Edie suspiciously like an animal's skull, complete with yellowing fangs. The other desk, behind which Dr Maberry is now rising, has only a blotter, ink bottle and a neat pile of papers on it.

Dr Maberry comes to shake Edie's hand. The tall Scottish doctor also looks thinner to Edie, if that could be possible.

'It's wonderful to see you,' Dr Maberry says. 'I'd love to stay for a wee while, hear everything that's been happening, Edie, but, alas, I'm due in surgery.' She exchanges a brief, tired smile with Dr Garland, and Edie is reminded that if it wasn't for these two women she wouldn't be alive today. The thought is humbling.

Dr Maberry hurries away, and Dr Garland drags a chair closer to her desk, urging Edie to sit and take the weight off her leg.

Edie lowers herself gratefully on to the cushion. When she's nervous her leg aches more.

'How have you been, my dear?' Dr Garland takes a seat at her messy desk, and Edie feels warmth bloom in her chest. This doctor, overloaded with work and responsibilities, still cares for Edie as a friend would.

'Harry and Mary have been so kind.'

'It's still working out well with them, is it?' Dr Garland scoops the little dog on to her lap, earning a lick on her cheek.

'I think so, yes.'

Dr Garland strokes the dog's ears. 'But how have you been?'

Edie finds she can't quite hold Dr Garland's gaze across the desk. 'I'm keeping busy, working with Harry,' she replies.

'That wasn't quite what I asked,' Dr Garland says gently. 'Harry's told me what an incredible help you are to him, and how much he admires your writing.'

'He has?'

Dr Garland nods, depositing the dog back on the floor. 'Into bed, Os,' she shoos, and he obediently trots off to a nest of rumpled blankets in the corner. 'Harry and I both think you're the perfect choice to write about this hospital,' she resumes. 'It's a unique opportunity to show the world what we're doing.'

Edie nods. *And a huge responsibility.*

'Do you know when Harry wants to publish?' Dr Garland asks.

'I'm not sure,' Edie replies. 'He mentioned me writing a weekly article.'

'You'll be our own little Dickens.' Dr Garland smiles.

Edie flushes. 'Harry suggested I write about a different area of the hospital each week.'

'Good idea. When would you like to start?'

The question is so direct, Edie is momentarily thrown. 'I don't mind. When would suit you?'

'We're ready whenever you are.' Dr Garland's smile deepens. 'You have our full support here.'

Edie swallows a knot in her throat.

'Unfortunately, Mr Croker is ill at present,' Dr Garland continues. 'He would have been the ideal candidate for your first interview.'

'Mr Croker?'

'The clerk of works. He's also a staunch supporter of our cause.'

Edie makes a mental note of Mr Croker's name, as Dr Garland talks on. 'When we first gained possession of this place, Mr Croker helped us clear rooms and move furniture, and has continued to go above and beyond his duty. He's rather exhausted himself, of course.' She gives Edie a wry smile. 'I'm sure he'll be right as rain in time.'

'Can you tell me about the other staff here?' Edie asks.

'Let me see.' Dr Garland ponders. 'Along with Dr Maberry and myself, we have fourteen other doctors, thirty-six nurses, and somewhere in the region of eighty orderlies, many of them volunteers.'

Edie digs in her satchel for her notepad and a pencil.

'You'll know that Dr Maberry and I brought our original team back from France at the beginning of the year,' Dr Garland goes on, 'during a winter lull in the fighting. The evacuation chain had become much more efficient by then.' The doctor rubs her temples. 'But now a new push is imminent, and it's estimated that even more beds will be needed soon.'

'How many does the hospital have at the moment?'

'Five hundred and twenty,' the doctor replies, 'spread throughout seventeen wards. Three of those wards contain our most severe cases. Those are situated in the south block.'

Edie scribbles notes, as Dr Garland begins to list the names of her staff.

'Dr Vera Woodman is our most experienced physician,' she says, 'after Dr Maberry and myself, of course. There are also our two assistant surgeons, Dr Gertrude Gazdar who worked with us in France, and Dr Jemima Short.

'Then we have Dr Anne Sheppard, our ophthalmic surgeon, and Dr Mary Chamberlain, our pathologist. Dr Chamberlain is passionate about the work she's doing here, identifying new strains of pathogen, and she'd be very happy to share her findings with you, I've no doubt.'

Edie's hand is beginning to cramp round the pencil.

'Miss Hale, our matron, is awfully efficient but can sometimes come across as a little brusque.' Dr Garland hesitates, choosing her words with care. 'Perhaps leave her until I've had a word.'

Edie places a cross next to the matron's name.

'Now, we have a number of nursing sisters, but I must warn you there are frequent clashes between our qualified nurses and the volunteers, the VADs. Both will no doubt wish to air their grievances.'

Edie wonders what grievances the nursing staff and their counterparts from the Voluntary Aid Detachment will want to share.

'Our nurses appreciate the VADs are necessary,' Dr Garland explains. 'But they also view them as privileged women, dropped at our front gate every day by their chauffeurs. Never mind that they scrub floors and empty bedpans and generally do the dirtiest jobs.' Dr Garland sighs. 'Many of these VADs have been expensively nurtured, it's true,' she goes on. 'The sort of women who've been ineffectually educated, who turn up at the hospital unequipped and untrained in any sort of medical capacity. Not much use, compared to our trained nursing staff.'

Why employ them then? Edie wants to ask.

'That said,' Dr Garland goes on, 'from what I've witnessed of them so far, these admittedly rather pampered women exhibit fine courage, resolution and intelligence, and generally tackle any difficult situation thrown at them.'

Edie makes a note to interview both nurses and VADs.

'In my opinion, the VADs are crucial to the running of this place,' Dr Garland concludes, 'but our nurses are proud of their skills, so please be mindful of this when you speak to both camps.'

'Thank you for the forewarning, Doctor.'

'Our orderlies are certainly essential,' Dr Garland continues. 'Miss Campbell is our capable quartermaster, ably assisted by Miss Hodgson. They will give you all the facts and figures regarding the stores and medical supplies and so on. Without our orderlies, our work here would not be possible.

'Last but not least,' Dr Garland says, with a smile, 'we mustn't forget the beating heart of our hospital.'

Edie looks up from her frantic note-taking. Beating heart? What did she mean?

'Our library,' Dr Garland says.

3

Josie – Atlantic Ocean

Out in the lobby a crowd has gathered, the stairways on either side of the twin elevators disgorging more passengers and crew from the lower decks. Josie tries to push her way through, but it's impossible to forge a path against the flow. Prevented from descending to F deck and the baggage hold, she's forced to change tack in her search for Jem. Choosing a different, more circuitous route, she shoves her way out on to the promenade deck. Here, she finds more passengers and crew crowding around the port-side lifeboats, a line of eleven pristine, white-painted tenders suspended on chains, woodwork gleaming in the sun.

Josie knows the same number of lifeboats are on the starboard side, but she's always thought twenty-two fragile wooden craft woefully inadequate for more than two thousand passengers.

The decks are fast filling with people, many women and children in tears, other passengers standing stunned as crewmen prepare the first of the boats for launching.

Josie clutches the nearest rail as the ship lists to starboard. The movement causes the lifeboats to swing further inboard, and Josie's heart plummets as she sees that the boats, hanging over the deck now, are practically impossible to launch on this side of the ship.

'Move away!' a crewman bellows at the surging crowd. His warnings are ignored, and Josie is shoved against the rail by a flow of desperate people. Below her, the waves churn and froth against the vast hull, as the *Lusitania* ploughs on.

The foghorn siren blasts, making her stumble backwards into the path of a crewman.

'What's happening?' Josie gasps at the steward, whose name she can't recall.

'We've been hit!' the man snaps. 'Get yourself a life vest!' He rushes away before Josie can respond. Left alone, the truth slams into her, a fist in the sternum.

The ship is sinking.

She seizes the rail again as the deck tilts further, panic threatening to engulf her. Everywhere she looks, people are running, shouting, while crew struggle to marshal the unruly crowds. The ship's emergency siren, blaring into the tranquil, cloudless sky, is abruptly interrupted by the squeal of the loudspeaker system, and then the captain's voice rings out: *Abandon ship! Abandon ship!*

The call Josie has dreaded hearing on every single voyage now echoes across the decks.

Oh God, we're going down.

This can't be happening. Her worst fear can't be coming true now, not when they were so close to land, not on her brother's first voyage. Josie's heart pounds like a fist beneath her starched uniform.

Stay calm, she counsels herself sternly. *Find Jem.*

Deep, shuddering groans emanate from the interior of the ship, a sound like nothing Josie has heard before, in all her time at sea, and a hot tightness builds in the base of her throat. She stands paralysed on the deck, a solitary static body amid a maelstrom of chaos, surrounded by crewmen grappling to release lifeboats, passengers clinging to each other, wailing and sobbing.

A junior officer mounts a davit close to Josie, shouting at people who are trying to clamber into a nearby lifeboat before it's been freed.

'Wait!' the officer cries, his voice hoarse. 'It can't be lowered yet!'

There comes the clang of metal on metal, and Josie's gaze is drawn to a lifeboat already full of people further along the deck. A young man in shirtsleeves is striking a hammer against the snubbing chain securing the boat to the deck, his arm rising and falling in a frenzied rhythm. The occupants of the lifeboat are imploring him to hurry, and suddenly his hammer strikes home, and the chain bursts free, releasing the boat. Josie watches, horrified, as the tender swings inward, crushing those passengers directly in its path, including the man with the hammer.

Sickened, Josie staggers a few steps towards the scene of carnage, but what can she do?

Nothing.

The officer on the davit shoves past her, rushing to a neighbouring lifeboat, where more men are trying to dislodge the release pin anchoring the craft.

'Stop! Wait!'

But he's too late. Josie can barely stand to watch, as

the scene plays out again, the lifeboat sliding along the deck, towing a grisly line of injured people behind it. The tender comes to a halt beneath the bridge wing viewing platform, where Josie can now see Captain Turner standing.

What was the captain doing? Why wasn't he stopping this bloodshed?

Josie can hear the officers on the bridge shouting at the crew below, as they grapple with ropes and chains, heaving the lifeboats over the rail. Terror sweeps through the ship like a storm, and Josie can hardly think. A screech of metal grinding against wood erupts from somewhere near the bow, as another boat breaks free of its chains, plummeting into the sea, and this last catastrophe jolts Josie from her numb stupor. A voice in her head is yelling at her: *Get off the port deck, get to the starboard side.*

She pushes her way back into the lift lobby and, moments later, the electric lights flicker and go out. The congested lobby is plunged into gloom, the twin elevators grinding to a halt between decks. With no power, their doors remain resolutely closed, trapping passengers inside. People begin thumping on them, the level of panic now at fever pitch.

Josie struggles to draw breath, bodies pressing in on her from all sides. Mere minutes have passed since the initial explosion, yet she feels as though she's lived a lifetime since.

She has to get out – she has to find Jem.

Fear lends her strength, and she manages to break free of the crowd, escaping on to the listing starboard deck. To her dismay, she discovers most of the lifeboats on this side have swung right out over the sea, creating a yawning gap between the *Lusitania*'s decks and the prospect of escape, an unbridgeable sixty-foot drop in between.

Screams from the portside decks are growing louder. The liner has ceased its starboard list, and beneath her feet Josie can feel the ship slowly begin to level. From somewhere towards the stern she hears the unmistakable sound of glass windows shattering, one after another after another.

Josie staggers further along the deck, her shoes soon soaked by water splashing over the teak boards, foaming around the bollards and capstans. The deck lurches as the ship descends, inch by steady inch, bow first into the waves.

The distant rumble of the vessel's last working engine fades away, the ship now moving at a crawl slow enough for the remaining lifeboats to be launched. The ship's forecastle sinks ever lower, observed by Captain Turner and his officers on the bridge wing. From what Josie can make out, no one seems to be issuing orders any more.

Within minutes, the *Lusitania*'s bows are entirely submerged, furniture, rigging and ropes floating free on the placid waves. Josie is left with no choice but to flee to the stern. She turns, the deck sloping up before her like a wooden hill, people everywhere, crying and shouting. She tries to think. Was Jem in a lifeboat already? Was he desperately searching for her?

Please, God, let him be safe.

'*Per favore* . . .' A hand grips Josie's arm, and she finds herself face to face with a woman clasping a crying baby in her arms, a little boy of four or five clinging to her skirts. She's with an older woman, the grandmother, Josie guesses, who's gripping the hand of a girl of perhaps ten.

'My children,' the mother implores in broken English. 'Please help them.'

The woman's eyes are wide with fear, brimming with unshed tears, and Josie's heart plunges to new depths. *What can she do for these poor people? Why aren't they in a lifeboat already?*

'Come with me,' she stammers. She desperately scans the deck for a fellow steward, and to her relief glimpses a crewman further along, hurling the remaining lifebelts over the side of the ship to people floundering in the water far below. Josie begs him to give her the last three cork vests; one for the grandmother, the mother, and the daughter. But there's nothing to fit the two smallest children. And none left for her.

'That's the lot,' the crewman says. 'That's all there is.'

Josie's voice fails her, but the mother is thanking the steward, '*Grazie, grazie, Dio ti benedica.*'

Josie pulls the family away, and they stumble along the pitching deck, heading for the stern, when the ship gives a long, protesting groan from every plate in her hull: a death rattle.

Panic grips Josie's lungs. Time is running out.

'Come on,' she urges, offering her hand to the little boy. To her surprise he takes it, and his tight grip triggers a flash of memory, of visiting Bronx Zoo with her mother and Jem, when Jem was only a toddler. A chimpanzee had poked its curiously humanlike fingers through the bars of the monkey cage and taken hold of Jem's hand.

At last, they reach one of the few lifeboats left, 'No. 13' painted on its side. A steward Josie knows, a friend of Nico's called Robert, a gentle, likeable young man, is brandishing a fire axe as women and children climb into the tender. Before Josie can gain Robert's attention, a man in a dark suit pushes past her and levels a handgun at Robert's head.

'Let me on!' the man demands.

'Women and children first.' Josie hardly recognizes Robert's uncommonly sharp tone.

'I've waited long enough! I won't wait no more!'

'Lower your gun, sir!'

'What's the point of fucking lifeboats,' the man yells, 'if you won't let people on 'em?'

'Women and children first.'

'To hell with that,' the man snarls, stabbing his gun in Robert's face. 'Let me off this fucking ship – now!'

'Sir!' Robert raises his axe, pushing the man back a step. 'Wait your turn!'

'Fuck you!' another man shouts. 'Can't you see we're sinking?'

The crowd surges, and Josie and the Italian family are jostled aside, as men begin clambering aboard the lifeboat. Soon, almost all the seats are filled, and Josie's heart is racing – she has to get these children on board.

'Rob!' she cries. But Nico's friend has gone, subsumed

in the flood of people. In a last-ditch attempt, Josie corrals the family, locking eyes with the mother. They both know it is now or never.

'Let the children on!' Josie cries, pushing through bodies, dragging the little boy with her, hoping the others are close behind. Somehow, by some miracle, enough space is found and the family scrambles into the lifeboat, moments before it begins its jerking, perilous descent. As the Italian family disappear from Josie's sight, the world dims. Fearing she's about to faint, she sinks to her knees, head dipped, breath ragged. All she can do is wait for this moment to pass, as above and around her the maelstrom continues, voices filling her head.

Josie!

She snaps alert.

'Jem?' She can barely manage a croak.

It takes everything she has to drag herself to her feet, clinging to the rail. She searches the deck, but there's no sign of her brother.

'Jem!'

She'd heard his voice, so clear.

'Jem!'

She stumbles on towards the last lifeboat, but is halted by a horrific scene: another tender has tipped over on its descent down the side of the ship, spilling its occupants into the sea. People are flailing in the water, crewmen desperately throwing them ropes and broken pieces of furniture. As Josie looks on, powerless to do anything, she sees another upended lifeboat being pulled along the side of the liner towards the huge blades of the propeller, now visible above the waterline. A scream lodges in Josie's throat, as the tender is smashed to matchsticks as though it were a toy.

A moment later the ship lurches, sending her stumbling into a man standing at the rail. He lends her a steadying hand, but shock steals any words of thanks from Josie's lips.

'Hold tight, lass,' the man says, with an odd calmness. 'Save yer strength.'

'My brother,' she stammers. 'I have to find him.' The stranger's cool stare terrifies Josie further. 'I have to find him,' she repeats, her lips numb.

'Time's running out, lass,' the man says, as though remarking on the weather. He makes no move to help or console Josie, instead turning back to face the sea. 'Look.' He gestures at the scene playing out below them.

Josie leans further out over the railing, scanning the water. She counts three lifeboats and four rafts afloat amid the wreckage of broken deckchairs, coffee tables, empty lifebelts, ropes and other debris. People are drowning everywhere she looks.

All the lifeboats but one have been deployed, and any chance of escaping the ship will soon be lost.

'We need to go,' Josie tells the man.

But he shakes his head, smiling benignly. 'Why fear death?' he mutters, as though talking to himself. 'It's only the most beautiful adventure in life.'

Josie realizes the man won't listen to her, no matter what she says.

Somehow she makes it to the final lifeboat on the

port deck, No. 21. She tries to see if Jem is on board, but there's no time to hesitate as she's bundled into one of the last spaces. She finds herself squeezed between a larger lady wearing a black lace shawl over her head, and the boat's wooden gunwale. Moments later, the dangerously full craft is winched over the side, swaying sickeningly on its descent.

'*Where's my baby?*' A scream comes from the bow, and Josie looks up to see a young woman on her feet, hysterical. '*Where is he? Where's my baby?*'

People near the woman reach out to her, tugging at her coat, trying to pull her down on to the bench. But she continues to scream, until a man shouts in her face, 'We ain't got no babies, lady! Sit down!'

The woman's cries stop, and then she's pushing her way to the side of the boat, causing it to rock and sway. Josie fears she is about to throw herself into the water, but at the last moment she's grabbed, and another woman is crying out, 'Your baby is safe, lady! I saw it! I saw it taken into another boat!'

The young mother allows herself to be helped back to her seat, and men take up the oars. Josie leans out over the gunwale, desperately searching the water. She counts four other lifeboats nearby. There must be more on the other side of the ship that she can't see. The sound of people sobbing, praying, calling out, drifts over the flat, calm ocean.

Josie's eye latches on the *Lusitania*. Mere minutes ago she was on board that floating city of veranda cafés and sun decks, smoking rooms and dining saloons, music lounges and drawing rooms. She'd thought she was safe in her beloved library.

Now, the forecastle is completely underwater, but she can see Captain Turner still at his post on the port bridge wing.

Josie rubs salt from her eyes, and when she looks again the captain is gone, swept into the water.

As the liner continues its relentless nosedive, her four funnels disappear beneath the waves, one after another, each accompanied by a muffled detonation. The underwater explosions propel fountains of water high into the sky, debris raining down on the survivors huddled in the lifeboats.

And then the RMS *Lusitania*, all 780 feet of her, is gone.

4

Edie – London

Stowing her notepad in her satchel, Edie follows Dr Garland out of the office.

'The library's on the third floor,' the doctor says, as she strides off. 'Not ideal, but a larger room was required.'

Edie's thigh muscles twinge as she hurries to keep up. The corridors are cool and winding, and every so often Edie catches a faint, yet horribly familiar scent, like meat on the turn. The smell of rotting flesh haunts her memories, and she tries not to breathe too deeply.

Further along a corridor, they encounter a trio of patients shuffling towards them, each man sporting a bandaged limb. Dr Garland dispenses encouraging words, speaking to the men in a manner that strikes Edie as professional yet deeply caring. In response, the men regard her with expressions of such reverence that Edie feels as though she's accompanying some queen on a regal tour.

'You're aware of the history of this place?' Dr Garland remarks to Edie, as they move on.

'It was a workhouse,' Edie manages. She recalls the black posts in the courtyard, suppressing a shudder as a childhood memory rises, of being herded outside with her mother and the other workhouse inmates, in all weathers, for their daily half-hour of exercise.

'The rooms were full of barbaric apparatus,' Dr Garland says, nodding a greeting at a passing medic. 'It was quite an undertaking to remove all the chains and padlocks and straps and whatnot. Did you know this place was the inspiration for *Oliver Twist*?'

Edie thinks of the forbidding grey buildings and can quite see why Dickens set his story here.

'It was closed as a workhouse some time ago,' Dr Garland continues, 'but was used to house Belgian refugees until fairly recently.' She intercepts an orderly hastening along the corridor towards them. The young woman is lugging two large metal pails overflowing with bloodied bandages.

'Where are the lids, Orderly Jenkins?' Dr Garland asks.

'There – there weren't any left, ma'am,' the orderly stammers, 'and Sister Bryony said I was to take 'em away.'

'You're removing surgical waste,' Dr Garland reminds the girl, with polite firmness. 'The pails must always be lidded.'

'Yes, ma'am.'

'The quartermaster should be informed of any equipment shortage, Jenkins.'

'Yes, ma'am. I'll do that, ma'am.'

The orderly hurries off, and Dr Garland resumes her stride, and it occurs to Edie that the doctor tends her hospital like a devoted mother her family: it's her life, her purpose. Her reason for being.

They pass through a set of double doors, and arrive at another corridor. The place is a rabbit warren, and Edie wonders again how she will ever find her way out without assistance.

'I can't show you everywhere today, obviously,' Dr Garland says. 'I'll get Orderly Hodgson to take you on a tour. She knows every nook and cranny, that girl.'

'Did you say there are seventeen wards?'

'There are indeed, and we've named them after female saints. We have St Anne, St Barbara, St Catherine and so on.' Dr Garland pauses to speak briefly with a nurse, and Edie resists the urge to lean against the wall, take the weight off her leg. She doesn't want to show weakness here, in a place of such intense and important industry.

Dr Garland concludes her conversation with the nurse, and leads Edie on. 'Let me show you St Margaret ward,' Dr Garland says. 'This one is for less serious cases, such as those convalescing from straightforward surgery.' She stops at a door. 'We did, however, have to change the name,' she adds in a lower voice. 'Originally, it was named for St Mary, but we suffered a series of strange occurrences . . .'

'How do you mean?' Edie asks, though she's not sure, if Dr Garland is referring to hauntings, she really wants to know. Eerie encounters were commonplace in the workhouse she was brought up in, but so far she's sensed no such dark atmosphere here, perhaps because the place is largely filled with people on a mission to get well and move on.

'I'm not one for superstitions,' Dr Garland says, 'but St Mary was considered by some here to be unsuitable, and it did appear that our patients suffered unusual complications more often. When we changed the name these stopped practically overnight.'

She offers no more information, and Edie has no chance to question her further as Dr Garland pushes open the door and leads her into the ward.

The walls are painted a fresh pale yellow, and Chinese paper lanterns hang suspended from the ceiling. Vases of pink cherry blossom adorn the bedside tables, and each of the dozen occupied beds is covered with a brightly coloured crocheted blanket. The patients, Edie notes, are dressed in pyjamas or the blue flannel uniform of the Endell Tommy. Tall sash windows admit warm sunlight, illuminating a peaceful scene of convalescence.

A couple of nurses are busy attending to patients, and Dr Garland nods to them from the doorway.

'Good morning, Doctor,' a man in a nearby bed calls. 'Have you brought us more visitors?' He gives Edie an appraising look, and she feels her cheeks warm.

'I have indeed, Mr Deacon.' Dr Garland leans to speak discreetly in Edie's ear. 'Mr Deacon was a private detective before the war.' She doesn't elaborate further, and Edie hasn't a chance to respond, as at that moment the calm atmosphere is broken by a man's raised voice, coming from beyond a privacy screen at the end of the ward. A nurse appears from behind the screen, spots Dr Garland and hastens down the aisle to her.

'Sorry to bother you, Doctor,' the nurse says. 'Can you spare a moment?'

'What seems to be the problem, Sister Moore?'

'We have a new patient, arrived only this morning,' the nurse says in a low voice. 'He's had an arm amputation, but not at this hospital. Says he can't remember anything about it, but just needs a rest.'

'Does he know his name?'

'Forester, he says. He came in without a referral.'

Dr Garland and the nurse head back to the screened bed, and Edie hesitates. Should she join them?

'Hurry up, or you'll miss the show,' Mr Deacon remarks cheerily. Edie grips her satchel as she follows Dr Garland, trying to prepare herself for what she might be about to witness.

The screen conceals a bed containing a middle-aged man in a shabby suit. Edie wonders why he's not wearing an Endell uniform like all the other patients. The man is bright-eyed and ruddy-cheeked, and Edie notes the empty left sleeve of his jacket has been pinned to the breast pocket of his suit, the material shiny with dirt or grease.

'Good day, Mr Forester,' Dr Garland greets the man. 'Can you remember your address, sir? Do you have any family we could contact?'

'Can't remember nothin',' Mr Forester replies flatly, his gaze swerving from the doctor to Edie. 'Who's that?'

'Miss Lawrence is one of our clerical staff,' Dr Garland replies smoothly. 'Can you recall your previous hospital, Mr Forester? Because our staff can find no record of your operation.'

'I said I can't remember nothin',' Mr Forester repeats.

'Sister Moore tells me you came here this morning, of your own volition.'

Mr Forester nods slowly. 'I did.'

'And you knew your name and date of birth, she tells me.'

Mr Forester nods again.

'We need to check your arm, Mr Forester,' Dr Garland says briskly. She turns to the nurse. 'Would you fetch a bowl of water please, Sister.'

The nurse bustles away, and Dr Garland turns back to the man. 'Can you remove your jacket, please, Mr Forester?'

'It's fine, Doctor,' the man says, shifting on the bed, half turning away. 'I just need a bit of a kip, like.'

'I'm sure you do,' Dr Garland says, 'but I would still like to check your arm. Amputations need careful attention.'

'Rather you didn't.' The man grips his jacket tighter.

'Why so coy, Mr Forester? Rest assured, I've seen far worse.'

Mr Forester seems to curl into himself, mumbling into his lap. 'Can't help being shy, can I?'

'A shy amnesiac still needs his injury checking, sir.'

The nurse returns, bearing a basin of water and a clean towel.

'Ah, thank you, Sister.' Dr Garland sets the basin on the chair next to the bed, and turns to face Mr Forester. 'Are you going to let Sister do her job now, sir? Or must I continue here?'

'Don't like to show my stump to ladies,' Mr Forester whines. 'Even lady doctors.'

Edie hears a snigger from somewhere beyond the screen.

'You need not be modest about an arm, Mr Forester.' Dr Garland leans closer to the man, peering at his left shoulder. She reaches out, and the man tries to move away, but the doctor is quicker.

After a moment, she releases her grip and takes a step back. 'Which arm did you say you'd lost, Mr Forester?' she asks, with cool composure. 'Because you appear to have the usual number.'

The man hangs his head as Dr Garland and the nurse exchange a look.

'Give Mr Forester a cup of tea, Sister Moore,' Dr Garland says. 'Perhaps then he will recall his lost arm.'

'It's surprisingly common for people to invent injuries or maladies,' Dr Garland tells Edie, as they exit the ward. 'If they can get themselves admitted for something minor, they can enjoy being waited on hand and foot for a time. Until they're found out, of course.'

'But *an arm*?' Edie can't quite believe what she's witnessed. Mr Forester's fake injury wasn't what she would call minor.

'He's not the first to try something like this,' Dr Garland says, as they climb stairs to the second floor, Edie struggling to keep up, the doctor bounding ahead like a mountain goat. Edie can't help but admire the older woman's stamina. 'And he won't be the last,' Dr

Garland says, over her shoulder, barely breathless. 'It no longer surprises me, the lengths to which people will go in order to sleep in a warm, dry bed.'

Edie silently agrees, having no breath to answer. They reach the next floor, and Dr Garland stops at a door. 'You look in need of refreshment yourself,' she says, giving a flushed Edie a knowing look. 'The library can wait for a moment.' She opens the door to a room Edie assumes is the staff mess. They join a handful of orderlies and nurses sitting at tables, eating and drinking.

Dr Garland calls across the room. 'Orderly Hodgson, can I trouble you a moment?'

A slight young woman with a bird's nest of hair spilling from her cap, looks up from her plate. On seeing Dr Garland, she jumps to her feet. 'Ma'am?'

'Hodgson, do you remember Edie Lawrence?' Dr Garland turns to Edie. 'Hodgson is one of my core team. She was with me in France.'

'I do remember you, miss.' The orderly grins at Edie. 'You were so brave, miss. How's your leg now?'

'Oh, it's –'

'Edie is writing about our hospital, Hodgson,' Dr Garland interjects. 'She needs a guide, and who better than you to show her around?'

'Happy to help.' Hodgson beams.

'Excellent,' Dr Garland pronounces. 'Could you conjure some refreshment for Edie too?' she adds.

'Course, ma'am.'

While Hodgson disappears into the kitchen in search of tea, Dr Garland draws Edie's attention to a notice-board on the wall. 'The War Office sends us weekly Purple Papers,' she explains, pointing at a number of pale mauve pieces of paper pinned to the board. 'Directives from on high.' She gives a dry laugh. 'They often make for an amusing read.'

SURGEONS	**SURGEONS**	**SURGEONS**
Don't use syringes without sterilizing them first in a little warm oil.	*Death under an anaesthetic is to be regarded as part of the treatment.*	*Don't make a practice of amputating the right arm, unless absolutely necessary to do so.*

'Presumably we female surgeons are incapable of remembering to clean our equipment,' Dr Garland says. 'And we spend our days lopping off arms hither and yon.'

The doctor's eyes flash with teasing humour, and Edie smiles.

Hodgson returns with a pot of tea, and Dr Garland announces she must return to her office. 'Can you show Edie to the library, Hodgson?'

'Course, ma'am.'

'Come and see me before you leave, Edie,' Dr Garland says. 'Hodgson will look after you now.'

Before Edie can react, the doctor is gone.

'Had a feeling I'd meet you again,' Hodgson tells Edie, as she leads her over to a table. 'I'm Mardie, by the way. I was in Dr Garland's hospital in Wimereux when you was brought in, all bashed up. Do you remember much of that?'

Edie sinks down on a chair. She remembers all too much of that time, most vividly the raid she'd been sent on with Stanley, Jackson and Bembridge, to scope out a possible German listening post. The subsequent attack by German soldiers had left Stanley and herself fighting for their lives. Orderly Hodgson's face is familiar to Edie, but her memories of the life-saving surgery on Dr Garland's operating table remain hazy.

'I thought you was awful brave,' Hodgson chatters on, 'fighting undercover with the men, and then facing that court-martial and everything.'

Edie sips her hot tea, unable to think how to answer. It's taking so much out of her just to stay calm in this hospital.

'So you're working for the chief now, are you?' Hodgson forges on, sharp eyes regarding Edie knowingly. 'Hard taskmaster, but she's fair. Dr Maberry's a brick too, but I find her a bit more standoffish.'

'I'm working for Harry Levinson,' Edie tells her. 'He's asked me to write some pieces on the hospital, for the newspapers.'

'You're a reporter, then?'

'Well . . .'

'That's a plum job, that is,' Hodgson pronounces, draining her cup of tea. 'What newspaper do you write for?'

'Depends on who wants the pieces,' Edie replies.

'*Daily Star* called us orderlies Amazons the other day.' Hodgson chuckles. She pushes back her chair and stands. 'Do I look like an Amazon to you?' The young woman is barely more than five foot, at least four inches shorter than Edie, and she can't help but laugh.

'The man what wrote the piece, he'd never set foot in here,' Hodgson says, sitting back down. 'He wrote all sorts of nonsense. Like us orderlies can catch any unruly patient and cart them off to prison. As if!'

'My pieces will be more truthful,' Edie promises.

'We're no saints,' Hodgson says, 'but we ain't no female warriors neither, ruling the wards with our *unnatural strength*.' She flexes her slim biceps, drawing a chuckle from Edie.

'It must be so interesting, being a reporter,' Hodgson remarks.

Edie can't think how to answer. It still feels surreal that a girl from the workhouse, like her, is writing for the press.

'Let's get you to the library now,' Hodgson says. 'It's the best thing here, I promise you.'

The library, they discover on arrival, is currently closed, but the doors are unlocked.

'Staff can go in whenever they want,' Hodgson assures Edie, leading her through into a large room. Mahogany bookcases stretch along the far wall, writing tables, stools and armchairs are scattered about, and a full-size billiard table stands in the middle of the space. At one end of the room a raised wooden platform is half shrouded by a pair of long navy curtains, the material stitched with the monogram WHC. Edie asks the orderly what the letters stands for.

'Women's Hospital Corps,' Hodgson answers.

A wooden painted sign has been mounted above the stage, proclaiming: *Deeds Not Words*. Edie recognizes the suffragettes' familiar motto.

'Wonder if Godson's about.' Hodgson taps on a narrow door sandwiched between the bookcases that Edie hadn't noticed. When there's no answer, the orderly tries the handle. 'Locked. She must be out.'

'The librarian?'

'Has Dr Garland warned you about her?'

Edie shakes her head.

Hodgson scratches her nose. 'Walls have ears,' she says, but the look she throws Edie suggests she's desperate to say more.

'What's she like?' Edie presses, keeping her voice low.

'Well,' Hodgson loud-whispers, 'she can be a bit of a dragon. Goes through assistants like a dose of salts, I've heard.'

'Oh.'

'But she might like you.'

Edie wonders why the orderly should think this, when she hardly knows her.

'Anyway, she's not here,' Hodgson says. 'Do you want to wait? She might be back soon.'

Edie would rather not. Her energy is waning, and she still has to navigate her way out of this place and back to the Levinsons'.

'I can show you the rest of the hospital, if you want,' Hodgson offers. 'Though you look a bit peaky, if you don't mind me saying.'

'Thanks, but I'll come back tomorrow,' Edie replies. Ready to meet the dragon.

Dr Garland isn't in her office, so Edie bids Orderly Hodgson goodbye in the courtyard, and limps through the gates. After the bustling industry of the hospital, Endell Street feels relatively subdued, the air tinged with the stench of the Thames to the south. A beggarwoman shambles past Edie on the pavement, and Edie suddenly thinks of her friend Sylvia Pankhurst, whom she hasn't seen for some weeks. Edie used to write about Sylvia's work with the poor women and children of the East End in the *Dreadnought* before the war. Perhaps Sylvia will let her publish some of her new hospital articles in the suffragette paper.

As Edie reaches the crossroads, a tumult of noise bears down on her, the clatter of carriage wheels over stone mixing with the shouts and cries of street sellers and cab-drivers. Her leg is growing painful as she limps in the direction of High Holborn, but she pushes herself on.

If she can just get back to Harry's, she'll be all right.

She spots a gap in the traffic, steps into the road – and something slams into her with such force it lifts her off her feet.

For a moment, she's airborne, satchel flying. And then she's falling, the road rising up to meet her. As her body strikes stone there is only blackness.

5

Josie – Atlantic Ocean

In the immediate aftermath of the sinking, a wretched hush descends among the survivors. Josie stares out over the empty ocean, her mind in freefall, unable to believe that on this calm, clear afternoon, with the lighthouse of Kinsale visible in the distance, they are shipwrecked. Moments ago, she was standing on the deck of a liner so fast, so sleek, it was known as the greyhound of the Atlantic. Now, she's trapped in an overcrowded thirty-foot wooden tender, surrounded by desperate people, miles from land and far from rescue.

Only five of the twenty-two lifeboats have successfully launched. Leaning over the gunwale, Josie desperately scans the water. A woman's stifled sobs, and a baby's sudden, plaintive wail, break the tense lull. As others continue calling for loved ones or friends, she screams Jem's name until she's hoarse. At last, the woman next to her lays a heavy, bejewelled hand on her arm. 'Take a breath, girl.'

For the first time since getting into the lifeboat, Josie takes notice of the owner of the fleshy body she's been pressed up against. As the woman lifts her lace head covering, Josie meets the shrewd gaze of Mrs Cavendish.

'Less than twenty minutes!' A man across from Josie has his pocket watch held aloft in a shaking hand for all to see. 'Took less than twenty minutes to go down!'

His words are met with stunned murmurs.

The lifeboats and the few collapsible rafts that have made it off the ship cluster together on the boundless, shimmering sea. While a couple of the boats are half empty, Josie's is overfull, riding low in the water. She spots one or two of her fellow stewards in the others, and wonders if her cabin mate, Lily, had made it to safety. Had Robert survived? Had any of them seen Jem? She feels sick with anguish.

From somewhere, a tin of biscuits is found and handed round. A digestive is pressed into Josie's hand but she can't eat it, can barely swallow.

Josie's attention is drawn to a full boat nearby, and among the passengers she spies the Italian family, the mother, grandmother and all three children clustered together in a small, tight knot. Josie's heart aches at the sight.

She's distracted by a man's cry: another survivor has been discovered clinging to wreckage. For a moment hope sparks in Josie's chest.

But it's not Jem.

An infinity of water stretches away to the horizon. The Atlantic Ocean cares not if she lives or dies, Josie knows. She's merely flotsam, one good wave from drowning in the eternal deep.

But she can't drown.

She has to find Jem.

Another survivor is spotted floating on a door. The corpulent, grey-faced man is dressed in a dinner suit and cries like a child as he's pulled into the safety of a lifeboat.

Eventually, a decision is made among the survivors to head towards the lighthouse. In Josie's tender four men take up the oars, and as the boat slowly retreats from the scene of the tragedy, Josie desperately searches the debris-strewn water for her brother. But she can only hope Jem's found something, a raft perhaps, to cling to. She lays her pounding head upon the gunwale, the wood warmed by the afternoon sun, only dimly aware of the boat moving, the slow, rhythmic grate of oars in rowlocks.

The sun continues its descent, and Josie closes her eyes against the glare, intending to rest only for a moment to gather her strength before resuming her search for Jem.

She's jerked alert by the sudden dip and sway of the boat. A man near the bow has risen to his feet, and is pointing at something in the distance. 'Look!'

There follows a scramble, people trying to glimpse whatever has been spotted. The lighthouse seems a little closer, Josie thinks. But that's not what the man is shouting about.

A fishing trawler is heading towards them, its wide brown sails flapping in the breeze.

'We're saved!' a woman cries. 'Oh, thank the Lord!'

Weak cheers erupt from the surrounding lifeboats,

and Josie's heart lifts at the prospect of rescue, and just as quickly sinks as thoughts of her missing brother assail her once more.

It seems to take an age for the *Wanderer* – a name Josie will remember for the rest of her life – to reach them. As the trawler comes alongside, Josie has an impression of a battered hull and weatherworn rigging, and wonders how many people the modest vessel can hold. Maybe two lifeboats at the most.

The *Wanderer*'s arrival is greeted with weary joy, and soon ropes are thrown down to Josie's boat, and a couple of crewmen from the *Lusitania* tie them off. One by one, passengers are hauled up into the fishing vessel, women and children first. Mrs Cavendish causes a minor scene, as several men are required to hoist her. At last, Josie is the only remaining female in the lifeboat. Her arms tremble, but somehow she manages to pull herself up the makeshift rope-ladder, on to the reeking deck.

She finds herself squashed next to the soft bulk of Mrs Cavendish again, as the crew of Irish fishermen work tirelessly to bring as many survivors as possible on board.

Someone passes Josie a tin cup of water, and she drains it dry. She hadn't known how thirsty she was. She hears the name 'Queenstown' muttered among the passengers around her, and tries to pick up what's being said.

'Nearest harbour,' a man asserts. 'They'll take us there.'

She has to find Jem.

Another survivor is spotted floating on a door. The corpulent, grey-faced man is dressed in a dinner suit and cries like a child as he's pulled into the safety of a lifeboat.

Eventually, a decision is made among the survivors to head towards the lighthouse. In Josie's tender four men take up the oars, and as the boat slowly retreats from the scene of the tragedy, Josie desperately searches the debris-strewn water for her brother. But she can only hope Jem's found something, a raft perhaps, to cling to. She lays her pounding head upon the gunwale, the wood warmed by the afternoon sun, only dimly aware of the boat moving, the slow, rhythmic grate of oars in rowlocks.

The sun continues its descent, and Josie closes her eyes against the glare, intending to rest only for a moment to gather her strength before resuming her search for Jem.

She's jerked alert by the sudden dip and sway of the boat. A man near the bow has risen to his feet, and is pointing at something in the distance. 'Look!'

There follows a scramble, people trying to glimpse whatever has been spotted. The lighthouse seems a little closer, Josie thinks. But that's not what the man is shouting about.

A fishing trawler is heading towards them, its wide brown sails flapping in the breeze.

'We're saved!' a woman cries. 'Oh, thank the Lord!'

Weak cheers erupt from the surrounding lifeboats,

and Josie's heart lifts at the prospect of rescue, and just as quickly sinks as thoughts of her missing brother assail her once more.

It seems to take an age for the *Wanderer* – a name Josie will remember for the rest of her life – to reach them. As the trawler comes alongside, Josie has an impression of a battered hull and weatherworn rigging, and wonders how many people the modest vessel can hold. Maybe two lifeboats at the most.

The *Wanderer*'s arrival is greeted with weary joy, and soon ropes are thrown down to Josie's boat, and a couple of crewmen from the *Lusitania* tie them off. One by one, passengers are hauled up into the fishing vessel, women and children first. Mrs Cavendish causes a minor scene, as several men are required to hoist her. At last, Josie is the only remaining female in the lifeboat. Her arms tremble, but somehow she manages to pull herself up the makeshift rope-ladder, on to the reeking deck.

She finds herself squashed next to the soft bulk of Mrs Cavendish again, as the crew of Irish fishermen work tirelessly to bring as many survivors as possible on board.

Someone passes Josie a tin cup of water, and she drains it dry. She hadn't known how thirsty she was. She hears the name 'Queenstown' muttered among the passengers around her, and tries to pick up what's being said.

'Nearest harbour,' a man asserts. 'They'll take us there.'

'Kinsale's nearer,' an Irish woman argues.

Josie doesn't care who's right: she wants only to reach land, and find Jem.

She soon loses all track of time, her only guide the sun dipping ever lower in the deepening blue, setting the ocean ablaze. A large naval steam tug appears, and *Wanderer*'s traumatized human cargo is decanted once again. Josie, Mrs Cavendish and the rest of their lifeboat join those rescued from other boats and rafts. There's barely room to sit anywhere, but a space is found for Mrs Cavendish in a sheltered corner of the bow, and the elderly widow insists Josie stay with her.

The tug moves at a steady clip, and soon they reach the entrance to Queenstown harbour, the rays of the setting sun casting a warm hue over the town beyond. Josie looks out at houses painted pastel shades of cream and pink and blue, the soft colours of candy. The place doesn't smell sweet, though. She breathes in a heady mix of fish and brine, and the green, land-borne scent that she misses on ocean voyages. A cool breeze has kicked up, and she shivers in her damp stewardess uniform and thin, torn stockings. Somehow, the copy of *Little Women* she took from the *Lusitania*'s library is still in her apron pocket, and she grips it with cold fingers. For the first time, she's grateful for the warm solidity of Mrs Cavendish beside her.

A crowd has gathered on the quayside, a straggling line of lamps held aloft, and Josie shivers anew at the scene. Voices call, *You're safe now, you're safe.*

Ropes are thrown and tied, and Josie waits with Mrs Cavendish, as the tug's crew lower the gangways. But the captain must report to the authorities before anyone can disembark.

'You'll let us off right this minute!' an American man close to Josie shouts, as the fishing crew obstruct the exit. 'My wife's pregnant! She needs to see a doctor!'

'Michael . . .' the man's wife moans, clutching at his sleeve.

'Captain's orders are to wait,' a crewman repeats. He's a wall of muscle.

'My father needs a doctor too,' a woman cries. She's supporting an elderly man who can barely stand. A crewman helps him on to a bench, and a few filthy blankets are found and wrapped around him.

Despite the medical emergencies, the exit remains barred: no one is allowed to disembark until permission is granted.

Boat horns blare out across the harbour, and people begin to cry, their voices mixing with the shouts of encouragement from the gathering townsfolk.

The ensuing wait is interminable, but at last the captain returns, and finally Josie steps on to dry land, Mrs Cavendish clinging to her arm, like a sea anchor. Faces white with shock surround them. Josie recognizes no one. Where are the rest of the *Lusitania*'s crew? Some survivors have bandages, or scarves, or scraps of material wrapped around their bleeding heads and limbs; others clutch broken arms in rudimentary slings. Everyone's clothing, including Josie's, is wet through.

Townsfolk approach them, offering blankets, water, food. Injured survivors are carried off on makeshift stretchers, loaded into waiting motor-cars and ambulances. Those who can walk are helped into carts, and Josie finds herself in the back of a horse-drawn wagon with Mrs Cavendish and a dozen others, a shawl draped around her shaking shoulders. Only now does she realize quite how frightened she's been. The relief of being off the water softens her bones, and only the bench prevents her from collapsing on to the straw-covered floor.

The wagon is soon full, and now they are moving off, jolting away from the harbour. Josie's thoughts are mired with exhaustion, and she's barely aware of Mrs Cavendish and the others discussing where they will be taken, what temporary accommodation might be offered.

The residents of Queenstown are opening their homes, welcoming the desperate strangers who have washed up on their shore. The wagon gradually empties as it trundles through the town, stopping at various houses, passengers disembarking singly and in pairs, stumbling away through warmly lit doorways.

They reach a hotel, the Rob Roy, and Mrs Cavendish declares she will stay there. 'Come, girl,' she says to Josie, as the driver lets down the back of the wagon for people to alight. For a moment, Josie resists. She has no money for a hotel, no money for anything, but Mrs Cavendish has cash in her purse, plenty of funds for both of them, and is determined to keep Josie by her side. They enter the hotel's foyer, and the American widow's formidable bearing and fat purse bring staff hurrying, offering hospitality. Josie's headache is worsening, the hotel's thick brown-patterned carpet undulating queasily beneath her feet. The faces surrounding her are beginning to blur, so many voices tangling in her head.

The manager appears, and Mrs Cavendish is given the largest twin suite the hotel has to offer, for herself and her 'companion'.

Josie is filled with a desperate longing to lie down and sleep, but not until she knows where Jem is.

'My brother,' she stammers. 'I have to find him.'

'You're in no fit state to do anything, girl,' the widow asserts. 'If your brother's made it, you'll find him in the morning.'

Mrs Cavendish's voice wakes Josie from a shallow slumber. It's late, though how late Josie has no idea. Someone has lit the oil lamp between the beds, and the room is burnished in its soft light. Josie hasn't slept properly, only dipped in and out of consciousness, waking at one point when a tray of food was brought up to the room. Mrs Cavendish has eaten, but Josie's appetite has left her.

'Did you hear me, girl?'

Josie can't answer, rendered mute by horrific scenes flickering through her mind.

'You can't sleep in your clothes, girl.'

How am I alive?

Ignoring the widow, Josie closes her eyes again and

rolls over to face the wall. She hears Mrs Cavendish hoisting herself off her bed, then shuffling across the room to the WC.

And, at last, Josie falls back into blessed oblivion.

She dreams she's back in lifeboat No. 21, but this time she and Jem are alone. The ocean is wreathed in thick, swirling fog, and Josie can't see anything beyond the edge of the boat. Only the muffled lapping of waves against the shallow hull, and the gentle rocking of the craft give any indication they are afloat. The world is entirely silent, no sign of other life.

They are rowing, side by side, Josie's oar strokes long and strong, but Jem's efforts are jerky and feeble. The boat is making no progress through the water, as though a giant's hand is holding the wooden craft in place, and no matter how hard Josie rows she can't shift it. The muscles in her arms are burning, her back in spasm, but she can't stop or they will never reach land.

She glances over her shoulder, glimpses a flash of light through the murk. They've been rowing for what feels like hours. They must be nearing land.

There comes a sudden clattering thud of wood hitting wood: Jem has dropped his oar and is bent over, head clasped in his hands, moaning into his knees.

Josie holds her own oar steady in the rowlock, noting with detachment how strangely dry the wood is. Why is it dry? 'What's the matter?' she snaps at her brother. 'Why have you stopped?'

'It's no good,' Jem sobs. 'Never gonna make it, Jo.'

Before Josie can respond, Jem lurches to his feet, the boat swaying beneath them.

'Sit down!' Josie drops her oar now, reaching for her brother's trouser leg. Her hand goes straight through the material, through Jem's shin, her fingers grasping nothing but air.

'Jem?' Josie snatches back her hand, staring up at her brother.

He looks at her at last, his wide green eyes despairing.

Waves are slapping at the hull, the sound like a wet hand striking the wood, over and over. Jem stumbles forward a step, tipping the boat.

'Sit down.' Josie fights to keep her voice level.

'It's no good, Jo.' Jem is shaking his head, russet hair plastered to his scalp.

'Don't be silly,' Josie pleads. 'Sit down, here, take your oar . . .'

But her brother ignores her, and before she can grab him he pitches over the side, immediately swallowed by the fog.

No!

With a cry, Josie lunges across the boat, lurching awake to find herself tangled in sheets in a strange room. As she struggles to sit up, the nightmare dissipates, subsumed by memories of yesterday's ordeal, the loss of Jem washing through her mind on a tide of disbelief.

In the opposite bed, Mrs Cavendish snores on.

One advantage of being shackled to the American widow, it occurs to Josie, is that the woman is indomitable and people do as she says. After a light breakfast in their room – Mrs Cavendish insisting Josie eat at least half a slice of toast – they set off by cab to the Cunard offices.

They arrive to find the place swarming with dishevelled survivors, as well as the townsfolk, relatives and good Samaritans who have come out in force to offer help and support.

Josie searches the crowd, but there's no sign of Jem.

Inside the ticket office clerks are barricaded behind their desks, consulting the ship's register: lists of staff and passengers, alive, dead or missing.

Josie croaks her name to a harried clerk. 'My brother . . .' she stammers. 'He was on the ship too, a baggage steward . . .'

'Name?'

'Jeremiah Everley.'

The clerk consults columns, running an ink-stained finger down the names, then shakes his head. 'No record here, miss.'

'Check again,' Mrs Cavendish demands. 'You have a full crew list, I presume?'

The clerk is fairly sure the register is complete. But, regardless, Jeremiah Everley is not marked as survivor, missing or deceased.

'You need to enquire next door, madam,' the clerk says, pointing across the room. 'Temporary morgue,' he adds. 'Some of the recovered bodies have been taken there for identification.'

The noise of the room dulls to a low hum in Josie's head, and she can only stare at the clerk. She barely hears Mrs Cavendish remonstrating with the man for his callous unhelpfulness. All she can think is: Jem can't possibly be in that room beyond the dark wood door.

But what if he is?

She lurches away from the desk, pushing her way through the crowd.

The door opens, and Josie stumbles through into a scene from a nightmare. The entire floor of the room is covered with sheeted mounds, rows and rows of bodies. The temperature feels cooler in here, the thick silence reminding Josie of a church crypt. A few people are moving among the bodies, occasionally crouching to attach tags to a wrist or an ankle.

Josie's horrified gaze lifts to the far side of the room, where a small group of people is clustered around a clerk at a desk.

She has to know.

As she stumbles through the bodies, she glimpses a curled fist, the mottled, bruised flesh of a leg, a foot that looks as though it's made of tallow, an arm so small it can only belong to a child. Bile rises in her throat, and she wills herself not to be sick.

Her voice is little more than a whisper as she gives Jem's details to the clerk. 'He was seventeen last week,' she hears herself stammer.

Her kid brother, who loved to spend all his spare dimes on chocolate bars and Cracker Jack.

The clerk consults another list, and Josie follows the man's finger, tracking down, down, until at last it pauses, hovering over a name.

'Jeremiah Everley?' The clerk meets Josie's eye for the first time, and it sets her heart beating against her ribs.

'Do you need to sit down, miss?'

'Where is he?' She doesn't recognize her own voice.

'Let me get someone to help you, miss . . .'

Josie allows herself to be steered away from the desk by a second clerk, who leads her back along the rows of mounds. If she doesn't look at the bodies, they aren't real. This is only a nightmare: she'll wake at any moment, and she'll be back on the *Lusitania*, back in her beloved library with her books.

The clerk pauses by a sheeted body. A hand, a young man's hand, the palm wide, the long, blunt-nailed fingers half curled, pokes from the cotton shroud.

Josie sinks to her knees.

6

Edie – London

'You're a cat with nine lives, Edie,' Dr Garland remarks, with a rueful smile. 'I've never known anyone as lucky as you.'

Edie doesn't feel lucky. She's lying on a trolley bed, in a little anteroom somewhere in the hospital, tucked beneath crisp clean sheets, head aching, ankle swelling. She has barely any recollection of the accident, only what Dr Garland has told her: that a bottle cart had taken a corner too fast and collided with her, knocking her unconscious for a short while. The result: mild concussion and a potentially sprained ankle.

She's still wearing her clothes, Edie is relieved to note, but someone has removed her shoes.

'Bed rest for the remainder of the day,' Dr Garland orders. 'Let's see how you are by teatime.'

'I have to get back to Harry's,' Edie mumbles. Her tongue feels oddly swollen and tender, as though she's bitten it.

'You aren't going anywhere,' Dr Garland says firmly. 'I'll send word to Harry, don't worry, and you can have some more pain relief in an hour if you need it. In the meantime, try to sleep. You've had a shock and your body needs time to recover.'

The doctor hurries away, leaving Edie alone.

You should be dead.

The thought swoops into her head, circling like a bird of prey. How has she dodged death again? When will her luck run out for good?

She sinks back on the pillows, closing her eyes, and an image of Stanley lying in the mud, his mouth spilling blood, flickers through her mind.

You should be dead.

She would have died in France if not for Stanley. All through that Godforsaken march up to the lines, he'd somehow kept her going. Many times she'd feared she couldn't take another step. He'd shared his precious rations with her, even his water when Edie's canteen had run dry. Stanley's friendship had kept her alive through a hell she hadn't thought she'd survive.

Her love for Stanley, born on the battlefield, had been a tiny, secret flame in her breast when all hope was cold to the bone.

Yet she'd left him in that enemy sap, seriously wounded and alone. She'd give anything to know where he was now. Although Harry had managed to discover that Stanley had been shipped back to Britain shortly after Edie had been rescued, his whereabouts since then have remained a mystery.

All at once Edie craves a cigarette, though she hasn't smoked since France. What wouldn't she give for one of Stan's thin roll-ups, the smoke harsh in her lungs, a reminder of him?

*

A knock at the door, and it swings open before she can react.

'We really should stop meeting like this, little scribe.'

'Harry?' Edie drags herself up on the pillows.

'Lucinda's just told me of your tussle with a bottle cart.' Harry raises a silvery eyebrow and smiles. 'Dicing with death again, young lady! We could be back in Wimereux.' He pulls a chair to Edie's bedside, depositing an armful of newspapers on the end of her bed.

Edie's heart lifts to see her friend, the reporter's energetic, solid presence instantly reassuring, dispelling all thoughts of Stanley, France and broken hearts. 'It's good to see you,' she croaks.

'When I said to research the hospital, I didn't quite intend to this degree.' Harry's smile is teasing, but his brow is carved with worry lines Edie hadn't noticed before. 'Oh, before I forget . . .' He digs in his coat pocket, producing a waxed-paper package. The warm scent of jam and pastry wafts to Edie. 'From Mary. She baked them for Lucinda and Florence, but apparently, according to them, jam tarts are a known remedy for injured little scribes who don't look where they're going when they cross busy roads.'

Bless the doctors for their kindness. 'Please thank them for me.'

'You can thank them yourself, when you're up and about again. Which, knowing you, won't be long.'

Edie flexes her foot, grimacing. 'Dr Garland thinks I've sprained my ankle.'

'You knocked yourself out too, don't forget. Count your blessings it wasn't worse.'

'I can't stay in here, Harry.' Edie's chest tightens at the thought.

'Well, if you decide to pick a fight with a bottle cart, this is what you have to endure.' Harry winks.

'I don't remember anything,' Edie mumbles. 'Maybe something smacking into me...'

'Out for the count, you were,' Harry supplies cheerily. 'Luckily for you, a couple of nurses were passing on their way back here for their evening shift. They got you scraped off the road and into bed.'

Pain sparks through Edie's ankle and she flinches.

Harry rustles open the fragrant parcel and offers its contents to Edie. 'I'm under strict instructions to make sure you eat.'

Edie can't help but smile, imagining Dr Garland and Dr Maberry in their office, reluctantly forgoing the baked goods. Of anyone, it was the doctors who deserved a sweet treat. 'I can't eat all of them...'

Harry gives her a mischievous look. 'I'll happily help you.' He delves into the bag and samples a tart, pronouncing it the best his wife has yet made.

Edie agrees. Hers is equally delicious.

'Glad you're intact.' Harry taps his nose. 'Your satchel broke your fall, Lucinda told me.'

Edie lifts a hand to her own nose. It's still skewed, but apart from some minor grazes it's no worse than before. At least she'd avoided smashing her face when she fell. 'I'll never win a beauty prize.'

'Even battle-scarred war heroes can be beautiful.'

Edie smiles wryly.

'This will put your accident into perspective.' Harry unfolds the top newspaper – the *Evening Standard*. 'At least you're not on the *Lusitania*.'

'The ship?'

'As was.' Harry passes Edie the paper. 'The Germans have sunk her.'

> Shortly after two o'clock on Friday afternoon, the great Cunard liner *Lusitania* was struck by torpedoes fired from a German submarine ...

Edie reads on, horrified.

> Saturday 1.30 a.m. First Officer Jones of the Cunard company wires from Queenstown as follows: About 500 to 600 passengers and crew have been saved. This is only an estimate. In the meantime, we're going through the hotels and lodging houses tonight, and will wire tomorrow fullest possible details. At present the injured and recovered dead are taking our attention.

Edie tries to imagine the scene, people struggling to save themselves. What must it be like to drown? Was it a quick, merciful death? Or did your lungs fill with water slowly, painfully, terrifyingly, as you sank beneath the surface?

'Edie?'

Gradually, she realizes Harry is speaking to her.

'You've gone the same colour as the sheets.'

Edie swallows. 'I'm thirsty, Harry.'

'Why didn't you say?' Harry leaps to his feet and disappears, returning a few minutes later with a cup of water. 'Sterilizing room's next door,' he reports. 'They're having a party in there.'

Edie drinks, as Harry reads the rest of the article to her.

> 'The *Wanderer* picked up around 160 survivors, and these were transferred to a navy tug out of Queenstown. The Admiralty reports that other vessels, including several trawlers, have collected a further 350 or more. The survivors are being put up at the hotels and boarding houses, but a list of names cannot be given before morning, as the survivors are in such a state that their immediate wants must be considered first. The nationalities on board included American, Canadian, Greek, Swedish, Mexican, Italian, Dutch, Russian, Belgian, French, Finnish, Scottish, English, Irish and Persian. The rescue boats are being landed at so many isolated parts of the coast, the exact number of survivors is difficult to ascertain.'

Harry lowers the paper and absently reaches for another tart.

Edie tugs a second newspaper from the pile. They all scream variations of the same headline: *Last moments on the doomed liner. White track of death across summer-like sea.*

What did Ma used to say? *Worse things happen at sea.*

'I'm not sure I should have shown you this, Edie.'

Edie's hands tremble but she can't stop reading. She pictures a ship afloat on a flat, calm sea; a sinister white arrow speeding through the waves; an explosion that rips through the hull; a tremendous crash shattering the peaceful scene.

> Mr Ernest Wallman, a Toronto journalist coming across to Liverpool with his editor on business, stated that a sharp lookout had been kept for enemy craft when Ireland was nearing. He was conversing with his editor at about two o'clock, when he glimpsed the conning tower of a submarine, off to starboard. They noticed the track of a torpedo, and the *Lusitania* was struck forward. A loud explosion followed, and portions of the hull splintered and flew into the air. Seconds later, a second torpedo struck, and the ship began to list to starboard shortly thereafter. The crew immediately proceeded to launch the lifeboats, and everything was done in an orderly manner.

Edie doubts Ernest Wallman has been quoted accurately. She reads on:

> Mr Wallman witnessed several members of the crew rescuing passengers, including a stewardess who selflessly gave up her own space on a lifeboat for a family, assisting the mother, grandmother and three children to safety.

What happened to the stewardess? Edie wonders. Did she make it into a lifeboat in the end? Harry is reading out another article.

> 'The course of the *Lusitania* was altered for land immediately after the torpedo struck. Captain Turner remained on the bridge to the last and went down with the ship, but

was rescued shortly after, having been kept afloat by a lifebelt.

'Apparently, the Cunard offices have been inundated,' Harry says. 'They've had to bring in police to guard the door. So many people want to know what's happened to their loved ones. I'll investigate further on my way home.'

'Where are the offices?'

'Cockspur Street. Not far.'

'I want to come with you.' Edie sets down the newspaper and pushes back the sheets.

Harry surges to his feet. 'Absolutely not. Lucinda would have my innards strung across the gates if I let you out of here.'

'But I'm fine.' To demonstrate this, Edie begins to swing her legs over the side of the bed, wincing as pain bites. Her head swims, and she puts a hand to the bedside table, dislodging a clipboard of medical notes, sending it clattering to the floor.

'You're in no fit state to go anywhere today, Edie.' Harry gently but firmly propels Edie down on to the pillows.

'I'm all right,' Edie persists. 'Nothing's broken.'

'A miracle,' Harry says drily. 'Even so, Lucinda has said you must rest.'

Edie sighs.

'Have another tart,' Harry urges, but Edie shakes her head. She's no longer hungry. 'There's something that might take your mind off sunken ships,' Harry says, after a moment. 'I might've made some progress in our search for your pal . . .'

Edie's spine stiffens. 'You've found Stan?' Her voice doesn't sound like her own. With every day that passes, her hope of being reunited with her dear friend grows a fraction more remote, yet the flame in her breast burns on. Stanley had been brought back to Britain: that much Harry had discovered from the hospital-ship records. But after that, he had vanished.

'I wish I could tell you I have,' Harry replies gently. 'But the good news is I've ruled out another tranche of institutions.'

Harry takes a notebook from his pocket, and reads off a list of London hospitals he's already checked: King George Hospital in Waterloo, Springfield War Hospital in Wandsworth, Paddington Military Hospital, West End Hospital, the Royal National Orthopaedic Hospital in Great Portland Street, the Military Orthopaedic Hospital in Shepherds Bush, the Metropolitan Hospital in Hackney, University College Hospital, the National Hospital for Diseases of the Heart in Westmoreland Street, Hampstead Military Hospital.

No trace of Stanley has been found in any of them.

'But I've also now ruled out Charterhouse Hospital,' Harry continues, 'Queen Mary's in Roehampton, and Rochester Row Hospital. Stanley wasn't admitted to any of those, either.'

So many hours of searching. Edie can't thank Harry enough for all his hard work.

'What if we never find him?' A desperate sob fills Edie's throat, and she swallows it.

'I've got my sources working hard,' Harry replies.

'Someone, somewhere, knows what happened to your pal. If he's suffering from shell shock – quite likely given what happened to you both – he could be in a private asylum.' He explains to Edie how pre-war asylums are being turned over for military use. 'And then there are the specialist hospitals, like the neurological and typhoid units, the numerous convalescent hospitals, many of which I have yet to investigate.'

Edie can think of nothing to say. The sheer extent of the task is overwhelming.

Harry leans back in the chair and regards her. 'You think about Stanley all the time, don't you?'

The question hangs in the air. Edie's throat tightens again.

'Don't you?' Harry presses, his voice low and emphatic, and there's something about his gaze that drags the truth from her.

She nods. Stanley's in her thoughts from the moment she wakes every day.

'His ghost threatens to come between you and the page.'

Edie shakes her head. Not Stan's ghost. His *spirit*. 'I have to know what happened to him.'

'We won't give up looking,' Harry says. 'We'll find him.'

Edie wishes she could believe him.

'I'm haunted too,' Harry says softly, 'by what's going on with our boys over in France.' He falls silent. Voices and laughter drift through the wall; the party in the sterilizing room next door is in full swing.

'There's something else I want to talk to you about, Edie.'

'I don't want to let you down,' she interrupts.

'What do you mean?'

'These pieces you've asked me to write on the hospital, I don't think I can do it.'

'You really did bump your head.' Harry chuckles. 'There's no question you can do it. You're the best apprentice reporter I know.'

'How many apprentice reporters do you know?'

'Well . . .' Harry pulls a face. 'All right, you have me there.'

They're both quiet for a moment.

And then: 'Mary doesn't want me to mention it, but I feel you should know, Edie.'

'Know what?'

Harry makes a show of reorganizing the medical notes on the clipboard.

'Know what, Harry?'

At last, he looks at her. 'I'm going back.'

It takes a moment for his words to register. 'You mean . . . back to France?'

Harry nods, not meeting her eye again. 'Mary's furious, and I don't blame her.'

'But you can't go!'

'I only decided this morning.' Harry sighs. 'Of course, freelance journalists like me are still banned from reporting anywhere near the front, too much of a liability, but an old friend in Paris owes me a favour . . . I leave first thing tomorrow.'

'You can't go back there!'

'It's my job, Edie. I have to.'

'Why now?' Edie cries. 'You're helping me look for Stan, but you can't if you leave.'

'I promise I'll carry on looking.' Harry gives her a hopeful smile. 'When I return.'

'Don't go, Harry.' She can't help the pleading note in her voice. The prospect of losing another friend is too much to bear.

'I'll be back before you know it,' Harry assures her. 'And I'll be very careful. Mary'd never forgive me if I came to grief out there.'

'Please . . .' It's an effort not to scream the word.

'You'll be so busy writing your pieces, you won't know I'm gone.'

'I can't do it without you.'

'Of course you can.' Harry reaches for Edie's hand and clasps it in both of his. 'The world needs to know about everything that's going on here in this hospital, and you're the one to tell them.'

Edie has no words. Silence stretches between them.

'I'll be back soon,' Harry says at last. 'Take care of Mary while I'm gone, and make sure you rest.'

He leaves Edie the newspapers, and the remaining jam tarts. She stares sightlessly at the closed door. All she can think is that she can't stay here.

At last, biting her lip against the pain in her ankle, she pushes herself up and off the bed. She stands swaying for a moment, and a memory comes to her of Sergeant Ratigan, Edie's commanding officer on the battlefield.

When the soldiers complained they needed a rest, Sergeant Ratigan's response was blunt and unsympathetic: *Rest is for the dead.*

7

Josie – Ireland

The church bells of Queenstown begin tolling again at first light. Each mournful knell resonates through Josie's aching head. She's barely slept in the past forty-eight hours, unable to stop thinking about her brother and how he died. Her last memory of Jem, when he'd come to find her in the *Lusitania*'s library, haunts her now as she accompanies Mrs Cavendish to the church. She should never have sent him back into the bowels of the ship. Her brother had been seasick and scared, and she'd let him down.

She can never forgive herself.

Queenstown's main thoroughfare is lined with men of the Connaught Rangers, the Royal Irish Rifles, and the navy. But Josie barely registers the troops as she follows the funeral procession along the street. All the windows have been shuttered, and despite the entire town turning out to pay their respects, dockworkers, farmers, shopkeepers, townsfolk and survivors crowding the pavements, a subdued silence lies heavy on the air.

Grave pits have been hastily dug on open ground above the town. Josie still can't accept that her brother is destined to lie there, in one of hundreds of coffins that squads of soldiers have carried all morning from the mortuary. When she'd first heard the strains of the funeral march, played by the town's brass band accompanying the coffins on their final journey, Josie's heart had threatened to burst.

Now, as she leaves the mild spring sunshine to step into the cool of the church, her heart is a stone in her chest. How will she ever get through this day?

'We'll sit here,' Mrs Cavendish decrees, steering Josie to a front-row pew.

Josie is too numb to resist. Part of her is glad of the widow's authoritarian presence, as there are hardly any faces she recognizes in the congregation. Barely any crew are here, and Josie's cabin mate Lily and steward friend Robert have drowned, she'd learned yesterday. Robert didn't even make it off the ship, helping others until the moment the liner went down.

Josie glances along the row, spotting a couple of the ship's officers. The grim-faced men are sitting with representatives of Cunard and a handful of local officials. Captain Turner is absent, gone to the coroner's court at Kinsale, Josie has heard. An image of the captain on the bridge flickers into her mind, and she closes her eyes briefly, as the vicar begins the sermon.

'Graciously hear us, Lord Jesus Christ, and deliver us from all evil . . .'

The drone of voices from the surrounding café tables ebbs and flows, but Josie hears nothing. In her mind, she's still standing at her brother's graveside, watching coffins being lowered, one on top of another. Too many of the wooden boxes had borne the chalked epigraph: 'Unidentified'. Mrs Cavendish had paid for Jem's coffin to have a nameplate, a kind gesture, but now Josie feels indebted to the widow.

'You haven't touched your food, girl.'

Josie prods her fork into the congealed fried egg. 'I'm not hungry.'

'So you keep saying.' Mrs Cavendish tuts. 'But a body needs sustenance.'

Some less than others. Josie hears her brother's voice in her head.

Mrs Cavendish orders a fresh pot of tea, and resumes perusing the local newspaper. *Lusitania Funeral – Bodies Laid to Rest*, the headline blares. 'We'll return to the Cunard offices,' the widow declares. 'They're issuing berths to New York again now.'

Josie's stomach churns at the thought of boarding another ship. The prospect of returning to America fills her with dread. She can't go back there, not without Jem. She doesn't even have Nico any more.

Mrs Cavendish reaches for Josie's hand, and she's too slow to react and is forced to submit to the widow's warm grip. 'I have a proposal for you, girl.'

Josie swallows. If the woman insists she accompany her back to New York, she doesn't trust herself not to scream.

'Are you listening, girl?'

Josie stares at her plate of uneaten food. Jem would've devoured this in seconds. Gradually, she realizes Mrs Cavendish is still talking. 'I need an assistant,' the widow says. 'Come and work for me.'

'I'm not going back.' The words are out before Josie has ordered her thoughts.

Mrs Cavendish draws in a sharp breath, her prow of a bosom rising beneath the layers of black lace. 'I beg your pardon?'

'I'm not going back,' Josie repeats, louder this time, provoking a few heads to turn at nearby tables. She can't go back, not without Jem. There's nothing left for her in America.

'Then what on earth will you do, girl?'

This question has been looming in Josie's mind since the funeral. Earlier, she'd found herself thinking of her aunt Pearl of all people. She hasn't seen her mother's older sister for years, not since Josie was eight. Before Jem was even born.

The chatter in the café melts away, as Josie's thoughts return to her aunt's narrow little second-hand-book shop in London, Josie's childhood home. Her mother, Amber, had moved in with her sister Pearl when Josie was a baby, soon after Josie's father, a steeplejack, had been killed falling from a factory chimney.

Josie had grown up immersed in books, her aunt's shop a haunt for bibliophiles, some of whom travelled from overseas in their search for a rare first edition that Pearl might have on her shelves.

Josie remembers when she was perhaps seven years old a man had visited the shop. He'd come all the way from Greece, looking for a particular book. Josie can't remember the title now, but she remembers the man clearly. Short in stature, with curly ash-blond hair, he'd spoken English but with such a pronounced accent that Aunt Pearl had struggled to understand him. Somehow, Josie had, though to this day she can't explain how. To Aunt Pearl's surprise, Josie had shed her habitual shyness and helped to decipher his words.

'You have clever girl, madam,' the Greek had told Aunt Pearl. 'She will go far in life.'

'Not yet, I hope,' Pearl had replied, drawing Josie close. 'She's my little apprentice.'

'Far,' the Greek had pronounced. He'd given Josie a twist of sherbet then, a parting gift for the clever girl.

The following month, another man, this time an American, came to Aunt Pearl's shop. Don Adams was a tobacco salesman, in London for work. He'd taken shelter in Pearl's shop one rainy Saturday, and met Amber, who was holding the fort that day while Pearl was ill in bed. Amber and Don had got talking, bonding over their shared love of jazz music, and Don had soon become a regular visitor to the shop.

Don had courted Amber with dogged intent, and before the year was out they were a couple. Then Amber had fallen pregnant with Jem. There followed a hurried register-office wedding, and plans to move into a place of their own.

But then Don's company had recalled him to New York. Somehow, despite Pearl's misgivings, Don had persuaded Amber to go with him, promising her a fresh start in America. Amber's decision to emigrate changed her life, and Josie's, for ever.

'Did you hear me, girl?' Mrs Cavendish leans across the table. 'Where will you go?'

'London,' Josie hears herself say.

'London?'

'I've got family there.' The only family she has left.

Mrs Cavendish regards her with a sharp eye. 'Your family are English?'

'My mother was.' She doesn't mention her stepfather.

'Was?'

No flies on you. Jem in her head again.

'My mother was born in London.' But died in New York, she doesn't add. Her family history is none of the widow's business, but if Josie had the strength she'd tell Mrs Cavendish about her aunt's beautiful bookshop, her childhood home. She'd tell her how her aunt had looked after her when Josie's mother had worked shifts at the match factory. She'd tell the widow how her aunt had taught her to read.

'What brought your mother to America?' Mrs Cavendish wants to know.

'She met a man.' Who'd swept her off her feet, showered her with attention and gifts, brought ribbons and sweets for her little daughter, quiet in the corner with her books. Then he had taken them far away across the ocean to a new life.

But Don had turned out to be a drinker, and when Jem had come along things had only got worse. Don's alcohol-fuelled rages were mostly directed at inanimate objects, walls and doors, and Josie's mother had done her best to shield Josie and Jem from the worst of his temper. Many times, Don had threatened to hit Josie, and though he never did, Josie grew so frightened of him she retreated further and further, seeking escape in the pages of whatever books she could find. Stories made the real world disappear for a time, and though books weren't always the safest place to hide, they offered Josie the solace she craved.

She'd vowed to herself never to tell a soul about those years of fear. Especially not the likes of Mrs Cavendish. Nor will she speak of the relief she'd felt when her stepfather had been killed, staggering from a drinking den one night. He'd been knifed in a fight, and breathed his last in the filth of a gutter two blocks from home.

Amber had always planned to bring Josie and Jem back to England, but there had never been enough money. The years had slipped by, and Josie had grown to young adulthood, Jem to a gangling adolescent, who towered over his sister and mother.

Josie's mother and aunt had written to each other every month and Josie can still remember the London address inked in her aunt's copperplate hand on the back of each envelope.

Then, last year, just when Josie had scraped together enough dollars to get all of them back to London to visit Pearl, Amber had caught a fever and died.

'Who do you have in England, girl?'

Mrs Cavendish's question pulls Josie back to the café, with its ambient chatter, and aroma of burned toast.

'My aunt.'

'Close, are you?'

Not for a long, long time.

Lightheaded, Josie forces herself to meet Mrs Cavendish's eye. The widow gives a slow, knowing nod.

They join a gathering of tearful relatives of the dead and missing, waiting patiently outside the Cunard offices. Josie sees a few crew members whose names she can't now recall. Volunteers from the town, armed with walking sticks and bundles of blankets, are preparing to spend another day searching for survivors along the coast. Josie can't understand how they can hope to find any more people alive, not after three days.

She finds herself thinking of the Italian family, the mother, the grandmother and those poor children. What had happened to them? Where were they now? She prays to a God she doesn't believe in that they're safe, that someone was helping them get home.

The warmth of the morning sun is a soft caress on Josie's cheek, yet she can't suppress a shiver as her thoughts darken, recalling Jem's coffin being lowered into the cold, dark ground.

Mrs Cavendish snares a passing clerk, demanding attention, and when the man discovers the widow's personal connection to the president of Cunard there is no more queuing in the heat for Mrs Cavendish or Josie.

The tea from breakfast swills in Josie's guts as they step inside the crowded offices. She finds herself before a desk, separated from Mrs Cavendish, and a harried clerk asks her name. He offers no sympathy for Josie's loss, no apology for the tragic circumstances that have brought her to him. 'Your posting as stewardess is transferable to another liner,' he tells Josie, barely looking up from his paperwork. 'The next ship to America will arrive tomorrow. You can sign on then.'

'No,' Josie croaks. Her voice doesn't sound like her own. 'I want to resign my post.'

The clerk's head lifts. 'You're under contract, Miss Everley.'

'I want to resign,' Josie repeats. Her bladder aches.

The clerk sucks his teeth. 'Wait here.' He disappears through a door behind him, and Josie has no choice but to wait.

Mrs Cavendish materializes at her side. 'My offer still stands, girl.'

Before Josie can react, the clerk returns, trailing an older man. 'Under normal circumstances, you'd have to honour your contract, Miss Everley,' the senior clerk intones.

'These are far from normal circumstances,' Mrs Cavendish snaps.

Josie tries to breathe. Three days ago she had a job she loved in a ship's library, and Jem was alive. Now, her beloved brother is gone for ever and she has nothing, and no one.

The senior clerk slides a sheet of paper covered with dense print across the desk. 'Sign here,' he says, pointing to a space at the bottom of the page. 'Then you're free to go.'

Before she can change her mind, Josie scrawls her name.

*

Back outside, Josie takes what feels like her first full breath in days. A quartet of young men pass by, heading for the volunteer station, and the loss of her brother rips at the wound in Josie's heart afresh.

She's adrift. Anchorless. Alone.

Questions and worries tumble through her brain. Has she done the right thing, ending her employment with Cunard? What will she do for work? How will she live?

On their way back to the hotel, Mrs Cavendish continues her efforts to persuade Josie to return to America with her. 'Free board and lodging, for secretarial work and occasional social engagements,' the widow presses. 'You won't get a better offer, girl.'

Josie bites the ragged skin around her nails until they bleed. It would be easier, not to mention safer, to stay with Mrs Cavendish. But though the widow's offer is tempting, Josie knows the pain in her heart will only worsen, surrounded by so many memories. The thought of returning to New York, without her mother, Jem and Nico, is unbearable.

All she craves is peace, a balm for her grief. Was finding her aunt the solution?

'Is there nothing I can say to make you change your mind, girl?'

Josie shakes her head, swallowing tears. It's an impossible decision to make, and she's terrified. She waits for the widow to denounce her, walk away.

Instead, Mrs Cavendish pats Josie's hand. 'Well, then, I wish you all the best, dear.'

8

Edie – London

Edie lifts her satchel on to the bed. The outer leather is scuffed and grimy from the accident, but to her relief her notebook inside is undamaged. Slowly, carefully, she pulls on her shoes, biting her lip as her ankle protests. At least it isn't broken. If she can get herself down to the courtyard, she can rest for a while in the sunshine. While she gathers her strength, she might even jot some notes on the patients and staff. And then, when she feels strong enough, she can make her way home to the Levinsons'. If she can catch Harry before he leaves for France, she has a chance to persuade him to stay, or at least ask him where she should continue the search for Stanley.

The need to find him consumes her, and she can't fully concentrate on Harry's writing assignment until she finds out what's happened to him.

There is a brisk rap at the door, and a tall, middle-aged woman in a VAD orderly uniform of white cap, apron and over-sleeves bustles into the room. She's carrying a vase filled with cheerful cornflowers. 'A gift from Dr Garland, dear,' the orderly says, by way of greeting, setting the flowers on the bedside table. Her smile wavers. 'Have I got the wrong room? I was told there was a patient in here who'd been knocked down in the street . . . Are you Miss Lawrence?'

Edie assures the woman she has the right room.

'But you're out of bed. Are you quite recovered, dear?'

Edie reassures the orderly she's quite well. To prove it, she tidies the newspapers Harry had left into a neat pile on the bed, and straightens the sheets.

'Terrible tragedy,' the orderly remarks, gesturing at the *Evening Standard* headline. 'It's the *Titanic* all over again, isn't it? Those poor souls.'

'Yes,' Edie agrees. It is a tragedy. She musters a smile, an attempt to offset the sad news, and is rewarded with a kind smile in return. As the VAD orderly turns to leave, a thought strikes Edie. 'Would you have a moment to spare?' she asks. 'I'm writing a piece on the hospital, and I need to interview some of the staff.'

The orderly hesitates. 'There are precious few spare moments in this place.' She gives a small sigh. 'I find there's barely time to draw breath.'

Edie nods in silent sympathy. Welcome to life in service, she wants to say to the orderly, but holds her tongue for fear of offence. The woman's diction betrays her higher class, her privilege, and Edie remembers what Dr Garland had told her about the VADs being dropped at the gates by their chauffeurs each day.

Edie retrieves her notebook, and invites the orderly to sit down for a few minutes.

'I haven't been off my feet all morning,' the woman

says. 'Are you a lady journalist?' She eyes Edie's notebook warily. 'I'm not sure I've ever met one before.'

'We're a rare breed,' Edie says.

'Now I understand why Dr Garland sent flowers.' The orderly smoothes her apron over her knees, sitting tall. 'What would you like to ask me, Miss Lawrence?'

'Would you mind telling me your name?' Edie begins.

'Not at all. Mrs Whitford-Gowers.'

'And how did you come to work here at Endell Street, Mrs Whitford-Gowers?'

'I answered the call of duty, of course.'

Of course.

'How long have you worked here?'

'A little over three weeks.'

'And what sort of tasks do you do, Mrs Whitford-Gowers?'

'Oh, goodness, anything and everything. Fetching and carrying for the patients, helping the nursing staff with their duties, making beds up, cleaning wards, delivering flowers to special patients.'

They share a smile.

'Preparing dressings,' Mrs Whitford-Gowers continues. 'Folding slings, emptying chamber pots, and anything else I'm needed for. I have to say, it's made me re-evaluate my own servants.'

'How many do you have, if you don't mind my asking?'

'Only my cook now. She's practically family. And our scullery maid, but she's been making noises to join the VADs herself. Wants to travel, apparently.' Mrs Whitford-Gowers gives a wry laugh. 'Girl's never been out of the borough.'

Edie thanks the orderly for her time, and the woman heaves herself to her feet.

'No rest for the wicked,' Mrs Whitford-Gowers says. She pauses in the doorway. 'Are you sure you're all right, Miss Lawrence? You're rather pale.'

'I'm fine,' Edie assures her, though her ankle is still aching and she's trying not to wince. The painkillers have worn off.

'If you're quite sure . . .'

As soon as the orderly has gone, Edie closes her notebook and shoulders her satchel. Fizzing with impatience to be outside, she limps to the window, looking down on the courtyard four storeys below. Down there is where she needs to be, amid the activity, where she can observe the nurses and orderlies busily tending the patients, recuperating in the fresh air. That's where she'll find the true heart of the hospital, not stuck here alone in this room.

The corridor is thankfully deserted, and she encounters no one until she reaches the staircase, where another VAD orderly is coming up the steps. The orderly's arms are laden with blankets, and she barely gives Edie a glance.

Emboldened, Edie makes her way downstairs, clinging to the banister. No one challenges her as she limps out into the busy courtyard. She pauses for a moment, sunshine warming her face as she takes in the scene. A pleasant herbal aroma reaches her from a nearby plant pot filled with rosemary, mint and thyme, and she counts more than thirty patients scattered about the yard, one or two in trolley beds. Most of the men are dressed in the distinctive blue hospital suits, a few officers in silk dressing-gowns.

Medics and orderlies hurry back and forth across the courtyard, checking patients, talking briefly with some, bringing refreshments to others. Edie glances towards the gates, where a pair of Endell Tommies are being signed out by a female porter. Some patients were obviously well enough to wander freely in and out of the hospital, which makes Edie feel less guilty for escaping her bed.

Without warning, a wave of giddiness swoops through her, the scene tilting and blurring. She manages to stagger the few steps to a nearby tub, and there she stays, clinging to its occupant, a pear tree, until gradually the world steadies and sharpens once more. After a few deep breaths, she moves to an empty table close by, shaded by a bright green sun canopy.

Once she's mastered her breathing again, she resumes her observation of the yard. At a nearby table a trio of young men are chatting, sharing cigarettes, and Edie's thoughts turn again to Stanley. If he was here he'd be snapping this scene with his camera, making her laugh with his silly comments and observations.

See that fellow over there, Lawrence? Only one leg, but he looks hoppy. D'you get it?

If only she had his camera with her, but she'd left it in Harry's study. She could have taken some pictures of these soldiers relaxing, like Stanley had when they'd first met during military training at Hurst Park.

Edie has a sudden vivid memory of Stanley raising his camera to his eye, and snapping a picture of her smoking a roll-up during an all-too-brief rest break.

Relax, Lawrence, it's not going to nick your soul.

In an effort to distract herself from thoughts of Stanley, Edie takes out her notebook and begins to jot brief descriptions of the people around her. She's on her third page, when an orderly pushing a patient in a wheeled chair approaches. The patient's left leg is encased in plaster and sticks out in front of him like a battering ram. Bringing the chair to a stop opposite Edie, the orderly applies the brake.

'Do you mind if we share your table, miss?' the woman asks with a tentative, tired smile.

'Not at all,' Edie replies.

The man says nothing, staring at Edie's notebook open on the table. His face has the pallid hue of someone who hasn't seen the sun for a while, his taut jaw and glassy stare making Edie wonder if he's quite all there. Was he suffering from shell shock? The man's fingers tap a persistent, nervous tattoo on the arms of his chair, but the rest of him remains frozen.

The orderly bends to say something in the man's ear, then hurries away.

Left alone, Edie waits for the man to acknowledge her, but he remains inert.

'I'm Edie,' she ventures, after several seconds of silence. Offering her first name seems apt in the circumstances. Less formal.

The man gives no indication he's heard her. Could he

be deaf? But the orderly had spoken to him, and why would she bother to do that if he couldn't hear her?

Just as Edie is wondering whether to leave the young man to his thoughts, he slowly lifts his head. His eyes, magnified behind wire-framed spectacles, remind Edie of an owl's, wide and haunted. His throat bobs above his hospital collar, but he says nothing.

'Have you been here long?' Edie tries.

The man fingers his knotted tie with a hand that visibly shakes, his gaze sharpening. Edie has the sense she's pulled him back from whatever abyss he was contemplating.

'Did you know this hospital is run entirely by women?' she hears herself say. 'All the doctors are women, and the support staff too. Apart from a few RAMC chaps on the gate.' To Edie, the hospital resembles a hive of bees, every worker performing her role, the male drones tended with efficient care, and Dr Garland as its reigning queen. She's wondering if she should share this observation with the man, when he gives a hoarse cough.

'Thought I hadn't a dog's chance,' he rasps.

Edie waits for him to go on.

'When I heard about this place, I didn't want to come.'

'Why was that?'

'I never thought it could be true.'

Edie is about to reply, when she spots the tall VAD orderly from earlier striding towards her.

'There you are, young lady!'

'Hello, Mrs Whitford-Gowers.'

'I've been searching the entire hospital for you, Miss Lawrence.'

'Have you?' Edie summons an innocent smile.

'Dr Garland insists you remain in bed,' the orderly replies. Her sharp eyes spot Edie's open notebook. 'Interviewing more people, I see.' She turns to the young man in the wheeled chair, but he's resumed tapping the armrest, staring into the distance.

'I needed some fresh air, Mrs Whitford-Gowers.'

'I'll have to tell Dr Garland you've left your room, Miss Lawrence.'

'Please don't worry her.' Edie makes a show of stowing away her notebook. 'I *will* rest, I promise.'

The orderly fixes her with a doubtful look, but to Edie's relief she doesn't insist Edie return to her bed. Instead, she's called away by a colleague, and hurries off.

Edie bids the young man good day, and hobbles towards the gates before anyone else can detain her.

It takes Edie twice as long as normal to reach the Levinsons', her ankle slowing her down. Approaching the house, she wonders if Mary is out, busy with her volunteering efforts. Is Harry still at home? How can she persuade him to stay, when the man lives for his work? Edie knows only too well how much he wants to report the truth from the battlefields because she once had the same drive. But now she wants only to find Stanley. The mystery of his disappearance has gone on long enough, and she feels sure they must be close to tracking him down. There can't be that many hospitals left to check.

She lets herself in through the back entrance, swaying

with fatigue in the kitchen doorway, to be greeted by a shocked Mary.

'What on earth are you doing here?' Mary advances on Edie, reaching her moments before her knees buckle. Deftly, Mary propels her to a chair. 'Harry said you'd had an accident. He told me you were being cared for at Endell.'

'I'm fine, Mary, really.'

Mary tuts. 'What can Lucinda be thinking, sending you away in your state?' She divests Edie of her satchel. 'You're white as a sheet, young lady! Tell me you didn't walk all the way from the hospital.'

'I forgot how far it was . . .'

'Have you lost your senses?' Mary plants her hands on her ample hips, reminding Edie of a plump, agitated chicken. 'You look ready to drop. I don't expect you've eaten anything, have you?'

Edie shakes her head, and Mary sets to, fetching a pot of tea and boiling an egg.

'Is Harry still here?' Edie asks.

'You've missed him,' Mary replies shortly, hacking at a loaf of bread. 'I hope you're not entertaining the idea of following him, young lady.'

'Would you let me go?'

'I most certainly would *not*,' Mary snaps. 'He left you this.' She tugs a folded slip of paper from her apron pocket.

Edie,
Apologies for the hurried note. Just heard from a source: try Queen Square Hospital.

Look after Mary while I'm gone.
Keep writing.
H.

Edie looks up to find Mary watching her. 'One of Harry's sources might have found Stanley,' she whispers.

'Oh, Edie.' Mary comes to her, wrapping her in a warm hug, and Edie is grateful she doesn't need to explain: Mary knows enough from what Harry has told her. Mary wasn't in France, but she knows of Edie's 'stunt', her terrible ordeal on the battlefields, her miraculous survival.

But no one, not even Harry, can truly understand how the loss of Stanley affects Edie. No one can understand the loyalty, the love, the lifeline that was forged between them in that hell. To be reunited with Stanley would restore the missing piece of Edie's soul.

'He says I should try Queen Square.'

'The National Hospital?'

Edie nods.

'Hasn't Harry checked there already?'

Edie shrugs, pushing the note across the table for Mary to read.

Mary rubs her brow. 'Typical Harry . . . so erratic.'

Edie's stomach growls, and Mary's eyebrows lift. 'I hope you're not thinking of going to Queen Square today, young lady.'

'I have to.'

'Another day won't change anything.'

But it might, Edie wants to cry. Anything can happen

in a day. Yet she knows in her heart that Mary's right: it would be wise to rest first.

'You can't go gallivanting about London in your state, Edie. I simply won't allow it.'

'Tomorrow, then,' Edie reluctantly agrees, earning herself another embrace from her friend.

9

Josie – London

Dusk is falling by the time the SS *Orduna* steams from Queenstown harbour. Josie stands on the upper stern deck, a bracing wind threatening to tug the cloche hat from her head. Soon she'll be forced to take shelter below decks, but not yet. She stares out over the water, at the Irish coastline diminishing in the distance, her guts churning like the ship's wake.

To be at sea is taking all her fortitude, every last modicum of courage she has. She slides a hand into the pocket of her coat, which, along with the hat, had been donated by a kind resident of Queenstown, and grips the leather coin purse stuffed with dollars.

Mrs Cavendish had insisted Josie accept the money. 'You can pay me back when you're settled,' she had asserted.

Josie had tried to resist, but Mrs Cavendish remained steadfast, and in the end, with no money of her own and no idea when her wages from Cunard might be paid, Josie had thanked Mrs Cavendish and taken the cash. She'd promised the widow she'd write as soon as she reached London, and repay her as quickly as possible.

The *Orduna* carries several hundred troops en route

from Canada, destined for the battlefields of France. Josie shares the deck with a number of these soldiers, their easy, relaxed banter at odds with the general atmosphere of tense exhaustion permeating the rest of the ship. Most of the other passengers are survivors from the *Lusitania* like her, identifiable by their ashen, haggard faces and the cork life vests they all wear.

When the wind grows too strong, Josie retreats below decks, seeking a corner of the second-class lounge to tuck herself away. Her nerves are as taut as a forestay in a gale, and she doubts she'll be able to sleep until the ship has safely docked in Liverpool. But at least she'll be warm inside. She debates whether or not to take off her life vest, and in the end decides she'll have to if she ever hopes to be comfortable enough to rest. It will serve in place of a pillow, at least.

A number of Canadian soldiers have commandeered the lounge, small groups of them playing cards, laughing and chatting. One or two are reading books, and Josie takes her pilfered library copy of *Little Women* from her apron pocket. By some miracle it's survived with only water damage to the cover, and a few torn pages. She hugs the bedraggled little book, and closes her eyes, imagining herself back in the library on the *Lusitania*. In her mind's eye, she drifts along the bookshelves, picturing the glossy spines of so many novels she'd been waiting to read. All are gone now, along with the polished mahogany writing desks, the velvet-upholstered chairs, the fountain pens and hand-cut writing paper. Everything gone.

When she'd first joined the *Lusitania* as a library stewardess six years ago, she knew she'd found her ideal vocation. To work with books was a dream, allowing her to continue an education cut tragically short.

After her stepfather Don died, her mother had worked three jobs to keep a roof over their heads. Josie had soon been forced to leave school and find work, mostly cleaning with her mother. But Amber had made sure Josie still had the chance to visit the neighbourhood Carnegie Library, a branch of the New York Public Library. Access to free books, and somewhere safe and warm to read them, had given Josie the literary knowledge to apply for the library-stewardess position with Cunard.

Her first shift on her maiden voyage remains seared on Josie's memory. The opulence and splendour of the liner's first-class library was beyond anything she'd experienced before, and it had taken her days to gain enough confidence to speak to the passengers. But as time passed, she came to realize an important truth: wealth did not necessarily equate to knowledge or wisdom. Many first-class passengers never opened a book, ignoring the shelves of literature waiting to be explored. Initially Josie had been shocked, but then simply sad.

There is no such luxury library on the SS *Orduna*.

The ship's engines rumble on, a muted, perpetual thunder. Huddled in a corner, wrapped in her coat, Josie thinks of her brother, who never had the chance to establish his sea legs. She should never have let him join her on the ships, but he'd been desperate to escape their rough neighbourhood, to follow his sister and travel the world.

She should have listened to Nico.

She will never forgive herself.

A sudden loud, metallic, ratcheting sound makes her flinch. Through the portside window, she can see crew preparing a lifeboat, releasing the craft to swing out over the side of the ship.

Josie's guts twist. They've been at sea barely an hour and night is falling. Why are the crew undergoing a lifeboat drill? Many of the Canadian soldiers are moving to the windows to observe proceedings, but Josie turns back to her book, unable to watch. She tells herself it's only a precaution, that it's better the crew know what to do in an emergency than not. It will be over soon, and the lifeboats will be returned to their rightful places, never to be moved again, God willing.

Much later, when she is proved right and everyone has settled, the ship fully under way, she goes in search of a drink of water, something to eat, the lavatory. She leaves her coat on the armchair, but wears her life vest.

Refreshed, she returns to her nook, and tries not to think of the worst that could happen.

A day and a half after leaving Queenstown, the *Orduna* reaches Liverpool, intact and on schedule. Josie has hardly moved from the armchair, and her limbs are stiff, her head aching from lack of sleep, unlike the Canadian troops, who slept like logs scattered over the floor of the lounge.

Exhaustion competes with hunger to sap Josie's strength, as she follows the stewards' directions up on deck, shielding her eyes against the bright early-morning sun. A sharp wind slaps her cheeks, and she pulls her coat tighter. In her pockets she carries a letter from Cunard confirming the termination of her contract, a purse of Mrs Cavendish's money, and a handwritten character reference from the widow. With Josie's possessions lost to the sea, these things are all she has left in the world, the precious letters standing in lieu of any identity papers she might be asked to produce.

The ship moors at a floating landing stage, and Josie is swept on a tide of passengers on to Prince's Dock. She stumbles along a covered walkway clogged with porters manoeuvring carts piled high with baggage and sacks of mail, and on towards a two-storey building. Passing through the entrance to the Liverpool Riverside station, her eye snags on a huge clock suspended on chains from the ceiling, its ornate hands pointing to eight.

On past the booking offices, waiting rooms and refreshment stands, she arrives at last at the ladies' washroom, where she freshens herself up as best she can.

At the money exchange, she waits in line to transfer Mrs Cavendish's dollars into pounds. But as she counts the notes, she's shocked to find the widow has given her a hundred dollars: a small fortune. She can't possibly change this much cash, she frets, as the queue shunts forward. Anyone would think she'd stolen the money. She'll be arrested for sure.

Discreetly, she extracts fifty dollars from the purse.

The exchange rate is chalked on a board – $4.76/ £1 – and Josie calculates in her head that fifty dollars equates to about ten pounds and ten shillings. More than enough to get her to London and, hopefully, to her aunt's house. She can worry about changing the rest of the money at a later stage.

With her English currency, she buys a train ticket to London's Euston, then treats herself to a cup of tea and a reviving bowl of carrot soup. Warmed, she waits on the busy platform for her nine-fifteen train. Everywhere she looks, people are reading papers, the front pages full of news of the tragic sinking. She can't bear to be reminded, and stands as far apart from the crowd as she can.

When at last her train arrives, all of the first- and second-class carriages are full, but to Josie's relief she finds a space in third. The journey from Liverpool to London will take at least five hours, but she tries not to think about it, instead letting her mind drift to her aunt, trying to imagine what Pearl might be doing at this precise moment. But she can barely picture her face.

As the railway guard's whistle sounds, and the train shunts into motion, Josie's thoughts darken. What if she can't find Aunt Pearl? What if she's . . . No, she can't finish that thought. Exhaustion weights her bones, and in the warm, rocking carriage, she grips the purse and papers in her coat pocket, fighting to stay awake. Her seat is by the window, and she longs to rest her head against the murky glass and close her eyes. The elderly man seated next to her soon succumbs to sleep, his whiskery head lolling on Josie's shoulder.

In an effort to stay alert, Josie takes herself back to her childhood in London, a city she hasn't visited for sixteen years. She can only dimly remember the place she was born, where she'd lived with her mother and Aunt Pearl. In her mind's eye, Josie enters her aunt's house and the front room, which served as the bookshop. While her memories of the rest of the house are murky, this room is clear in her mind. The walls were lined with bookshelves, a small settee whose arms leaked stuffing sat before the hearth, and a couple of low tables displayed her aunt's newest books. It was a place of love and safety, and Josie's home for the first eight years of her life.

Josie's mother had been the younger, more conventionally beautiful of the two sisters, but there was something beguiling about Pearl. She would help anyone, warmly welcoming visitors into her shop, and Josie smiles to herself as she remembers 'assisting' Pearl as she served her customers. Josie's happiest memories were of shelving books with her aunt, learning her alphabet by sorting the books, author by author, tracing the letters on the spines of novels with a stubby finger.

Josie's mother hadn't shared Pearl's love of books. Instead Amber loved music and dancing, a passion that had led her to Josie's stepfather, the man who would take Josie away from Pearl, the bookshop and everything she held dear.

As a young child, Josie had been borne along on the tide of her mother and stepfather's ambitions. Their new life in New York, at first an adventure, had soon turned sour. But by then Jem had come along, and

Don had been killed, and Josie and her mother and brother had been trapped, renting a room in a tenement they could barely afford. But despite everything, Amber and Pearl had written to each other with sisterly regularity, and Josie thinks of those letters now, left behind in that mouldy tenement in the Bronx. Lost to her.

For a moment, she senses Jem's presence in the carriage, a strange feeling of warmth that spreads from her pulsing temples to her stiff toes. Next to her, the old man slumbers on, white head nodding in unison with the swaying of the train. Josie turns back to the window, her unshed tears blurring the view beyond the sooty glass.

It's mid-afternoon by the time Josie's train pulls into Euston station. She baulks at the sight of the crowded platform, fighting the urge to remain in the relative safety of the carriage. Finding her way out to the street, she takes shelter against the station wall, allowing herself a moment to catch her breath and gain her bearings. Only now does it strike her that all her memories of London are filtered through an eight-year-old's eyes, and to her dismay nothing looks familiar.

The city teems with people – servicemen, workers, street sellers, families. Josie steels herself to join the traffic. Omnibuses, wagons, carriages and motor vehicles are swarming everywhere she looks, a cacophony of noise and smoke to rival anything in New York.

She decides to hire a cab, surely the quickest, easiest way to find her aunt's address.

Reaching into her coat pocket, she draws out Mrs

Cavendish's purse, and is fumbling to open it when a young man rushes past, clipping Josie's arm, sending the purse flying.

'Oh!' Josie gasps, as the man who collided with her scoops the purse from the pavement. She's about to thank him, when he sprints away.

'No!' she cries. 'Stop!'

She stumbles after the thief, but within seconds he's lost in the crowds milling around the station entrance.

Josie staggers to a halt, heart beating in her throat.

How could she be so stupid as to get robbed?

What was she going to do now?

Her shock gradually gives way to a smouldering anger. The thief had targeted her, she now realizes. He'd spotted a lone, defenceless woman, fresh off the train, and had gone in for the kill. Why had no one stopped him? Why had no one helped her?

Because you're on your own now, Jo.

Forced to ask directions of three separate strangers, Josie eventually finds her aunt's street, off Tottenham Court Road. Her throat is parched, her legs aching, and the soles of her feet are burning by the time she finally reaches Pearl's house. Since leaving the train, all that's kept Josie going is the thought of her aunt, the only person in the city she can trust to help her. It gives her a dizzy feeling to think how alone she is now.

Here at last is the familiar terraced house, except there's no bookshop sign above the door, and the front window is obscured by drapes. The royal-blue-painted door Josie remembers so fondly is peeling, the brass dragonfly knocker tarnished.

The place looks run-down, and Josie suffers a pang of doubt. Was this the right address?

The knocker gives a hollow clang. She waits, longing to sink down on the step. But that wouldn't do. Instead, she cups her hands against the bay window, peering through a chink in the curtains. She can just make out the shape of bookshelves in the darkness beyond, but there's no sign of movement.

One more minute, she tells herself. She'll give it one more minute.

And then what?

She startles as she hears the scrape of a key in the lock. The door cracks open, revealing the pale, lined face of a stranger.

10

Edie – London

Thick clouds the colour of ash greet Edie as she limps from the Levinsons' house the next morning. The air is uncomfortably close, thunder rumbling from the direction of Hampstead Heath. The sound reminds her unnervingly of distant artillery, and she grips her satchel tighter. A summer storm is on the way, and as she reaches the bus stop at the end of the street the first spots of rain arrive. Edie berates herself for not thinking to bring Mary's umbrella with her.

A voice in her head is willing her to turn back, to stay with Mary and Susan in the warm kitchen until the storm has passed. But now the bus is lurching to a stop, and there's no chance to change her mind.

On the journey, she tries to prepare herself for disappointment. There's no guarantee Stanley will be in Queen Square Hospital. In fact, Edie tells herself, there's a far greater chance that he won't be. It's been almost six months since they fought together in France. If Stanley had survived, as the hospital-ship records seemed to indicate, then surely he would be at home now, wherever that may be. Not in some hospital. Or perhaps he was even in France, fighting. Edie pushes that thought to the back of her mind.

The only thing she can do is continue to follow up on Harry's leads, in the hope someone might have some information, an address maybe.

The bus deposits her on the corner of leafy Queen Square, and there is the National Hospital, a grand, five-storey red-brick building. Mary had a friend whose son was a doctor here, she'd told Edie last night. The hospital is pioneering the treatment of diseases of the nervous system, particularly something called neurasthenia. Shell shock.

If Harry's source is correct, and Stanley is here, does this mean he's suffering from shell shock? What state of mind will he be in? Edie worries, as she climbs the steps to the entrance. Will he want to see her? Will he even recognize her? The last time they were together, she was Private Eddie Lawrence. He'd only ever known her as that.

Visiting hours are from ten until noon, a clerk informs Edie at the reception desk. She waits, biting a thumbnail to the quick, while the clerk checks patient names in a ledger.

His name won't be there. His name won't be there.

'Here we are,' the clerk says at last. 'Private S. Chay, Ward D.' There is no more information.

Edie tries to concentrate as the clerk gives her directions to the ward, but she's finding it hard to breathe now. Could she really have found him at last? Could Stanley be somewhere in this building? The thought of seeing him again consumes her with almost overwhelming fear and longing.

She wants suddenly to flee from this place, to run back to the Levinsons' and forget Stanley, forget everything that happened in France.

Instead, she hears herself thank the clerk and heads towards Ward D.

The ward, when she finds it, is a large, plain room containing a dozen beds, generously spaced. Two nurses are busy tending patients, and no one notices Edie hesitating in the doorway. She scans the room. All the beds are occupied as far as she can see. Despite the humid weather, the patients are bundled under sheets and blankets, unmoving as corpses. Edie can't make out any of their faces clearly so can't tell if any is Stanley.

'Can I help you, miss?' A tired-eyed nurse bearing a kidney dish filled with bloody water appears before Edie. 'Who are you here to see?'

Before Edie can answer her, a man in one of the middle beds suddenly rises up, crying out, as though waking from a nightmare. His terrified sobbing carries through the ward, and the nurse sighs, setting the kidney dish on a table. She joins her colleague in trying to settle the patient, leaving Edie by the door.

Thunder crackles and the electric lights in the ward and the corridor flicker. The crying man lets out a guttural scream, throwing off his blankets again, half falling out of the bed. Before the nurses can stop him, he is lurching down the aisle, heading straight for Edie.

She stands frozen as the man stumbles nearer, his eyes staring yet unseeing.

'Come now, Mr Rudd.' The swifter of the two nurses catches hold of the man's arm, and he stops abruptly at her touch, emitting a terrible groan. His haunted eyes pin Edie, but after a long, tense moment he allows the nurse to turn him gently round.

'It's only a spot of thunder,' the nurse soothes, guiding the man back to his bed. 'Nothing to be frightened of.'

Edie can only look on as the nurses settle Mr Rudd back in his bed, tucking the blankets tight. Gradually, his sobs diminish to whimpers.

'Are you all right, miss?' The nurse is back, scooping up her kidney dish as though nothing has happened.

Edie manages a nod.

'Perhaps you should sit a minute.' The nurse drags a chair across, and Edie sinks down on it.

'Who are you here for?' the nurse asks again.

Edie swallows, moistens her dry lips. 'Stanley Chay.'

'Relative, are you?'

'Cousin,' Edie hears herself say. This nurse would never believe her if she told her the truth.

The nurse gestures to the furthest bed. 'He hasn't woken properly since he was brought in here two days ago,' she tells Edie. 'It's nearly the end of visiting time, you know.'

But Edie is no longer listening. She pushes herself to her feet, suppressing a grimace as pain flares in her ankle, and limps towards the figure in the last bed. The man is lying curled on his side, facing the wall, auburn curls slick with sweat, his concave cheek stubbled.

It's him.

It's Stanley.

The friend she'd thought she'd lost for ever.

Her knees threaten to give.

'It can be a shock.' The nurse has reappeared at Edie's side. 'Especially if you haven't been in a hospital like this before.'

Another chair is produced, and Edie sits again, unable to tear her eyes from Stanley.

'Can he . . . Is he aware . . .'

'Your cousin had to be sedated,' the nurse says. 'Yesterday he became distressed and it was decided for his own safety he should be given a stronger sleeping draught. When the doctors made their rounds last night, he still hadn't woken.'

'Has he spoken at all?'

Has he called for her, for his pal Lawrence?

'Not to my knowledge,' the nurse replies. 'He's not unusual in that regard. Most of the patients in here are mute, or if they do speak we can't understand what they say.'

'Can he hear us?'

'Possibly,' the nurse replies. 'With shell shock, the men are sometimes so afflicted by nerves they have to be drugged. But they often report afterwards that they could hear our voices even when they were insensible.'

'So he has shell shock?'

'Intermittent, we believe,' the nurse replies. 'Your cousin's diagnosis is neurasthenia, but he was discharged from hospital some months ago.'

'But he's back . . .'

'He had a relapse,' the nurse explains. 'At home.'

'A relapse?'

'I don't know any more, miss, I'm sorry.'

There is a sudden commotion from further down the ward, and the nurse dashes off to deal with the crisis – an overturned bedpan.

Stanley lies unmoving, and Edie wants to reach out and touch him, prove to herself that he's not a figment of her imagination. She lays a hand gently on his forearm, and he gives a faint twitch but remains asleep.

Except he doesn't appear to be in a restful sleep, more like someone out cold. The nurse had said he could possibly hear, so Edie leans closer, speaking quietly.

'Stan? It's me, Lawrence.'

Will he recognize her voice? She no longer has to disguise it as she did when they were serving together, and her timbre is a little higher. She's wearing women's clothing too. If he wakes, will he know who she is?

'Stan, can you hear me?'

Stanley's eyelids flicker, but remain closed. It's all the sign Edie needs.

'I can't believe I've found you,' she whispers hoarsely. 'It's taken so long, too bloody long, but Harry and I never gave up, Stan. We've been searching all over London for you.'

Stanley gives a faint groan, and Edie's hand tightens on his arm. 'It's all right, Stan. It's only me, you can wake up.'

I came back.

She bites the words back. That confession is for another time.

Stanley moans again, louder, and now his eyes are blinking open. Edie searches for his familiar, cheery gaze, and her lungs empty of air. Stanley's eyes are lifeless, blank and staring. A terrifying void.

'Stan?' Edie takes her hand from his arm, hardly able to speak. 'It's me, Lawrence.'

Stanley continues to stare at her in silence. Then he lifts his head, his shoulders, his torso, rising in the bed. The sheets fall away, and Edie is shocked by how much weight he's lost, his pyjamas hanging from him. He leans towards her, a look of terror twisting his features.

'You're not Lawrence,' he gasps.

Edie forces herself to remain in the chair, her eyes brimming. Her worst fears are being realized. He doesn't know her.

'It *is* me, Stan,' she stammers. 'I know I look different.' She gestures at her skirt, her hair. 'I can explain.'

'Get away from me.' Stanley's threat is spoken with such quiet menace, Edie can't move.

'I said, get away from me!'

Stanley's roar brings both nurses rushing to his bedside. Edie stumbles back, stunned, as Stanley continues to shout nonsensically at her. She's never seen him like this before. In all the time they'd suffered the horror of the battlefields together, she'd never seen Stanley so angry. It's as though he's turned into someone else. They are strangers to each other, and the fact of this sinks through Edie's veins like poison.

'Please go, miss,' one of the nurses says to Edie. 'Your presence is making him worse.'

There is nothing Edie can say to this. Leaving the nurses trying to calm Stanley, she retreats from the ward.

11

Josie – London

The door opens wider, and Josie stares at the small, grey-haired, stoop-shouldered woman framed in the doorway. There is a tense moment of silence, until suddenly the woman's wary expression transforms into a smile of joyous disbelief.

'Josie?' Pearl's familiar voice and vibrant brown eyes weaken Josie's knees, and she can't speak for relief.

Her aunt steps closer. 'Is it really you?'

'It's me, Auntie.' Josie's voice is thick with unshed tears.

'Oh, my love,' Pearl gasps. 'I dreamed you'd come home one day.'

Josie falls into her aunt's embrace, and she can feel the older woman's bones through her frayed cardigan. It's like hugging a bird. At last they draw apart, and Josie wipes her eyes on her sleeve.

'I can't believe you're here, love.' Pearl's shining eyes take in Josie as she draws her over the threshold. Josie breathes in the familiar smell of old books, a scent that instantly takes her back to her childhood. Yet this is not quite the homely, bright place Josie remembers. The dimly lit front room is empty of customers, and although shelves still line the walls, they contain only a scattering of books.

Pearl's bony hand finds Josie's. 'You look exhausted, love. Come and sit down, and you can tell me everything.'

Josie lets her aunt lead her through to the narrow galley kitchen at the back of the house, where she sinks down on a rickety chair. The kitchen table is covered with scraps of paper, bills and letters, and the white-painted dresser that fills almost the whole of the opposite wall is just as Josie remembers it, the shelves cluttered with mismatched china teacups, bowls and plates. Josie wonders if the drawers are still stuffed with crayons, sticks of chalk, balls of twine. Another flash of memory: learning to read at this table, sitting on her aunt's lap, books and paper and crayons spread before them.

For the first time in days, Josie feels her body relax. Her aunt's home is a haven, a sanctuary, an island in a roiling sea, and she is finally safe. Pearl hovers close, asking if she wants tea, something to eat, perhaps. She has some bread, some cheese . . .

'Anything, thank you,' Josie says. She's so famished she can hardly think straight.

Pearl gathers together a simple meal, chattering on about how she's missed Josie and Jem and, of course, poor dear Amber. Josie's concentration drifts, as the past rolls over her.

She was last in this kitchen sixteen years ago. Over the years, family news had regularly passed across the Atlantic, in letters and on postcards, and Pearl had always remembered Josie and Jem's birthdays. But never once had she made the crossing to America, even when Jem was born. A fear of travelling overseas had kept Pearl from her family, all this time, and when Josie had signed up with Cunard and begun working on the ships, Pearl had written to say she was beside herself with worry.

Now, as she watches her aunt fill the kettle, Josie wonders if Pearl has heard the tragic news. Surely everyone knows about *Lusitania*'s sinking.

The thought of having to tell her aunt tightens Josie's chest, shortening her breath, and the corners of the narrow room begin to darken.

'Josie?' Pearl is at her side, brow puckered with concern. 'What's the matter, love?'

Josie drags in a breath, and her aunt enfolds her in a hug.

For a while, Josie's head is too heavy to lift from her aunt's shoulder. All she wants is to be held.

Tell her.

Jem's voice.

You have to tell her.

It takes everything Josie has to lift her head and meet Pearl's fearful gaze. Her aunt strokes a lock of Josie's hair behind her ear, and Josie closes her eyes.

'Jem's gone.'

Recounting the horror of the past days steals the last of Josie's strength. Pearl listens, weeps with her, holds her close, and for a time Josie finds peace of sorts.

As dusk falls, Pearl prepares a vegetable stew, and

Josie manages a small bowl, but she can barely keep her eyes open by the time she's finished. She wearily follows Pearl up to the attic garret she'd once shared with her mother, all those years ago, to find the room has barely changed.

Pearl lights a candle, apologizing for the lack of electricity, but the landlord has never had it installed. She lends Josie a spare nightdress, finds her a washcloth, brings her warm water and soap. 'Is there anything else you need, love?'

Josie is too exhausted to think, and can only shake her head.

'If you need me, love, just call.'

They embrace once more, then Pearl is closing the door, and Josie is alone.

She hardly has the energy left to undress. She washes her face, climbs into bed and pulls the blankets around her. But though she's never felt more tired, sleep is elusive. As the candle burns down to a stub, she stares up at the cobwebbed cracks in the rafters, and she's a child again, and her mother is alive, laughing with her aunt downstairs.

With her mind full of warm memories, Josie finally drifts away.

Her fractured sleep is plagued by dark dreams. She wakes early, to warm sunlight leaching through the thin muslin curtain, and for a reeling moment she has no idea where she is. She sits up, blinking the contours of the room into focus, and with the force of a wave her memory returns: the ship, the rescue, the robbery, Pearl.

Jem.

For minutes she can't move, can barely breathe. Gradually, she gains control of herself. Her mouth is parched. A terrible thirst comes over her, and it is this that compels her to rise and dress. She makes her way downstairs on legs she doesn't entirely trust to hold her, and finds her aunt already up and busy in the kitchen.

'You always were a little lark,' Pearl greets her. 'How did you sleep, love?'

'Like a log,' Josie fibs, the nightmares she'd suffered lingering in her mind. In the last of them, she'd been back on lifeboat No. 21, and Jem had been floundering in the water, drowning. She'd reached for her brother, but the gap between them had kept widening. No one else in the lifeboat had taken any notice of their desperate cries, and she'd woken herself up, a scream lodged in her throat, the unmistakable tang of the sea in her nostrils.

Though she'd washed her hands and face last night, a briny scent clings to her, and she can still feel the gritty trace of salt in her hair, on her skin. Her stewardess uniform is stiff with dried salt, and it's as though the sea is on her and in her, washing through her veins, and she'll never be rid of it.

Pearl sets a cup of tea and a bowl of steaming porridge before her.

To Josie's dismay, her eyes brim at the memory of her mother burning oats every morning. 'Mom never could make it like you, Aunt Pearl.'

'She never knew my secret ingredient.' Pearl winks.

Josie swallows a mouthful of creamy oats, and all at once is ravenous. Will her aunt share her secret?

'I can't tell you, can I?' Pearl says, feigning shock. 'It's a *secret*.'

This draws a smile from Josie.

'You're to eat that up, young lady,' Pearl says. 'Put some meat on them bones.'

Josie dutifully does as she's told as Pearl bustles about the kitchen, spooning fresh tea leaves into the pot, fetching milk from a small zinc-lined cabinet in the corner. The kettle on the stove begins to steam, the sound a ghostly echo of the *Lusitania*'s muster whistle, and Josie stiffens.

The tears when they come take her by surprise. Pearl comes to sit beside her, offering a handkerchief.

'I'm sorry,' Josie croaks.

'There's nothing to be sorry about, love.'

At last Josie's tears abate, and the two women sit without speaking for a time, until Josie finds herself telling her aunt about Mrs Cavendish, and the money, and how she'd been robbed outside the station.

Pearl's hands ball into fists, and she mutters a curse word so filthy it provokes a laugh from both of them.

'I need to find work,' Josie says, when she's regained her composure. 'And find somewhere to live.'

'Here,' Pearl says swiftly. 'You can live here with me.'

'That's so kind of you, Auntie. But I have to pay my way. Help with the rent. And I must repay Mrs Cavendish, just as soon as I can. I don't like to be in debt to her.'

'You don't need to pay me any rent yet,' Pearl assures her. 'You've got to find something first.'

'Maybe I could help with the bookshop?'

Pearl is silent for a moment. 'It's too late,' she says at last. 'I've had to sell most of the stock.'

'What?' Had Josie heard right? 'Why?'

Pearl sighs. 'The landlord's been threatening to sell up for years, but now he says he means it. I can't afford to buy him out.'

Josie stares at her, scrabbling for something to say.

'I couldn't tell you yesterday,' Pearl says quietly.

'Is there nothing we can do?' Josie asks. 'How much does the landlord want?'

'Oh, love.' Pearl smiles sadly. 'Far more than I can ever give him. But I don't have to move yet. Might be months before he gets his act together. He's a lazy devil, which for once could be a good thing.'

Josie can't believe how relaxed her aunt seems, yet Pearl must know her landlord well enough so maybe she's right not to worry unduly.

'But there's something you might be interested in,' Pearl says. 'I saw this the other day, and was thinking of applying . . .' She searches among the scraps of paper on the table, and passes Josie an advert torn from a week-old newspaper.

EDUCATED LADY WANTED
For post of Asst. Librarian, Endell Street Hospital.
Apply in Person to Miss Godson, Chief Librarian.

'A hospital?' Josie swallows.

'I've heard great things about the place,' Pearl says. 'It's run by women, apparently.'

'Really?'

'Apart from a few chaps from the Royal Army Medical Corps. All the doctors and nurses, even the orderlies, they're all women, the librarian, too.'

Josie tries to picture a hospital run entirely by women, but her tired brain is unable to imagine such a novel place.

'I reckon this Miss Godson would snap you up,' Pearl goes on. 'You've library experience, a passion for books, youthful energy . . .'

Josie meets her aunt's eye. Can Pearl not see how exhausted she is?

'It won't be like the library on the ship, love,' Pearl says gently. 'You'll be working with books again, but in a completely different situation.'

Josie bites at a ragged fingernail. Could she face working in a library again?

The following day, Josie helps her aunt in the shop, sorting through the stock that's left. Pearl has decided to donate the remaining books to the library at Endell Street, for the use of the patients and staff there.

Josie contemplates the barren shelves that once contained her childhood dreams. Her love of books was born here, and the thought that her aunt will soon have to leave her home is heartbreaking, for herself and Pearl. So many cherished memories are woven into the fabric of the place.

'I'm so glad you're here, love,' Pearl says, wiping her eyes. 'I don't know what I'd do if you weren't.'

That's one blessing, at least, Josie thinks. Her beloved aunt is all she has in the world, and she must somehow be strong for Pearl.

By lunchtime, Josie has finished packing the books, and seven full tea chests are stacked, ready to go. She wonders how her aunt intends to get them to the hospital.

'They're being collected this afternoon,' Pearl says. 'I wish I could go with them, make sure they're delivered safely.'

A thought occurs to Josie, a seed taking root in her mind. Perhaps if she pays a visit to this hospital her aunt speaks so highly of, she could see what the place is like, and maybe meet Miss Godson the librarian. She has to find a job somewhere. She shares her thoughts with her aunt, offering to accompany the books to ensure they reach their destination.

'You'll need some fresh clothes, love,' Pearl says, eyeing Josie's salt-stained uniform and grubby apron. 'Let's find you something decent to wear.'

Upstairs in Pearl's bedroom, Josie sits on the edge of the bed as her aunt opens her neat walnut wardrobe, releasing a faint aroma of lavender and camphor. She pulls clothes from hangers, laying them on the bed: a pale blue chiffon dress, a cotton shirt, a knitted cardigan, a tweed skirt, a cream blouse.

'Everything's at least a decade out of fashion,' Pearl apologizes.

Will any of it fit me? Josie wonders. Her aunt is shorter than her by several inches.

'Try the cardigan,' Pearl urges. 'It's lambswool. And this skirt, it's too big for me.'

Pearl goes back down to the kitchen to make tea, leaving Josie alone. She takes off her stewardess uniform, dumping it on the floor, and pulls on the blouse and skirt, finding to her relief that both fit her well enough. Though she's lost weight recently, the cardigan is a little tight across the shoulders, but the length is adequate, and the shade of blue is pretty. Dressed in Pearl's clothes, Josie surveys herself in the dressing-table mirror, and her aunt stares back.

Later that afternoon, a horse-drawn cab arrives to collect the chests of books. Josie stands on the pavement with her aunt, watching the driver load the last box, and tries to picture them arriving at Endell Street, being unloaded and dumped somewhere for strangers to sort through.

Next to Josie, Pearl is quiet, subdued. Her aunt hasn't mentioned the job at the hospital library again, but Josie has churned over the idea in her mind. In her heart, she knows she shouldn't let the opportunity slip past.

'I'd like to come with you, please,' she tells the driver. The man gives a terse nod, and Pearl squeezes Josie's hand. No words are required.

The cab lurches along unfamiliar streets, and Josie stares through the window, recognizing nothing, wishing Pearl was with her. But her aunt had looked so tired, Josie had insisted she rest. Pearl has given her instructions on which omnibus to catch for the return journey, and she's drawn her a rough little map so she won't get lost.

At last, the cab rumbles to a stop before a large pair of gates emblazoned with the white-painted words: ENDELL STREET MILITARY HOSPITAL.

An RAMC guard admits the cab through the gates, and Josie disembarks to find herself in a spacious courtyard. The place is busy with men in blue suits, a few sitting in wheeled chairs, others playing cards and smoking at several shaded tables. Women in uniform flit among them – orderlies and nurses, Josie presumes.

While the boxes of books are unloaded, to be conveyed by orderlies to the library, Josie signs her name in the visitor's ledger.

'Who are you here to see?' a uniformed female porter asks her.

'The librarian,' Josie replies. 'Miss Godson.'

The portress raises her eyebrows, as if in sympathy, and points the way across the courtyard. 'Third floor. Ask anyone, and they'll show you, miss.'

A covered walkway bisects the yard, and as Josie looks towards the hospital entrance the hairs on the nape of her neck tingle. Her gaze sweeps over the patients and staff. Some of the men have arms in slings or legs in plaster boots, and the heads of one or two are wrapped in bandages, but most appear surprisingly relaxed and cheery.

The courtyard exudes an odd holiday atmosphere,

and reminds Josie unnervingly of the *Lusitania*. It's as though she's been transported back to the saloon deck, and any minute now she'll be summoned by a passenger to fetch them a drink, or a bottle of ink, or a fresh copy of the ship's newspaper.

'You all right, miss?' The portress's voice brings her back.

'Yes,' Josie manages. 'Thank you.'

It takes everything she has not to turn and flee, back through the gates. Instead she squares her shoulders and sets off across the courtyard.

12

Edie – London

Returning to the Levinsons', Edie longs for a moment alone with Mary to unburden herself of the disastrous reunion with Stanley. There is no one else she can confide in since Harry has gone, but as Edie lets herself into the house, she's greeted by the shrieks of children at play, familiar voices and laughter emanating from the drawing room. The Levinsons' two daughters, Abigail and Alexandra, have arrived during Edie's absence, and there is no escape until the usual pleasantries have been exchanged.

Edie finds herself perched on a chair, as Abigail, the elder daughter, a tall, confident woman who takes after her father in looks and manner, questions her at length about how things are going in her role as Harry's assistant.

'Mother tells me you're writing about a military hospital,' Abigail says, passing Edie a plate of biscuits. Edie's mouth is so dry, her stomach a closed fist, that she can only hold a biscuit in her lap. She mumbles a reply, how she's only just begun and there's much work to be done yet.

'I do admire you, Edie,' Abigail says, to Edie's surprise.

'When I was eight or nine, Father commissioned me to write a piece on our old cat, Chestnut – do you remember, Mother?'

Mary, occupied with trying to disentangle her youngest granddaughter's hands from a length of wool she's managed to wrap around herself, shakes her head. Alexandra laughs at her sister, and claps her hands. 'Oh, Lord, it was awful, Abby.'

'It took me simply ages,' Abigail continues, struggling not to laugh too. 'At least an hour. And Father took one look at the page – which if I remember rightly was rather ink-stained and torn – and declared it unpublishable. Well, as you can all imagine, I cried!'

'You sobbed for hours.' This from Alexandra.

'I don't remember it at all,' Mary mutters, unravelling wool. 'How on earth did you come to tie yourself up like this, Georgina?'

'Marianne did it, Grandmama.'

'Clearly, Father has very high standards,' Abigail says, favouring Edie with a smile disarmingly like Harry's. 'His assistants have to be very good writers to pass muster.'

Edie feels her cheeks warm, the biscuit crumbling in her hand, and the other women laugh good-naturedly. To Edie's relief, Susan appears, bearing yet more refreshments, and while Mary and her daughters gather the children, distributing cake and water, Edie makes her excuses and slips away.

She spends the rest of the day, and long into the evening, up in her room trying to decide what to do.

If Stanley doesn't recognize her, if her very presence causes him distress, should she simply leave him be?

And yet.

The nurse had said he had moments of lucidity. Perhaps if she went back, tried again, this time he would know her.

She decides to return to Queen Square the next morning.

In Edie's satchel, two freshly baked currant buns from the kitchen are wrapped in greaseproof paper. Mary's daughters and grandchildren are still abed, and so, too, is Mary. Susan is busy lighting the fire in the dining room – Edie can hear the maid grumbling quietly to herself. Nobody notices her unbolting the back door, and making her way round the side of the house. The street is quiet of traffic, and at last Edie can breathe freely again. The Levinson family are so kind and welcoming to her, yet Edie still finds the noise and turmoil they bring with them hard to tolerate at times.

Part of her wishes she could have spoken privately with Mary about Stanley, but another part of her resists the prospect of sharing this troubling turn of events. To voice her fears aloud is to make them real.

On her way to Queen Square, Edie continues to ruminate on the events of the previous day, reflecting on her lingering shock at Stanley's outburst. She can't rid her mind of his face, his affable features contorted with fear. He'd been a stranger to her in that moment.

Passing a newspaper vendor, Edie buys a copy of the

London Illustrated News to distract herself. The headline declares: *Lusitania inquest: Kaiser guilty of wilful murder.*

She scans the front page, then tucks the paper into her satchel, along with the buns and a copy of *Kidnapped* borrowed from Harry's bookshelves. Though she would much rather walk, Edie fears the journey would be too much for her ankle so boards a bus to take her as far as Euston station. Disembarking there amid the seething crowds, she manages to navigate the final short distance to Great Ormond Street, and on to Queen Square.

Arriving at last at the hospital, Edie makes her way to Stanley's ward and is greeted by a scene largely unchanged from the previous day. A couple of different nurses are tending the patients, most of whom look to be sleeping. One patient is sitting on the side of his bed, wearing only stained long johns. He is swaying from side to side, eyes closed, as though moving to some silent, internal music.

'We watched the elms . . .' the man sings out tunelessly, to no one in particular. 'We watched the rooks . . .'

A nurse approaches him. 'I'm sure you did, Mr Wallis,' she says briskly, as she manoeuvres him gently but firmly between the sheets.

Edie makes her way along the aisle towards Stanley's bed, acknowledging the nurse with a nod. With the exception of Mr Wallis, the other patients lie silent, and Edie arrives at Stanley's bedside to find him similarly unresponsive. His eyes are closed, chest barely moving beneath the sheets, skin sallow and drawn. Edie sets down her satchel and draws a chair close.

'Stan?' She leans closer, keeping her voice low. 'Stan?

Can you hear me?' She reaches for his hand, and his fingers twitch, and Edie's veins run chill as a memory of lying wounded in the trench in France shudders through her. She'd held Stanley's hand then, and for a time her mind is consumed by darkness and regret.

Voices bring Edie back to the ward. A man in a nearby bed has woken, sobbing, and both nurses are attempting to placate him.

Edie takes the newspaper from her satchel, hoping that reading to Stanley might prompt a response from him. Perhaps he will wake if he hears her voice. 'The Germans have sunk a liner, Stan,' she tells him, eyes scanning the pages. She learns that of the 1,906 passengers on that fateful voyage, 764 have been saved, but 1,142 are dead or missing. Stanley sleeps on, as Edie reads quietly of an inquest held in an eighteenth-century courthouse in a place called Kinsale.

> 'The district coroner, court officials, jurymen, and a score of local residents were present. Captain Turner climbed with assistance into a chair that had been placed on a table as an improvised witness box. As chief witness, he stated that he had special instructions, but refused to divulge what they were. He denied seeing a submarine. He carried out his orders, and stated that he would do so again.'

Edie reads on, discovering that the *Lusitania* had not been convoyed at the time of the attack: '*The resources available to the Admiralty do not allow for escorts of the hundreds of merchant and passenger ships that travel daily.*'

The inquest, the article concludes, brought a verdict

of wilful and wholesale murder against the Kaiser and the German government.

Edie lowers the paper. She can't read any more, but she remembers the buns and the novel, and retrieves them from her bag. 'I brought you something to eat,' she whispers, setting the greaseproof parcel on the bedside table. 'And a book I think you'll enjoy.'

In truth, she has no idea if Stanley likes seafaring stories of pirates, and wonders if he's even read a whole novel in his life. But she'll read to him, for what's left of visiting time.

She opens the book.

'*Chapter One.*' She swallows, suddenly self-conscious, but no one is looking her way, the nurses busy with their tasks. '*I will begin the story of my adventure with a certain morning early in the month of June, the year of grace 1751, when I took the key for the last time out of the door of my father's house . . .*'

As Edie reads on, the sounds of the ward, the nurses' footsteps, the calls and cries of patients, drop away, until it's only her own voice she can hear and Stanley's gentle breaths.

Edie turns the page, glancing at his face. Can he even hear her?

'*Mr Campbell, the minister of Essendean,*' she continues, '*was waiting for me by the garden gate, good man. He asked me if I had breakfasted; and hearing that I lacked for nothing, he took my hand in both of his and clapped it kindly under his arm . . .*' Edie pauses, eyeing the currant buns. When did Stanley last eat anything? The nurses would know, but she doesn't like to disturb them when they're so busy.

She bows her head to the book again, reading on.

'Excuse me, miss?'

Edie starts, losing her place in the story. An orderly has appeared, curly red hair escaping her cap, her cheeks dusted with pimples. 'Would you like a drink, miss?' She gestures to a trolley parked in the aisle. How had Edie missed its arrival?

'Oh, thank you.' Edie's parched, and a cup of water would be welcome.

While the orderly is busy at her trolley, Edie takes Stanley's hand again. His stiff fingers are bent like claws, but they loosen slightly as she strokes his rough knuckles.

'You're the first what's stayed,' the orderly says, passing Edie a cup.

'Sorry?'

'He's had a couple of visitors afore, but you're the only one what's stayed.'

Edie wonders who had come. Had it been Stanley's family? Edie has never met them, but she remembers Stanley once mentioning his parents, though she can't recall any more than that.

She wants to ask the orderly if she knows when Stanley last had a visitor, but the girl is already trundling her trolley out of the ward.

Edie sips her water, musing on the unknown visitors. Family or friends or . . . ? A thought strikes: could Stanley have a sweetheart? He'd never mentioned anyone, but they hadn't really talked much about their lives beyond the army. Edie had barely talked at all, terrified that Stanley and the other men would see through her disguise, and denounce her as a woman in their midst. She'd kept her mouth shut for the most part, and the others had simply thought her shy or withdrawn.

To know that Stanley has had visitors apart from her lifts Edie's heart, and at the same time burdens it. How can her heart be light and heavy at the same time?

All through Edie's exchange with the orderly, Stanley has remained unresponsive, seemingly asleep. Edie picks up her book.

She reads on, until at last visiting time is over. More nurses are bustling about the ward now; a change of shift looks to be occurring. Edie reluctantly packs away the book, squeezes Stanley's hand goodbye. To her shock, his fingers curl about hers, and his eyelids flicker.

'Stan?' she gasps. 'Can you hear me?'

Stanley's head slowly turns towards Edie's voice.

'Stan . . .' She grips his hand tighter, and his eyes crack open.

Edie ceases to breathe, leaning closer, the noises of the ward diminishing to a faraway hum. 'Stan? It's me,' she stammers. 'Lawrence. I came back . . .' Her voice breaks, and she can't go on.

Stanley's eyes close, then open again, and a faint moan escapes his lips. Did he recognize her?

'It's me, Stan,' she says again. 'Lawrence.' She wonders if he's deafened. Her own hearing has taken a long time to return, damaged by the proximity to the blasting guns, and she still suffers an occasional tinny ringing in her ears.

Stanley swallows, and his fingers grip Edie's. His

dry lips part, and Edie glimpses a broken front tooth. 'Lawrence?' he rasps.

'Oh, Stan, thank God . . .' Edie can hardly speak for joy. 'It's me, I came back . . .'

'Lawrence?' A look of bewilderment clouds Stanley's face, and his hand slips free of Edie's. 'Where did you . . . ?' He falters, coughs. Beads of sweat break out on his brow.

'I never meant to leave you, Stan,' Edie gabbles. 'I never meant to lie to you . . .'

'What?'

'Time to leave, please, miss.'

Edie spins round, to find a nurse at her elbow. A second nurse is beetling towards them.

'Mr Chay needs his medication, miss. Visiting time is over . . .'

Edie is shunted out of the way, as the two nurses administer pills and water.

'You're quite safe now,' Edie hears one say, as she wipes Stanley's sweating brow with a flannel. 'Just sleep. There's nothing here that can hurt you.'

Edie can only look on, helpless, as Stanley's eyes close again, and he slips away.

The nurse turns to Edie. 'Visiting time is over,' she repeats, with an impatient sigh. 'Are you a relative?'

Edie clears her throat. 'Cousin,' she lies again.

The nurse's scowl softens.

'What did you just give him?' Edie asks. She has a sudden sickening mental image of Stanley lying in the trench, unconscious, blood flowing into the mud.

'Something to make him sleep for a good while,' the nurse replies. 'I'll let you have one more minute with your *cousin*, but then you have to go . . .'

Edie nods, perching on the chair. Moments later, she hears a commotion further down the ward, and looks up to find a middle-aged couple coming along the aisle. The man is wearing a dark blue suit. The shape of his jaw and his curly brown hair are unnervingly familiar to Edie. A few steps behind him is a woman, her shoulders hunched beneath a grey coat, clutching a handkerchief and dabbing at her eyes.

Edie grabs her satchel and rises as the couple reach the bed.

'Who are you?' the man demands.

'Edie Lawrence,' she stammers, her brain tumbling as she realizes these people must be Stanley's parents.

'How do you know our son, Miss Lawrence?'

'Excuse me.' The nurse is back. 'Visiting time is over, Mr Chay. You'll have to return tomorrow.'

'We couldn't get here any quicker,' Mr Chay snaps at the nurse. 'Why have you let this woman in anyway?'

Edie's face burns. Stanley's parents have no idea who she is or the part she played in their son's fate. 'Sir,' she stammers. 'I've been searching for your son for months. He's a good friend. Harry Levinson has been helping me.'

'Harry who?' Mr Chay glances at his wife, but she's moved to Stanley's bedside, displacing Edie, and is stroking her son's inert hand.

'Our son has never spoken of a Harry,' Mr Chay

tells Edie. 'And neither has he mentioned you, Miss Lawrence. I don't know who you are, but I do know that your presence is disturbing our son's rest, and I'd like you to leave.'

For a moment, Edie can't move, and then the nurse is gently leading her away.

'I'm sorry,' Edie whispers, but no one hears her, least of all Stanley.

13

Josie – London

The hospital's white-painted corridors, the walls hung with storm lanterns and metal fire buckets, remind Josie unnervingly of the *Lusitania*. But no ship she'd ever worked on smelt like this, a blend of harsh carbolic mixed with other, unidentifiable, smells. Medical staff in uniforms of white and grey, and patients in blue suits or pyjamas and dressing-gowns pass Josie as she makes her way deeper into the main building.

She soon becomes lost, and has to ask directions of an orderly, who helpfully leads her up flights of stairs, along yet more corridors, until at last they reach the library.

'Librarian should be about somewhere,' the orderly says. 'Good luck, miss.' The young woman hastens away, leaving Josie to push open the heavy oak doors. She steps into a spacious, double-sized room, electric light-bulbs hanging from the high ceiling. There's no need for them this afternoon, as sunshine streams through tall windows at one end of the room.

At the opposite end a low-rise platform reminds Josie of the music-lounge stage on the *Lusitania*. A pair of saxe-blue curtains, with the monogram WHC in black and orange fabric, is half drawn across it. A hand-painted sign above the stage proclaims *Deeds Not Words*.

Josie surveys the rest of the room, taking in the floor, which is littered with crates, boxes, tea chests and anthill-like towers of books. A billiard table sits in the centre of the library, its baize surface also strewn with books and piles of magazines. A pair of huge wood and glass bookcases spans the entire back wall. In the gap between them Josie spots a narrow door, which suddenly opens. A short, stout woman, her steel-grey hair escaping its bun, emerges from a back room. She's carrying a stack of books along one arm, in the manner of a hod-carrier ferrying bricks. Spying Josie, she hesitates in the doorway, frowning. 'Can I help you, miss?'

The woman is rather breathless, high colour in her cheeks, and Josie worries she might be about to collapse under the weight of her load. 'Are – are you the librarian?'

'For my sins,' the woman returns. She staggers past Josie, and deposits her armful on a patch of bare floor beneath the windows. Josie fancies she hears the creak of stays under duress as the woman straightens again, rubbing the small of her back with a grimace.

'My name is Josie Everley,' Josie says. 'I've come about the job.'

'Have you now?' The librarian's blunt response takes Josie straight back to the library on the *Lusitania*. She steadies her breath. Years of dealing with first-class passengers have armed her against brusqueness and bad manners.

'Are you still needing a library assistant, ma'am?' she asks.

'Regrettably, I am.' Miss Godson sighs. She fumbles for her spectacles, dangling on a chain over her formidable bust, and peers at Josie. 'Do you have any library experience?'

'I worked as a library stewardess,' Josie replies, 'for Cunard...'

'A stewardess?'

'On the transatlantic liners.' Josie can't bring herself to speak the name of the ship in front of this frowning woman.

'If you've only worked on ships, Miss Everley, what makes you think you're suitable for this position?'

I know more about books than you think, Josie wants to snap. 'I was responsible for the ship's first-class library, ma'am,' she hears herself say instead. 'I kept the books in order, made sure they were shelved correctly.'

'Are you fit?' Miss Godson interrupts. 'You look rather... wan.'

Wan? Josie bites back a retort. 'I could help you sort these, ma'am. Help you shelve them...' She gestures to the books spilling from boxes and crates. The entire room could do with a good dusting, she thinks.

'Are you *American*?' Miss Godson asks. 'You don't sound English.'

'I'm from New York, ma'am.'

The librarian's lip curls at this information, and Josie braces herself for rejection.

'Do you know your alphabet, Miss Everley?'

Josie bristles at the question. 'I could read before I went to school, ma'am,' she replies coolly. Perhaps it had been a mistake to come here. This woman doesn't want her.

'Well,' Miss Godson says at last, 'I suppose I could offer you a day's trial.' She consults her pocket watch. 'You can work until five, and then I will decide if you're of any use to me.'

The librarian turns on her heel, and heads through the doorway. Josie hesitates. Should she follow?

An impatient voice issues from the back room. 'Well, come along, girl!'

Josie crosses the threshold, and is instantly assailed by a familiar musty smell: a blend of old books, glue and dust. The stockroom is far smaller than the main library, the space filled mostly with books. Several hundred, Josie estimates, crammed every-which-way on overflowing shelves sagging on the walls, while more books fill numerous chests and crates, and yet more are piled on the floor. The librarian is standing behind a desk, its surface a mess of books, newspapers and journals. She beckons impatiently, and Josie negotiates a path through the book-strewn terrain.

'This,' Miss Godson says, waving an arm over the contents of the desk, 'needs sorting today.'

Josie contemplates the task, and a memory of the *Lusitania*'s opulent, pristine library, with its cupola skylight, ivory-white panelling, and plush velvet and mahogany furniture drifts into her mind. She pictures the gleaming bookcases bearing new and barely read texts, each carefully shelved in alphabetical order. A world away from this chaotic cave.

'Are you sure you're up to this, Miss Everley?' The librarian's sharp gaze travels the length of Josie. 'Running a library is strenuous work. Most people have no idea.'

'Let me show you what I can do, ma'am,' Josie hears herself say.

The librarian's nostrils flare, but she proceeds to explain to Josie the rather haphazard, and to Josie frankly nonsensical, method of sorting the book donations. She soon stops listening, distracted by the sheer amount of literature surrounding her. So many stories waiting to be read.

Perfect for an ink drinker like you.

Jem's voice in her head. He was always teasing her about her voracious appetite for reading.

Miss Godson drones on, and Josie tries to concentrate, but all she can think is that even if she lived to be a hundred she'd never get through a fraction of these books. She wants to read them all, savour their contents, curl up in a corner and lose herself in their pages. Was there any better way to escape life?

'Any questions?' the librarian concludes, jolting Josie back to the moment.

Josie tries to think. 'Is the library open for people . . . for patients to use?'

'Only at specific times,' Miss Godson replies.

Josie waits for the librarian to elaborate further, but instead she heads for the door again. 'I have an appointment,' Miss Godson throws over her shoulder. 'I won't be long.'

Without further explanation or instruction, the librarian strides away.

Josie exhales, her shoulders relaxing a notch.

She surveys the chaos of the desk, and the enormity of the task she's been left with hits her like a ton of dime novels. Where on earth should she start?

Shrugging off her aunt's borrowed cardigan, she rolls up the sleeves of her blouse, and only now does it occur to her that she should have brought an apron. She makes a mental note to bring one next time. If, of course, there is a next time.

She picks up a book at random. *Little Lord Fauntleroy* by F. H. Burnett, she reads on the spine. She opens the cover. It's an illustrated copy printed in 1907, with pretty patterned endpapers, and a name inked in a childish hand inside the front cover. *Eliza*. No surname. No date.

Josie sets it down, and takes up another book, this one bound in blue cloth. *The Throne of David* by the Reverend J. H. Ingraham. Its smooth pages appear unread. She picks up a third. *The Mightily Past* by Florence Dalgleish. This one is older, the bookplate inside announcing it as a Sunday School prize from 1852.

Book by book, Josie works her way through the piles on the desk, sorting the grubby, damaged ones from those she deems of good enough quality to present on a shelf. Her standards are too high, she soon realizes, as the tower of discarded books grows bigger and bigger at her side. So she begins a third stack, this time of books that could perhaps be repaired, rebound. *Rescued*.

Time ticks on, but Josie has no heed of the passing

hours, engrossed in her endless undertaking. She finds herself reading sentences, whole passages sometimes, words catching her eye and hooking her in, and for a while her mind is free of sorrow.

Until she comes to the last book on the desk: *The Open Road, A Little Book for Wayfarers* by E. V. Lucas. The cover is a dark glossy blue with gilt embossing. On first inspection, it looks in good condition. Josie opens it.

The inscription on the title page stops the breath in her lungs.

> *Life is sweet, brother...*
> *There's day and night, brother, both sweet things.*
> *Sun, moon, and stars...*

Josie stares sightlessly at the page, unable to move, heart weighted with grief once more.

Oh, Jem.

A noise at the door: Miss Godson has returned. Josie tenses, rising from the chair as the librarian approaches the now considerably neater desk.

'I see you've been busy,' Miss Godson mutters, her eyes appraising the stacks of books arranged around the desk.

'I've gone through all that was on here, and in this box,' Josie indicates a tea chest nearby, 'I put the books into three piles: keep, repair, discard. I hope that was all right?'

Miss Godson nods slowly, inspecting the top few books of each stack. 'I'll have to check, of course, but this all seems...'

The clang of a bell issues from the courtyard.

'Perfect timing, yet again.' Miss Godson groans. 'Another lunchtime disrupted.'

'What's happening?' Josie asks, as the bell continues to ring. She can hear shouting, and the sharp, urgent blasts of a distant whistle.

Miss Godson is gathering up pens and a bottle of ink. 'Ambulance convoy,' she snaps. 'Another.' She strides to the door, and Josie has no clue if she should follow.

'Come on, girl!'

She hurries after the librarian, through the warren of corridors, an atmosphere of barely contained panic sending ice through Josie's veins. A stream of medics and orderlies is flowing in the same direction, some carrying rolls of bandages, others metal pails, water containers, blankets.

Reaching the courtyard, Josie can make little sense of the chaotic scene. People are swarming everywhere, like an ant heap that's been prodded with a stick. The librarian forges a path through the maelstrom, heading for the main gates, and Josie swallows a sour taste rising in her throat as she chases after her.

At least half a dozen motor ambulances are parked at the entrance to the hospital, their rear doors open, disgorging their contents. Female orderlies are lifting stretchers from the vehicles, one after another after another, and Josie can't help but gape at their strength. They work swiftly, calmly, clearly used to performing this task. Each stretcher with its broken human load is carried carefully through the gates with brisk efficiency.

Josie follows Miss Godson to a line of trestle tables near the gates, but her gaze keeps returning to the activity around the ambulances. The female stretcher-bearers are ferrying more and more men into the courtyard, but now a crowd of onlookers has amassed on the street, their raised voices mingling with the rumble of engines and the shouts of the medics. Some well-wishers thrust handfuls of flowers and cigarettes at the wounded soldiers, most of whom are too senseless to receive them. Petals flutter, stems crushed underfoot. A couple of RAMC guards and a female porter are attempting to keep back the horde of well-wishers but it's a losing battle.

A sickly sweetish stench, like rotten meat, reaches Josie's nostrils. She can't breathe, thrown back to the mortuary in Queenstown, the rows and rows of bodies . . .

'Make yourself useful, Miss Everley!'

The librarian gesticulates towards the far trestle tables, where orderlies are hurriedly filling canisters of water from a huge urn. Josie stumbles over, and someone shoves a bucket of water and a couple of tin mugs into her hands. 'Start over there.' The orderly points across the courtyard to a line of stretchers on the ground. A pair of women doctors and a nurse are moving among them, assessing injuries. The groans and cries from the wounded men are an assault on Josie's senses, and the stench is worsening, but somehow she forces herself to crouch by the side of the nearest soldier. The man lies unmoving as an effigy, his legs wrapped in filthy bandages, a ragged bunch of flowers splayed over his torso. As Josie dips a cup and scoops water, the man's eyes open in his smoke-blackened face, and he moans something, but Josie can't catch the words over the noise around them.

She reads terror in the man's eyes, his gaze fixed on her.

'Would you like some water?' Josie stammers. The man tries to lift his head, and Josie supports his shoulders, holding the cup to his burned, peeling lips. He gulps a mouthful, chokes, swallows, coughs.

'Slowly . . .' Josie urges. But the man pulls the cup to his lips again, draining it dry. Spent, he collapses back, rose petals scattering, and Josie staggers to her feet.

Wounded and dying men surround her, everywhere she looks.

A single thought fills her head: she'll never have enough water for them all.

14

Edie – London

She makes it to Russell Square before her legs give out and she collapses on to a bench. The tears she'd managed to hold back at Stanley's bedside now blur her vision, and she presses the heels of her hands hard into her eyes.

The encounter with Stanley's parents, the shock of their reaction to her presence at his bedside, hollows Edie's insides. Now she's found Stanley at long last, the fear of being prevented from seeing him again threatens to overwhelm her.

If only she could talk to Harry ... Edie feels a stab of frustration at his abandonment. Never more than now has she needed his rational, calm advice. Overcome with despair, she begins to cry, stifling her sobs with her sleeve.

A couple are strolling towards her through the square, arm in arm, and eye her warily as they pass. She must look a sight, Edie thinks dully, as she roughly wipes tears from her cheeks. Berating herself for her weakness, she pushes herself to her feet. All the starch has leached from her bones, and it will be a slow journey back to the Levinsons'.

*

Mary takes one look at Edie as she stumbles through the front door, and ushers her into the kitchen.

'Where on earth have you been?' Mary wants to know.

They sit at the table, the sweet smell of baking permeating the air. Now it occurs to Edie that the house is quiet. Mary's daughters and grandchildren must be out. It's the first time Edie has had Mary to herself for days, and she haltingly explains to her how she'd found Stanley at Queen Square, and returned to visit him again today.

'Well, that's wonderful news,' Mary says. She leans closer. 'Isn't it?'

Edie swallows. 'He didn't recognize me at first.' She forces herself to go on. 'But then he did, and it was . . .'

'It was what, my dear?'

Edie meets Mary's eye, unable to find the words to convey the depth of her despair. Mary reaches across the table, gently taking Edie's trembling hands in her own. Nothing is said for a long moment.

'What happened then?' Mary says softly.

'His parents came.'

'His parents? Did you explain who you were?'

'They didn't give me the chance.'

'What do you mean?'

'His father said Stan needed to rest and I shouldn't bother him again.'

'Oh, Edie,' Mary murmurs. 'Look at me, my dear.'

It takes an effort to lift her head. There's a silent message in the older woman's kind gaze: she understands.

'I'm sure, in time, you'll be able to visit him again,' Mary says. 'What would Harry say, if he was here?'

'He's not here, though, is he?' Edie's hands curl into fists, an urge to strike the table sweeping through her. 'I should've gone with him.'

'He couldn't have taken you, Edie. You know that.'

Edie's eyes burn, her heart a wooden weight in her chest.

'At least you know Stanley's alive,' Mary says. 'That's something, isn't it?'

It's almost worse, Edie wants to scream. Separated from the one person she loves beyond all others in the world, her pain is beyond grief. It's torture.

Edie suffers a broken night, and wakes with a yearning to see Dr Garland. In the absence of Harry, she needs the doctor to tell her, in her measured manner, that all will be well. Only Dr Garland truly understands what she and Stanley suffered in France. Dr Garland saved her life, and the lives of so many other wounded soldiers, and knows more than most what a miracle it is to survive the battlefields.

She slips from the house, avoiding the kitchen where she can hear Mary and Susan preparing breakfast. Abigail, Alexandra and their children are returning to their own homes today, and Edie knows she'll be expected to join them all for this final family meal. But she can't face it.

She considers taking the bus as far as Euston, but the crush of bodies would be too much to bear. So she walks, wary of her weak ankle, reaching the British Museum, then passing the shops on New Oxford Street, negotiating the straggling lines of people queuing for food. A distinctive, cloying stench of offal wafts from a butcher's shop, blood running in the gutter, and sour bile rises in Edie's gullet as she limps on.

Reaching Endell Street, she's admitted through the gates by a porter, and it occurs to Edie now that Dr Garland is likely too busy to see her. She's probably in surgery, or performing her ward rounds, or in a meeting. Edie braces herself for no reply as she knocks on the doctor's office door but, to her relief, she hears a dog's answering bark followed by a brisk familiar voice calling, 'Come in!'

Dr Garland's terrier jumps up at Edie as she opens the door, licking her hand in welcome.

'Os! Naughty boy, get down!' the doctor scolds, rising from her desk. 'Edie, I wasn't expecting to see you. I heard you were convalescing at Harry's, against my orders I must add.'

The doctor's worried frown almost undoes Edie, and for a moment she can't speak.

'Is everything all right, my dear?'

'I'm sorry for disturbing you,' Edie manages. 'I know how busy you are.'

'Nothing new there,' the doctor says, with a dismissive wave of her hand. 'Now, what on earth has happened?'

Edie takes a steadying breath. 'I found Stanley,' she stammers. 'He was admitted to Queen Square Hospital, a few days ago.'

'I see.'

There is no need to say more, and Edie is grateful for that small mercy. Dr Garland is fully aware of the months of searching she and Harry have endured. The doctor also knows how much Stanley means to Edie, how their shared ordeal in France haunts her.

'He didn't know me at first.'

'He was unconscious, you mean?'

'The first time I visited, he was. And when he woke up he got . . . upset.'

'What's his diagnosis, do you know?'

'Intermittent shell shock. He had to be sedated when I was there.'

'Neurasthenia.' Dr Garland nods. 'Well, he's certainly in the best place. Queen Square is renowned for its treatment of nervous exhaustion and other psychogenic disorders.'

'The second time I visited, I read to him.'

Dr Garland's gaze softens. 'I'm sure Stanley appreciated that.'

'Then his parents came,' Edie goes on.

'From my experience, those soldiers suffering shell shock fare best when surrounded by friends and family. Visit him as much as you can, talk to him, let him know you're there for him.'

'His family don't want me to visit.'

There follows a moment of silence, as Dr Garland considers this. 'Did they say why?'

'They don't want him upset.'

Dr Garland rubs her chin, ruminatively. 'Did you explain how you knew their son?'

Edie shakes her head.

'No, of course you couldn't have,' Dr Garland

corrects herself. 'Well, all you can do is wait for them to come round. When Stanley is well enough, you can both explain to them.'

Edie's heart sinks at the realization that no one, not even Dr Garland, can help her.

'I should let you get on,' she says, gathering her satchel and rising.

'How's the writing going, my dear?' Dr Garland says, as Edie reaches the door.

Edie has barely written a word, but she can't admit it.

'Have you begun a piece on our library yet?' Dr Garland's little dog paws at her hip, and the doctor pushes him off gently. 'Have you met Miss Godson?'

Edie confesses she hasn't.

'She doesn't suffer fools,' Dr Garland says, with a tight smile. 'A morning shadowing her in the library might be the distraction you need, Edie.'

I don't need distracting, Edie wants to cry. *I need to see Stan.* Now she's caught her breath, all the things she should have said to his parents crowd her head. Why did she run away? She should never have left him.

Dr Garland is talking to her. 'The librarian is creating an apothecary of "Brontëan balms", so she tells me. "Tolstoyan tourniquets" and "Shakespearean salves". The place is a veritable medicine chest of literature. I really think you should meet her today, Edie.'

They are interrupted by the arrival of a nurse at the door. 'Sorry to disturb you, Doctor,' the nurse says breathlessly. 'You're needed in theatre.'

'I'm coming, Sister Whiteman.'

The nurse dashes away, and Dr Garland rises. 'Let me know how you get on, Edie.'

Edie makes her way up to the library, Dr Garland's words echoing in her mind, to find the place deserted. There are far fewer piles of books littering the floor than when she'd last been here with Orderly Hodgson. Edie finds herself drawn to the bookcases on the back wall, the shelves partly filled with all manner of novels. Someone, presumably the librarian, has carefully arranged the books in alphabetical order by author. Edie runs a finger along the spines: *Allen, Arnold, Barrie.*

She's read hardly any of these authors, despite plundering Harry's bookshelves.

Her stomach twists. How can she call herself a writer if she knows barely anything of literature?

The hairs on the back of her neck prickle, as if someone is watching her.

'Hello?'

Edie spins round, to find a young woman observing her from the doorway. She is perhaps a few years older than Edie, slight and pale, with hair the colour of autumn leaves. All this Edie registers in a heartbeat.

'Can I help you?' the young woman asks, in an accent Edie can't place. Definitely not a Londoner, she thinks. Was she the formidable librarian?

'Are you Miss Godson?' Edie ventures.

The young woman gives a small laugh, quickly collecting herself. 'I'm not,' she says. 'Did you want to speak to the librarian?'

'Is she available?'

'She's out just now, and I'm not sure when she'll be back. You could maybe wait for her?' The woman glances over her shoulder, as though she's expecting the librarian to materialize from thin air.

'Do you work here?' Edie asks.

'I'm the library assistant, yes,' the woman replies. She wipes her hands on her dusty apron. 'Josie Everley,' she introduces herself. 'I'm new here . . . Sorry, I didn't catch your name, miss.'

'Edie Lawrence,' Edie says, extending a hand. They briefly shake, and the library assistant steps away again, her reaction putting Edie in mind of a nervous doe.

'I'm sorry, Miss Lawrence,' Josie says, after an awkward pause. 'Do you mind if I get on?' She tips her head towards the doorway. 'Book donations. They keep coming.'

'Is there anything I can do to help?' Edie asks. A behind-the-scenes glimpse at how the library is run will be useful for her piece, and she suddenly craves something practical to do. Anything to take her mind off Stanley.

A wary look crosses Josie's face.

'I don't know much about books, but I'm a hard worker,' Edie adds.

'Why would you want to help me, Miss Lawrence?'

'Please, call me Edie. I'm sorry, I should have explained. I'm a journalist. Dr Garland has asked me to write about the library here.'

'Does Miss Godson know?' Josie's face pales further.

'Dr Garland has spoken to the librarian, so she knows,' Edie replies, hoping this is true.

'Well, I'd sure appreciate some help.' Josie's smile is hesitant. 'If you don't mind getting your hands dirty . . .'

'I'm used to that, don't worry.'

Edie follows Josie into a stockroom filled with books. A desk stands like an island in the middle of the room, heaped with yet more books and stacks of newspapers, all vying for space with assorted repair paraphernalia.

'Could you maybe stamp these books here?' Josie leads Edie to the desk, and explains the various piles. She shows Edie the library stamp, a small block of wood embossed with the words: PROPERTY OF ENDELL ST. LIBRARY.

'You might have to practise with the ink pad,' Josie says. She takes a scrap of paper and rolls the stamp in the ink, then swiftly presses it down. 'Too hard, and the ink bleeds through,' she cautions. 'I found that out the hard way.'

'Where are you from?' Edie finds herself asking, as she selects the first book and rolls the stamp as Josie has shown her.

'New York.' Josie's voice is quiet, and she offers no more information as she sorts a stack of *Country Life* magazines.

'Have you always been a library assistant?' Edie tries.

'Before here, I was a library stewardess,' Josie replies. 'On the ships.'

'That must have been interesting,' Edie says. 'Which ones?'

Josie doesn't answer, her expression troubled, and it takes Edie a moment to guess why. She recalls the recent news headlines of the tragedy in the Atlantic, and meets Josie's eye, wishing she could take back the question.

'I'm so sorry,' Edie says uselessly.

Josie visibly swallows. 'It's all right,' she mutters. 'Please, tell me what it's like to be a journalist . . .'

The hours pass swiftly, and Edie finds herself enjoying Josie's reserved company. Working in the quiet, sun-warmed library, the war seems so distant, almost mythical. A collective bad dream from which they will all wake any day now. Even the awful scene at Stanley's bedside has lost a little of its sting, Edie finds, her mind now occupied with books. She ventures an occasional careful question, but Josie reveals little of her history, and Edie senses the young woman is doing her best to hold herself together. They talk about the hospital instead, and how wonderful Dr Garland and Dr Maberry are to allow a library such as this to exist.

Gradually, the piles of books are sorted, stamped and shelved, and they finally take a break. Josie insists on sharing her lunch of soup and cheese rolls with Edie.

'My aunt's trying to feed me up,' she says, with a rueful smile. 'How much cheese can one woman be expected to eat?'

Miss Godson still hasn't returned by the time they've finished, but this doesn't bother Edie. She can interview the librarian later. Josie has shown her so much of the library that there's plenty for her to write about already.

Dusk is falling by the time she takes her leave of Josie, promising to return soon. 'I've enjoyed today,' she confesses.

'I've enjoyed it too,' Josie replies shyly. 'Thank you for all your help.'

As Edie passes back through the gates, out into the busy London streets, her thoughts return to the newspaper accounts she's read of the *Lusitania* tragedy. She can't help but imagine Josie trapped on the ship, at the mercy of the ocean, and how terrifying that must have been. No wonder the woman doesn't want to talk about it.

Her thoughts turn to Stanley. She'll write to him, she decides. Explain everything. And hope that someone kind will read the letter to him, if need be, and that his parents come to their senses soon.

Nearing Harry's road, her blood chills. She can hear a sonorous droning noise. Recognizing it, she looks up: a huge grey cigar-shaped Zeppelin is hovering over the rooftops in the near distance. Though some streets away, the enemy aircraft is heading in her direction, and she frantically picks up her pace. But she's gone barely a few steps when a crashing boom, so loud her eardrums thrum, causes her to stumble.

She glances back, to see flames flaring beyond the rooftops, thick black smoke filling the evening sky. Another crash follows, and now she hears faint screams.

For a moment, Edie stands paralysed. She knows she should run to safety, away from the horror unfolding a few streets away, but another voice is telling her the opposite: a proper reporter wouldn't flee. Harry wouldn't retreat, if he was here.

Before she can talk herself out of it, she changes course, heading towards the plumes of smoke, following the sound of clamouring bells: the fire brigade must be on their way.

The Zeppelin is steadily drifting away, as Edie reaches the scene of the attack. A bomb has been dropped on a house in the middle of a terrace, crashing through the roof, setting the timber ablaze. The inhabitants of the terrace are out on the street, children crying, families in shock. Edie joins the growing crowd, offering to do anything she can to help.

But now a horse-drawn fire engine barrels around the corner, men clinging to the outside of the vehicle. It clatters to a halt in a tumult of bells and hoofs and shouts, smoke billowing from the engine's chimney.

The firemen spring into action, a stoker feeding coal into a firebox, others unrolling hoses, seizing buckets. The driver deftly unhitches the horses, leading them a safe distance away, as the steam engine pumps and wheezes.

Edie is transfixed by the fire team's synchronized actions. As one man hooks a pipe to a water cistern at the end of the street, two of his colleagues deftly unroll a length of hose attached to the fire engine while another galvanizes residents to fetch buckets of water. Edie joins the effort, filling pots and pails at a standpipe. Soon a supply wagon laden with coal and wood lumbers alongside the fire engine. Stokers begin transferring the contents of the wagon into the firebox, and the leather hoses continue to discharge gallon upon gallon of water into the gradually diminishing blaze.

At last, the fire is doused, and the foreman issues the order to 'take up'. Within minutes, the firemen have rolled up their hoses, re-hitched the horses, and are heading back to the station.

Edie's throat is scorched from the smoky air, but a grateful resident presses a cup of lemonade into her hands, and she swallows the contents in two gulps.

Night is descending, and the street is emptying of onlookers now the emergency is over and the firemen have gone. With nothing left to do, Edie retrieves her satchel from the gutter, and slowly makes her way home.

15

Josie – London

Josie sips her tea, thinking of Edie Lawrence. She pictures the young journalist's misshapen nose, which looked as though someone had punched her, and the vivid blue eyes that missed nothing. Edie had been so helpful yesterday, and had promised to visit Josie in the library again today. The prospect of seeing her is helping to dispel darker thoughts, memories of the ambulance convoy at Endell, the courtyard full of wounded and dying men, and her lack of water to give them.

'Should you be going to work today?' Pearl asks, setting a plate of toast before Josie. 'You look exhausted, love.'

'I didn't sleep too well,' Josie admits, 'but I'm fine, honestly.'

'That librarian, is she working you too hard?'

'She can't help it, Auntie,' Josie says. 'She's very busy herself, so I'm left on my own quite a lot.'

'That's not right, love,' Pearl argues. 'And you should never have had to help with those ambulances.'

Yesterday, over dinner, Josie had tried to describe the ambulance convoy to her aunt, but had been unable to find the words. She couldn't make Pearl understand that Miss Godson had had no choice but to help. In a hospital, when the alarm bell rings everyone has to pitch in. There is nowhere to hide, not even in the library.

'Why don't we visit the market today?' Pearl suggests, topping up Josie's tea. 'Find you some new clothes.'

'I'd love to,' Josie says, 'but Miss Godson needs me.'

'Surely she can cope without you for half a day. She should let you have a bit of time for yourself.'

'I have to go in, Auntie.'

'But you need time to recover, love,' Pearl insists. 'You're worn out!'

Josie bites her lip. Her aunt's talk of exhaustion and loss comes nowhere close to describing the pain Josie suffers every morning when she wakes and the fact of Jem's death crashes down on her once more. Loss means missing something, sure, but losing Jem is so much more than merely missing him.

Each time her mind grazes the finality of her brother's death it terrifies her. Without Jem, her life is unanchored, drifting, but working at the Endell Street Hospital has given her something to focus on. The chance to rescue others.

'I'm fine, Auntie,' Josie repeats, draining her tea. 'It's better I keep busy.'

'I've heard Miss Godson's a funny old stick,' Pearl comments, running water into the sink.

Josie has to agree. The librarian is definitely a little peculiar, wearing her professionalism like an extra corset, unyielding and rigid. She intimidates Josie with her encyclopaedic knowledge of literature, but Josie senses kindness beneath the hard exterior.

'She's certainly a character,' Josie allows. She musters a smile for her aunt's benefit, but doubts and fears skulk in her mind, like mice in the wainscoting. Miss Godson's standards are very high, and Josie dreads falling short of her expectations.

'Do the patients use the library much?' Pearl asks. 'And the staff, what are they like?'

'People are always coming to the library,' Josie replies, 'but I'm working in the stockroom mostly. I met a woman journalist yesterday. Her name's Edie Lawrence, and she's writing about the hospital and the library. She'd come to interview Miss Godson, but ended up helping me instead.'

'A woman journalist?'

'She knows Dr Garland,' Josie says. 'They met in France, when Dr Garland operated on her leg.' Josie briefly relays to her aunt what Edie told her: how she'd attempted a stunt to report from the battlefields, how she'd disguised herself as a soldier, and trained and fought with the men.

'You're having me on,' Pearl gasps.

Josie shakes her head. 'She wouldn't tell me much more than that, but that's how she came to know Dr Garland apparently. The doctor saved her life.'

'Blimey,' Pearl breathes. She dries her hands on a towel, frowning. 'I'm worried this library job's too much for you, love.'

Josie shakes her head again. 'I need it, Auntie.' More than Pearl could ever know.

*

Josie nods a greeting to the female porter on gate duty, and hurries through the bustling courtyard. Nothing remains of the ambulance convoy, of course, and she tries not to think about it.

As she makes her way along the corridors, she finds herself walking the passageways of the *Lusitania* in her mind, and her thoughts return to Dr Garland, the woman who'd saved Edie's life. When would she meet the famed captain of this hospital?

Miss Godson had shared snippets of information about Dr Garland and her colleague, Dr Maberry. According to the librarian, Dr Garland, the chief surgeon, was devoted to her staff and patients. 'But she'll work herself into an early grave, you mark my words,' Miss Godson had added darkly.

Dr Maberry was equally committed to the work of the hospital. 'She's a no-nonsense Scot,' Miss Godson had told Josie. 'Sensible woman. I've a lot of time for her. She brooks no argument, has no truck with time wasters, and can smell a malingerer at a hundred paces.'

Just as on a ship, there are spheres of existence here, Josie is discovering. The staff occupy one sphere, the patients another. But even within the spheres, there are divisions that can't be crossed. Officers are treated separately from ordinary soldiers; doctors, nurses and orderlies have their strict duties and responsibilities.

The fact that the staff are all women, and the hospital's captain and first officer are women too, is not only novel but quite wonderful, in Josie's opinion. She's never worked under female command before, but from what she's witnessed here the hospital runs at least as smoothly, and the staff work as hard, as if it was presided over by men.

And as on a ship, there are multiple rules to remember.

As Josie reaches the library, she thinks of Miss Godson's. Smoking around the books is expressly forbidden, which Josie approves of, unlike some of the patrons. She's heard men arguing with Miss Godson in the library about why they weren't allowed to smoke when they could enjoy a cigarette or pipe in the wards while reading the library books in bed.

'My library, my rules,' was Miss Godson's constant refrain.

The librarian's similar ban on eating in the library also annoys the patients, as the men aren't forbidden to read while eating in the dining room, or when taking their meals in bed.

Josie passes through the deserted library, the air cool as a chapel's, and lets herself into the stockroom. Miss Godson's handbag and coat are present, but not the librarian, and Josie welcomes the solitude as she settles herself at the desk, surrounded by piles of books to be sorted. Soon, she's lost in her work, her mind focused on repairing, stamping and shelving, a blessed reprieve from thoughts of Jem.

An hour passes, and Josie is beginning to wonder if the librarian will appear at all this morning, when there is a knock at the door. She looks up to find a tall, rake-thin woman in a grey doctor's uniform striding towards her.

'Is Miss Godson about?' the woman says, by way of greeting.

Josie registers the Scottish accent, and scrambles to her feet. 'Good morning, Dr Maberry, ma'am,' she stammers. 'Miss Godson isn't here just now.'

'Do you know where I might find her?' Dr Maberry's gaze sweeps over the room, and Josie berates herself for addressing the doctor as 'ma'am'.

'I'm afraid I don't know, ma'am – I mean *Doctor*.'

'Are you the new library assistant?' Dr Maberry's sharp eyes home in on Josie.

'Yes, I'm Josie Everley, Doctor.'

'And how are you finding our library, Miss Everley?' Dr Maberry's gaze softens, and Josie remembers to breathe.

'It's . . . it's lifesaving,' she hears herself stammer.

'Lifesaving?' Dr Maberry considers this for a moment, as Josie wills the floor to swallow her. *Lifesaving?* Why had she said that, of all things? Dr Maberry will think she's trying to equate her work in the library with lifesaving surgery and medicine.

'Interesting,' Dr Maberry says at last. 'I agree. You're prescribing books to the patients, aren't you? Providing relevant remedies for certain ills.'

'The books seem to give the men comfort, Doctor,' Josie says. 'That's all I meant.'

'Don't underestimate your impact, Miss Everley. The work of the library is as important as any other in this hospital.'

'Yes, Doctor.'

'I'll leave you to get on with your lifesaving work, Miss Everley.' Dr Maberry's eyes gleam with knowing humour, and Josie finds herself revising her initial opinion of the Scot as intimidating. 'Please tell Miss Godson I'd like a quick word, when you next see her. Nothing urgent. Good day to you.'

For another hour, Josie continues to work her way through the book donations, taking a brief break to eat the sandwiches Pearl had made for her. She returns from a visit to the washroom, to find Miss Godson has arrived. The librarian had been in a meeting with a private benefactor, she tells Josie, who wished to donate their home library, comprising over five hundred books, to Endell Street Hospital. Josie wonders where on earth Miss Godson thinks they will put another five hundred.

'You've been busy, I see,' the librarian remarks, perusing the tidy desk. 'If you've finished here, you can come with me to the wards.'

'The wards?'

'Delivering books to the patients,' the librarian says. 'I'll distribute the requested literature, while you give out the reservation slips. You'll need a notepad, too. The patients will no doubt have lots of orders.'

Josie's heart stumbles at the prospect of having to talk to patients. Tucked away in the library's stockroom, she's so far had minimal contact with the rest of the hospital, relishing the seclusion it affords her.

'Don't look so appalled, Miss Everley,' the librarian says, not unkindly. 'It's an important part of our role here, to serve those invalids who can't visit the library themselves.'

'I don't know if —'

'Fetch the trolley over here, please,' Miss Godson instructs, ignoring Josie's weak resistance. 'There are seventeen wards,' Miss Godson tells her, as they contemplate the cumbersome mahogany cart, its compartments and shelves waiting to be stocked with books, magazines, stationery, cigarettes and matches. 'We'll visit three today.'

The librarian tasks Josie with sourcing as many Nat Gould novels and similar adventure stories as she can find. Endell Street, Josie discovers, mostly caters for the lower rank of soldier, many of whom love a good, thrilling adventure.

'A lot of the men,' the librarian says, 'prefer cockles to caviar.'

It takes Josie a moment to understand the librarian's meaning.

'A number of them are practically illiterate,' Miss Godson explains. 'Terrified of reading, some of them. A novella, or an illustrated magazine perhaps, is often all they can handle.'

Nat Gould books, according to the librarian, are as valuable to some men as a year's supply of Woodbines.

But classics were also in demand, Josie learns.

'Always make sure there's a Wells novel on the trolley,' Miss Godson instructs. '*The History of Mr Polly* goes down particularly well with men who think they're a failure.'

As the book cart is gradually filled, Josie tries to remember the librarian's recommendations for various ailments and mental afflictions.

Crime and Punishment for those with a guilty conscience, Miss Godson advises. 'Tormented heroes, always popular.'

The Odyssey, for those with 'itchy feet'. 'Those who still have their feet, of course. Make sure you check, Miss Everley, before mentioning anything to do with walking.'

Peter Pan, for those who have lost limbs. 'It's not just a children's book,' Miss Godson reminds her.

The Secret Garden, for those with a touch of hypochondria. 'A surprising number of them suffer from this,' the librarian remarks, with a raised eyebrow.

Robinson Crusoe, for the more pessimistic souls.

For futile dreams, Miss Godson recommends *Far from the Madding Crowd*. 'I never dream,' she adds. 'Waste of sleep.'

'Ah, good, we have both volumes,' Miss Godson says, brandishing a calf-bound copy of *Les Misérables*. 'You're familiar with Hugo, I assume?'

Josie nods. She'd read the novel last year, and the story haunts her still.

'It's well over a thousand pages,' the librarian says, 'which might put some of the men off. But I still recommend it to build a man's patience and stoicism.'

At last, the beast on wheels is full, and Miss Godson casts a critical eye over the shelves. 'Well-crafted stories not only enable a patient to connect with the protagonist's transformative odyssey,' the librarian explains, 'but they also inspire an introspective odyssey of their own.' She gestures to the trolley. 'Typically, a character in any of these novels follows a trajectory, emerging as an improved version of themselves. By immersing himself in the stories, a patient is inspired to re-evaluate what he deems significant in his own life.'

Josie nods, impressed that the librarian has voiced something she has long recognized in her own reading journey.

'This will have to suffice,' the librarian mutters, regarding the trolley with a shrewd eye. She holds open the door, and it takes all Josie's strength to push the laden trolley over the threshold. Miss Godson is already striding off, and Josie can't hope to keep up. She wonders how they will manage to get the trolley up and down the stairs, then remembers that the hospital has an external elevator for carrying stretchers, and this will no doubt be the method Miss Godson uses.

The muscles in Josie's arms are already protesting as she shunts the heavy cart on its casters in the librarian's wake, receiving some amused and sympathetic glances from passing staff.

A young man on crutches limps by. 'Too much heavy readin's bad for you,' he jokes. He throws Josie a wink over his shoulder and lurches on.

Cheeks flushed, breathing hard, she reaches St Anne's ward. The librarian gestures for Josie to park the cart in the central aisle. She follows her directions, barely able to look at the men recumbent in their beds on either side of the room.

Miss Godson hands Josie a small pile of request slips. 'Give these out,' she instructs. 'We'll collect them tomorrow. Some of the men might want you to write letters for them, but there isn't time today. We have this ward to do and two others, remember.' The librarian begins selecting books off the trolley, ignoring Josie's anxious look.

Josie scans the large, bright ward, open windows at the far end admitting a fresh warm breeze. The walls have been painted a pretty pale green, and there are standard lamps between the beds. Vases of flowers adorn almost every bedside table, lending a homely air to the place. The beds each have a colourful knitted blanket tucked neatly over crisp white sheets, and it strikes Josie that they look a little like books lined up on shelves, each patient containing a unique life story.

It's this thought alone that gives her the courage to begin.

16

Edie – London

The morning's newspapers are full of the Zeppelin attack. Edie breakfasts alone in the dining room, barely tasting her food as she reads the various accounts in *The Times*, the *Daily Express*, and the *News of the World*. Mary and Susan are busy in the kitchen preparing refreshments for a Women's Volunteer Reserve meeting Mary is due to host, and Edie is left undisturbed. She learns that yesterday's enemy airship, laden with incendiary devices, wasn't the first to be spotted over London in recent days.

She reads on, forgetting her toast and tea, hooked by the increasingly provocative wording of the various bylines.

ZEPPELIN RAID DANGER!
CITIZENS MUST TAKE PRECAUTIONARY MEASURES!

One article goes on to expand on the true menace of the enemy's Thermite-charged bombs, a terrible compound that, upon ignition, immediately generates enough heat to melt cast steel. It is the after-danger from fire that Londoners need to fear, and Edie thinks of the firemen last night who'd swiftly and bravely tackled the blaze, preventing what could have been a much worse tragedy.

As ever, the newspapers continue to peddle advertisements pandering to the public's fears, and Edie's eye is caught by a particularly unscrupulous offering: an invention of something called an 'Antizep'. Every household should have one, she reads. A simple drawing shows what looks to Edie like a hand grenade, filled with a 'secret compound', the ingredients of which are not divulged in the text.

Whatever it contains, the Antizep promises to 'extinguish any fire caused by enemy aircraft'. But how anyone can think this is a defence against Zeppelin bomb attacks, like the one yesterday evening, Edie has no idea. Promising people such things is dangerously deceitful, she thinks. Yet when people are scared, they're more likely to believe what they're told.

A more interesting article fills the opposite page:

> From Police Headquarters, instructions have been issued bidding all to seek shelter indoors, or underground in cellars, or in the central Tube stations, in the event of further air raids on the city.

Edie thinks of London's growing homeless population, who have no other place to go than the Tube stations. She reads on.

> If some system for the reception and care of those who seek shelter is organized, this would provide a very fine defensive works. If no system is organized, those who go to the Tube stations for protection will jeopardize their lives more than if they remained in the open thoroughfares.

Edie pictures floods of terrified people, pouring down into the Underground, transforming a place of safety into a potential death trap. The author of the article suggests that the Tube stations be used exclusively for the protection of women and children:

> This will give the men an opportunity for exhibiting that chivalrousness of conduct for which the English are famous, and will give those sturdy youths who have a conscientious objection to taking their places in the firing line the privilege of coming under fire at home.

The article goes on to suggest that a corps of specially trained female constables be enrolled to manage the reception of women and children into the Underground stations.

> There are in London, and indeed throughout Britain, a large number of strong women, anxious to have their services used, who would be ideal for the work. A female constable should be in constant attendance at each station. In the event of an air raid she should be assisted by other female constables, specially trained, who live in the vicinity.

The emergency stairways should be used for incoming women and children, and those men in the trains or on the platforms at the time of the attack should exit without delay. Edie wonders what the men might think of this. And what about the lighting, the ventilation, and the electrical current running through the rails? Have the authors of this article considered such things, and their potential impact on those forced to use the Tube as shelter?

> The Tube system could provide those who are menaced from the skies with protection beneath the ground, and afford our citizens the same feeling of security that the forts gave in feudal times.

'Edie?'

Mary's voice snaps her back.

'Your toast's getting cold, dear.'

Edie lowers the paper, takes a bite, then drains her tea. A noise from behind startles her, but it's only Susan tripping in the doorway, spilling a salt cellar over the floor.

The young maid mutters a curse, and Mary admonishes her mildly, and while the mess is cleared up Edie turns her attention back to the paper, her eye caught by another byline: *Captain and crew give evidence at* Lusitania *sinking inquiry*.

The article proclaims that a Lord Mersey has been put in charge of the inquiry, and there is much confusing evidence for him to sift through. The ship's cargo had apparently included ammunition and shell cases, packed in the hold, although this had not been common knowledge to the passengers or most of the crew.

Edie thinks of Josie, wondering if the library assistant had known what the ship was carrying, and if so what had made her risk the crossing.

Edie reads on, learning that Captain Turner had been unaware that many of the lifeboats would fail to launch successfully due to the ship's design.

Mary taps her shoulder, professing disappointment that Edie's breakfast remains uneaten.

'I'm reading about the *Lusitania*,' Edie explains. 'I met a library assistant at Endell – she's one of the survivors.'

'Lucky woman,' Mary says. 'But what a terrible thing to go through. How did she come to be at Endell?'

'She didn't say,' Edie admits. 'She was very reserved. Made me wonder if she'd lost someone on the ship.'

'Such a tragedy. I remember the *Titanic* as though it were yesterday.'

'It says here,' Edie taps the page, 'the captain didn't know his ship had been struck for several minutes. At first no one realized it was sinking.'

'How awful. It must have been sheer chaos.'

Edie agrees, trying not to think about the horrors the library assistant must have witnessed. No wonder the young woman was so reticent to speak of it.

Edie retreats to Harry's study, her intention to write up her own account of the Zeppelin attack as she'd witnessed it, and record the brave actions of the firemen. After that, she'll draft her first piece on the hospital library. But though she has everything she needs – a comfortable armchair, fresh sheets of paper, sharpened pencils – she struggles to concentrate, her thoughts turning to Stanley and his parents.

For once, her writing fails to lift the heaviness in her heart. The prospect of not being able to see Stanley again is unbearable. His companionship in France had kept her alive, but his sacrifice has left a shadow on her soul. She has to make peace with him, tell him the truth, before the darkness of their shared ordeal consumes them.

She rubs her eyes roughly, then reaches for a fresh sheet of paper.

Dear Stanley,

She grips the pencil so hard it threatens to snap.

I visited you, but you might not remember.

She rubs the words out with a pumice stone she finds on Harry's desk, almost tearing the page.

Call yourself a writer, Lawrence? Stanley's voice comes clear to her, and she pictures his nut-brown eyes and teasing grin. *Bloody spit it out, kid.*

She chews the end of her pencil, thinking. The fear that this might be her only chance weighs heavy, but she has to try.

Dear Stan,

I think about you all the time, wishing I could turn back the clock. There is so much I need to tell you. Please write to me. I have your camera safe.

Your friend, Edie Lawrence

It's only as she signs her name that it hits her: he doesn't know her as Edie, only as Eddie. But she can't bring herself to add the extra *d*. She's lied to him enough.

Before she can change her mind, she folds the letter, addresses an envelope to Queen Square Hospital, Ward D.

What memories did Stanley have of that night in the enemy trench? She should have told him the truth then, but would he have believed her?

Did he remember her with any fondness, or did he consider her the worst sort of traitor for abandoning him when he most needed her? The events of that trench raid are branded on her memory, and when she closes her eyes at night Bembridge and Jackson's faces loom behind her eyelids, and Stanley's too, all of them crouched in that enemy sap. Every night, she relives the enemy's surprise attack, the shots that felled Stanley, the German soldier's bloodied hands gripping Edie's neck, squeezing the life from her.

At death's door herself, there had been nothing she could do for Stanley, she knows this in her heart. Yet the knowledge doesn't make things any easier.

Their friendship had meant everything to Edie then, but only now does she understand the true depth of her feelings. Would Stan ever feel the same love for her?

She posts the letter on her way to Endell Street Hospital before she loses her nerve. It's all she can think to do. If Stanley's family don't want her to see him she has to respect their wishes, at least for now. Hopefully, when Stanley is better he will read her note, and then everything might resolve itself, and if it doesn't . . . She closes off the thought.

At the hospital, Edie heads for Dr Garland's office, hoping to brief her on the progress of the library piece. If the doctor seems amenable, Edie will mention her new idea, one that only came to her yesterday. Rather than limiting herself to writing a few articles, Edie wonders if she could produce a regular library newsletter. An ambitious idea, but it would keep her busy, a distraction from her grief.

Voices emanate from beyond the office door, and Edie's heart sinks. The doctor has visitors. She decides to knock anyway, now she's here, though she'll have to keep her idea to herself for a while longer.

'Ah, perfect timing,' Dr Garland says, by way of welcome. Her little dog jumps up at Edie, wagging his tail. She pats his head.

'We were just talking about you,' Dr Garland says. She clicks her fingers at the dog, and he trots obediently back to his nest of blankets in the corner. 'Come in, my dear.'

Two strangers are seated before Dr Garland's messy desk, and both men now rise to their feet as Edie enters the room.

The first, a smartly suited man in his forties, shakes her hand. 'Dr Johnson,' he introduces himself. 'I'm truly honoured to meet you, ma'am.' Johnson's accent is American, Edie guesses, his voice a rich, slow drawl. She catches Dr Garland's eye. What did this man mean, it was an honour to meet her?

'Dr Johnson hails from Texas,' Dr Garland says. 'He and I met in Paris last autumn, when Dr Maberry and I were first establishing the Women's Hospital Corps. Dr Johnson has extensive experience of running military hospitals abroad, and his knowledge has proved invaluable to us. He's come to see how we're getting on here.'

'You flatter me, Doctor,' Johnson says, with a deep chuckle.

The second man is elderly, with a shock of white hair and a wintry expression.

'Mr Marsh is the deputy director of medical services for this district,' Dr Garland informs Edie.

Marsh extends a bony hand, and Edie dutifully shakes it.

'Dr Garland has been telling us about your exploits across the Channel,' Marsh crackles, as they take their seats. He clears his throat. 'How you pulled quite a stunt.'

'I'm not sure I used the word *stunt*, Mr Marsh,' Dr Garland interjects.

The older gentleman ignores her, frowning intently at Edie. 'What compelled you to risk your life in such a perilous way, young lady?'

Edie bristles at the man's tone, and bites her still tender tongue. She wants to snap back that he knows nothing about her, or what she's been through, but respect for Dr Garland keeps the words locked inside her head. For the moment, at least.

'Edie is one of the bravest young women I know,' Dr Garland says, breaking the strained silence. 'As I was telling you, she risked her life, as we all did, for a greater good.'

Dr Johnson nods, smiling at Edie. She feels her cheeks warm in response.

'And what precisely was that greater good?' Mr Marsh presses, pinning Edie with a sharp glare. 'Women are forbidden to be on the battlefields, yet you placed yourself in mortal danger and almost lost your life, Dr Garland informs us. Only her surgical skills saved you. I fail to understand why someone would act in such a reckless way.'

Edie scrambles for a response, baffled as to why Dr Garland has told these men about her at all. What interest could they possibly have in her? And why wasn't the doctor putting an end to this interrogation?

'With respect, sir,' Edie replies, dismayed to hear her voice break, but forging on regardless, 'I wanted to be a journalist.'

'A noble endeavour,' Dr Johnson remarks, his warm dark eyes flashing.

'But that profession was closed to me as a woman,' Edie continues.

'You considered risking your life on the battlefield would somehow help your journalistic aspirations, Miss Lawrence?' Marsh leans back in his chair, awaiting Edie's response.

Edie meets Dr Garland's eye across the paper-strewn desk. How can she convey the inequality inherent in everything to this man who knows only privilege?

'Only by risking her life in such a fashion could Miss Lawrence be taken seriously as a journalist,' Dr Garland offers. 'She's proved beyond doubt that women can report from war, and I have every confidence she will bring her skill with words to good use at our hospital.'

Edie braces herself for Marsh's riposte, but to her surprise the older man's glare softens, and the hint of a smile hovers on his thin lips. 'Dr Johnson and I trust your judgement, Dr Garland,' Marsh replies at last. 'Therefore we are content to commission Miss Lawrence to write the official reports of Endell Street Hospital, on behalf of the War Office.'

Dr Garland beams at Edie, who can only gape, as the man's words slowly percolate into her brain.

'Miss Lawrence, you will submit your reports to Dr Garland, who will pass them directly to myself for review,' Marsh continues. 'Dr Garland, you have my permission to equip Miss Lawrence with anything she may need to undertake this duty.'

'And I will showcase your account as an example of good practice when I return to France,' Dr Johnson adds. 'If that's acceptable to you, Miss Lawrence?'

He waits politely for Edie's response, but she can't speak. To write articles on the hospital for Harry is one thing, but to write for the War Office? That was entirely beyond her. She can't do it – *she can't*. She opens her mouth to say this, but Dr Garland is already speaking for her. 'You won't be disappointed, gentlemen,' the doctor says, turning to Edie and smiling. 'Miss Lawrence will do us all proud, I have no doubt.'

17

Josie – London

Josie works her way through St Anne's ward, following in Miss Godson's wake. She hands out request slips as the librarian had instructed, and collects those books the men have finished with, greeting each patient with a shy, smiling nod. A patient with both arms immobilized in plaster casts asks her, with polite earnestness, if she could write a letter for him to his sweetheart. 'Only if you have the time, miss.'

Josie has precious little time. Miss Godson has already finished her circulation of the ward, swiftly completing her literary prescriptions, and is waiting for Josie in the next ward. She'll soon be wondering where Josie has got to. But the young man's beseeching eyes, so like Jem's, are too much for Josie to resist.

'Sure,' she says. To her relief, the man has only a few heart-rending lines to dictate, and soon she's able to move on to the last two beds. She musters a warm smile for her penultimate customers, but only one, an olive-skinned soldier from a New Zealand regiment, is awake. His right shoulder is bandaged, but otherwise he looks unscathed to Josie.

'Good morning, sir,' she greets him. 'Do you like to read?'

The New Zealander grins at her, revealing a missing incisor. 'Depends what you got, miss.'

'Let me see.' Josie considers the remaining books on the trolley, its shelves a mess of returns mixed with un-issued novels and an assortment of magazines. She picks out a well-thumbed Nat Gould – *A Gamble for Love*. She adds to this a book on English cricket, and another on woodwork. Some of the men prefer non-fiction, she's learned.

The New Zealander shakes his head politely at each of her suggestions. 'You got any classics?'

Josie hadn't expected this response, and hopes her face doesn't betray her surprise. 'I've got a couple by Dickens,' she says, 'a Brontë and a Hardy.'

'Give me something that'll make me look good if I cark it before the end, eh.' His eyes gleam, and Josie flushes. She chooses *The Return of the Native*, remembering that Miss Godson had recommended this one for those men who felt out of place.

'Books are the best distraction, eh?' the man remarks, examining the novel's cover. 'Well, *nearly* the best dis-traction.' He smiles up at Josie, his eyebrows twitching.

'Have you read any Hardy before?' Josie asks, doing her best to ignore the man's teasing tone. In the past, on the ships, men who flirted with her hadn't bothered her much. But now her skin feels thinner, her fragile emotions barely contained beneath a surface of civility.

'Nope. What's this one about?'

'How society treats outsiders,' she replies. 'Among other things.'

'Sounds interesting, eh,' the man says doubtfully. 'Ta.' He shifts on his pillows and a wince of pain mars his smooth features. 'What's your name, miss?'

'Josie.'

'Pretty name,' the man says. 'Got a cousin back home called Josephine.'

'I'm just Josie.'

'All right, Just-Josie. I'm Stuart, or Stu to me mates.' He runs his fingers through his greasy hair, his grin widening and Josie returns his smile shyly. Her attention shifts to the man in the neighbouring bed, but he remains asleep.

'He won't answer ya,' Stuart tells her. 'Gone mute, poor bastard.'

'Mute?'

'Shot in the flank, hasn't spoken a word to anyone since.'

Josie can't imagine the pain of being shot.

'I mean, I'm not a great one for the words meself, if I'm honest, miss,' Stuart chats on, 'but old Theo, he's the quiet one . . .'

As Stuart talks, Josie studies Theo's sallow face, his closely shorn, raven-black hair. How far from home he is, many thousands of miles. New Zealand is so remote as to be fantastical to her, existing only as an imaginary place of cloud-topped mountains, tattooed tribes and mythical beasts.

'You got any papers on that trolley of yours, Just-Josie?' Stuart's question breaks into Josie's thoughts.

'Dying to get my hands on a *Wellington Post*, eh.'

'No, I'm sorry, but I can put a request in for you?'
'Ta, Just-Josie.'
'Miss Everley.'

A voice close behind Josie makes her start. She turns to find Miss Godson has materialized, her face a stony mask. 'Bring the trolley, Miss Everley. We're behind schedule.'

'See ya, Just-Josie,' Stuart calls after her, as Josie hurries to follow the librarian.

The moment they are in the corridor, Miss Godson seizes Josie's elbow in a vice-like grip. 'I would advise you not to be overly familiar with the patients, Miss Everley,' the older woman warns, her voice low. 'We must remain professional at all times.'

Josie feels her face warm. 'I *was* being professional, Miss Godson –'

'Fraternizing with the patients, Miss Everley, will not be condoned,' the librarian interrupts. 'Our job is to provide reading material, not loose conversation. Now, come along, we're late.'

For the remainder of the morning, Miss Godson hovers on Josie's periphery, overseeing each brief exchange. At last, the book deliveries are complete and Josie wheels the trolley back to the library, sweating under her blouse, her shoulder-blades so tense they ache. The librarian has vanished again, leaving Josie with a vague promise that she'll return later to 'check things'.

Pushing the cart through the doors, Josie is surprised to find a well-dressed woman in her late fifties or well-preserved early sixties, Josie guesses, idly leafing through a *Country Life* magazine at the billiard table. She is wearing a black fur coat despite the mild weather.

'Can I help you?' Josie croaks.

'Mrs Vera Stanten,' the woman introduces herself, her manner forthright. 'Eugenia mentioned she had a new assistant. Another. Would that be you?'

Eugenia? It takes Josie a moment to realize that the woman is referring to Miss Godson. That the eminent librarian has a first name hadn't occurred to her. 'I'm Miss Godson's library assistant, yes, ma'am,' Josie replies.

'What's your name?'

Josie tells her, and Mrs Stanten extends a well-manicured hand. 'May I call you Josie?'

'Of course,' Josie stammers.

'Where do you want me to start?' Mrs Stanten sweeps her gaze about the library.

'Oh, you're here to . . . help?'

Miss Godson had said nothing about a 'friend' coming to help. The unexpected arrival of this woman, whose confident bearing and well-heeled shoes remind her unnervingly of Mrs Cavendish, makes Josie feel shy. For the first time, she finds herself wishing that the librarian was here.

'That trolley looks terribly heavy,' Mrs Stanten remarks. 'Has Eugenia had you pushing that thing around the wards?'

Josie admits, yes, that is where she's just come from.

'Where is Eugenia?' Mrs Stanten wants to know.

'Miss Godson has gone to supervise a new delivery of donations, ma'am,' Josie tells her. 'She's very busy,' she adds redundantly.

'Leaving you to deal with everything else?' Mrs Stanten smiles, one eyelid lowering in a near-wink.

'Oh, it's all right, ma'am,' Josie mumbles, before remembering her manners. 'Would you like something to drink? I have to restock the trolley, but I can make you some tea first.'

'That would be marvellous.'

Josie shunts the trolley into the stockroom, Mrs Stanten following on her heels.

'It's a little messy,' Josie apologizes. The understatement of the year. For the first time, she considers the room from a visitor's point of view. Mrs Stanten must think a maniac has run amok in here, so many books, magazines and boxes strewn everywhere.

'You're American,' Mrs Stanten remarks, divesting herself of the fur coat. There's no clear surface to put it down. 'Whereabouts in the country are you from?'

Josie takes Mrs Stanten's coat from her, the fur heavy and warm in her arms, trying not to think of the animal to which it had once belonged. She drapes it over the back of the desk chair. 'New York,' she replies, moving to the little tea-making table, willing the woman not to ask any more questions. 'How do you like your tea, ma'am?' She locates a cleanish enamel mug and gives it a quick wipe with a tea-towel.

'On second thoughts,' Mrs Stanten says, eyeing the mug, 'perhaps later. Now, why don't you tell me how this place works? Eugenia was quite . . . vague, shall we say, when we last spoke.'

To Josie's relief, Mrs Stanten doesn't ask her anything more about America, or how she came to be working for Miss Godson in the hospital library. Instead, she makes a show of listening, her gaze roving distractedly around the stockroom, as Josie tries to explain the complicated system the librarian has devised for sorting the book donations.

'Eugenia always was too clever for the rest of us,' Mrs Stanten mutters obscurely, when Josie has finished.

Josie decides to give Mrs Stanten the relatively simple job of sorting through a tea chest of books that was recently delivered, the contents of which she hasn't managed to investigate.

'How long have you been a library assistant?' Mrs Stanten asks, watching with raised eyebrows as Josie levers up the lid of the chest with a screwdriver.

'Oh, a little while,' Josie replies evasively. She avoids Mrs Stanten's eye, as it occurs to her that Miss Godson has yet to appoint her officially as library assistant. She's assumed she's passed the librarian's 'test', as Miss Godson has kept her on so far. There's been a vague mention of monthly wages, and a rough timetable drawn up, but apart from tasking Josie with sorting and repairing books, and keeping the trolley stocked, Miss Godson hasn't made any formal promise of permanent employment.

'Let me fetch you an apron, Mrs Stanten,' Josie says, before the woman can probe any further. 'The books can be dusty.' Has the woman ever worn an apron in her life?

'Marvellous,' Mrs Stanten murmurs, with a frown, and proceeds to grapple with the apron strings, sighing gratefully when Josie steps in to tie them around her waist.

To Josie's surprise Mrs Stanten sets to work with fervour, a pair of gold half-moon spectacles balanced precariously on her nose. Josie is left to concentrate on her own tasks, and as they work, the sounds of the hospital, the voices of staff and patients in the courtyard drift to them. The hive, as Josie thinks of Endell Street Hospital, is functioning as it should, and she takes comfort from this.

The room is growing stuffy, and Josie moves to open the stiff sash window, when a flash of white through the glass stops her. A gull alights on the narrow sill, and Josie's heart trips, the sight of it taking her straight back to the *Lusitania*. The seabirds, with their pristine white feathers and intelligent yellow-ringed eyes, would strut about the decks as though they owned the ship. Most of the passengers and crew abhorred them, viewing them as winged vermin, but Josie loved them, and would sometimes stand at the rail and watch the gulls soaring above her in the blue, envying their grace and freedom.

'So many Austens,' Mrs Stanten remarks, tugging Josie back to the stockroom. 'Have you read any?' She brandishes *Mansfield Park*.

'Only *Pride and Prejudice*,' Josie mutters, turning away from the window.

'Some would say that's Austen's best,' Mrs Stanten says. Josie glances over to find the older woman regarding her. 'Her novels reflect such a different world from ours.' She holds Josie's gaze for a moment longer, then sets the book down and reaches for another in the tea chest. 'Eugenia always advocated that books are the most wonderful way to take one's mind off unpleasant things.'

Josie wonders what unpleasant things Mrs Stanten has had to bear in her life. A spider in her coat pocket? A scuff on her shoe? She holds her tongue.

'Eugenia is an enormous Austen fan,' Mrs Stanten continues. 'Now where did I put that sheet?' She hunts about on the table next to her, pouncing on the rule sheet Josie had shown her: Miss Godson's guide to prescribing books.

'Let us consult the oracle.' Mrs Stanten adjusts her spectacles, which have slipped down her long nose. 'Is Austen good or bad medicine, according to our esteemed librarian?'

Josie abandons her magazines, as Mrs Stanten begins to read out Miss Godson's list of rules concerning the selection of suitable reading material.

'*Objectivity of Plot*,' Mrs Stanten begins. '*Stories preferably of action that carry the reader along zestfully, and give him no time for retrospective bypaths.* Does this sound like Austen's plots, do you think?'

'Well . . .'

'Ah, but the second point is more promising,' Mrs Stanten forges on. '*Stories with an emphasis on characters who win love and spur emulation.*'

That sounds more like a Jane Austen novel, Josie thinks.

'According to Eugenia, we must *avoid literature that contains pathological characters and illnesses,*' Mrs Stanten reads on. '*Religious or ethical propaganda, or experimentations in moral fields are also doubtful nourishment for the sick.*' She looks up from the sheet. 'We're all emotionally biased, I suppose, and an ill person is particularly vulnerable to bombardments of this nature.'

Josie's feeling is that everyone is susceptible, but she keeps this thought to herself.

'I can't see how Eugenia believes that books alone can have the power to cure the patients, though,' Mrs Stanten remarks, with a sniff. 'How can one hope to mend such broken men with only words?'

Josie thinks of something Miss Godson had told her, almost in passing: that librarians must accept their influence is limited, largely unknowable and immeasurable, unlike conventional medicine. But vital, nonetheless.

'How do you know Miss Godson?' Josie ventures to ask.

'Oh, we go back years,' Mrs Stanten replies. 'I met Eugenia when we both worked at the British Museum.'

Josie listens, intrigued, as Mrs Stanten regales her with the story of her husband, an eminent Egyptologist. Mrs Stanten had worked – unofficially, she is keen to impress on Josie – as her husband's project curator, helping to showcase the fruits of his archaeological work at the museum.

'Eugenia was an archivist at the same time I was there,'

she tells Josie. 'There weren't many of us women so we naturally formed a friendship. I say friendship, although Eugenia isn't what I would call a sociable person. But we became friends of sorts, and have remained so ever since.'

They continue with their tasks, and it soon becomes apparent that Mrs Stanten's tea chest contains more than Jane Austen novels.

'*Venus in Furs*,' Mrs Stanten declares, showing Josie a battered hardback. '*Moby-Dick. Bartleby, the Scrivener.* There's a veritable treasure trove in here . . .'

Approaching noon, Josie makes a pot of tea, and this time Mrs Stanten accepts the stained mug without a murmur.

'Thirsty work,' Mrs Stanten pronounces. 'Eugenia certainly likes to keep people busy. But, then, she always was rather a bossy boots.'

Josie swallows tea, hiding her smile.

'Comes of being a spinster, I suppose,' Mrs Stanten continues. 'I say, while the cat's away, shall the mice play?'

'How do you mean, ma'am?'

'Shall we liven things up a little?'

Josie is given no chance to reply, as Mrs Stanten is already setting down her tea and moving to a cluttered table across the room. As Josie looks on, she opens the lid of a box. Instead of books Josie glimpses a round turntable, and now Mrs Stanten is lifting out a tin horn, and cranking a handle on the side of the box.

A gramophone!

The first few scratchy notes of a waltz rise into the

dusty air, and simultaneously there comes a knock on the stockroom door. Josie turns to find Edie Lawrence in the doorway, clutching her satchel.

'Hello.' Mrs Stanten greets Edie, as the familiar strains of 'The Blue Danube' fill the room. 'Have you come to help too?'

The young journalist's reply is lost to Josie. The unforgettable music has sucked the air from her lungs, and the room begins to blur, then darken, as though someone has switched off the sun. She feels herself sway, as the blood drains from her head, and as the floor comes up to meet her there's nothing she can do to stop it.

| Issue No. 1 | # The Daily Dose | Price FREE |

A WAR HOSPITAL RUN BY WOMEN WHERE THE ONLY MEN ARE PATIENTS

Endell Street is the only military hospital entirely staffed by women under the War Office. It's the result of the pioneering work of the Women's Hospital Corps, founded at the start of the war by Dr Lucinda Garland and Dr Florence Maberry.

'They are more than wonderful doctors and nurses, they are caring and tender-hearted ladies.'

This is how the staff at Endell Street – from the chief surgeon, down to the porter on the gate – are described by soldiers wounded at the front who are brought to the hospital every day.

In these dark days of war, this hospital has become a beacon, a haven, a leading light, its success proving the justification of women's enduring fight to participate in the world of medicine.

E. Lawrence

Book Recommendations

Burroughs, John.
Birds and Poets; Locusts and Wild Honey; Signs and Seasons; Ways of Nature.

Wister, Owen.
The Virginian.
(The best of all cowboy tales.)

Burnett, Mrs F. H.
Little Lord Fauntleroy.
(A boy born in poverty in America becomes the heir of his grandfather, an English earl, and is transplanted to England, where he soon endears himself to everyone he meets.)

Henry, O. (Sidney Porter).
Whirligigs; Rolling Stones; Roads of Destiny.
(Humorous short stories, fun and racy.)

PEOPLE WE TAKE OUR HATS OFF TO:

The French – merci beaucoup!

For Sale, Cheap: Desirable Bed. Climate warm, fine view through window. Splendid amenities. Good neighbours. Owner going abroad. Apply: Fedup, St Ursula's Ward, Endell St.

COMPETITION

Can you complete this well-known proverb?

D_ _T/J_D_E/_/B_O_/B_/IT_/C-V-R.

18

Edie – London

Edie drops her satchel, rushing to Josie's side, as the final notes of the waltz fade away. The library assistant's face is parchment white, and Edie swallows her panic as she tugs off her coat and gently slips it beneath Josie's head.

'Oh, my goodness,' the lady working with Josie gasps. 'The poor dear.'

'She's breathing,' Edie mutters, taking up Josie's slack wrist, feeling for a pulse. A fluttery beat thrums beneath her fingers. *Thank God.*

'Are you medically trained?' the woman asks, doubt in her eyes.

Edie almost laughs at the thought. 'No,' she replies. 'I'm a writer. I'm writing about the hospital, and the library.'

'Oh,' the woman says. 'You know Josie, then? Vera Stanten.' She introduces herself. 'I've only been working here a short while.'

'Edie Lawrence.'

They regard the library assistant, unmoving on the floor. 'I wonder why she fainted,' Edie says. 'Has she been unwell?'

'Only a little quiet,' Mrs Stanten replies. 'Reserved, I should say. But then I only met her today.'

'We should fetch a nurse.'

'I'll go.' Mrs Stanten rises and hurries away.

Edie manoeuvres herself more comfortably on to her knees, keeping hold of Josie's hand, wondering what had caused her to collapse. Had her arrival shocked Josie somehow? But that made no sense, and anyway, Josie hadn't seemed to notice her. Instead she'd been staring at something across the room.

Was it the music? Had the waltz induced a memory? Edie glances over at her satchel, lying by the door, thinking of her notebook inside. Trapped within its pages were the nightmare images that swarm her mind, whenever she catches the bars of a marching tune like 'Tipperary'. Certain music has the power to return her to the hell of the battlefield. Sometimes the memory of a song the men used to sing jolts her awake in the small hours, sweat-soaked and shaking, the melody circling in her head. Then she has to pour her darkest thoughts into her notebook, her words in place of tears on the page, until she's calm again.

Could this music have had the same effect on the library assistant?

'Josie?' Edie strokes the young woman's rough, ink-stained fingers. Her nails are bitten to the quick. 'Josie? Can you hear me?'

Josie gives a weak moan, and at that moment a nurse bustles into the room, Mrs Stanten close behind.

'Did she hit her head when she fell?' the nurse asks briskly, kneeling next to Edie.

'I don't think so.' Edie shifts to the side, giving the nurse space. 'I don't really know what happened.'

'She simply dropped to the floor,' Mrs Stanten replies. 'Gave us no warning whatsoever. I'd just put a record on the gramophone, and a second later she was down.'

'What's her name?' the nurse asks, as she takes up the library assistant's slim, freckled arm and deftly feels for a pulse.

'Josie,' Edie supplies.

The nurse taps Josie's cheeks lightly. 'Time to wake up, Josie.' Another tap, a little more vigorous, and Josie's eyelids flicker open.

'Ah, there you are,' the nurse says, with a smile. 'Back in the land of the living.'

Josie blinks at the woman, fear flashing in her eyes.

The nurse speaks with a soothing firmness. 'Let's get you up off the floor, lovey.'

Edie drags a chair over, and Josie is helped into it.

'How do you feel?' the nurse asks, pressing the back of her hand to Josie's forehead. 'No fever,' she mutters.

'A bit . . . giddy,' Josie answers.

'Best you sit here a while, until that passes,' the nurse advises. She turns to Edie and Mrs Stanten. 'A drink of water wouldn't go amiss. I have to get ready for the pageant now, but come and find me if she swoons again.'

'Oh, gosh, yes, the pageant,' Mrs Stanten says. 'Eugenia told me about it, but I'd forgotten.'

Edie fetches a cup of water, and the colour begins to return to Josie's cheeks.

'I'm sorry, Mrs Stanten,' Josie rasps. 'I hope I didn't alarm you.'

'No need to apologize, dear,' Mrs Stanten says. 'You couldn't help it. But are you feeling better now?'

'A little, thanks.' Josie gives her a weak smile, and turns to Edie. 'You came back.'

Edie returns her smile.

'So you're a fellow writer, Miss Lawrence,' Mrs Stanten says. 'I write too, plays mostly. In fact, I'm penning one at the moment for the staff to perform. Did you say you were writing about this library?'

'Yes, among other things,' Edie replies. 'But I wouldn't know where to start, writing a play.'

'Oh, it's enormous fun,' Mrs Stanten says, refilling Josie's cup. 'Dr Garland has given me the task of organizing the hospital entertainment, which is going to be rather a challenge, but I simply can't wait.' She consults her gold wristwatch. 'The pageant's due to begin soon, and Eugenia did say it might visit the library. Will you help me move some furniture, Miss Lawrence?'

'I can do it,' Josie gasps, pushing herself unsteadily to her feet. 'Miss Godson is particular where the chairs and tables go.'

'Oh, no, dear,' Mrs Stanten insists, easing Josie back down on to the chair. 'You must rest. Miss Lawrence and I can manage by ourselves.'

Josie reluctantly accedes, but keeps her chin lifted, and Edie admires her spirit. But she can't help noting the tremor in the young woman's hand as she brushes a stray lock of hair from her eyes.

'What needs to be done?' Edie asks Mrs Stanten.

'Eugenia asked that the tables and chairs be moved to one side . . . and the stage has to be clear for the saints to do whatever saints do . . .'

The sound of a choir drifts up from the courtyard, women's voices singing 'There Is A Happy Land'.

'I must see the pageant,' Josie says weakly.

'You can watch from the window,' Mrs Stanten asserts. 'Better you stay here, in case you feel queer again.'

A drum begins to beat, and is joined by a tin whistle, slightly out of time.

'We should hurry,' Mrs Stanten says to Edie. 'It's starting already.'

'I'll move the furniture in the main room,' Edie promises Josie. 'Will you be all right on your own?'

'I'll be fine,' Josie says, mustering a smile. 'Thank you.'

'I'll be back as soon as I can.' Edie grabs her satchel and hurries out of the stockroom after Mrs Stanten.

Down in the courtyard, the music and singing have stopped, and patients and staff are milling around a raised wooden dais. Edie joins Mrs Stanten at the edge of the crowd, watching as Dr Garland mounts the few steps to stand on the platform. The naturally reserved doctor is wearing a stoic expression, and Edie suspects this is taking a lot of courage. Dr Garland has said she is more comfortable at her operating table than addressing a crowd. The courtyard bell rings out, and gradually the hubbub diminishes enough for the doctor's voice to be heard.

'Thank you, everyone,' Dr Garland calls. 'I'm very much looking forward to celebrating our inaugural saint's pageant with you today. All the staff involved have worked tirelessly to bring this to fruition, and we wish them the very best for a wonderful spectacle. Let the pageant begin!'

A great cheer erupts, and now a second woman joins Dr Garland on the platform.

'That's Matron,' Mrs Stanten informs Edie.

The matron is bedecked in a long white dress and ankle-length blue cape.

'I believe she's supposed to be St Mary,' Mrs Stanten adds.

The matron's deep, carrying voice is a contrast to Dr Garland's, as she calls the procession to order. A number of women in various costumes are assembling themselves into a loose line. The matron shakes Dr Garland's hand, steps down from the dais, and sets off on a circuit of the courtyard. A train of assorted female saints follows her, each woman preceded by a pair of banner-bearers, holding between them a stretch of material embroidered with their saint's name.

Edie fumbles her notebook from her bag. She'll write this up later for the hospital newsletter, and maybe Harry will be able to get it published somewhere too. She wonders how Josie is faring, left alone in the library, and looks up at what she guesses is the library window, glimpsing a shadowy figure beyond the glass. The shouts and cheers of the crowd are growing louder, and Edie begins to wish she was back in the library too.

'There goes St Barbara.' Mrs Stanten points. 'The patron saint of artillerymen, did you know?'

Edie didn't, and commits this fact to her notebook.

'Oh, look, and there's St Felicitas,' Mrs Stanten remarks. 'With her seven sons.' A gaggle of the youngest orderlies, dressed as 'boys' in short trousers and ragged shirts, are trailing after their 'mother', whom Edie recognizes as the Irish nurse who'd helped her in France, Sister Bryony. The nurse waves at Edie as she swishes past, but there's no chance to talk properly. Edie makes a mental note to ask Sister Bryony for an interview later.

Behind the last of the 'boys', a stocky older woman is dressed in the black habit of a nun, flanked by two orderlies bearing a banner stitched with the name St Hildegarde.

'Perhaps the most contentious of our saints,' Mrs Stanten informs Edie. 'She was a German Benedictine abbess, but also a medical writer during the Middle Ages. She practised medicine too.'

Edie scribbles down this snippet, wondering if she should omit the German fact from the final copy. A question for Harry when he returns from France, whenever that might be.

The ward sister who had helped Josie earlier now passes by. She's dressed in paper chainmail and a wig made from crow feathers. St Joan of Arc winks at Edie as she passes.

More saints process past, accompanied by whoops of laughter and applause. The mood is jubilant, and Edie begins to appreciate the purpose of the spectacle.

Entertainment such as this is a welcome distraction for the patients, whose bodies are so often locked in pain, their nerves taut as wire. Most of the men she can see are smiling, some clapping and whistling as the women go past, and Edie hopes they can forget their suffering for a short while.

Bringing up the rear of the procession is St Ursula, with a band of half a dozen maidens in tow.

'That one came to rather a grisly end,' Mrs Stanten informs Edie, in a low voice.

In what way? Edie would like to know, but Mrs Stanten can't tell her any more.

The vibrant spectacle wends its way inside the hospital, the audience of staff and patients following in its wake.

'They'll tour the wards now,' Mrs Stanten says.

Edie pictures the procession trailing along crowded corridors, up and down staircases, the saints and their attendants visiting the various wards, where men who are well enough are sitting up in their beds. She can already hear faint cheers and singing coming from inside the building. The last of the patients, those wheeled-chair-bound or on crutches, follow the parade inside, leaving the courtyard practically deserted.

'How long will the pageant go on for?' Edie asks Mrs Stanten.

'Until they've visited most of the wards, I should think,' Mrs Stanten replies. 'They'll finish with a show in the library. Eugenia mentioned a photographer coming to take a group picture. I do hope she turns up soon.'

'I'll check that Josie's all right,' Edie says.

'Good idea,' Mrs Stanten agrees. 'I'll join you shortly.'

Edie slips into the hospital through the tradesmen's entrance. Her sense of direction is slowly improving, and she finds her way up to the third floor. Reaching the library at last, she wonders how long it will be before the carnival procession reaches this corner of the hospital. Ten minutes? Half an hour? An hour? She has no way of knowing, but she can at least warn Josie.

Edie finds her in the stockroom, gazing through the window.

'You weren't very long,' Josie says. 'How's the pageant going?'

'The saints are touring the wards,' Edie tells her, depositing her satchel on the floor. 'They're heading this way.'

'Already?' Panic flares in Josie's eyes.

'They'll be a while yet,' Edie tries to reassure her.

Josie chews her lip, and Edie racks her brain for something distracting to say, but all she can think is to ask her how she's feeling.

Josie sinks down at the book-strewn desk. 'Much better, thank you. I don't know what came over me.'

Something in the way Josie can't quite meet her eye tells Edie the American is not being altogether truthful. 'Perhaps you're tired,' she ventures. She briefly considers sharing her own struggles with Josie, confessing how exhaustion dogs her too. But, no, her past trauma must stay buried, for what good would come of opening old wounds?

Josie doesn't answer, as she makes a show of tidying the books on the desk.

'At least it's peaceful in here,' Edie offers. The stockroom is a sanctuary of sorts, despite the lack of space.

'The saints won't come in here, will they?' Josie worries.

'Into the stockroom?' Edie smothers a chuckle, as they both contemplate the overflowing shelves, the corners stacked with boxes and crates. There's barely room to swing a cat, as her ma would have said. 'I doubt they'd fit,' she reassures Josie.

The young woman smiles hesitantly. 'I find too many people overwhelming.'

'Me too,' Edie confesses.

From out in the main library they hear voices. Had the pageant arrived already? Josie moves to the door and opens it a crack, peering out.

'Miss Godson's here.'

A moment later the librarian enters the stockroom, bosom heaving.

'I've just been informed a royal party has arrived,' Miss Godson says, breathless. 'Queen Alexandra and her daughters. An unscheduled visit.'

'Royalty?' Josie stammers.

'Dr Garland and Dr Maberry are welcoming them now,' Miss Godson says. 'Her Majesty and Their Royal Highnesses will visit at least a few of the wards, no doubt, but they may also grace the library with their presence.'

Edie exchanges a glance with Josie. There's no time

to panic as the sound of women singing a hymn – 'Lift Up Your Hearts!' – issues from beyond the library doors.

Miss Godson and Mrs Stanten hurry to receive the visitors, but Edie hesitates, suddenly overcome with nerves. She's never met royalty before.

The voices are growing louder, and Edie watches with Josie from the stockroom doorway, as the saints file into the library and arrange themselves on the stage, continuing to sing a medley of rousing tunes. An audience of staff and patients has followed them in, and they clap and whistle their approval, until all at once a reverent hush descends.

The royals have arrived.

The crowd parts, and Edie glimpses the Queen dressed in black, flanked by two of her daughters, their plumed heads bobbing, as they proceed into the library.

'I can't believe the Queen is here,' Edie whispers to Josie, but the American doesn't seem to hear, her gaze fixed on the crowd as it closes around the royal party. As the saints on the stage begin to sing again, Josie retreats into the stockroom.

Before Edie can follow, Mrs Stanten appears, her face flushed. 'It's not every day you get a royal visit,' she remarks. 'This will make all the papers in the morning.'

Edie has to agree, it's quite the occasion. In her mind's eye she's already compiling a piece for the hospital newsletter, something she'll be proud to show Harry.

All too soon, the royal party departs, and the library gradually empties again. Miss Godson and Mrs Stanten disappear, leaving Edie and Josie alone. They both give a long, heartfelt sigh of relief.

It's past supper, by the time Edie returns to the Levinsons'. Exhausted and starving, she seeks out Mary, busy baking in the kitchen, desperate to share the news of the royal visit.

'The wanderer returns,' Mary greets her, wiping floury hands on her apron. 'What's happened today?'

'Queen Alexandra, Princess Victoria and Princess Maud visited Endell Street,' Edie tells her. She still can't quite believe the events of the day.

Mary wants to know every last detail, plying Edie with questions about what the royal party were like, what they were wearing.

'The Queen was in black,' Edie reports, 'and had on a huge black plumed hat. So did one of the princesses, but the other one, she had on a white ermine stole and a white plumed hat.'

'How long did they stay?'

'Not very long. It was an unplanned visit.'

'Were they impressed with the hospital, do you think?'

'They seemed interested,' Edie replies. 'They came to the library, and the saints in the pageant sang for them, and then they watched a little show put on by a troupe of children from Miss Conti's School of Music and Dancing, and then they went off.'

'I wish I'd been there.' Mary sighs. 'Oh, some post came for you earlier.' She gestures to a letter on the sideboard. 'Have you eaten?'

Edie turns over the envelope, contemplating the unfamiliar handwriting. Who could be writing to her? She's never received post here before. Very few people know she's living with the Levinsons, only Sylvia Pankhurst and Dr Garland, and she can't imagine why either of them would want to write to her.

'Edie?'

'Sorry, I didn't hear what you said.'

'Have you eaten anything? You look rather peaky.'

'Oh, no, I haven't, but I'm fine, thank you.'

'You most certainly are not fine, young lady,' Mary scolds. 'There's cold ham and potatoes, left over from dinner. I'll put some on a plate.'

'Do you mind if I change first?' Edie says, and makes her escape before Mary can stop her.

Climbing the stairs to her attic room, it occurs to Edie that someone else knows where she lives. Stanley. Can this letter be from him?

Her hand trembles, as she opens the envelope.

Dear Miss Lawrence,

Please call at the above address, at your convenience,

Yours,
Mr and Mrs G. Chay

19

Josie – London

The after-effects of her collapse yesterday linger like a hangover, and Josie struggles to resist Pearl's attempts to keep her at home.

'I've seen more colour on a ghost,' her aunt bluntly informs her at breakfast. Josie flinches at the insensitivity of Pearl's words, but understands her aunt is only concerned for her.

Josie knows she looks rough, but she can't let Miss Godson down. The librarian was run ragged attending committee meetings, and also Mrs Stanten had warned that she was busy today at her husband's retirement event. Without Josie, the library couldn't open, and she'd tried to explain this to her aunt, but Pearl had remained unconvinced.

Josie hadn't added the true reason she wanted to go in to work: that the library was the only thing keeping her grief at bay, and without it she was lost.

She hopes the walk to Endell Street Hospital will help clear her head.

A female porter on the gates admits Josie with a nod and a smile, and Josie crosses the shaded courtyard, the sun's warmth yet to reach the enclosed space. Soon, it will come alive with patients and staff, but for now it is quiet.

A blend of smells – carbolic, drains, and the familiar chemical-metallic aroma typical of medical buildings – assails her as she makes her way up to the third floor. She's slowly growing accustomed to the place, but is grateful the corridors are less busy at this early hour, and she encounters only two nurses and an orderly, murmuring greetings as they pass.

Unlocking the library doors, Josie breathes in the peaceful, dusty air. To be alone in here, if only for a short while, soothes her frayed nerves. The books require no conversation from her, make no demands on her. Grief clings to her like a second skin, but tucked away in this calm space she can forget her sorrows for a time.

She begins assembling her book-repair equipment – a roll of linen tape, waxed binder's thread, a fresh pot of wheat-flour paste, razor blades, a cork cutting mat. Arranging everything on the desk, she selects a book waiting to be repaired – a copy of *Jane Eyre* – and carefully wipes a clinging cobweb from the dull ruby-red pictorial cloth. The book has lost its front endpaper somewhere in its lifetime, and she flicks slowly through the rest of the pages, noting their slight discoloration and thumbed edges. She examines the hinges of the spine, finding them cracked with some loose binding, but still mostly intact. The book shows signs of wear, the lettering on the spine bleached by the sun, and she suspects it's been shelved by a window. Whose home has it come from? Whose hands have held it before hers?

She loses herself to the task of restoring the novel to something resembling its former glory. It takes concentration to thread a needle with hands that possess a faint yet constant tremor, but she manages it at last, and begins to stitch loose pages together. It's like suturing a wound, she finds herself thinking. She's performing surgery on this book, saving its life, and the thought gives her a warm feeling.

Dr Josie.

Jem's voice comes to her, so clear. A flicker of movement snags her eye, but when she glances at the window it's only a pigeon pecking at the glass. She turns back to her task, and her heart jolts: her brother is right there, lolling in a chair before the desk, his long legs stretched out in a familiar relaxed pose, eyes closed.

Jem.

The needle and thread drop from Josie's fingers. She clamps her eyes shut, prises them open again.

Her brother is gone, replaced by a stack of books.

'Josie?'

Mrs Stanten has appeared in the doorway, and now Josie is aware of her own stuttering breaths. Had she spoken Jem's name out loud?

'I didn't mean to startle you.' Mrs Stanten shrugs off her fur coat, as Josie wrestles control of her senses.

The chair remains empty. Jem was never there, she tells herself. What she saw was a figment of her imagination, a waking fever dream.

'You're not feeling queer again, are you?' Mrs Stanten considers Josie, her sculpted eyebrows raised. 'You're terribly pale.'

'You surprised me, that's all,' Josie manages. 'I thought you weren't coming in today?'

'My husband has flu, apparently, so his party's had to be postponed,' Mrs Stanten says, with a roll of her eyes. 'I'll make a pot of tea, shall I?' Without waiting for Josie to reply, she bustles off to fetch water from the kitchens downstairs.

Gathering herself, Josie moves to the window, tugging it open a crack. The pigeon is gone, and she looks down on the courtyard. The first of the patients are emerging, their voices floating up to her on the mild morning breeze. The scene steadies her heart, and after a moment she's able to return to the desk and continue her work.

Mrs Stanten's cook has produced a batch of Shrewsbury cakes, and at midday Mrs Stanten insists Josie have a break and share some with her.

'They're terribly moreish, dear, and if you don't eat them I'm afraid I will, and that wouldn't be wise with my hips.'

Replenished, Josie prepares to embark on the afternoon book-delivery rounds. Miss Godson has sent word that she'll be absent until tomorrow, so Josie must face the task alone. Mrs Stanten offers to cover the library desk in her absence.

'Will you be all right on your own, Mrs Stanten?' Josie asks, earning herself a sharp look.

'You forget, my dear, I helped run the first excavations organized by the Egypt Exploration Fund,' the older woman replies. 'I was copying inscriptions, reliefs and monuments, and drawing illustrations for my husband's publications, all while raising four children. I think I can handle a few customers.'

While Mrs Stanten stocks the book cart with stationery, pencils, matches and the like, Josie concentrates on fulfilling the patients' book requests. She selects Thackeray's *Vanity Fair* for an officer who has jotted on his request slip his ambition 'to become a novelist when I leave Endell'.

Mrs Stanten suggests Wilde's *The Picture of Dorian Gray* for a Scottish rifleman, who has scribbled 'in search of distracting literature' on the back of his slip.

Josie chooses *Wuthering Heights* for a soldier who has scrawled on his slip that he's never read a classic in his whole twenty-two years.

At last the requests are complete, the trolley groaning under the weight of fresh books, and the two women prepare to open the main library. As Mrs Stanten turns on the lights, Josie wheels the trolley out of the stockroom. Opening the main library doors, she's greeted by a line of patients waiting in the corridor, a few of the men leaning on crutches, one in a wheeled chair.

Invited in, the men begin perusing the bookcases, settling themselves for an afternoon of reading. Mrs Stanten is soon put to work handing out newspapers and locating texts, and Josie takes her leave.

St Ursula's ward, Josie's first port of call, is a scene of

calm industry. She nods a greeting at the nursing staff busy attending to patients, exchanges a smile with an orderly collecting lunch trays. A man on crutches makes a beeline for Josie, as she parks the cart at the foot of the first bed.

'The trolley of delights,' the man says, tapping the cart's wonky front wheel with his crutch. 'Any books on there for me?'

Josie opens the record of requests. 'What's your name, sir?'

'Mansfield. I've been waiting for a book of poems by Eastaway.'

Josie checks her notes. Miss Godson's handwriting is tiny and hard to decipher in places, but at last she finds the book in question.

'Here we are, sir.'

The man thanks Josie, pocketing the book and lurching back to his bed. The exchange is so matter-of-fact, so polite and cheerful, it's only the man's limp that reminds Josie of the wreckage beneath the veneer.

Before continuing, she briefly consults Miss Godson's instructions about various patients in the ward. Private Trowbridge, the first patient on the list, was a concert pianist before the war, Josie learns. But Miss Godson's note is heartbreaking: he'll likely never play again, having suffered multiple bone fractures in his left wrist following a mortar attack near Ypres.

Josie greets Private Trowbridge with her best smile, and offers him the contents of the book cart.

Trowbridge stares back at her in sombre silence.

'How about a Gould?' Josie holds up *A Fortune at Stake*, but Trowbridge turns his head away.

'No, thank you,' he mutters.

Josie fights the impulse to retreat, remembering something the librarian had said to her: that for some men, the very thought of a book was worse than a bomb.

She takes a step closer, trying not to look at his bandaged wrist. 'Are you sure there's nothing that might interest you, sir?'

'Why didn't the doctor let me die?' the soldier mumbles. He refuses to look at Josie, and in the charged silence she tries to think of a suitable reply. Her desperate gaze falls on a sheet of paper and a pen on the bedside table.

'Would you like me to write a letter for you?' she ventures. He must have a mother, a family, a sweetheart perhaps? She ought to be moving on, with so many book deliveries to make, but she can't bring herself to walk away.

'No.' Trowbridge's eyes well, and Josie feels an overwhelming urge to reveal her own tragedy, to confide in this broken man that she's hurting too, but the words stick in her throat. She reaches for the trolley, steadying herself.

'Why didn't the doctor let me die?' Trowbridge repeats, weeping openly now. Josie desperately searches for something useful to say to this grown man, crying like a lost child.

'Because it's not your time,' she hears herself reply. 'You have lots of music still to make.'

Was that the right thing to say?

Trowbridge shakes his head miserably, and the movement provokes a hacking cough. Josie stands helpless, as the young man struggles to breathe. To her relief, a nurse hurries over, deftly adjusting pillows, offering water.

Josie is about to wheel her trolley away, when something snags her memory. She searches among the books, until she finds what she's looking for: *The Life of Chopin*.

She sets the book on the young man's bedside table, and retreats.

On her way to St Anne's ward she negotiates hurrying staff, and several patients wandering the corridors like gaunt ghosts. Rounding a corner, she narrowly avoids colliding with a small group of women coming in the opposite direction. She recognizes the leader – Lady Anderson. The woman had come into the library recently to enquire about knitting patterns. Lady Anderson and her entourage of female volunteers organized needlework, basket weaving and knitting lessons for the patients.

Josie has heard that many of the men have proved unexpectedly good at crafts, and those with any real aptitude for needlework weren't restricted to sewing regimental badges. Instead, Lady Anderson and her volunteers were teaching the men how to fashion scenes copied from pictures. Lady Anderson pauses to share one such image with Josie now.

'Have you ever seen anything so exquisite, my dear?' Lady Anderson says, flourishing a wooden embroidery hoop stitched with a detailed garden scene, full of flowers intricately rendered in different-coloured threads. Josie has to agree: it is beautiful.

'Made by a young private who'd never stitched a thing in his life before,' Lady Anderson pronounces proudly. 'Our men have hidden talents.' She and her women sweep past Josie, like a charm of goldfinches, heading for the next ward.

A polite cheer goes up as Josie wheels the book cart into St Anne's ward, and she feels her cheeks redden.

'Here she is at last!' the man in the first bed proclaims. His left leg has been amputated at the knee, Josie notices, and she gives him an extra warm smile as she checks his name against her record of requests.

'Prescription literature.' The soldier smiles, as Josie hands him a copy of *Where Angels Fear to Tread*.

'I hope you enjoy it,' Josie says, moving on down the aisle.

Bed by bed, she makes her way through the ward, issuing and collecting books, accepting new request slips, exchanging pleasantries. *Bleak House*, *Gulliver's Travels*, *Silas Marner*, *The Wings of the Dove*, one by one the books are dispensed, until the trolley is half empty.

A last she reaches the final two beds, where she finds the New Zealand soldiers both awake, Stuart greeting her arrival with a grin. 'Anything left for us, Just-Josie?'

'I do have something, actually.' She unearths from the trolley a week-old copy of the *Wellington Post*, which Stuart accepts with a joyous whistle.

'Been waiting for this for ages, eh.'

'Would you like something from the cart?' Josie asks Theo. His ink-dark eyes watch her closely, reminding her of a crow. He clears his throat, and Josie waits for him to answer, but instead he reaches towards the bedside table, and turns back to Josie with a thin book in his hand. He offers it to her, as though bestowing a gift. It's not an Endell Street library book. *Māori Myths and Legends* is embossed in flaking gold lettering on the narrow spine. A name is printed inside the cover: T. Aitken.

At first glance, Josie can see that the stories are written in English, but the inscription on the title page is in a language she can't read.

'What does this say?' she asks.

'It's Māori,' Stuart supplies. '"Farewell young men",' he translates. '"Go and uphold the name of our warrior ancestors. Fear God. And honour the king."'

'This belongs to you?' Josie asks Theo. 'Are you Māori?'

'His ma and mine are both Māori,' Stuart answers. 'Will you read to us, Just-Josie?'

Was he teasing her? Would he dare ask this of Miss Godson if she was here?

'I'm not sure that's —'

'Please,' Stuart presses. 'Your voice is heaps better than my old croak, eh.' He nods towards Theo. 'Poor old fella could do with a story, eh.'

'Well . . .' Josie bites her lip, hearing the librarian's voice in her head. *No fraternizing with the patients, Miss Everley.*

'Reckon it'd do you good to hear a yarn from home, eh, Theo mate?' Stuart persists.

Theo nods.

'Well, if you really want me to read to you . . .'

Stuart grins at her, victorious, as Josie opens the book. The first story is entitled: 'How The Moon Was Made'. It's only a page long, Josie notes with relief.

'Just one,' she relents.

Stuart beams, but Theo remains quietly watchful, as Josie sits down on the chair between the two beds. '*In the beginning,*' she begins, pushing through the shyness that threatens to stopper her throat, '*before the route to the afterlife was sealed to mortals, two women wondered about what went on in the Raro . . . Raro . . .*' She stumbles on the unfamiliar word.

'Rarohenga,' Stuart supplies. 'It's Māori for the Underworld.'

'Oh.' Josie suppresses a shudder. Should she be reading a story about death?

'Please, go on,' Stuart urges.

'*The friends gathered provisions of dried kumara . . .*' Josie pauses again, looking up.

'Sweet potato,' Stuart supplies.

'*. . . and began their quest to reach the Rei . . . Reinga.*' She falters again.

'It's where the spirits leap off into the Underworld,' Stuart says.

Josie reads on, heart aching with the memory of reading bedtime stories like this to Jem when he was a little boy. '*The women found themselves in a dark cave. They could see a faint light, and as they ventured nearer they found three grey spirits hunched around a fire. The women longed for the spirit-fire. It would warm their homes for ever, so one of them snatched up a burning log. The friends ran back to the Reinga, but the spirits chased them, catching them before they could escape. In her panic, the woman holding the burning brand threw it high in the air, and there it caught in Rangi's robe, where it glows for ever more as Marama the moon.'*

Josie reaches the end of the story. She can hear an RAMC guard barking orders down in the courtyard, drilling a team of orderlies.

'Line up! Look sharp!'

She closes the book and finds Theo's gaze fixed on her.

'Thank you,' he rasps.

'Bloody hell.' Stuart laughs. 'You're a little miracle worker, Just-Josie.'

She smiles bashfully and rises, returning the book to Theo.

'I'll come back tomorrow,' she promises, and begins to wheel the trolley away.

'We'll hold you to that,' Stuart calls after her.

Josie smiles to herself.

Issue No. 2 | # The Daily Dose | Price FREE

There was much merrymaking at Endell Street Hospital recently, with a procession of female saints, after which the wards are named.

The saintly pageant, beautiful and poignant to behold, was very well received, and will linger long in the memory of everyone who witnessed it.

Furthermore, the hospital's cup of happiness was filled to overflowing by the presence of Queen Alexandra, who arrived without notification, and toured the wards informally with her daughters Princess Victoria and Princess Maud.

E. Lawrence

Book Recommendations

Franck, H. A.
A Vagabond Journey around the World. Illus.

(A young man just out of college makes a bet that he can start without a cent in his pocket and work his way around the world. This is the record of how he did it, and is a most interesting book of travel.)

Davis, R. H.
In the Fog.

(A baffling murder mystery, which might have happened in a London fog.)

Doyle, A. C.
Adventures of Sherlock Holmes.

(Detective stories of absorbing interest in which the solution of the mystery is the question, rather than the details of the crime.)

Haines, A. C.
Partners for Fair.

(A boy and his dog and their wanderings with a travelling circus.)

PEOPLE WE TAKE OUR HATS OFF TO:

The Canadians.

LECTURE

**Dr Jemima Short begs to announce her new course of medical lectures.
Her next lecture will be given on Tuesday next, in the Library, on the 3rd floor.
Subject: Disorders of Sleep.
All welcome.**

COMPETITION

Can you complete this well-known proverb?

A/B_O_/I_/T_E/H_N_/I_/W_R_H/T_O/_N/T_E/S_E_F

**FOR SALE
1914 Premier Model No.6 Lady's bicycle.
Price: 6 shillings.**

20

Edie – London

Stanley's parents live in Kentish Town, a part of London unfamiliar to Edie. She considers asking Mary for help with directions, but she fears her friend will try to convince her not to go. She can hear Mary's voice in her head, imploring her to ignore the letter, to let sleeping dogs lie. Instead Edie waits until after lunch, when Mary is occupied in the back garden, pottering in the rose beds, to slip from the house unnoticed.

She's wrapped Stanley's pocket camera in a piece of cloth to protect it, along with the small bundle of photographs Harry had managed to develop for her. They may be her only chance to persuade Stanley's family of her integrity. The camera and the photographs are the one physical proof she can offer them that she's telling the truth. She can hardly bring herself to consider the consequences if they don't believe her, and has no earthly idea what she'll do if they continue to refuse to let her visit Stanley.

All she can do is try.

She hurries along the street, her satchel with its precious contents bumping against her hip, a sour taste lingering in her mouth. Mary will soon wonder where she's gone, but with luck she'll be back before teatime at the latest. If Mary asks where she's been, she'll have to pretend she's visited the hospital library again. The prospect of lying to Mary leaves Edie cold, but it's better this way, she tries to tell herself. What Mary doesn't know can't hurt her, and she worries about Edie as though she were another of her daughters.

Edie boards a bus, hugging her satchel on her lap as the vehicle wends its way towards Kentish Town. She stares out at the streets reeling past the dirty window, and finds herself thinking of how London has changed from the vibrant, bustling city of a few months ago to a place she barely recognizes.

Most museums and galleries have closed their doors, many coffee houses and pubs following suit. Shop windows reflect a shortage of goods, shelves half bare of fresh fruit, vegetables and meat. During the day the roads are clogged with vehicles, bicycles, the pavements thronging with Londoners, as well as troops from across the Empire, and so many 'Blighty' soldiers. But as evening falls, the roads and squares and parks rapidly empty, windows are blacked out, and eerie searchlights sweep the night sky for enemy aircraft.

Edie's bus is being driven by a woman, a fact that both thrills and worries her, though she's mostly impressed by the woman's driving skills. The vehicle shudders through the streets, negotiating pedestrians, cyclists, cabs and carriages, and Edie can't fault the driver's ability to remain calm.

The bus conductor is also a young woman, and her

presence makes Edie wonder about all the women now working at men's jobs, in hotels and factories, offices and hospitals. So many orderlies, cooks, cleaners and clerks. Even well-off women, with no need to draw a wage, are volunteering with agencies, doing their bit for the war wounded, the poor, the refugees flooding in from a war-torn Continent.

London is a city run increasingly by women, Edie thinks, and the notion stirs her in a way she can't quite define. It feels as though a new world is being born from the carnage and destruction of war, but at the cost of how many lives?

After almost an hour of travelling, Edie arrives at the Chays' street. She finds the address, a three-storey mid-terrace house with a narrow, overgrown front garden, and fumbles to open the rusted iron gate. Dandelions and chickweed sprout from cracks in the path, and the red front door is dulled, its stained-glass lights dusty.

She glances at the bay window, but the panes are swathed in blackout curtains. On such a pleasantly sunny day they give the house an abandoned air, and Edie half expects her knock to go unanswered.

She waits, her blouse sticking to her back with sweat, her mouth parched. Now she's here, the nerves she's kept at bay since she left the Levinsons' threaten to sabotage her.

But it's too late to retreat. The door opens, and Edie finds herself facing the man she'd encountered at

Stanley's bedside in Queen Square. She straightens her spine, mustering her courage.

'Mr Chay? I'm Edie Lawrence.'

'You came.' There is no welcoming smile, as Mr Chay admits Edie into a gloomy hallway. Portrait pictures line the walls, but Edie has no chance to take them in.

'Have you travelled far?' Mr Chay enquires, as he ushers Edie into the front room, a similarly dingy space lit by a single gas lamp. Edie mumbles a reply, glancing at the tightly drawn curtains, wanting to ask the man why they were closed. She starts, as a small, middle-aged woman rises from a settee in a shadowed corner of the room, and comes towards her. Edie recognizes her as Stanley's mother.

'Helena, this is Miss Lawrence,' Mr Chay says.

The woman regards Edie with frowning distrust, her amber eyes reminding Edie unnervingly of Stanley's.

'Pleased to meet you, Mrs Chay,' Edie stammers, tentatively extending a hand. After an awkward pause, Stanley's mother offers limp, clammy fingers in return.

'How about some tea, Helena?' Mr Chay touches his wife's shoulder, and Mrs Chay bows her head and shuffles from the room.

Mr Chay gestures to Edie to take a seat on a threadbare armchair, but he remains standing by the empty hearth.

'My son keeps asking for someone called Lawrence,' he says, without preamble. 'Is he a relative of yours? A brother perhaps?'

Edie shakes her head, forcing herself to meet the man's probing gaze. 'He means me, sir. I'm Lawrence.'

The long silence that follows is broken by the faint clatter of crockery drifting from somewhere in the depths of the house. A clock on the mantelpiece chimes the hour, and Edie finds herself holding her breath, the walls of the room beginning to encroach on her, the air thick with unspoken words.

Mr Chay scratches at a greying sideburn, in a manner that reminds Edie disarmingly of Stanley. 'I don't understand,' he says at last.

There is nothing for it but to speak the truth.

'I met your son when we were both training at Hurst Park,' Edie replies. 'We fought together in France.'

Mr Chay opens his mouth to respond, but is interrupted by the return of his wife, bearing a tray piled haphazardly with tea things. She sets it on a low table, her movements slow and shaky, and retreats to the settee in the corner.

'This woman says she knew Stanley in France,' Mr Chay informs his wife.

'France?' Mrs Chay's voice is little more than a whisper. Edie begins to wonder if she's quite all there. There's something off about her: she exudes a nervous energy, yet she seems so feeble.

'This woman says she fought with our boy, in the army.'

This woman. Our boy.

'I know it sounds unbelievable,' Edie interjects, 'but I promise you it's the truth. I'm the Lawrence your son's been asking for. If you'd just let me explain . . .'

'How do you know our son?' Mrs Chay surges to her

feet, and Edie flinches. The woman's voice has risen, on the edge of hysteria.

'Calm yourself, Helena.' Mr Chay moves to his wife's side but she refuses to sit down.

'Ma'am, I'm telling the truth,' Edie stammers. 'If Stanley was here, he'd tell you –'

'He's suffered worse than Hell,' Mrs Chay cries, cutting Edie off. 'He's a broken man. He can't sleep, barely eats. His hands shake so bad he can't even hold a cup. You don't understand the strain we're under . . .' She begins to sob, and Mr Chay places an arm around her shoulders, glowering at Edie.

'Tell us how you know our son,' he demands. 'Since he came home he's told us nothing.'

'He's been discharged?' Edie glances towards the door leading to the stairs. 'Is he here? Can I see him?'

Mr Chay shakes his head, his frown deepening. 'He's not receiving visitors.'

'He'll want to see me, sir,' Edie says. 'I have something of his to give back to him.' She fumbles open her satchel, and unwraps the camera on her lap.

Mr Chay's eyes widen and his wife's sobs peter out. 'Where did you get that?' Mr Chay barks.

'I'm trying to tell you, sir,' Edie replies. 'I fought with your son in France, and when he was wounded I kept his camera safe.'

'You were really there?' Mrs Chay gasps. 'You were with my boy, when he was—'

'How can I trust that's really Stanley's?' Mr Chay interrupts.

'I'm not lying, sir.' Close to tears, Edie digs the photographs out of her bag. 'Stanley was wounded,' she stammers. 'Shot in the leg . . . I was there, I was injured too . . .' Her thigh aches, and she resists the urge to lift her skirt, show these people the unsightly scar she will bear for the rest of her life. With shaking hands, she unties the string around the bundle of photographs, and passes them over.

A heavy silence descends, as Mr and Mrs Chay examine the first picture, the grainy image of Edie crouched among the troops on Southampton docks, her rifle gripped between her knees.

'Stanley took the picture,' Edie says, her voice hoarse. 'We were waiting to board a troopship, the SS *Winifred*.' She's haunted by memories of that momentous day, her fear and excitement on the journey to the battlefields. Her utter ignorance of what was to come.

Mr Chay's eyes flick from the photograph to Edie, and back to the photo. He makes no comment, his expression unfathomable. Mrs Chay holds a handkerchief to her mouth, her whole body trembling.

Edie can do nothing but wait, longing for more tea, her mouth so dry from nerves her lips are tacky.

At last, Mr Chay gathers the photographs together. 'These pictures,' he says. 'Tell me again how you came by them.'

Edie takes a breath. Her story will take some telling. But tell it she must.

'I've always wanted to be a journalist,' she begins. Mr and Mrs Chay listen in awed silence, as Edie hesitantly confesses her 'stunt', how she'd managed to enlist in the army, met Stanley, travelled to France with his platoon. How they were sent to search an enemy outpost. She falters here, the memories too raw still. To their credit, Mr and Mrs Chay are patient, and when Edie at last concludes her account, Mr Chay murmurs something to his wife, who gives a single, silent nod.

Mr Chay turns back to Edie. 'Stanley's upstairs,' he says.

She climbs the narrow staircase, pausing for a moment on the shadowy landing. Four doors stretch away into the gloom, behind one of which is Stanley. Edie grasps the banister, beset by a wave of doubt that threatens to floor her.

She takes a shaky breath, willing her heart to cease its frantic thumping. The nearest door is ajar. She steps to it, peers through the crack, and though she can make out little of the darkened room beyond, she somehow knows Stanley is near.

She taps on the door, then nudges it further open, and as her eyes adjust to the low light she sees a figure lying in a narrow bed.

'Stanley?'

No movement or sound. Edie hesitates. Should she leave him to sleep? But there's no guarantee his parents will let her see him again. She must take the opportunity now, tell Stanley the truth. It's the only way they can begin to move on from this living nightmare.

'Stanley?' She raises her voice slightly. 'It's me,

Lawrence.' This garners no response from the bed so, taking another breath, Edie steps over the threshold.

The curtains are drawn, and she crosses the room and tugs them open. Sunlight floods the bedroom, revealing a washstand with ewer and bowl, a chest of drawers, its surface cluttered with medicine bottles, a kidney dish, a jug of water. A framed photograph of a football team hangs on one wall, with a display of newspaper clippings and a few pictures cut out of magazines of boxers sparring and a cricket team. A cloying, medicinal tang lies heavy on the air, and Edie wonders if she should open the window a crack.

A cough comes from the bed and she jerks round, to find Stanley awake, pushing himself up on his pillows, staring at her.

'Stan?'

His ashen skin is drawn tight over the prominent bones of his skull, yet the sight of him lifts Edie's heart like a summer breeze.

'Lawrence . . .' Stanley's voice is a faint rasp. 'What took you so bloody long?'

His slow grin brings tears to Edie's eyes, as she stumbles to his bedside, and drops to her knees.

21

Josie – London

Josie hauls the book cart back to the library, her ward deliveries completed at last. She finds the place deserted, no sign of Mrs Stanten, or her fur coat. But a note has been tucked under a corner of the cutting mat on the desk.

Dear Josie,

Had to dash. Will see you tomorrow.
Don't work too late.

V

Josie wonders when Miss Godson will return from whatever meeting she's been called to this time. She's beginning to feel some sympathy for the librarian: the poor woman's so busy she barely has time to breathe, let alone read. At least Mrs Stanten helps, part-time though she is, and Josie is gradually getting used to her ebullient company.

She sets about making herself a cup of tea, nibbling a stale oat cake while she waits for the kettle to come to the boil. In her mind's eye she replays the encounter with the New Zealand soldiers: Stuart with his bold grin, Theo with his haunted eyes. She remembers what Stuart had said, that Theo had been shot in the flank, and it makes her shudder to think of the pain he must be suffering. How do any of the men bear their injuries so stoically?

Stuart had called Theo a 'lucky blighter', fortunate to be alive. The bullet could so easily have hit a vital organ.

Lucky is one way of viewing it, Josie reflects, as she sips her black tea. But lucky isn't how she would feel, to be wounded in battle, then trapped indefinitely in a hospital bed thousands of miles from home and family.

But, then, perhaps Theo *was* lucky, when so many soldiers never made it off the battlefield at all. The light is beginning to wane, and Josie flicks on the stockroom's bare electric bulb. Soon, she'll have to return to her aunt's for dinner, but first she must finish sorting the trolley, in case Miss Godson arrives early tomorrow.

She begins methodically checking each returned book on her list, ticking them off one by one, before ferrying armfuls of them through into the main library. As she works, her thoughts are calmed by the repetitive task of shelving the books, and gradually a sense of peace suffuses her.

She lets her mind drift as she contemplates the huge number of stories the library contains, any one of which offers the potential to ease her heartache, if only for a short while.

As the trolley gradually empties, Josie's thoughts wander further.

She ought to write to Mrs Cavendish, to let the American widow know she'd reached London safely, and to thank her for lending her the money. Soon, she'll be able to start repaying her, as Miss Godson has at last confirmed her wages, and Josie is now officially on the hospital staff payroll.

As if she's summoned Miss Godson by the power of thought alone, the library doors squeal, and she turns to find the librarian beetling towards her.

'I wasn't expecting you still to be here, Miss Everley,' Miss Godson says, by way of greeting.

'I'm almost done with the trolley, ma'am,' Josie replies. 'There were a lot of requests.'

'Did you record them all?'

'Yes,' Josie says, slotting the final book into place on the shelf.

'Good work.' Miss Godson disappears into the stockroom.

Closing the bookcases, Josie follows her, to find the librarian seated at the desk, pince-nez balanced on her nose, scrutinizing a copy of *Middlemarch*. 'Some leaves need stitching in this,' Miss Godson remarks.

'I haven't finished repairing it yet,' Josie tries to explain, but the librarian seems not to be listening. Her attention has turned to the record of requests, and she runs a finger down the lists of names and book titles, muttering under her breath.

Josie hesitates by the door, braced for criticism, but instead Miss Godson beckons her closer, and gestures for her to draw up a stool.

'I see here you visited Private Trowbridge earlier today,' the librarian says.

'Yes.' Josie recalls the young man's bandaged wrists and aura of hopelessness. Why was she so interested in this particular soldier?

Miss Godson squints at Josie over the top of her spectacles. 'You gave him a book about Chopin.'

'It was the only thing I could think of,' Josie replies. 'He was so despondent, I couldn't interest him in anything else.'

Miss Godson's gaze is piercing, and Josie's palms grow damp as the silence deepens between them.

'An astute choice,' Miss Godson says at last.

'I'm not so sure . . .' Josie murmurs. 'Next time I'll try harder to find out what he likes. I was in a hurry . . .'

'That won't be necessary,' Miss Godson says quietly. 'Private Trowbridge died this afternoon. Matron informed me as I arrived.'

It feels to Josie as though the temperature in the room has dropped several degrees.

'Marcus Trowbridge was my neighbour's son,' Miss Godson goes on, her eyes glistening. 'I've known him since he was born.'

'I'm so sorry, ma'am.'

'Matron told me he'd been enjoying the book you gave him before he died. It gave Marcus solace at the end, Miss Everley.'

Miss Godson digs a handkerchief from her sleeve and blows her nose. 'I must congratulate you, Miss Everley,' she says, more briskly. 'You appear to possess a librarian's knack.'

'Pardon, ma'am?'

'Uniting patients with the books they need,' the librarian explains. 'It usually takes years of training. But you seem to have an aptitude for it.'

Was Miss Godson complimenting her? It seems so unlikely, Josie wonders if she's misunderstood the woman.

'I'll be reporting your progress to Dr Garland and Dr Maberry,' Miss Godson continues.

'Thank you, ma'am.'

'Are you happy with your duties?'

'Happy, ma'am?'

'You seem rather . . . distracted, Miss Everley. Is everything all right?'

'It's . . . I mean . . . Trowbridge . . .' Josie's sentence peters out. She has no idea what she wants to say.

'Very sad, yes,' Miss Godson concedes. 'The world has lost a rare talent.'

'I'm so sorry, ma'am,' Josie says again, words failing her.

'The inevitable legacy of war.' Miss Godson clears her throat, removes her spectacles and rubs the reddened bridge of her nose. 'You should go home, Miss Everley, before it gets dark.'

Josie rises. Pearl will be growing worried, especially since the recent spate of Zeppelin attacks on the city.

'Goodnight then, ma'am.' The words have barely left her mouth, when from somewhere outside the bounds of the hospital she hears the echoing retort of a cannon, firing a trilogy of shots in rapid succession.

The colour leaches from Miss Godson's face. 'Sound rockets.'

'What are they, ma'am?'

'Haven't you read about them in the newspaper? They're the new air-raid warning.' The librarian pushes back her chair. 'If enemy airships are sighted over London, they discharge salvos from the roofs of the fire stations in the area.'

There's no chance for Josie to ask further questions, as now an ominous rumbling is coming from beyond the window. The low percussive thudding grows steadily louder, as though thunder approaches, except Josie knows in her bones that this is no natural storm.

An ear-splitting roar, followed a moment later by a deep, resonating crash, sends the walls of the stockroom shaking. Josie cries out as flakes of plaster rain down from the cracked ceiling, the light-bulb swinging wildly on its frayed cord.

'Get down,' Miss Godson cries, and Josie drops to the floor. The two women crouch beneath the shelter of the desk, as gradually the rumbling fades away, to be replaced with distant shouting and the urgent clang of the courtyard bell.

'That sounded like the hospital's been hit,' Miss Godson gasps, a hand to her chest, as the bell continues its portentous alarm. Minutes pass, and Josie struggles to breathe, fear gripping her by the throat. How can this be happening to her again?

'Are you all right, Miss Everley?' The librarian's face is ashen in the muted light.

Josie's hands are damp with sweat, and her knees are cramping. 'What's going on?' she manages to croak. 'What should we do?'

'Stay calm,' Miss Godson replies. 'It sounds as though the worst is over.' She hauls herself to her feet, and Josie follows her lead, wincing as the blood returns to her stiff legs. They survey the stockroom, unscathed apart from a layer of plaster dust coating the desk, the shelves, the piles of books.

Josie crosses to the window, peering down at the courtyard, the scene below reminding her of the time the ambulance convoy arrived. People are dashing everywhere, while RAMC guards on the gate unfurl a fire hose. A succession of orderlies rushes in and out of the main entrance, lugging buckets of water.

Josie turns away, to find Miss Godson at the door. 'We have to help, Miss Everley.'

Josie is seized with an overwhelming urge to pull the librarian back into the stockroom.

I can't do this, she wants to scream. *I can't face this again.*

But Miss Godson is already dashing out of the library, and Josie has no choice but to stumble after her.

Hurrying along the corridor, Josie learns from passing staff that three of the wards, including St Anne's, have sustained bomb damage. The windows of St Anne's have blown in, and part of the ceiling has collapsed, and a sudden thought tears through Josie's numbed brain: Stuart and Theo's beds are by the window.

Nurses and orderlies are ferrying those men who can

walk out of St Anne's ward, and Josie flattens herself against the wall as a stream of patients and staff pass by.

Miss Godson has moved further away along the corridor, and is talking with Dr Garland and Dr Maberry. She is gesticulating towards the library, and both doctors are nodding, but before Josie can move a nurse appears before her, a grimace of barely suppressed panic on her face. 'Don't just stand there,' the nurse snaps. 'Help us.'

Josie follows the nurse into the ward, the air so full of dust she can see no further than the first few beds. The nurse rushes to help a patient collapsed on the floor, and Josie joins two orderlies struggling to push a bed containing a man whose legs are encased in plaster out into the corridor. The metal frame holding the patient's limbs in place has broken, the contraption lying tangled on the bedcovers.

With Josie's help, the orderlies manage to shunt the bed over the threshold, the man crying out with pain at every jolt of the wheels. There's no space in the choked corridor to park the bed, and no one seems to know what to do with the evacuated patients.

Miss Godson materializes at Josie's side. 'The walking wounded are being herded down to the basement,' she says, 'but those who can't leave their beds will have to go into the library.' She coughs into her sleeve. 'Dr Garland has agreed this is the best option. Clear some space in there, and I'll join you shortly.' She hurries away again.

The lights along the corridor flicker, then go out,

plunging the windowless passage into darkness. Someone near Josie swears, and further away to her left a strident Scottish voice calls, 'Stay calm!'

It's a few long moments before lanterns are lit, and light is restored. Josie stumbles back into the library, the electricity still working in here somehow, and begins to clear desks and chairs to the edges of the room, as the first few beds are wheeled through the doors.

There's barely a chance to worry about Theo and Stuart, as she's put to work shifting furniture, fetching medical provisions and fresh water. But to her relief, she returns from a trip to the kitchens to find the New Zealanders are safe, their beds having been moved into the library. Josie brings the men water, and Theo asks her shyly if she's all right.

Josie raises a hand to her hair, the messy bun she'd hastily fashioned this morning now escaping its pins. Her fingers come away covered with dust.

'I'm fine,' Josie lies. Now the panic is largely over, her legs are threatening to give, and she rests a steadying hand on a nearby bookcase.

'Old Fritz thought he'd got us, eh?' Stuart says. 'Not this time –'

He breaks off as the lights flicker, and a moment later all the bulbs die, throwing the library into shadow.

Josie clamps a hand over her mouth, heart thumping, as around her rise terrified moans and cries.

'Bloody hell!' Stuart curses loudly. 'Can't Fritz take a bloody day off?' The comment serves to lighten the mood, and there follows a smattering of laughter.

'Stay calm!' someone calls through the library doors. 'The electric's blown . . .'

Josie exhales, as those around her breathe a collective sigh of relief at the knowledge they're not under renewed attack by the Germans. The discordant chimes of the courtyard bell have long grown silent, but only now does the blunt shock that's so far deadened Josie's nerves begin to dissipate, leaving her weak and shaky.

With an effort of will, she holds herself together. Gradually, she realizes Theo has pulled himself up on his pillows and is saying something to her.

'You're bleeding.' He indicates Josie's face. She touches her cheek, her fingers coming away sticky with blood.

'It's only a scratch,' Theo adds. 'Here.' He hands her a clean, folded handkerchief, and Josie wipes her face.

'Thank you.' She has no time to wonder how she came to cut her face, as Orderly Hodgson is rushing through the doors, calling her name.

'What's the matter?' Josie manages.

'It's Miss Godson,' Hodgson says, breathless. 'You need to come quick.'

| Issue No. 3 | # The Daily Dose | Price FREE |

Let our Librarians take you on a tour of the wards, here at Endell Street Hospital.

The 'Book Trolley of Delights' is stocked with all manner of literature, from novels to periodicals – the most welcome prescription for our war-torn patients.

The joyous response of the wounded men, as the book cart is wheeled to their bedsides, is a pleasure in itself to behold.

Any visitor to our wards will see for themselves the truth of the reading cure in operation here at Endell Street.

The Librarians prescribe books as carefully as the doctors write prescriptions.

Of all the remedies applied to our wounded men, reading is the only one they accept naturally.

The patients gladly accept literature as one of the most important tools of mental therapy, absorbing the curative quality of reading with all their hearts, as their journey to healing begins.

E. Lawrence

Book Recommendations

Threadgill, H. M.
The Sea and the Jungle. Illus.

(The story of a tramp steamer from England that sails across to Brazil and up the Amazon River to the rubber plantations. As well as a thrilling narrative of a storm at sea and life in the tropics.)

Rinehart, Mary Roberts.
The Circular Staircase.

(Humorous detective mystery in which a circular staircase features.)

PEOPLE WE TAKE OUR
HATS OFF TO:

The ANZACS

ARREST ALL DIRT

**And CLEANSE Everything By Using HUDSON'S EXTRACT OF SOAP.
Reward: Purity, Health, Daily Satisfaction.**

COMPETITION

Can you complete this well-known proverb?

U_R_A_/B_O_S/M_K_/H_L_O_/M_N_S

22

Edie – London

Edie makes her way downstairs, listening for Susan going about her morning duties elsewhere in the house. But only the arthritic tick of the grandfather clock in the hall disturbs the quiet, the sun's early rays illuminating the peacock fanlight above the front door.

She wonders if Stanley is awake at this hour too, and her sternum aches at the thought of him. Being reunited with him feels like a dream now, their time together woefully brief. Stanley's father had been insistent that Edie shouldn't tire his son, and the only way Edie could persuade Mr Chay to let her return was by leaving Stanley's bedside after a mere ten minutes.

There had been no opportunity to talk freely, honestly, about all that had happened, so much remained unsaid, but Edie is determined to see him again. It's only a question of time. Until then, all she can think to do is try to distract herself with writing.

Like a shadow, she slips into Harry's darkened study and pulls the door to behind her. Leaving the curtains closed for now, she lights the lamp on the desk, then curls up in the old leather armchair, her notebook in her lap.

Now she takes a deep breath. She opens her notebook to a fresh page, and sets pencil to paper.

Best Hospital in London, she writes, then underlines the heading twice.

The military hospital in Endell St, London, is 'manned' by the Women's Hospital Corps.

Edie chews her pencil, as she ponders *manned*. Could she use *'womaned'* instead? What would Harry say? If only he were here to ask.

Her eyes drift to Harry's desk, where his trusted typing machine sits gathering dust amid glass phials of India ink, scraps of paper, and his favourite fountain pen lying where he'd left it on the blotter. Her gaze comes to rest on his empty chair, the seat cushion still bearing his imprint. She could never sit in it.

If only she knew when he'd return, but there's been no word from him, which doesn't seem to bother Mary as much as it does Edie. She turns her attention back to her notebook, the pages full of scribbled information she's gleaned from Dr Garland and the few other members of hospital staff she's been able to interview so far. Somehow she must wrangle these jottings into a serviceable piece good enough to pass muster with Mr Marsh and the War Office.

The Women's Hospital Corps, Edie reads, *'WHC' – known as the 'What Ho Corps' by the patients*. She doubts Mr Marsh at the War Office will be impressed to learn this.

The doctors all take military rank.
Dr Maberry, doctor-in-charge = Colonel.

Dr Garland, chief surgeon = Major.
15 surgeons, 1 physician, 1 ophthalmologist, 1 radiologist, 2 dental surgeons, all = captain.

Edie pauses, wondering if she's spelled *ophthalmologist* correctly.

36 nursing sisters, 80 + orderlies, (many of them London Society women). Many are volunteers, some employed as female 'Tommies' and receive army pay of 3s 2d a day.

Edie thinks of Mrs Whitford-Gowers, the VAD orderly she'd met following her road accident. She hadn't needed an army wage, she'd told Edie. She was happy to volunteer her time; she saw it as her patriotic duty.

The hospital has 550 beds, 17 wards.
  Wards with 30 beds+ = 1 day sister + 4 voluntary nurses + 1 night sister + 1 nurse helper.
  Voluntary nurses assist with dressings, making beds, sweeping & dusting, attending to meals, washing up, etc. Some are married women, with husbands at the front.

Edie skims over her notes. So far, she's barely written anything the War Office doesn't already know.

Some staff live at the hospital, others return home every day.
  Each morning = motor-cars arrive at hospital gates when VADs are due to start work, and again in the evening at the end of shift.

Edie leans her head against the soft leather of the armchair, staring into the hearth. Susan hasn't lit the fire in here while the weather is mild, but Edie can't imagine being cold in Harry's study, with its book-lined walls and shadowy corners. The armchair holds her in its supple embrace, and it occurs to her that there's nowhere she feels safer.

A knock at the door, and Mary appears, bearing a vase of delicate bell-shaped white flowers. Sweet perfume fills the room.

'I didn't realize you were awake,' Mary says, with a smile. 'I expect you haven't had breakfast yet, have you?'

'Not yet,' Edie admits, and her stomach growls on cue.

Mary gives her a knowing look. 'What are you writing today?'

'A piece on the hospital,' Edie replies. 'I'm going back there later.'

Mary contemplates Harry's disordered desk. 'How on earth my husband manages to get anything done, I haven't a clue,' she mutters, shunting paperwork to one side and setting down the vase.

'They smell nice,' Edie says. 'What are they?'

'Lily-of-the-valley.' Mary tidies more papers, and Edie looks on worriedly. Harry hated anyone tidying up after him. Will he think she'd been interfering with his work?

'It's said that the flowers first bloomed where Eve's tears fell as she left the Garden of Eden,' Mary chatters on. 'Harry loves them – they were his mother's favourite, God rest her soul. That's why I grow them.'

'Your garden is beautiful.'

'A labour of love.' Mary sits on Harry's chair, oblivious to Edie's discomfort at her choice of seating. 'Now, I hope you don't think I'm prying, Edie dear, but how did your visit to Stanley go yesterday? I didn't see you last night to ask.'

'Oh, well . . .' Edie closes her notebook, searching for the right words to describe the enormity of seeing Stanley again. How to explain to Mary what it had meant to her? 'He was much better than he was when I last saw him.'

'How do you mean better?' Mary presses. 'Did he remember you this time?'

Stanley had been like a different person from the one she'd visited in Queen Square. He hadn't questioned her new image, but Edie knew he'd want answers soon. She grips the notebook in her lap. 'Yes,' she answers.

'That's progress, isn't it?' Mary says gently. 'The poor man's been through so much. You both have.'

More than you can ever imagine, Edie thinks. 'His parents were suspicious,' she finds herself admitting. 'They wouldn't let me see him at first.'

'Did they know who you were?'

'I tried to explain, but they didn't believe me. It was only when I gave them Stan's camera that they were finally persuaded, and then they let me see him, but only briefly.'

'That's understandable.'

'What do you mean?'

'Well, it must be hard, when your son is suffering –'

'How does denying him visitors help?' Edie rises from the armchair, her notebook clutched to her chest.

'I didn't mean to upset you, dear. I only meant that I can understand how his parents must feel.'

Edie bites her lip. Stanley's parents have some understanding of their son's ordeal in France, but Edie lived through it with him. If they let her, she knows she could help him recover.

'It may take some time,' Mary says, 'for them to learn what you mean to Stanley.'

Edie wishes she could share Mary's optimism, but as far as Stanley's parents were concerned, he was ill and needed complete rest. She can understand how they might be frightened that she could upset their son further. But Stanley had wanted her to stay, yet his father had asked her to leave.

'I gave Stan his camera back,' she tells Mary. 'The photographs too.'

'His parents saw them?'

Edie nods. 'It took them a while to accept it was me in the pictures.'

'I find it hard to believe the hell you survived,' Mary murmurs. 'And yet here you are.'

Edie wonders if she did the right thing in leaving all the photographs with Stanley, even though technically they belong to him. Now she has no proof at all of her time on the battlefields of France, apart from her war-torn notebook. Stanley's precious photos had captured the ordinary truth of the war, in all its horror, and she's let them slip through her fingers. In a far recess of her mind, she'd imagined looking through the pictures with Stanley, talking about them, trying to come to terms with what they'd both gone through.

But his parents had not given them enough time.

'You must try to be patient,' Mary says. 'They'll come round to you.'

Edie longs to believe this, but all she can think of is Stanley's father escorting her politely but firmly out of his house.

'Perhaps his parents are worried you'll convince him to go back,' Mary suggests.

'To fight?' Edie stares at her friend. How can she think that? 'They didn't know what to make of me,' Edie admits. 'Even with the photos, I knew they found it hard to believe what I was telling them.'

'Your story is unique, Edie.'

'I'm going back,' Edie says. 'I'm going to visit Stan again.'

Mary frowns, but makes no reply.

'I have to, Mary.'

'That's all very well, dear, but you can't upset his family.'

'He's a grown man.'

'Convalescing in his parents' house.' Mary gives Edie a sympathetic look. 'I know how you must be feeling.'

Do you? Edie wants to cry.

'Give it a day or two,' Mary says. 'I'm sure in time Stanley's parents will grasp what a good influence you are on their son, and all will be resolved.' She rises, moves to the door. 'Let's see what culinary delight Susan's produced for breakfast, shall we?'

*

Over hot rolls, slathered in precious honey donated by one of Harry's beekeeper friends, Mary regales Edie with news of her latest fundraising venture: the Women's Volunteer Reserve.

'If I were a few years younger,' Mary says, 'I'd join their ranks myself. I've seen them march on Hampstead Heath in their smart uniforms, drilling like a regular army.'

Edie has also seen the WVR in action recently, and she shares Mary's excitement at the opportunities opening up for women. They both agree that the WVR will be a valuable addition to home defence, although the organization has mainly been established to raise funds for the war effort, and provide services such as canteens and clubs for soldiers. Edie keeps her darker thoughts to herself: that the WVR might think of themselves as an army, but the women have no idea of the reality of war, the brutality of the battlefield, and God forbid they ever should.

The front doorbell rings, and Susan goes to answer it.

'Do you really think Stanley's parents will accept me?' Edie asks Mary, as she collects their bowls and plates for the maid to wash up.

'I have no doubt that when they get to know you, Edie, they will come to love you.'

But what if they don't want me in their life at all? Edie worries. What if, when she goes back, they turn her away for good?

'In war you can't give much thought to tomorrow,' Mary says, patting Edie's shoulder. 'That way lies madness.'

Susan comes back into the kitchen, her face pale. 'Telegram, ma'am.'

Mary blanches, as she rips open the envelope.

Edie's thoughts turn immediately to Harry. Was this news from him? Or, worse, news *of* him? But the telegram isn't black-edged.

'Endell Street has been hit,' Mary reads. 'A Zeppelin attack last night.' She passes the telegram to Edie. 'Dr Garland is asking for our help.'

Edie tries to make sense of the words on the card. How can the Germans have bombed Dr Garland's hospital? Her mind spins, lost for a moment in imagining what must have happened, the damage, the terror. Had anyone been injured, or killed? There are no other details on the telegram, no clues as to how serious the attack was.

'I'll go there straight away,' Edie decides.

Mary promises to follow as soon as she can.

Edie arrives at the gates of the hospital to be met with a scene of frantic activity, the courtyard seething with more staff and patients than she's ever seen before.

Nobody can tell her precisely where Dr Garland and Dr Maberry might be, only that they are somewhere in the hospital, assessing the damage and treating injuries.

'Three wards were hit,' an orderly informs Edie.

'Were many people hurt?' Edie asks.

'A few,' the orderly replies. 'They got most of the patients down to the basement. Or, at least, those that could move went down there. But there are loads in the library. That might be where the doctors are.'

Edie thanks the orderly, who dashes away.

As she heads to the library, negotiating corridors full of staff, patients and firemen, Edie finds herself questioning her ability to help. She isn't medically trained, hardly even knows her way about the place.

But then she thinks of the young library assistant, Josie. The poor woman must be terrified, faced with another disaster so soon after the *Lusitania* tragedy. This thought alone is enough to propel Edie up the stairs to the third floor.

She pushes open the library doors, to find the main room packed with beds, at least twenty, barely space between them for a person to stand. The billiard table has been pushed against one wall, its baize surface covered with all manner of medical paraphernalia, piles of gauze bandages and bedding.

Edie edges her way further into the room, exchanging nods with a passing orderly. 'Is Dr Garland here?' Edie asks the girl.

'She was, a little while ago,' the orderly replies. 'Dunno where she is now.'

Edie thanks her, and is wondering what she can do to help, when she spots the library assistant at a bedside across the room.

Before Edie can take another step, a patient in a nearby bed grasps her sleeve, and she finds herself staring down at a young man whose face is covered with bandages, dried blood crusting his lips. 'Am I gonna die soon?' he rasps.

'Oh, no,' Edie stammers. 'Can I get you anything? Some water?'

'Chaplain says I gotta be prepared, miss.'

'I'm sure he only meant you to prepare to get better,' Edie says.

'Do you really think that's what he meant, miss?'

'I do.'

The young man closes his unbandaged eye, and Edie gently extracts her sleeve from his grasp. She hears someone say her name, and turns to find Josie at her side.

'You're here,' Josie breathes, as though Edie is some sort of apparition and might vanish at any moment.

'Are you all right?' Edie immediately regrets asking such a redundant question. Things are clearly far from all right. 'Were you here when the attack happened?'

Josie nods, visibly swallowing. 'Miss Godson and I tried to help . . .'

'You've been here all night?'

Josie gives another weary nod, and Edie sets a hand on her arm. 'You must be exhausted,' she says. 'Have you had anything to eat? What about a drink?'

Josie waves Edie's concern away. 'Miss Godson . . .' She falters.

'Is she here too?' Edie looks around the library, but can see no one who resembles the formidable librarian.

'She didn't make it.'

Edie turns back to Josie. 'What do you mean?'

Josie takes a shaky breath. 'She was injured. A window in one of the wards shattered as she was helping to move a patient. She was cut . . .'

'Oh, Josie.'

'The doctors did everything they could,' Josie says. 'They stopped the bleeding, and we thought she'd be all right, but her heart –'

They are interrupted by voices at the door, and Dr Garland enters the library. She's accompanied by a trio of official-looking men. The doctor spies Edie across the room, and beckons her over.

'I won't be a moment,' Edie promises Josie.

She joins Dr Garland, and is shocked at the doctor's grey face and bruised eyes. She looks to Edie has though she hasn't slept. 'Thank you for coming, Edie,' Dr Garland says, drawing her to one side. 'I trust you've heard about Miss Godson?'

'Only just now, Doctor. Awful news.'

'A terrible business. We did everything we could, but in the end she'd lost so much blood and her heart wasn't strong enough. She wasn't the only one to lose her life.'

There are no words. Edie glances at Josie, frozen in the stockroom doorway.

'I need your assistance, Edie.' Dr Garland introduces the men, whose names Edie instantly forgets. They're from the War Office, and have come to assess the damage.

'It would help me enormously if you could take notes, Edie,' Dr Garland says. 'These gentlemen are here to compile their official damage reports, but I'd like a record for ourselves. Please can you escort them around the hospital, and meet me back in my office in an hour?'

'Of course, Doctor.'

'Thank you. That's a tremendous help.' Dr Garland bids the officials goodbye, and hurries away.

Edie turns to the men. 'Will you excuse me for a moment, please?'

She leaves the trio conversing, and makes her way back to Josie. 'I'll be back to help you as soon as I can,' Edie promises.

'Thank you,' Josie whispers.

23

Josie – London

In the following days, while the rest of the hospital gradually returns to normal, the library stays closed out of respect for Miss Godson's untimely death. It shocks Josie how much she misses her. It wasn't as though Miss Godson had been her friend, or even particularly friendly. But her immense knowledge of literature, her boundless passion for books, her tireless work at Endell Street Hospital had inspired Josie beyond words.

Even if the woman herself had been hard to warm to.

'She unnerved me, if I'm honest,' Josie admits to Edie, as they shelve the last of the displaced books. A week has passed since the air-raid attack, and Josie is preparing to reopen the library at last. She's immensely grateful for Edie's assistance this morning. Yesterday Mrs Stanten had pulled a muscle lifting an overfull tea chest, and she won't be returning to work for a few days. Josie has been left to run the library alone.

'Unnerved you?' Edie wipes her brow with the back of a grubby hand. It's hot in the library, despite the breeze blowing through the open windows. 'In what way?'

'I don't think she was aware of the effect she had,' Josie tries to explain. 'We both knew I couldn't ever be her equal. Did you know she was once Queen Victoria's chief librarian at Windsor? And Mrs Stanten told me she worked as an archivist at the British Museum too.'

'All that means is Miss Godson had her own area of expertise and knowledge, and you have yours.'

'She made sure I never strayed over the line, you know.' Edie smiles.

'But,' Josie goes on, slotting the final book into place on the shelf, 'I think she was quite shy, really. Lonely, for sure.'

'That's not the impression she gave me,' Edie confesses. 'She unnerved me too, but I didn't have to work with her, like you.'

'She liked to control things, in her own way,' Josie replies. 'It took me a while, but I came to see there was a sort of *vulnerability* about her bossiness. I think maybe she would have liked us to work more together, but she couldn't bring herself to admit that. Like I said, I fell short of her standards.'

'But she must have thought highly of you,' Edie argues, as they return to the stockroom for refreshments. 'She wouldn't have left you in charge of this place if she didn't.'

'I don't know . . .'

'Will there be a funeral?'

'I guess,' Josie replies. She can't face a service but keeps the thought to herself. 'Can I show you something?' She takes a stack of papers tied with string from the bottom drawer of the desk. 'Did you know Miss Godson was a writer?'

Josie hands her the package, and Edie unties it to reveal what appears to be a manuscript – hundreds and hundreds of sheets of paper covered with a dense, spidery script. On the title page is printed: OUT OF THE ASHES WE RISE by E. GODSON.

'Her novel,' Josie explains. 'One of several. Have a look at it, while I fetch some water.'

When Josie returns, she finds Edie immersed in the first chapter. 'Have you read any of this?' she asks.

Josie pours water into the kettle. 'Only the first few pages. I didn't know anything about it until yesterday. Dr Garland showed me a letter Miss Godson had given her, back when she first joined the hospital, which left everything to the library if she died in service.'

'I don't suppose she expected to die quite so soon,' Edie reflects.

'She didn't only write novels,' Josie says. 'Look at this.' She passes Edie a slim volume, on the front page of which is written in ink: A GUIDE FOR THE SELECTION OF WHOLESOME LITERATURE FOR THOSE WHO ARE ILL OR INJURED.

Edie opens the booklet, and begins to read.

This guide aims to suggest titles for use in hospitals, keeping the following points in mind:

1. *Books in a hospital are for recreation rather than instruction, and should include fiction, travel books, biographies, popular science and outdoor books.*
2. *Books must be wholesome – not morbid, gruesome or*

depressing. Good detective stories and tales of adventure must not be horrible, or make vice attractive.

3. Magazines are invaluable: a patient too ill to read will often look at pictures.

4. New fiction is important, but old favourites and classics remain much in demand.

5. It is not enough to provide books for those who wish to read. There will always be patients who are unable to take any initiative towards selecting any form of literary entertainment, and for these must be provided light, simple stories which will not tax the brain or require much concentration of attention, but instead will serve to stimulate their interest in things outside themselves.

'Miss Godson was a living library,' Josie remarks. 'She knew every novel in here, and got to know the patients surprisingly well. She'd leave me detailed notes on which books I was to give to which men.'

Edie turns the pages of Miss Godson's guide.

'It's strange, though,' Josie mutters, spooning tea leaves into Miss Godson's beloved pot. 'I hadn't a clue she'd written anything, until I got this.' She pulls a slip of paper from her apron pocket and hands it to Edie.

In the event of my death, I entrust my literary works, in their entirety, to Endell Street Hospital library, to be used as Miss Everley sees fit.

E Godson
May 1915

'Did she give you this herself?' Edie asks.

'No, I found it the other day,' Josie replies, fiddling with the little stove, coaxing the temperamental flame. 'Tucked under a book on the desk there.'

'She must have thought very highly of you,' Edie says, 'to entrust her writing to your care.'

'It doesn't make sense. I mean, Mrs Stanten was Miss Godson's closest friend. She's going to be pretty miffed when she finds out, I reckon.'

'I'm sure she'll understand,' Edie replies. 'At least you haven't got to think about her for a couple of days, while she's not here.'

'I guess,' Josie says.

'What are you going to do with all this?' Edie riffles through the stack of pages. 'How many books did Miss Godson write?'

Josie admits she doesn't know for sure, but she's found at least two more manuscripts tucked away in other drawers. 'I guess I'll have to read them all first, then see if any of them can be published. But I haven't a clue how to do anything like that.'

'I might be able to help,' Edie says. 'Well, I have a friend who might be able to help. If he ever comes back, that is.'

'Who?'

'Harry Levinson. He's a journalist, and my mentor. He knows everyone, and has contacts in the publishing world.'

'Would he help me?'

'Harry'll help anyone.' Edie peruses more of the

librarian's pages, then glances up and meets Josie's eye. 'I'd love to help. If you want me to, that is.'

The offer makes Josie smile, and warmth spreads in her chest that has nothing to do with the balmy weather. 'Thank you,' she says.

The smashed window in St Anne's ward has been boarded over, a temporary repair until the glazier has finished his work in St Dymphna's. With no natural light coming in, standard lamps have been borrowed from other wards, and Josie wheels her trolley into a room suffused with a golden glow.

The ambient light takes Josie back to the library on the *Lusitania*, muted sunshine burning through the papered-over skylights, and she suffers a moment of helpless, disabling grief. She grips the trolley, unable to move, until voices bring her back to her senses.

'Miss, have you remembered my paper?'

'Got any more Goulds, miss?'

The men's needs distract Josie enough for her to carry on, and she makes her way through the ward. Her first patron is a Private Seymour. Miss Godson's notes are scant, only telling Josie the basics: that the young soldier had been grievously wounded in battle.

That the memory still haunts Seymour is evident in his dazed, lustreless eyes. Speaking softly, Josie asks if he'd like to choose any reading material from the cart, but he stares at her mutely, so instead she brings a small selection of books to his bedside.

'This one is about a man who thinks he's not very

brave,' she tells Seymour, offering a novel entitled *Four Feathers*. Miss Godson had classed this as an 'anti-hero' novel. 'Though he's in the army,' Josie forges on, 'he's received four white feathers from his so-called friends. So he goes to Egypt and performs heroic deeds, and returns the feathers, one by one.'

This earns no response from Seymour, so Josie offers Jack London's *The Call of the Wild*, thinking he might be interested in dogs, and when this garners no reaction either, she tries Jeffery Farnol's *The Broad Highway*. 'It's about a young Englishman who goes on adventures,' she tells Seymour. 'He's determined to seek his fortune, rather than stick to the terms of his uncle's will.'

Seymour remains silent, but his neighbour in the next bed likes the sound of that one, so Josie gives it to him instead.

Nothing seems to appeal to the young man, and Josie is about to concede defeat, when she tries one final book. Lytton's *Last Days of Pompeii*. 'It's about Roman society in the first century,' she explains. A popular book, especially with the officer class, according to Miss Godson's records, but Josie doesn't mention this.

Her last-ditch suggestion rouses Seymour, his stony countenance transformed as he pushes himself up in the bed, reaching out a trembling hand. Josie gives him the book with a smile, and moves on.

At last, she reaches the final two beds, where she discovers that Stuart's is empty, and Theo is sitting up in his, awake and alert.

'Just-Josie,' Theo greets her. They smile shyly at one

another. Stuart's absence has thrown Josie somewhat: she's come to anticipate his teasing manner.

'He's gone for some fresh air,' Theo tells her. 'Prob'ly a smoke too.'

'How are you?' Josie asks. 'Would you like some fresh air too?' Perhaps she can organize a chair for him. She scans the ward, but there are no orderlies to ask.

'I'm all right here, ta,' Theo replies quietly.

Josie suspects he's fibbing. 'I saved the latest *Wellington Post* for you.'

'That's made my day, Just-Josie.'

As Theo scans the headlines, she wonders if she can ask him about his home, his family, or whether personal questions would upset him. What would Miss Godson do? What would she ask, without seeming to pry?

'Whereabouts in New Zealand are you from?' Josie ventures. 'I don't know anything about your country.'

'Few people do,' Theo says, with a forgiving smile. 'I'm from a small town near Auckland, in the North Island. I'd tell you the name, but you won't have heard of it.'

'I expect you miss your family . . .' Josie instantly regrets her unthinking remark, inwardly wincing.

'I miss Ma,' Theo replies. 'She's been on her own, since my father died.'

'I have some postcards, or writing paper, if you wanted to write to her.'

'She can't read,' Theo says. 'But I've been thinking of sending a card anyway. Someone'll read it to her, eh.'

Josie fetches a selection of postcards, and Theo

chooses a silk-embroidered one, stitched with the words 'To My Dear Mother, From Your Loving Son'.

Theo thanks her, and his gaze sends a quiver through Josie's veins. Just as quickly it's gone.

'Can I get you anything else before I go?'

'How about another story?' Theo's smile is hopeful, as he offers her his book of Māori myths. 'If you're not too busy.'

'One story,' Josie relents, taking a seat. She flicks through the pages, searching for a short chapter. 'How about this – "The Shining Ones"?'

'My favourite,' Theo murmurs.

Josie begins to read: *'Many years ago, when our ancestors believed the world was flat, and the sun circled the earth, a Māori looked up into the clear night sky, and he was curious. He saw the robe of Rangi, twinkling with starlight. The other Māoris called the stars the Children of Light, playing in the sky. Sometimes a light would tumble out of the folds of Rangi's robe, falling in a flash through the sky . . .'*

Josie reads on, the words lifting off the page, her voice invoking tropical creatures, azure seas and warring tribes. The strange Māori words transport her away from the ward and the hospital, the story somehow conjuring a spell to hold real life at bay. She reaches the end, and notices that Theo's eyes have closed, a peaceful expression on his drawn, sallow face.

Something Pearl once said comes back to her: *Books weave magic.*

'Thank you,' Theo whispers, alert again. His dark eyes shine.

'I'll come back for the postcard later,' Josie says, wishing she could stay by his bedside for longer.

'I'll be here.' Theo holds the book of myths to his heart, and meets Josie's gaze. Something passes between them, a frisson in the air, and is gone again.

As Josie pushes the book cart out of the ward, she finds herself thinking of *Little Women*, safe in her bedside drawer back at her aunt's house. The book is ragged and water-damaged, and only she will ever want to read it. But it's the most precious thing she owns, and it strikes her then that as long as there are stories left in the world there's hope.

| Issue No. 4 | # The Daily Dose | Price FREE |

OBITUARY
CHIEF LIBRARIAN

Endell Street Hospital today mourns the death of Chief Librarian,
Miss Eugenia Godson,
aged 70.

Miss Godson had presided over the library at Endell Sreet
since its opening in March.

It was in 1870, at the age of 25, that Miss Godson was appointed
by Queen Victoria to oversee the Windsor Library, one of the finest
collections of books in the world.

Miss Godson was a great favourite with the monarchy,
who referred to her as a 'Walking Library'.

Previously, Miss Godson was an assistant at the British Museum,
and an amateur novelist, and her personal literary collection has
been donated to the Endell Street Hospital library.

E. Lawrence

24

Edie – London

Edie aches with the need to visit Stanley again. Their reunion, so frustratingly brief, has left so much unspoken, so many questions unanswered. Will he ever forgive her for lying to him? Can she find the courage to share her true feelings for him?

She thinks about writing to Stanley's parents, putting down on paper all that she hadn't been able to convey in person. She's a writer, after all, and surely she can find the words to make them understand what she and Stanley shared in France.

But, in her heart, she knows a letter won't be enough.

It crosses Edie's mind that she might have to resort to scaling a drainpipe, if Mr and Mrs Chay continue to restrict visiting rights to Stanley. The scar on her leg aches at the thought.

A light yet persistent rain is falling as Edie sets off on the journey to Kentish Town. An overturned wagon on Grafton Road is causing a blockage in the traffic, delaying Edie's bus, and it's gone eleven by the time she arrives at Stanley's house.

The curtains are still drawn, and she knocks tentatively

on the front door. Worry has dogged her all the way here. Is she making a big mistake?

What if Stanley has changed his mind? What will she do if he's decided he doesn't want to hear her side of the story?

Edie's nerve threatens to break, and she's on the brink of retreating, when she hears footsteps beyond the door, and then it's opening, and there is Stanley. Dear Stan, thin and pale. Surprise steals Edie's breath. He'd seemed so weak the last time she'd seen him, and now he was standing in front of her.

For the space of one heartbeat, two, three, they stare at one another. Stanley's shirt hangs off him, trousers bagging at the knees. But his familiar nut-brown eyes are vibrant. Alive.

'Lawrence,' he breathes. 'You came back.'

Edie returns his hesitant smile, but her voice, she finds, has deserted her.

'Come in,' Stanley says at last. He steps back, holding open the door.

Edie removes her straw hat, the rim bent out of shape by the rain, and follows him into the living room. Although the curtains remain drawn, it feels like an entirely different space from when she was last here. Warm lamplight illuminates an armchair draped with blankets, newspapers piled on the floor next to it, a cup without a saucer resting on the arm. Stanley claims the chair, motioning for Edie to take the settee opposite. She peels off her coat, makes herself as comfortable as her damp skirt permits.

'You came back,' Stanley says again. He pulls a tobacco pouch from his trouser pocket and begins to roll a crooked cigarette. Tobacco flakes spill from his trembling fingers, but he seems not to notice. 'I wasn't sure if you would.'

'Of course I came back.' Edie's voice doesn't sound quite like her own.

A motor-car passes along the street outside, the muffled *put-put-put* of its engine breaking the silence in the room.

'Where are your parents?' Edie asks, after a moment. Were they about to burst in here, demand she leave?

'My uncle's sick,' Stanley tells her. 'He's been on his own, since my aunt died. Three nippers under twelve.' He picks up a box of Vespas from the floor. 'Mother's staying to lend a hand for a few days, and Father's gone with her.'

Edie mutters words of sympathy. The truth is, she doesn't care where Mr and Mrs Chay have gone, only that they're not here.

It occurs to her that this is the first time she's been alone with Stanley since that fateful trench raid. She has to know if he's forgiven her.

'You look like you're about to be sick, Lawrence.'

'What? Oh, no, I'm fine – just, you know . . .' She can't find the words.

'Here, want a fag?'

Yes, she does, even though she hasn't smoked since France, wouldn't dream of lighting up in front of Harry or Mary.

The first few drags are harsh on her tender lungs, making her cough, but she smokes on, and soon a familiar giddy sensation swoops over her, and she begins to relax. They smoke in silence, Stanley flicking ash into the hearth, Edie tapping her cigarette on a tea-stained saucer.

Rain patters against the windowpanes, gusts of wind rattling the glass. Was it a sign? Edie worries. A storm in July. A warning she shouldn't have come here.

'I thought you were dead, Lawrence.' Stanley stares at a frayed patch of rug between them, his cigarette smouldering, forgotten.

Edie swallows bile, no longer able to smoke for the nausea. 'I thought you were too,' she mutters, when she can trust herself to speak. *I couldn't bear the thought of you gone. I wanted to be the one to die.*

'We both survived, Lawrence. A fucking miracle.'

The swear word hangs in the smoky air, but Stanley makes no apology, and Edie finds she respects him all the more for this.

'Your nose,' Stanley says. He takes a long, shaky drag of his cigarette. 'I dunno, but it looks . . . better.'

They exchange a look, and Edie doesn't know what to say to this. Her grazes from the road accident have mostly healed, but her nose will always be crooked. She thinks of the game Stanley had played, trying to make her laugh by guessing how she'd come to break it. She'd never told him the truth about that either, how she'd been imprisoned in Holloway for assaulting a police constable at a suffrage rally, though she'd only been defending herself.

While on hunger strike in prison, a particularly vicious wardress had smashed a fist into her face, breaking her nose; a punishment for simply breathing.

'I'm sorry,' she hears herself say.

'What for, Lawrence? Walking wet shoes on my mum's clean rugs?' Stanley tosses his cigarette butt into the hearth. 'She won't care.'

'I'm sorry for lying to you.' Now she *is* going to be sick. She stubs out her cigarette in the saucer and swallows. 'I should have told you the truth, but I couldn't risk it, not at the start. If it'd got out that I was a woman, fighting . . .' She falls silent. Stanley is staring at her, and she finds she can't meet his eye. 'I'm sorry for leaving you in that trench.'

I'm so sorry.
I vowed I'd stay with you.
I didn't want to leave you.
I broke that vow.

She waits for Stanley to say something, but he remains silently staring at her.

'Well, I'm sorry, that's all,' she says at last, as the truth hits: he'll never forgive her. She can't blame him. If their roles were reversed, if she'd been the one left abandoned in that trench, would she forgive him?

She's on her feet, grabbing her coat, when suddenly Stanley is before her, barely an arm's length away.

'What you got to be sorry about, Lawrence?'

Edie can't move.

'Weren't none of it your fault.'

And now he moves closer. Closer still. And the settee

is butting up against the backs of Edie's knees, and she has nowhere to go. Stanley holds her gaze.

'Don't you care that I lied to you?' Her voice is no more than a whisper. 'You thought I was *Eddie* . . .'

'I always knew.'

He knew?

Stanley's slow smile is tinged with sadness. 'From the start, Lawrence.'

'Was it that obvious?' But it can't have been: the rest of the platoon would have ripped her to shreds if they'd known a woman was in their midst.

'Not obvious, unless you looked close.'

'I thought you didn't know . . .'

'I didn't *want* to know, Lawrence. I was a coward . . .'

'No!' She spits the word. 'You're the only reason I'm alive.'

Stanley says nothing for a moment. And then: 'They want to send me back.'

No. She can't bear it.

'If I refuse, they'll electrocute me.'

'*What?*'

'Shell-shock treatment.' Stanley is so near, Edie can see flecks of amber in his brown eyes, a pulse throbbing in his neck.

'They can't send you back.'

Stanley closes his eyes, swaying slightly on his heels. He opens his eyes again, and the force of his gaze dries Edie's mouth.

'They can, Lawrence.'

'Not if you're –' She breaks off.

'Mad? You can say it, Lawrence. Don't be shy.'

'Not mad,' she stammers. 'Injured.'

'Leg's on the mend.' Stanley sways again. 'No peg leg for me.' His laugh is brief, harsh. 'And the *shell shock*.' He spits the words as though they're dirt in his mouth. 'They can cure it now, the doctors reckon.'

He falls quiet, and in the silence that drops over them, like a shroud, Edie can hear her own heartbeat pounding in her ears, louder than the rain outside.

Stanley's gaze is burning now, and Edie wants so badly to hold him, to be held by him.

'I knew you were different, Lawrence.' Stanley lifts a hand, strokes a knuckle along Edie's cheek, setting fire to her skin.

Rain drums against the glass, but Edie is no longer aware of anything but the sensation of Stanley's touch. His fingers ignite feelings in her she's long suppressed. She'd thought her affection for him was a bond between pals. And yet, all along, she'd craved *this*.

'I missed you, Lawrence.'

It's all she's longed to hear.

The pavements shine, washed clean by the rain, and Edie lifts her face to a watery sun as she lets herself out of Stanley's house. At the gate, she glances back to see him standing at the sitting-room window, his spare figure partly obscured by the curtain, and she aches to go back, fold herself into his embrace. And, this time, never leave.

She's lightheaded, unsteady on her legs as she makes

her way back to the bus stop. The last few hours have been a dream, an interlude of such profound bliss it's left her feeling drunk. It's taking every ounce of concentration she possesses to continue walking in a straight line, when all her body yearns to do is veer around and go back.

They'd promised each other they'd meet again first thing tomorrow. Edie would return, and together they'd tell Stanley's parents everything that had happened in France.

By the time Edie reaches the gates of Endell Street Hospital, her racing heart has calmed somewhat, and she's regained a fragile composure. She stumbles past an RAMC guard deep in conversation with an orderly, and makes her way up to the library. She's hoping to find Josie on her own, the quiet library assistant unlikely to demand much conversation while she tries to gather herself. Maybe later she'll have the chance to ask Josie about some aspects of her role at the hospital.

To Edie's relief, the closed sign is hanging on the library door, and no one is waiting in the corridor. She slips inside, and is brought up short by what she slowly understands is some sort of shrine made of books, arranged on a round table in the centre of the room. She steps closer, peering at a large portrait photograph of Miss Godson as a much younger woman, posing on a wooden bench in a bucolic garden scene. The photograph has been propped up in the middle of the book shrine, a focal point framed by dried roses and lavender, the scents of the flowers mingling in the peaceful air.

'Hello, Edie.'

She glances up, to find Josie emerging from the stockroom.

'Hello,' Edie greets her. 'I was just admiring your . . .'

'Shrine?' Josie smiles bashfully. 'It wasn't my idea. Some patients did it. I only helped with the books. They're all Miss Godson's favourite novels, apparently.' She looks utterly exhausted, crescents of purple beneath her eyes. But her smile is bright. 'I'm glad you've come,' she says. 'Mrs Stanten had to go home again – her back's hurting – but she's left some lemonade. It's delicious – d'you want some?'

Edie follows Josie into the stockroom, and is pleasantly surprised to find the place somewhat tidied. The rambling heaps of books she remembers littering the floor have been cleared away, and now only a few neat piles remain. Josie must have been working very hard. Perhaps too hard, Edie worries.

Josie pours lemonade, and hands a cup to Edie.

'You look like you've been busy,' Edie says, trying not to gulp the lemonade. She hadn't realized how thirsty she was.

Josie nods. 'Mrs Stanten's sure been a big help.'

'Have you a few minutes to answer some questions, for my next piece?' Edie asks. 'Please say if you'd rather I came back another time.'

'Oh, no, I don't mind. I could do with a break, to be honest.'

'Shall we sit outside?' Edie suggests. Josie looks like she needs some sun on her face.

They take their drinks down to the courtyard, and find a table tucked in a sun-warmed corner. The yard is unexpectedly quiet, only a few patients sharing the space. A trio of orderlies are slapping paint on a wooden bench, the young women's giggles drifting on the late-afternoon breeze.

Edie rolls her eyes comically at Josie, eliciting a shy laugh. The library assistant cradles her lemonade, and Edie notices she's trying not to look directly at Edie's nose.

'It doesn't hurt,' Edie says, with a smile.

Josie swallows some lemonade and coughs. 'What? Oh, you mean . . . sorry, I . . .' She flushes.

'It was broken a long time ago.'

Josie takes another sip of her lemonade.

'People usually want to know how,' Edie says after a moment, thinking of Stanley and his constant, ridiculous guesses.

'Oh.' Josie drains her cup. 'You don't have to tell me.'

Edie is startled into a laugh. 'You're the first person who's said that.'

Now it's Josie's turn to grin.

'I was punched by a wardress,' Edie says. 'In gaol.'

Josie's cup slips in her hand and clatters on to the table. 'Oh.'

'I was on hunger strike, last summer, just before war was declared,' Edie explains. 'They tried to force a tube down my throat.'

Josie stares at her. 'My God.'

'A doctor and three wardresses held me down.'

Josie's eyes widen.

'I fought them off.' Edie gestures to her crooked nose, and then at her chopped hair. 'This was my reward.'

'Jesus . . .' Josie exhales. 'That's lousy.'

'It's the best thing that happened to me,' Edie counters. 'That punch was the spur for everything after.'

Across the courtyard, the orderlies have finished painting, and are heading back into the building. The sun dips behind the main block, throwing Edie and Josie's corner into shade.

'Is it true?' Josie asks, after a moment. 'What I've heard about you?'

'Well, that depends,' Edie says. 'What have you heard?'

'That you fought with the men in France, and nearly got killed.'

'Who told you that?'

'Dr Garland.'

Edie nods slowly. 'It's true.'

'But . . . why would you do that?'

Edie leans down to her satchel resting against the chair leg, and extracts her notebook. She lays it on the table between their empty cups. 'I'll tell you my story,' she says, 'if you'll tell me yours.'

25

Josie – London

'I've never known a year pass so fast,' Mrs Stanten remarks to Josie one morning in mid-August. The two women have joined Dr Garland, Dr Maberry and a large number of staff and patients in St Nicholas Church for a service to mark the first anniversary of the war.

Josie silently agrees. It makes her dizzy to think of all that has happened, all that has changed in her life in such a short time.

The chaplain leading the service is new to the parish, but speaks with compassion for all those present, 'whose patriotism is clearly evident in the brave work of Endell Street Hospital'.

'We have entered the second year of the greatest and most deplorable war,' the chaplain preaches, 'and none of us can tell how much longer it may continue. We must give thanks for our tenacious doctors and nurses, for the splendid patience of our fleet's vigil, the courage and endurance of our men in the trenches.'

Josie tries to imagine what Theo and Stuart had endured on the battlefield, but her mind refuses to go there. Instead, she thinks of the piece she'd read in the paper that morning about a Crimean veteran who'd donated his war medals to the Red Cross, and the eighty-eight-year-old widow, who'd sent the Red Cross the gold wedding ring she'd worn for sixty years but wished to be used for the benefit of wounded soldiers.

How could the world be full of slaughter and grief, yet include such examples of generosity and hope?

'Time is our great ally,' the chaplain goes on. 'It is something to know that we are holding our own. That there is among us a deepening sense of the gravity of the ordeal through which we still have to pass.'

After the service, Josie returns to the library, half listening to Mrs Stanten chattering about a play she's writing.

'It will be performed in the hospital at Christmas,' Mrs Stanten informs her, as they begin their work, sorting through a stack of backdated *Illustrated London News*. 'A pantomime to raise everyone's spirits.'

The temperature in the stockroom is rising, and Josie rolls the sleeves of her blouse above her elbows. She thinks of Miss Godson, and suffers a pang of sadness that the librarian is not here to chastise her for slovenly behaviour. 'What's a pantomime?' she asks Mrs Stanten, her mind shying from thoughts of Christmas without Jem.

Mrs Stanten is aghast. 'You've never seen a panto?'

Josie shakes her head, shrugs.

'A panto is basically a play,' Mrs Stanten explains, 'with singing, dancing and buffoonery.'

'Like a show in the theatre?' Josie experiences a

sudden flashback to the *Lusitania*, Mr Welch and Mr Frankum performing their comic songs in the third-class dining saloon. A few nights before the disaster, Josie had sneaked Jem in to hear the duo singing; she'd hoped a laugh would distract her brother from his seasickness, and it had worked for perhaps half an hour.

'Yes, a show,' Mrs Stanten replies. '*Aladdin*. You know the story, I trust?'

Of course Josie knows the story of Aladdin: a boy, a magic lamp, a genie, three wishes. What she would give for a magic lamp.

First wish: bring Jem back.

'I've found my principal boy already,' Mrs Stanten chatters on. 'Miss Janey Woolton — sublime singer. A little on the short side, and rather androgynous in a certain light, but that only plays to her advantage, of course.'

Josie wonders when Mrs Stanten has found time to hold the auditions, and where they happened. Not here in the library, or she would have known about it.

'My evil-magician role was snapped up by you'll never guess who.'

Josie hasn't a clue. 'Dr Maberry?' she ventures, only half joking. The tall, thin Scottish medic strikes her as the more intimidating of the two head doctors.

Mrs Stanten gasps, hand to her heart. 'How can you suggest such a thing, Miss Everley?'

Mortified, Josie begins to stammer her excuses, until she realizes Mrs Stanten is joking and begins to laugh too.

'I shouldn't tease you,' Mrs Stanten says, when she's

able to speak again. 'But I couldn't resist.'

'Who is it, then?' Josie asks. 'The magician?'

'Have you met that rather big, soft RAMC guard? Charlie his name is. Half the staff appear to be in love with him, if you believe the gossip.'

Josie has heard no romantic gossip, least of all about Charlie, but she knows who Mrs Stanten is talking about, and can't imagine the man playing an evil role in any pantomime.

'He auditioned for Aladdin, bless him,' Mrs Stanten says. 'It had to be explained to him that the principal boy is traditionally played by a girl. He was rather confused by this, but happily accepted the role of the magician.'

The two women make their way into the main library, to begin preparations for opening. A pile of fresh newspapers has been left outside the doors, and Josie lugs them inside while Mrs Stanten re-inks the stamp pad and gives the card index a quick flick to check all is in order.

'Widow Twankey, on the other hand,' Mrs Stanten forges on, 'that was a different kettle of fish.'

Josie hasn't a clue what the woman is talking about.

'Mr Threadgill practically snapped my hand off when I offered him the part,' Mrs Stanten tells her.

'Mr Threadgill?'

'Ernest Threadgill, a friend of mine from the West End. He's played all the pantomime dames in his time, both of the Ugly Sisters and several stepmothers, Mother Goose, even the queen in *Puss in Boots* once.'

Josie finds herself nodding, though none of what Mrs Stanten is saying makes sense.

'I'm still searching for my princess, though...'

Josie looks up from folding the newspapers to find Mrs Stanten regarding her from across the issues desk.

'I have an image in my mind,' Mrs Stanten says, 'of a pretty young woman with auburn hair and the greenest eyes... You don't happen to know of anyone who fits that description, do you?'

Is Mrs Stanten teasing her again? The woman can't possibly mean what Josie thinks she means. Mrs Stanten is smiling at her with rather too many teeth.

'There must be someone on the staff,' Josie suggests desperately.

'But you'd be perfect, dear.'

No, oh, no. Josie shakes her head firmly. She couldn't possibly.

'I heard you singing the other day, when you thought no one was listening,' Mrs Stanten presses. 'You've a beautiful voice.'

Josie scrambles for a response that won't make the situation worse. She's never sung in front of anyone before, only to Jem when he was a baby and needed soothing to sleep. The thought of Mrs Stanten overhearing makes her cringe inside.

Another memory surfaces, of her mother falling ill for the final time. Josie had sometimes sat at her bedside and sung her favourite tunes to her – 'Moonlight Bay', 'You Made Me Love You', 'If I Had My Way'. But she's never had the desire to perform to an audience.

'Promise me you'll at least consider it,' Mrs Stanten says, moving to the door and flipping the CLOSED sign to OPEN. Moments later, patients begin shuffling into the library, and Mrs Stanten greets each man brightly.

'Good morning, Mr Chadwick. You're looking very dapper in that suit.'

'Thank you, Mrs Stanten. Have the papers arrived yet?'

'They have indeed. Miss Everley has them . . .'

Josie hears no more, as she retreats into the stockroom, closing the door with a soft click behind her.

After lunch Mrs Stanten oversees the library, while Josie wheels the trolley round the wards. There are several book requests for St Anne's, but Josie decides to leave those until last: she wants to spend a little extra time with Theo at the end. She trundles her book cart through the hospital, delivering requests, occasionally consulting Miss Godson's helpful 'fever chart' of therapeutic books, at the apex of which lie the novels of Jane Austen.

Mostly, she dispenses her own brand of medicine: novels by Sexton Blake, Rex Beach, Marie Corelli; a few poetry collections; Montaigne, Shakespeare, Wordsworth.

For a patient suffering from debilitating anxiety and insomnia, Josie prescribes *The Portrait of a Lady*. 'A balm for the anxious mind,' she tells the young soldier. 'And it's my personal favourite of Henry James's novels.'

'What's it about, miss?'

'It opens with afternoon tea in an English country garden,' Josie tells him. 'Imagine the scene: rugs and cushions and books strewn on a sun-dappled lawn . . .'

She leaves the soldier happily reading.

In St Ursula's she meets a restless officer, frustrated at being kept in bed until his broken leg heals sufficiently.

'He's snappy, that one,' a nurse whispers to Josie in passing.

The snappy young officer is initially dismissive of Josie's attempts to interest him in the contents of the trolley. 'I only read the classics,' he informs her.

Hardy's *Under the Greenwood Tree* is rejected, as are *Moby-Dick* and several other novels he's already read. In desperation, Josie consults Miss Godson's guide, and suggests *Pride and Prejudice*. To her surprise, the officer accepts Austen, and as Josie pushes her trolley away, she wonders if Elizabeth Bennet cutting Mr Darcy down to size will resonate with him at all.

Her next patient is afflicted with an extensive facial wound, half his head swathed in bandages. He's also suffering from heartbreak, Josie learns, as his fiancée has broken off their engagement. 'We were going to get married when the war ended,' the soldier tells Josie. 'No chance of that happening now.'

Josie's heart aches for him, and all the other men in the hospital whose futures have been upended. She leaves him with a copy of *Jane Eyre*.

By the time Josie finally arrives at St Anne's ward, she's emotionally exhausted. Her heart sinks further when she discovers Theo's bed is empty.

'He's gone to find you in the library,' Stuart tells her.

'Dunno why he didn't just wait.'

Josie hurries to complete the last of her requests, and wheels her cart back to the library. Mrs Stanten, serving behind the issues desk, beckons her over. 'You have a visitor,' she whispers, nodding towards a man sitting alone at a table by the window, a book open before him.

Theo.

Josie parks her cart by the desk, and makes her way over to him. 'Hello,' she says, feeling suddenly and inexplicably shy.

Theo's face brightens, like the sun breaking through cloud. He's dressed in hospital blues, the flannel suit a size too big, the red tie loose about his neck. His smile lifts Josie's heart, and she finds herself smiling too.

'Can you sit with me?' Theo says.

Josie takes a seat. She can't see the title of the book he's reading, and words crowd her tongue, but all she can think to say is 'I thought you weren't allowed out of bed yet. How did you get past the ward sister?'

Theo's honeyed look makes Josie's heart flip.

'I wanted to see you,' he says. His gaze is steady, and the air tautens between them. 'If my life were a book,' he says, 'meeting you would be my favourite chapter.'

No one, not even Nico at his most erudite, has ever said anything like this to Josie before.

From down in the courtyard they hear the bell ringing: it's five o'clock and the end of visiting. It will soon be time for the library to close too, and Mrs Stanten is already serving the last of the patrons, as the place gradually empties. Josie waits for her to come over and tell Theo he has to leave, but instead she winks at Josie, before closing the library doors and slipping away into the stockroom.

'I should let you close up, eh,' Theo says quietly. 'You'll want to get home.'

Never before has Josie wished time to slow. 'It's all right,' she says. 'There's no rush.'

'I have to go, Just-Josie.'

'Really, there's no hurry . . .'

'I mean, I have to go home soon.'

For a moment, Josie can only stare at Theo. He reaches across the table, brushing the back of her hand with his fingertips.

Josie can't move, can't speak, Theo's touch taking her back to a time she has pushed to the deepest recesses of her mind. She hasn't thought of Nico in so long. Nico with his hazel eyes, his fumbled embraces, the way he would sometimes press her up against a wall and smother her with kisses.

During Josie's time on the ships, several male passengers – and once, on one bizarre occasion, a drunken woman – had touched her, flirted with her. She's learned to deflect unwanted attention, dodge a roving hand, maintain a professional demeanour at all times.

But she has no defence against Theo's tender touch. His eyes are dark pools and Josie gazes into their depths, utterly unmoored.

'What I feel for you, I have no words for,' Theo says softly. 'All I know is I don't want to leave you.'

He cups her cheek, and Josie leans into him, closing

her eyes. She doesn't want to be parted from him either. But what can they do?

She pulls away, putting space between them once more. Losing Theo will break her already fractured heart all over again.

She can't weather the pain.

'I guess I should help Mrs Stanten,' she hears herself say, pushing back her chair and rising. 'Will you be all right to get back to the ward on your own?'

'I . . . yes . . .'

Josie gives him no chance to finish, no opportunity to make this moment worse. Instead, she forces herself to turn away, fleeing to the sanctuary of the stockroom.

Issue No. 5

The Daily Dose

Price FREE

The staff here at Endell Street includes 16 doctors, 36 nurses, and over 80 orderlies – all of them women.

Chief Surgeon, Dr Garland, and her staff are often engaged in the operating theatre for 12 hours continuously, with barely a break.

'Of course, we should never get through it all if not for the splendid spirit of the patients,' the Chief Surgeon says. 'The men are all so brave and good.'

The hospital has no garden, but instead an open-air courtyard. Patients are wheeled out in their chairs and beds every day to read, play cards, and enjoy the fresh air. The plants that adorn the space are tended by women gardeners. The gate is guarded by a female porter.

Said a badly wounded soldier, as his stretcher was carried into the courtyard by a female orderly: 'I asked to come here; they told me on the other side I'd be well looked after.'

E. Lawrence

Book Recommendations

Muir, John.
Stickeen.

(A short book about a dog, a glacier and Mr Muir.)

Elliott, Maud Howe.
Roma beata. Illus.

(Very charming home letters written during six years of residence in Rome.)

Le Roux, Gaston.
The Mystery of the Yellow Room.

(Detective story: a locked room, a badly wounded woman, who did it?)

THINGS WE WANT TO KNOW:

When will the war be over?

When you require the BEST TONIC MEDICINE, get a BOOK.
A proven remedy for:
Nervous debility; Lassitude; Headaches; Hysteria; Indigestion; Insomnia; Exhaustion; Faintness; Loss of Appetite; Shell Shock.
Literature provides the elements which repair the shattered nerve endings, until the system is fully charged with the vital force to heal the mind.
Books come in paper form. They can be used on Active Service, at any time, anywhere, as no water is needed.

LECTURE

Dr Jemima Short begs to announce the start of a new course of medical lectures. Her first lecture will be given on Wednesday next, in the Library, on the 3rd floor.
Subject: Microscopic germs:
How to see the invisible.
All welcome.

26

Edie – London

She can't sleep for thinking of Stanley. Was he thinking of her too? Over and over again Edie returns in her mind to the house in Kentish Town, imagining herself back with Stanley, safe at last.

Over the past weeks she's managed to visit him a handful of times. Gradually, Mr and Mrs Chay have come to understand what their son endured in France, and that Edie had been there with him, suffering alongside him.

Edie's reappearance in Stanley's life has been transformative, his recovery from neurasthenia progressing with almost miraculous speed. So much so that Edie has begun to fear he will soon be called up again to fight. Every time she leaves him to return to the Levinsons' she's terrified it will be for the last time.

Being apart from him is a form of torture for which she has no defence. It robs her of appetite and rest. Writing is the only thing preventing her from breaking down.

Below her, the house is quiet at this early hour, the only sound a faint scraping as Susan clears the ashes from the kitchen range. Soon the household will wake, and Edie will have to face another day. Another day thinking of Stanley, worrying if this will be the day he receives the call.

She has no appetite for breakfast, and instead shuts herself away in Harry's study. In an effort to distract herself, she decides to write up the notes she's taken during her conversations with Josie at the hospital: *Miss Everley the librarian is often taken into the confidence of the soldiers she serves, when they share their harrowing stories with her and sometimes their hopes and fears.*

Edie pauses, recalling a morning recently when she'd accompanied Josie on one of her ward rounds. She'd observed the young woman's gentle, attentive conversations with the patients, as she tried to find suitable reading material for them. The men often confided in her, Edie had noticed.

One young private, only nineteen years old and far from his home in Wales, had wept for his mother. Josie had sat at his bedside, held his hand, talked to him of favourite pastimes. The comfort she gave him was unhurried, thoughtful, and Edie witnessed the difference this made. The soldier had dried his eyes, and gratefully accepted Josie's literary recommendation of a book of poetry by John Morris-Jones.

Edie had seen Josie perform her book therapy time and again, lifting the spirits of so many men who'd been wounded in body and mind, numbed by the horrors they'd endured. They so often seemed to come back to life when she supplied them with works on subjects that interested them.

'I think of the library as a sort of medicine cabinet,' Josie had told Edie. 'Not one stocked with pills and drugs, but with curative literature. Does that make sense?'

'Perfectly,' Edie had replied.

'More than once,' Josie had continued, 'soldiers have told me that the books I bring them mean more to them than food.'

The morning slips past, and at last Edie leaves the sanctuary of the study in search of refreshment. But as soon as she's eaten she retreats to her bolthole, curling up in Harry's armchair, pondering the library at Endell Street. An idea is beginning to percolate in her mind. Not only did the library provide stories, but the place was itself a story.

'Miss?'

Edie starts, she hadn't heard Susan's knock. The maid hovers in the doorway, wiping her hands on her soot-streaked apron. 'Yes, Susan?'

'Gentleman to see you, miss. I've put him in the drawing room.'

Edie blinks at the maid. What man wanted to see her? 'Did he give a name?'

'Chay, miss.'

Stanley was here? Edie surges to her feet, dropping her notebook.

'Is everything all right, miss?'

'Oh, yes, thank you, Susan,' Edie stammers. She can't get out of Harry's study quickly enough.

In the drawing room, she finds Stanley leaning on a

walking cane, examining the framed family portraits of the Levinsons ranged along the mantelpiece. He turns when Edie closes the door, and for a moment neither of them speaks. And then Edie is across the room, and Stanley is folding her into an embrace.

At last, they pull apart, and Edie tries to think of what to say, but the very fact of Stanley's presence renders her speechless.

'Thought I'd surprise you, Lawrence.' Stanley's gaze drifts around the room, over the polished dark wood furniture, the various oil paintings. 'Nice gaff.'

Edie clears her throat. 'The Levinsons have been so kind to me.'

Stanley nods.

'I don't know what I'd've done without Harry and Mary.' There's so much more she wants to say, but she remembers her manners at last. 'Please . . .' She gestures to a chair, and Stanley sits with a sigh.

'The old leg's bearing up,' he says, patting his thigh. 'But I can't stand for too long or it threatens to snap off . . .'

'How did you get here? You didn't walk?'

'What do you take me for, Lawrence?' He grins. 'Got the bus, though I reckon I could've walked here faster. Driver didn't know where she was going.'

It's Edie's turn to grin. She doesn't doubt Stanley's walking stamina.

Susan appears in the doorway, to ask if Edie would like tea for her visitor.

'Thank you, Susan. That would be lovely.'

The maid slips away, and there's a moment of charged silence. Edie wonders if Stanley has come to break bad news. She pushes the thought to the back of her mind.

'Ever been to the zoo, Lawrence?'

Stanley's question is so unexpected that Edie can only shake her head.

"Bout time I took you, then,' he says.

'To the zoo?' Edie gapes at him. It isn't a place she's ever thought to go.

'Don't look so shocked, Lawrence.' Stanley chuckles. 'You'll love it, I reckon.'

Tuesday is half-price day, Edie learns, which is why Stanley has chosen today. She considers teasing him about being a cheapskate, but she doesn't want to risk insulting him. As they pass through the entrance, Stanley turns to her, an excited and at the same time bashful look in his eye.

'Always wanted to work here,' he says, 'from when I was a nipper, and my dad brought me to see the aquarium being built.'

Stretching away to their left is Terrace Walk. Edie can see several other couples strolling arm in arm, and she fleetingly pictures herself and Stanley joining them. As if reading her mind, Stanley offers his arm, and Edie slips her hand through his bent elbow, like a key in a lock.

'So many things I want to show you, Lawrence,' Stanley says, leading her along a path, apologizing for his weakened leg slowing them.

'There's no rush,' Edie reassures him. Her leg aches

too, but she's determined to ignore it. 'We have all day.' She can think of nowhere she'd rather be than here with him.

Strange, unfamiliar animal calls drift on the breeze, and Edie gazes around, trying to locate where the various squawks and neighs and barks are coming from.

'Birds are this way.' Stanley steers her to a row of huge iron cages, pointing out the tropical birds, their colourful plumage like nothing Edie has seen before. They bear no resemblance to the plain feathered pigeons, crows, blackbirds and sparrows she's used to. Even the birds' names sound romantic to her ear – *macaws, weavers, mynahs, toucans*. She wonders at the birds' origins. What exotic countries had they come from?

Stanley doesn't know, but he's keen to show her more. 'Come on, Lawrence, I want you to meet a mate of mine.'

'Does he work here?' Edie has noticed a few zoo-keepers wandering around with brooms and buckets, but not many. She wonders if most have joined up, and if their absence has left the zoo short of manpower.

'You could say that.' Stanley leads her round a corner, and Edie finds herself before another series of large enclosures. These contain not birds, but a variety of different monkeys and apes. Edie reads the names printed on the signs attached to their cages: baboons and macaques and chimpanzees.

She's never seen any sort of monkey in real life before, only ever read about them in books. It fascinates her, the way they swing and jump about the branches. A couple of tamarins are grooming each other's hair, and

Edie can't take her eyes from their nimble, human-like fingers. She could happily sit for hours on this conveniently placed bench and simply watch the monkeys until closing time.

But Stanley has other ideas.

'Come and meet George.' He takes Edie by the hand and pulls her towards an enclosure. Sitting on a log is a substantial monkey with shaggy greyish fur, a thick white ruff, and the most extraordinary blue and red nose.

'Meet George,' Stanley says. 'He's got a hooter almost as beautiful as yours, Lawrence.'

Edie can't help but laugh.

Stanley produces his camera from his suit pocket, and snaps a picture of George, and then one of Edie.

'There's a darkroom behind the wolf den,' he tells her. 'The keeper in charge knows my father, and before the war he let me use it sometimes. Good bloke.'

They pass through the monkey and ape house, on into the stork and ostrich habitat next door, and out to the terraces. Edie lifts her face to a flawless blue sky, the sun warming her cheeks. If they are going to be walking around the zoo all day, she's grateful for her straw hat. Her stomach growls, so loudly she wonders if Stanley can hear it, but he's pointing to some creatures in a paddock. At first glance they resemble half a dozen giant rodents, with coats of sharp spines. Too big to be hedgehogs, Edie thinks, but she doesn't like to admit her ignorance.

'Porcupines,' Stanley helpfully informs her. 'People like you write with their quills.'

They stroll on, towards a sequence of ponds, around which flock a variety of waterfowl: ducks, geese and swans. These, at least, Edie recognizes.

'They must've moved the penguins since I was last here,' Stanley remarks, as they reach the largest of the ponds. A sizeable crowd has gathered to watch two sealions being fed by a keeper. The man is balanced on a precarious-looking platform, a bucket at his feet, dangling fish over the pond. The sealions are taking it in turns to climb on to a wooden chair positioned in front of the platform, lunging to catch each fish as it's tossed into the air.

The audience gasps and claps each time a sealion completes the trick, but Edie can't help feeling sorry for the creatures. Being forced to perform for food seems demeaning, but Stanley is clapping and whistling so Edie keeps the thought to herself.

Beyond the pond are more paddocks and buildings. A female zookeeper, dressed in olive-green overalls and a grey straw hat, is leading a lion cub across the grass in front of the lion house. Some children are waiting to pet it, and squeals of delight erupt as the cub is introduced to them.

Stanley steers Edie on, towards a neighbouring paddock, where two keepers are exercising a pair of sun bears on long chains.

'People think they make good house pets,' Stanley tells Edie. 'They're the smallest bears.' He lifts his camera and takes a photograph. One of the bears rises to its hind legs, the crescent of orange on its chest resembling a garish bib to Edie. Its stance makes it look remarkably human-like. For the first time, it occurs to her that these creatures have endured the recent Zeppelin attacks too, just like she has. What did they make of the explosions over London, the searchlights strafing the night sky?

They reach the redbrick reptile house, and enter a porch filled with glass cases ranged along the walls. All manner of fish and amphibians are on display, and Edie marvels at the frogs, toads, lizards, electric eels, mudfish. So many species she never knew existed before today.

Inside the main building, the humidity hits her like a warm wet flannel in the face. Potted palm trees lend a tropical air to the place, and several visitors have removed their hats. Edie considers following suit as Stanley leads her to a row of large glass cases fixed to the wall. But her hair is still startlingly short, and she doesn't want to draw attention to herself, so she keeps her straw hat on as she studies the chameleons, puff adders and rattlesnakes.

'Come and see the crocs.' Stanley urges her towards three large pools in the middle of the space, each water feature separated by low iron railings. What Edie had at first taken to be rocks, now transpire to be an alligator, two crocodiles, and a creature she learns is a speckled caiman. It originates in the Americas, Stanley tells her, and its name comes from the bony ridge between its eyes, which gives the appearance of a pair of spectacles.

Edie grips the rail, transfixed by the caiman's jade-green irises and wrinkled eyelids. It stares back at her, unblinking.

'Oh, look!' a woman exclaims.

Edie turns to find an enormous tortoise inching its way across the floor, followed by a keeper clutching an armful of greens. 'Methusaleh!' the keeper calls. 'Don't you want your dinner?'

The visitors laugh and point, as the tortoise forges on, and as it passes Edie she sees someone has painted on the creature's substantial carapace the words: WE CAN'T DO WITHOUT OUR SHELLS.

Stanley snaps a picture, and promises the keeper he'll send it to the newspapers.

Outside again, Edie breathes in the fresher air, while Stanley spots a postcard dispenser on the wall. He slots a penny, cranks a tiny handle, and a card with a picture of a bear cub on it drops into the chute.

'For you,' he says, presenting the postcard to Edie. 'A memento of our day.'

'Thank you.' Edie smiles. 'But we haven't actually seen any bears. Only those little pet sun bears.'

'That's because I've saved the best till last, Lawrence.'

They continue along the terrace, admiring the views across the zoo, watching elephants lumbering along the path below.

'Are there any actual bears here?' Edie asks.

'Not just any old bears, Lawrence.' Stanley tucks her arm through his again. 'Wait till you meet Winnie.'

'That's a pretty name.'

'She's a pretty little bear,' Stanley replies. ''Cept, of course, she won't stay little for ever.'

Winnie was the unofficial mascot to the Second

Canadian Infantry Brigade, Edie learns. She was a gift to the zoo from her owner, a Lieutenant Colebourne, who'd rescued Winnie from the hunter in Ontario who'd killed her mother. Colebourne had named the cub 'Winnie' after his hometown, Winnipeg.

'When Colebourne was sent for training in England last year,' Stanley tells Edie, 'he brought the cub with him, but had to leave her at the zoo when he took up a commission in France.'

They pass the big-cat enclosure, hyenas and lions pacing behind their bars, up and down, up and down. And now, at last, they are at the bear pit.

Stanley buys a couple of stale buns from a kiosk. 'Not for you to eat, Lawrence.'

Up some steps, and they come to a low brick wall enclosing what looks at first glance to Edie like a huge well. Stanley is jamming the buns on to the ends of two long sticks, and he hands one of these to Edie, holding his own over the pit.

'Be careful,' Edie gasps, as Stanley leans further out over the brick border, his hat slipping. She peers over the lip, into a shadowed shaft stretching down twenty feet or more. Sitting at the bottom, leaning against a long, wooden pole, is a small black bear.

'Hey, Winnie,' Stanley calls, and the bear obligingly raises her head. Edie's breath stalls, as the bear spots the bun dangling on Stanley's stick, and begins to climb the pole. As soon as she reaches striking distance, she swipes a paw at the bun, and has it in her mouth before Edie can blink.

'Give her yours, Lawrence.'

The bear rips Edie's bun from the stick, and then is slithering back down the pole, down into the umbral depths of the pit.

Edie turns to Stanley, to find him closer than he had been a moment before. His sweet-chestnut eyes, focused on her, make Edie's heart trip faster.

'Do you think she's lonely, Lawrence?' Stanley asks, as they make their way back down the steps.

Yes, Edie thinks. The little bear must feel lonely, down there in the dark of her pit, all alone, waiting for people to dangle buns to her. She must miss her home, her mother. Her freedom.

'No one should be lonely,' Stanley says. He pauses on the path, leaning stiffly on his walking cane, and takes Edie's hand, setting a blaze in her belly.

'With you in my life,' Stanley says, 'I'll never be lonely.'

27

Josie – London

She's on her own in the library this morning, at least until Mrs Stanten arrives, whenever that might be. Josie finds herself longing for the woman's merry chatter and constant questions; anything to take her mind off Theo.

His words circle her mind. *If my life were a book, meeting you would be my favourite chapter.*

He would be gone tomorrow, back to New Zealand. It's more than likely she'll never see him or hear from him again. The thought makes Josie's chest tighten. Her hands are shaking, and she spills ink on the issues desk while re-inking the stamp pad. She makes more mess trying to clear it up, and can't get the ink stains off her fingers. Giving up, she turns instead to the book trolley.

She has yesterday's returned books to shelve, and the latest patient requests to process. The pile of slips grows bigger every day, and Josie is endlessly surprised by how diverse the men's tastes are. On today's trolley she's collecting reference books on a wide range of subjects, from ancient philosophy to zoology, as well as illustrated books on sculpture, travel guides to distant places – many of which Josie has never heard of – musical scores, booklets of ballads, and poetry collections by Keats, Browning, Kipling.

One by one, Josie methodically locates each requested book, gradually filling the shelves of her cart. Half of her mind is on the task at hand, the other at Theo's bedside.

She can never face him again, yet the more she ruminates on what he said, and how she reacted, the more she doubts herself.

He's going to leave her, like Nico, she tells herself. Promises might be made, only to be broken, and she can't bear the pain. She can't.

It's better to be alone.

All she can do is work. Soon, her fragile equilibrium is broken by the arrival of a pair of orderlies, Annie and Mabel, who are sorry to interrupt Josie's work, but they've been sent to ask for her specific assistance.

'Sure,' Josie says, somewhat baffled. 'How can I help?'

A competition to find the best-decorated ward has been launched that morning, the orderlies explain, and they're on the hunt for any books that might complement the themes, especially any that the men might enjoy reading.

'What sort of themes?' Josie asks.

'All kinds,' Annie says unhelpfully. 'Each ward has a different one.'

'St Therese's are going for an English garden in springtime,' Mabel replies. 'We wondered what books you had on gardening, or flowers, that sort of thing.'

'Quite a few, I think,' Josie replies, trying to rally her fractured thoughts. After a brief search of the shelves, she duly supplies the orderlies with several texts, including Keeler's *Our Garden Flowers and Shrubs*, Matthews's *Field Book of British Flowers*, Rexford's *Four Seasons in the Garden*.

St Deborah's had chosen a Japanese theme, Annie tells Josie. Together, the three women peruse the area of the stockroom that Josie has loosely set aside for travel books. Here, they find such gems as Abraham's *The Surgeon's Log; Impressions of the Far East*, Isabella Bird's *Unbeaten Tracks in Japan*, Brownell's *Heart of Japan*.

'What's this one about?' Annie asks, brandishing a small book bound in blue cloth.

Josie examines it: Inazo Nitobe's *Bushido; The Soul of Japan*. 'It says here that *bushido* is the Japanese equivalent of chivalry,' she reads from the introduction. 'This is about the Samurai.'

'Sam who?' Mabel asks.

'Samurai – the warrior class of Japan,' Josie explains.

The orderlies have never heard of the Samurai, but after a short discussion it's decided that the patients might well want to read about warriors in another culture, so the book is added to the pile.

At last, Annie and Mabel conclude they have enough material. With profuse thanks, and promises to return the books later, they hurry away. Josie watches them go, wondering what she'll find when she finally has to visit Theo's ward.

Mrs Stanten arrives just before noon. Josie, still gathering requests, is glad to see her colleague.

'Have you been labouring all morning, young lady?' Mrs Stanten says, shedding her coat and hanging it behind the door on a hook Josie had fixed up. By her own admission, she's becoming uncommonly handy with tools, having repaired the book cart's wonky wheel, and installed several new shelves in the stockroom.

Josie admits she hasn't left the library, her work impeded by a steady stream of orderlies and the occasional roving invalid, all on the hunt for books and magazines on various themes. She plans to start the ward deliveries now that Mrs Stanten is here to hold the fort.

'I had a bit of an accident with the ink stamp,' she confesses. 'I tried to clear it up, but I think I've made it worse . . .'

Mrs Stanten regards her with a keen eye. 'Is everything all right, dear?'

Josie longs to confide in the older woman, let the pain in her heart spill out. But what good would come of that? Mrs Stanten can do nothing to help with a wound so deep. She takes a steadying breath. 'Just a little tired. I'll be fine.'

'I would have got here sooner, but I stopped by St Anne's ward to see a friend of mine,' Mrs Stanten says. 'Mrs Akroyd only started as a VAD today, and I wanted to tell her to pop up to the library when she gets her break later. Anyway, you'll never believe this, dear, but they've decked the ward out in the manner of a farmyard!' Mrs Stanten gives a rich chuckle. 'I had to climb over a stile – a stile! – before I could get through the door. The patients were all in costume – there was the farmer, and a couple of cows, and some pigs, and one man had done himself up as a sheep with so much cotton wool on his head I'm sure Matron will have a turn when she sees him.'

The comical image Mrs Stanten paints makes Josie smile, loosening the ache in her heart. But the moment is interrupted by a knock on the stockroom door.

For a second, Josie doesn't recognize the man in the doorway. Stuart is dressed not in his customary hospital blues, but instead in an ill-fitting jacket and trousers, a wide-brimmed leather hat clutched in his hands.

'Hoped I'd catch you, Just-Josie.' Stuart notices Mrs Stanten at the stove, and gives her a wary nod. 'Sorry to disturb you both, eh.'

'Can we help you?' Mrs Stanten says, catching Josie's eye. 'The library isn't quite open yet, but you're welcome to wait . . .'

Stuart steps over the threshold, holding something towards Josie. 'I only came to give you this. From Theo.'

Josie has no choice but to take the folded note.

'He would've given it to you himself, but he's been taken crook . . .'

'What do you mean?'

'We're supposed to be going home tomorrow, but they've moved him to another ward.' Stuart twists his hat in his hands. 'I tried to see him earlier, but they won't let me in. Nurse said he's got a raging fever and can't be disturbed.'

'But – but he was better. He's going home,' Josie stammers.

'He took badly late last night,' Stuart replies. 'Happened bloody quick. One minute he was talking to me, the next he said he felt hot, and then he couldn't catch his breath.'

'Have the doctors seen him?' Mrs Stanten asks, and Josie is grateful for her steady presence.

'It was Dr Garland who took him away,' Stuart replies.

'Where?' Josie's voice cracks.

'St Barbara's,' Stuart says.

The fever ward.

'That sounds rather serious,' Mrs Stanten says redundantly. 'Would you like a cup of tea, dear?' She busies herself at the stove, as Josie stares mutely at Stuart.

St Barbara's, she knows, is closed off to all but authorized staff. No visitors are allowed, and even Miss Godson hadn't been permitted to take her trolley to the patients there.

'Reckon you're precious as *pounamu* to him, eh.' Stuart gestures at the note Josie clutches.

'*Pounamu*?'

'Our Māori sacred stone,' Stuart says.

The kettle begins to steam, its thin whistle filling the silence. Mrs Stanten lifts it off the flame, as Josie unfolds the note.

Kahore he pouri ekore etaea ete aroha.

She looks up at Stuart. 'I don't understand . . .' She shows him the note. 'What does it say?'

'There is no darkness love cannot light,' Stuart translates.

Josie holds his gaze. 'I have to see him,' she says.

*

After her ward rounds, Josie leaves Mrs Stanten to close up the library and process the incoming requests. Promising not to be long, Josie hurries away, finally tracking down Dr Garland in the pathology lab, in conversation with another doctor. The women's heads are bent over a microscope, examining the contents of a slide.

'Dr Garland?'

The doctor glances up. 'Miss Everley? What brings you here?'

Josie tries to ignore the hint of sharpness in Dr Garland's tone: the woman is simply busy and doesn't have time for interruptions.

'I'm so sorry to disturb you,' Josie stammers, 'but may I speak with you briefly? Please?'

They step out into the empty corridor, and Josie pleads her case to visit Theo. Unable to confess the feelings she has for him, she instead tells the doctor that Theo's precious and beloved book of Māori myths will give him solace, if she can only read to him, just one story.

Dr Garland listens closely, her expression tired but sympathetic, and Josie's heart lifts with hope.

'I shouldn't allow you to visit the patient,' Dr Garland says, when Josie has finished. 'The fever ward is for highly vulnerable, potentially contagious patients, and we must control the spread of germs as much as possible, as I'm sure you understand, Miss Everley.'

Josie swallows a stone lodged in her throat. 'But I have to see him, ma'am. Just for a few minutes. Please.'

The doctor regards her steadily, and Josie has the

sensation the woman can see right into the darkest corners of her mind.

'If I grant you access, you must promise not to touch the patient.'

'I promise.'

'And you must remain no longer than ten minutes at most. Have I your word?'

'Yes, ma'am. Thank you so much, ma'am.'

The fever ward is in the south block at the end of a long, dimly lit corridor. Josie counts only six patients in residence, attended by two nurses wearing cotton masks and ankle-length white gowns. They resemble spectres, gliding between the beds. The blinds have been pulled across the windows, and the only light comes from shaded lamps that cast a muted, sombre glow.

Josie shows one of the nurses the scribbled permission note from Dr Garland, and is admitted across the threshold. A blend of smells assails her: antiseptic, a hint of sweetish pus, the ferrous underlay of blood.

'Wash your hands at the basin,' the nurse directs Josie. 'There's soap and a towel.'

Josie does as she's bade, and as she's drying her hands she notices how quiet and sterile the ward is. Unlike the other wards she's visited today, here in the fever ward no one is talking, or laughing. There's no banter between the men, no cries of pain. All the patients appear to be asleep, and the nurse has to lead Josie to Theo's bedside.

His face is a sickly shade of grey, his breathing fitful

and shallow, faintly rattling on each exhalation.

'Theo?' Josie whispers, not daring to touch him. 'It's me. Just Josie. Can you hear me?'

Theo's eyelids flicker, and Josie holds her breath, willing him to wake.

She senses the nurses' eyes on her from across the ward. Soon they will ask her to leave. She has only minutes. She draws out the little book of Māori myths that Stuart had given her earlier, and flicks to the very last story. It's the shortest, only a page.

She swallows, and in a quiet voice begins to read: *'Hinemoa was the daughter of a great chief who lived on the shores of Lake Rotorua. She was very beautiful, and many young men desired her as their wife.'*

A dense hush permeates the ward, broken only by the soft tread of the nurses' shoes, and Josie's hesitant voice.

'Tūtānekai,' she reads on, carefully sounding out the unfamiliar Māori name, *'a would-be suitor, lived on Mokoia Island, in the middle of Lake Rotorua. He knew his rank was too low for Hinemoa's father to accept him, so Tūtānekai hid his love for Hinemoa for a long time. He could see her only at meetings of the tribe, when he would gaze at her from a distance, and sometimes she would return his looks.'*

Theo's breath rattles, and Josie pauses, watching the rise and fall of his chest beneath the sheets. She wills him to breathe, as she reads on.

'Now Hinemoa did love Tūtānekai, but she too hid her love, thinking he didn't feel the same. This continued for many meetings, during which they spoke only with their eyes, until at last

Tūtānekai sent a message to Hinemoa, and she replied in joy: "Have we both then loved alike?"

Josie glances up again, to find the spectre of a nurse hovering. 'I can only give you another minute, miss,' the nurse says, her voice muffled by the mask.

Josie nods. '*Tūtānekai told Hinemoa to listen for the sound of his flute at night,*' she resumes reading, '*calling her to his island. When she heard it, she must take her canoe and leave her home. Hinemoa agreed, for she only wanted to be with Tūtānekai.*

'*Every night, Tūtānekai sat on a high hill and played his flute, and the wind carried his music across the lake to Hinemoa's home. But she did not come. Her people had suspected her intention, and pulled all the canoes high up on the shore.*'

Hectic spots of colour bloom on Theo's cheeks, his breaths rasping.

From the corner of her eye, Josie sees the nurse heading towards her again.

'*Every night, Hinemoa heard the sound of Tūtānekai's flute and wept because she could not go to him,*' Josie forges on. '*Eventually, she decided to swim across the lake to her lover. She took six hollow gourds and lashed them to her body to buoy her up. The night was dark and the great lake cold.*'

'Miss, you have to leave now . . .'

'Please, not yet,' Josie hears herself say, the taste of salt on her tongue.

She couldn't help Jem, but she can help Theo.

She will stay, until this tale is over.

She won't leave him.

'*In the darkness she could see no land.*' Josie's voice is no more than a whisper now. The second nurse joins the first, and the two women stand at the foot of Theo's bed, conferring in low voices. Josie does her best to ignore them.

'Her heart was beating with terror, but the flute played on, and she entered the water and began to swim.'

'It's time, miss.'

No.

She won't leave him.

'Having only Tūtānekai's flute to guide her, she was led by that sweet sound, and arrived at the island, where at last the lovers were reunited.'

The nurses loom over her, as Josie closes the book.

'Kahore he pouri ekore etaea ete aroha,' she whispers to Theo.

There is no darkness love cannot light.

| Issue No. 6 | # The Daily Dose | Price FREE |

What do our wounded soldiers here at Endell Street read?

Almost anything printed and bound within covers, is the answer given by the Librarians.

The Library is a model of its kind, its aim to provide what the wounded men want, not what they think is good for them.

All manner of books are demanded and supplied – fiction, poetry, magazines, technical works.

Literary novels are never forced on the soldiers, but are always available. Experience has shown that when a man begins on a better class of book he does not as a rule return to the old worthless trash.

Magazines, too, are much in demand, notably *The Strand*, *The Windsor*, *Pearson's*, *The Wide World*, *The Red*, *The Illustrated London News* and *The Sketch*.

Recently, the Library has had to invest in a large number of Nat Gould's adventure stories, as these escapist stories are proving addictive to many of our wounded men.

E. Lawrence

Book Recommendations

Stevenson, R. L.
Across the Plains.
(Lay Morals. Memories and Portraits.)

Grey, Zane.
Last of the Plainsmen.
(The story of Buffalo Jones, the preserver of the American bison.)

Robins, Elizabeth.
The Magnetic North.
Gold Seekers in the Klondike.

Jerome, J. K.
Diary of a Pilgrimage.
Idle Thoughts of an Idle Fellow.
Three Men in a Boat.

Runkle, Bertha.
The Scarlet Rider.
(Tale of a mysterious highwayman, full of spirit and adventure.)

PEOPLE WE TAKE OUR HATS OFF TO:

The British Navy. Ahoy there!

LECTURE

**Dr Jemima Short begs to announce her new course of medical lectures.
Tuesday next, in the Library,
on the 3rd floor.
Subject: Neuritis, and other
nervous diseases.
All welcome.**

COMPETITION

Can you complete this well-known proverb?

B_O_S/A_D/F_E_D/S_O_L_/B_/F_W/B_T/G_O_/

28

Edie – London

The peaceful, tempered ambience within St Nicholas Church is in stark contrast to the turbulent, uncertain world beyond its doors. As Edie inhales the scents of beeswax candles and dust, breathing in the atmosphere of reflection and sorrow, she finds herself thinking of the wounded soldiers next door at Endell. Hundreds of injured and traumatized men, each enduring unimaginable pain, each fighting for their lives, the medical staff battling alongside them, willing them to survive. Sometimes they succeeded, but too often lives were lost. Edie can't begin to imagine how Dr Garland and her colleagues bear so many deaths, day after day.

Five soldiers are being laid to rest this morning. As she's not officially on the hospital staff, or a patient or a family member, Edie hasn't had to attend Endell Street Hospital's compulsory church parades, imposed by Army Order, before. Neither has she witnessed any of the weekly funeral services. She's present today only to support Josie.

Edie steals a glance along the pew. Pallid and fragile, Josie sits flanked by the wiry figure of Dr Garland and the stouter bulk of Mrs Stanten. The young librarian has taken the death of a New Zealand soldier particularly badly, Mrs Stanten had confided to Edie a few days ago.

'Dr Garland and I are rather worried for her,' Mrs Stanten had said. 'Considering the loss the poor girl has already suffered.'

Edie had wondered how much Mrs Stanten was aware of Josie's past. She herself knew precious little, only that Josie had lost her younger brother in the *Lusitania* tragedy, and blamed herself for his death.

'She considers you a friend,' Mrs Stanten had gone on. 'I think she'd draw strength from your company, dear.'

Edie had nodded. Although she hadn't known Josie long, she'd felt an instant connection with her, a kinship of sorts. Edie had never had a close female friend before, a new terrain she's keen to navigate. What were friends for, if not to offer comfort and hope in times of need? Her thoughts turn to Stanley. There's no doubt in her heart that his friendship had saved her life.

As the last of the congregation take their seats, and the shuffling and whispering diminish to a heavy, expectant silence, shadowy memories rise in Edie's mind.

The stark stone walls of the church remind her of the workhouse chapel, in which she'd spent too many Sundays as a child, cold and hungry and bored. Church service had been compulsory for all workhouse inmates, unless there was some cast-iron excuse not to attend. If anyone was found to be improperly absent, their name was inked into the governor's Book of Names, and God help them.

Even after so many years, she can still conjure the governor's voice in her head, intoning grace before meals, reciting his interminable prayers at breakfast, and before every meagre supper.

The chaplain conducting today's service looks to Edie to be in his forties at least, and reminds her of a particular clergyman who'd preached for a time at the workhouse. Father Simon had had his own Book of Names, in which he'd recorded the moral and religious state of the inmates, as well as the progress and condition of the children he examined.

A sudden, clear image of the Lord's Prayer sampler that had hung on the wall of Father Simon's private office comes into Edie's head; she mentally slams the door on a slew of dark memories this evokes, looming from the shadows of the past.

The chaplain at the lectern concludes his opening address, and invites the congregation to join him for the first hymn, 'The Lord Is My Shepherd'.

The flock begin shuffling to their feet, and Edie glances around her, taking in the pews filled with hospital staff and patients. The men in their blue suits stand rigid, their gaze fixed on the chaplain with an appearance of attention. The women seem less attentive, many of the orderlies and nurses smothering yawns, their eyes heavy-lidded. Next to Edie, Dr Garland stands erect as a pillar, her drawn, wan face belying her exhaustion.

Edie turns her attention back to the chaplain, croaking the words of the hymn, as around her the voices of the gathering rise and fall in ragged harmony.

The service lumbers on, Edie barely listening as the clergyman regales his audience with allegories, likening his faithful Bible to an entrenching tool, his prayer book to a soldier's precious mess tin. Edie senses the men behind her shifting in the pews, muttering to each other. The talk of war doesn't sit well with them, Edie can tell. How can this clergyman not sense it too?

He soon changes tack, and begins to preach on what he terms the 'new womanhood'. Edie's ears prick up. What on earth was the man going to say on the subject?

'Do not regard those women in charge of the hospital as "playthings",' the clergyman intones, clearly addressing his remarks to the men in the audience.

Edie glances at Dr Garland. Her expression is stony, and Edie has a sudden image of her performing surgery in her operating theatre, surrounded by white-gowned female medics, men waiting on stretchers, the place a beehive of intensity, not one single whit of playfulness about the scene.

'Instead,' the clergyman drones on, 'I exhort you to regard the women as your own equals in every respect.'

From somewhere behind Edie comes a barely stifled sigh. Edie wonders if the clergyman is aware that Dr Garland, Dr Maberry and their medical colleagues are superior in terms of army ranking to their male patients. The War Office has made no secret of this, so why the clergyman is wasting his breath on the subject instead of talking about the poor dead men in the coffins behind him, Edie has no idea.

'Life must be taken as a whole, the sorrows and the joys . . .' the clergyman ploughs on, but Edie has ceased to listen, her mind turning again to Stanley.

She'll never forget their day at the zoo. It still feels like a dream. His declaration of love for her remains a secret flame, held safe in Edie's heart, hers and hers alone.

At last, the funeral service is over. As Edie steps outside she's greeted by the sun breaking through rolling cloud, like a blessing. The congregation rapidly disperses, Dr Garland, her staff and patients heading back through the hospital's gates. Edie remains with Mrs Stanten and Josie, the latter pale in the sunlight, her eyes reddened. She looks beyond exhausted to Edie. Grief-stricken.

Edie tries to think what she can say that might lift Josie's spirits. 'Would you like to go for a walk?' she ventures.

'A breath of fresh air will do you good, dear,' Mrs Stanten urges Josie. 'I can manage quite well in the library.'

Josie dips her head, which Edie takes as silent assent, and she flashes the older woman a grateful smile, promising they'll return to the hospital soon. She gently steers Josie away, south along Endell Street, a plan forming in her head. She'll take Josie to the river, it's not far, a chance to escape the crowds.

As they negotiate the busy streets, Edie expects Josie to ask where they're going, but she says nothing, her gaze fixed on the pavement.

They reach Bow Street, and Edie's steps slow as they approach the Royal Opera House. She touches Josie's arm, and they pause to gaze up at the grand classical portico.

'I've never been inside,' Edie admits. Neither has Josie, Edie learns. The American has seen almost nothing of London beyond her aunt's home, and Endell Street, of course.

They regard the opera house. The building has been requisitioned by the Ministry of Works, Edie has heard, and is now a furniture repository. She's telling Josie this when, as if on cue, a horse-drawn wagon carrying a team of labouring men appears. Edie and Josie retreat, as the men proceed to unload tables, desks and chairs from the back of the vehicle.

Glancing across the street, Edie spots two women coming down the steps of the police station. Both are wearing a uniform of skirt, belted tunic and a wide-brimmed black felt hat with the distinctive 'WPS' shield badge on the front. The members of the Women's Police Service stride off along Bow Street, watched by Edie and Josie, and a few of the labourers, who have ceased in their furniture removal to stare.

'Do you have women police in New York?' Edie asks Josie, as they walk on.

'There are matrons who help the police,' she replies, her voice dull and quiet, 'and I've heard some women do detective work. But they don't wear uniforms.'

They leave Bow Street, dodging vehicles at the treacherously busy crossroads, and carry on into Wellington Street. Edie can smell the river now, its distinctive brackish, sewage stench telling her it's low tide.

Perfect.

Five minutes later, they pass the Lyceum Theatre, and

Josie stops to read the billboard advertising the current play: *In Time of War*.

Edie has read about Charles Watson Mill's 'stirring military drama' in the newspapers. By all accounts, the play employs various devious tricks to recruit men to fight. In the interval, a message is flashed on the fire screen:

> *Your King and Country Need You.*
> *Lord Kitchener Wants You.*
> *Come and Enlist.*

Then a recruiting sergeant major steps on to the stage and gives a short speech about local enlistment. The four-act play is concerned with the urgent need for recruits to fill the numerous gaps caused by casualties in the present crisis, and at the end of the performance recruiting officers are poised to sign up enthused audience members as they leave the theatre.

Edie's stomach turns at the thought of innocent young men being lured to enlist, and pulls Josie away.

'Where are we going?' Josie asks at last.

'I want to show you something.'

They reach Waterloo Pier, and the arched bridge spanning the Thames. Edie leads Josie to a half-concealed flight of wooden steps, and on down to the strip of deserted foreshore. Before them spreads the vast river, glittering in the late-morning sun. Boats and ships ply the waters, and the cries of gulls and faint calls of the boatmen on the pier tending their craft carry to the women on the gentle breeze.

The river has always held a strange allure for Edie, its dark, forbidding depths hiding secrets she would never know. What did her ma used to say?

You can't step in the same river twice.

It had taken years for Edie to understand what she meant. A river was like life, constantly changing. Sometimes calm, sometimes rough.

'I used to come here as a nipper,' Edie tells Josie. 'Mudlarking. Found all sorts of things . . .' She waits for Josie's response, but the other woman is staring out at the water, arms wrapped around herself, silent. What is she thinking?

'Josie?'

Her gaze remains fixed on the river, as though hypnotized.

Edie's blood runs cold, as it comes to her now how Josie's brother had lost his life. She should never have brought Josie to the river, in the shadow of a bridge notorious for its suicides. She opens her mouth to suggest they leave, head back up the damp-rotten steps, when Josie turns to her, meeting her eye for the first time.

'I'd forgotten about the mudlarks,' she says. 'I used to watch them when I was a kid, looking for stuff in the mud, but my mom never let me join in.'

'I forgot you were born here,' Edie says. 'When did you move to America?'

'I was eight. Before Jem.'

They stand together in silence, watching the passing boat traffic, the sun glinting on the water. The breeze off the river is chill, and after a while Edie begins to shiver.

She's about to suggest they should head back to the hospital, when Josie speaks: 'What did you find?'

'Oh, all sorts,' Edie says. 'Coal and wood for the fire, mostly. But bits of treasure sometimes, too. I once found a broken clay pipe with a picture of Mr Punch painted on the bowl. And a porcelain eggcup. And pottery fragments from Roman times.' She scuffs the stony ground with the toe of her boot, resisting the urge to begin mudlarking right now. The freshly revealed shore is littered with broken terracotta tiles, lumps of chalk and flint, chips of glass, slivers of bone. 'Once, I found a complete set of false teeth,' Edie says, the grisly memory making her laugh now.

To her delight, Josie's eyes widen and she laughs too. 'What did you do with them?'

'Threw them back in the river,' Edie admits.

Josie's attention drifts to the boats beneath Waterloo Bridge, and she falls silent again.

'Do you mind me bringing you here?' Edie asks, after a moment.

Josie shakes her head.

'I'm sorry about Theo,' Edie offers, unable to think of anything more comforting to say that isn't trite or patronizing.

'Me too,' Josie murmurs. 'He would have loved the river, I think.' She pulls a slim book from her coat pocket, holds it out to Edie. 'This was his. Do you think I should send it to his family?'

Edie turns the pages of the little book of myths. 'Do you want to?'

Josie shakes her head again.

'Then I think you should keep it,' Edie suggests. 'For your library. Something to remember him by.'

Josie tucks the book away again, takes a deep breath, lifts her chin to meet Edie's tentative smile. 'Will you find me some treasure, Miss Mudlark?'

Edie's smile widens. 'How about we find some together, Lady Library?'

29

Josie – London

As the new year is born, hopes of an end to the war grow ever more remote. In the first week of 1916, newspapers report that HMS *King Edward VII*, the lead battleship of the Royal Navy, has been mined off the coast of Scotland. As January progresses, enemy airship raids continue over the country, and elsewhere in Europe Allied troops are evacuating from the ill-fated Gallipoli campaign.

Josie reads accounts of the expanding refugee crisis, and the endless lists of men killed, wounded or missing in action, and her heart aches. The weather reflects the dismal news. A bright, crisp December has declined into a dank, depressing January, with days of freezing rain and hardly a glimmer of sun.

But despite the gloom, nothing can dampen the mood at Endell Street Hospital, on the opening night of *Aladdin*.

Josie suspects half the hospital is involved in Mrs Stanten's pantomime. All week, the library has been busy with recitals and costume fittings, the place filled with industry and a feverish atmosphere of anticipation. Various members of staff, from the youngest orderlies to the most senior doctors, many of the more mobile patients, and several of Mrs Stanten's thespian friends have convened among the books to practise their scenes. Even the RAMC guards have been drafted in to help prepare the stage, paint the scenery boards, and hang paper decorations from the ceiling.

Somehow, Josie has managed to continue with her library work, keeping out of the way as much as possible, hiding whenever Mr Threadgill, cast in the role of Widow Twankey, looms in her orbit. The fleshy, florid man was born for the role, in Josie's opinion, filling the library with his booming voice and larger-than-life presence, making everyone laugh with his risqué humour.

To Josie's embarrassment, Mr Threadgill has taken quite a shine to her, unashamedly determined to coax Josie out of her shell and persuade her to sing a number in the forthcoming performance. Josie privately curses Mrs Stanten for telling Mr Threadgill about her 'beautiful' voice.

'How's my belle of New York?' Mr Threadgill had greeted her at this morning's dress rehearsal, snaring Josie as she edged her way into the over-crowded stockroom. Mr Threadgill had been half dressed in a voluminous pink frock and lace-frilled bloomers, his hair greased to his scalp. Widow Twankey's ridiculous horsehair wig was splayed on Josie's desk.

Janey Woolton, the actress playing Aladdin, was seated next to Mr Threadgill's hairpiece. Janey had paused in rubbing greasepaint into her face to roll her eyes at

Josie. *Here we go again*, the actress signalled, with a flash of a smile. Josie had smiled shyly back, as she mumbled a good morning to Mr Threadgill, and negotiated a path through the milling performers to the sanctuary she's constructed in the corner: her little bolt-hole surrounded by piles of books.

Janey Woolton takes no nonsense from Mr Threadgill or anyone else, Josie had noticed. Deemed a 'proper actress' by Mrs Stanten, Janey had played most of the theatres in London, always taking the principal boy's role, and Josie can see why. Janey may be slight, but she exudes a wiry strength, and her androgynous looks and tumbling dark hair naturally draw the eye.

With the performance only a few hours away, the atmosphere in the library grows ever more tense and excitable. The stockroom fills with children of various ages, students from Miss Conti's School of Music and Dance. The children are dressed as fairies and forest animals, though how these should feature in the story of *Aladdin* Josie hasn't been able to work out. A harassed music teacher is trying to corral the children, checking headdresses are on straight, shoelaces are tied, but her voice is lost in the rising chatter.

'Josie?'

She hears her name called, spots Edie at the door, and her heart lifts to see her friend. Edie beats a path through the capering creatures, joining Josie in the relative sanctuary by the window.

'Can you escape for a minute?' Edie asks.

Josie is halfway through re-stocking the book cart, but

the press of people has grown unbearable. She seizes Edie's offer of rescue, and they make their way out of the stockroom. In the corridor they meet Dr Garland and Dr Maberry. The doctors have finally managed to snatch half an hour free to rehearse their cameo parts.

'How are things progressing?' Dr Garland asks Josie. 'Is Mrs Stanten bearing up under the strain?'

Josie gives the doctor a half-truth: all is going well, considering. She omits to add that Mrs Stanten has wept on her shoulder on more than one occasion over the past few days, lamenting the ongoing problems besetting the pantomime: how the genie keeps forgetting his lines and granting too many wishes, parts of the scenery still remain unpainted, and too many costumes are still not finished.

'Are the rumours correct, Miss Everley?' Dr Maberry asks.

'Rumours, ma'am?' Josie meets the tall Scot's eye.

'That you've been persuaded to sing the finale?' Dr Maberry's eyes gleam.

'Oh, um . . .' Josie longs for the floor to open and swallow her. She's saved by the arrival of Mrs Stanten, who hurries the doctors away for their rehearsal.

'Now's our chance,' Edie whispers, and Josie gratefully follows her friend out of the library.

In the courtyard, the wind is too fresh to sit out comfortably, so Edie suggests they visit a teashop in Broad Street, one of only a handful still open.

'I've been asked to write about the pantomime,' Edie

tells Josie, as they make their way through the gates. 'Stan's coming to the hospital later, with his camera, to take some pictures. He wanted me to ask if you have any books on photography.'

Josie promises to have a look, as soon as the stockroom is free again.

'I've been wondering about the audience tonight,' Josie says, as they turn into Broad Street. 'All those seriously injured patients who can't leave their beds, it seems a shame they'll miss out, don't you think?'

'What about the new electrophones?'

Josie hasn't heard of these.

'They've installed a couple in the two officers' wards,' Edie tells her, though she admits she hasn't seen one in action yet. 'Dr Garland told me the men fasten receivers over their ears, and then they can listen to a play, or whatever else they fancy.'

'Like a gramophone, you mean?'

'Not really. The performance is relayed live to the men through their headphones, over the telephone lines, as it happens.'

This sounds extraordinarily complicated to Josie. She wonders if Edie has got the gist of it quite right.

They arrive at the teashop, and enter a welcoming fug of aromatic steam. Edie orders a pot of tea to share.

'Just think,' she says, 'if you sing tonight, your voice might come down the telephone lines, and all the men in the wards will be able to hear you at once.'

Josie pulls a fearful face. 'Why do people think I'll sing?'

Edie settles back in her chair, fixing Josie with her blue gaze. 'Don't tell me you're scared, Lady Library.'

'I'm not scared.'

'Really?' Edie teases.

'I'm not!'

'Prove it, then.'

'Is that a dare, Miss Mudlark?'

'I'm famous for my dares,' Edie replies, with mock solemnity, making Josie chuckle.

'Has anyone ever told you,' Edie remarks, pouring tea, 'you have a very dirty laugh for a librarian?'

'Stop it.' Josie presses a napkin to her mouth, trying to compose herself. Around them, the few other customers pay them no attention.

'So, will you sing?' Edie presses. 'You'd make Widow Twankey's night if you do.'

'You never give up, do you?'

Edie grins. 'Never,' she pronounces. 'And neither do you.'

Josie stands in the wings, peeping through a slit in the curtains, looking out over a sea of faces. The library has never been busier, the entire space packed with staff, patients and visitors. Most of the audience are seated in chairs requisitioned from all over the hospital, but more people are standing at the back, and there are even a few patients on trolley beds. At least a hundred people, she thinks. Her aunt Pearl is somewhere in the crowd, but Josie can't see her. So many eyes, all of which will be looking at her soon. Earlier, when Edie had found her hiding in the stockroom and had asked if she needed anything, Josie had been so nervous she could hardly speak.

It's too late for nerves now.

'Ladies and gentlemen!' Dr Garland calls over the hubbub of voices. A rustling, shushing quiet descends over the audience. Dr Garland, though slight in figure, exudes presence. 'It gives me the greatest pleasure to welcome you all to our library tonight, for what promises to be a wondrous spectacle of comedy and music.' She pauses, takes a steadying breath, and Josie is reminded that the doctor, like her, is unused to performing to such a crowd. She might be cool and calm when faced with a life-or-death operation, but standing on a stage requires nerves of quite a different sort.

'I would like to take this opportunity before we start to thank everyone for their hard work,' Dr Garland goes on. 'Thank you to Mrs Stanten, for penning the performance you are about to enjoy, and for all her efforts with the hospital's entertainment. Thank you to all the staff and patients for your support, and also our good friends of the RAMC, for lending a practical hand.'

Dr Garland pauses to allow a round of applause.

'But above all, I would like to give thanks for our wonderful library.' She spreads her arms to encompass the room. 'This place of sanctuary and hope has been a labour of love, and tonight, safe within its warm surrounds, you're invited to escape your worries, indeed, to escape the war itself, for a short while.'

A few cheers of 'hear, hear,' from the back of the room.

'So, without further delay, sit back and enjoy Endell Street Hospital's first ever pantomime – *Aladdin*!'

Act by act, the pantomime plays out, and Josie watches it from her corner, tucked away in the wings. She laughs at Widow Twankey's unashamedly camp buffoonery, gasps at the puff of smoke that magically accompanies the appearance of the genie from the lamp, looks on in awe as Aladdin holds the audience in the palm of her dainty, perfectly manicured hand.

When a troop of pretty young orderlies in soldiers' uniform march on to the stage to the barked orders of an RAMC officer, the audience whistle and whoop. Widow Twankey evokes roars of laughter in her pursuit of the officer, who finds himself subsumed by her enormous, lace-bedecked bosom, unable to escape the dame's clutches. His troop of orderlies abandons him to his fate, cavorting off the stage to ecstatic applause.

The fairies and forest animals caper about the scenery, getting under the cast's feet, but no one seems to mind, and as the pantomime rolls to its conclusion, Josie finds she's enjoyed the experience so much her nerves have almost entirely abated.

As her moment in the spotlight arrives, she's no longer afraid. Mr Carr strikes the first chords to 'The Belle of New York' on the piano, and Josie takes a readying breath.

'"When I was born,"' she sings, '"the stars stood still and blinked their eyes with wonder . . ."'

At once, her voice is eclipsed by applause. She sings

on, opening her lungs, and now the choir of nurses behind her join their voices to hers, and Mr Carr's music can hardly be heard above the women singing, the audience clapping and whistling and cheering.

And, for a moment, Josie's heart soars free.

| Issue No. 7 | # The Daily Dose | Price FREE |

Chief Librarian Miss Josie Everley's debut book *The Reading Cure* will be published by Messrs Methuen on 6 June 1916.

Miss Everley, a survivor of the *Lusitania* tragedy that occurred exactly one year ago today, has lately been in charge of the library here at the Endell Street Hospital.

She has dedicated her book to the memory of her brother, Jeremiah, and all those who lost their lives on the liner.

E. Lawrence

Book Recommendations

Beach, Rex.
The Ne-er-do-well.

(The story of a son of a millionaire, who is spirited away to Panama as a practical joke. His father casts him off and he is thrown on his own resources. Lively adventures ensue, with the hero falling in love with a beautiful Spanish girl.)

Porter, Eleanor H.
Miss Billy.

(In which the youthful hero proves to be a girl, much to the consternation of the three bachelor brothers who have undertaken to adopt 'him'.)

Nicholson, Meredith.
The Houses of a Thousand Candles.

(Underground passages, villains, love and mystery.)

FOR SALE
Picture Postcards – ½ d each – available to buy every morning 10 – 12, in the Library.

LECTURE

Dr Short begs to announce her new course of medical lectures.
This Tuesday, in the Library,
on the 3rd floor.
Subject: The Nature of Asthma.
All welcome.

COMPETITION

Can you complete this humorous limerick?

There was a fair doctor from Endell,
Who tried her utmost to mend all.
When men bashed her style,
She exclaimed with a smile,

30

Edie – London

Through the dank, dark days of February, Edie finds warmth and hope in Stanley's company. She can hardly believe her good fortune. The longed-for reunion heralds the end to her night terrors, and for the first time in months she begins to sleep through the night. Stanley's health is also fortified, his nervous attacks almost gone.

He doesn't believe in Fate, he tells Edie, but he does believe in second chances. 'You're my second chance, Lawrence,' he says.

'And you're mine,' Edie whispers.

As the days of cold and rain continue, Edie thinks of the poor soldiers in the trenches of France and Belgium, suffering in a sea of mud, and is grateful to be safe and dry by Stanley's fireside. While he reads books on photography borrowed from Endell Street Hospital library, Edie works on her hospital pieces. So far, the War Office has been impressed with the reports she's submitted, and Dr Garland has asked her to continue chronicling the progress of the hospital, to Edie's relief. If only Harry was here to share in her joy.

As Stanley's health gradually improves so, too, does

his parents' attitude towards Edie. No longer do they treat her as an outsider, but instead accept that Edie is crucial to their son's recovery. The damaged muscle in Stanley's leg, however, has left him with a permanent limp. His mobility is so impaired that it comes as a relief to them all when he's officially discharged from military service.

The question of what he will do now is discussed at length around the Chays' dinner table. Stanley's father, a railway engineer, offers to put in a word for him at the depot. 'They're short of drivers, son,' Mr Chay says. 'You'd only have to turn up and the job's yours.'

'I'll give it some thought,' Stanley promises.

'You do that, son.'

'Thinking about it, if I worked at Maida Vale, you could work with me,' Stanley says, grinning at Edie across the table.

'The Ladies' Tube Station?' Mrs Chay chips in. 'Run by women, isn't it?'

'Been operational since last summer,' Mr Chay confirms. 'The ladies do a grand job, but of course they can't drive the trains.'

Not yet maybe, Edie thinks, but soon they will.

She meets Stanley's shining eyes, and they share a smile.

At the end of February, with the newspapers full of the Battle of Verdun, Harry finally returns home. His unexpected appearance at breakfast one morning is such a shock, Edie fears she's seeing his ghost in the doorway.

Mary recovers faster, and bursts into tears as Harry folds her into an embrace.

Edie looks on, as the couple hold each other. 'I'm so sorry, Mary,' Harry says. 'I meant to send word, but I've hardly had time to draw breath.'

They release each other, and Mary shows her forgiveness by preparing Harry a huge breakfast, using the last of the eggs and a rare rasher of bacon she'd been saving for dinner.

'How have you been?' Harry says, turning to Edie.

She can still hardly speak for shock. 'I found Stan,' she manages.

Harry is silent a moment, digesting Edie's words. 'I couldn't have asked for better news,' he says at last. His keen eyes hold hers. 'And how is your pal?'

'He's had shell shock,' Edie tells him. 'He was recovering at home, which was why we couldn't find him. But then he had a relapse, and Queen Square took him in, and that's where I found him. But he's much better now, and his father is going to get him a job on the railways . . .'

'I might have another suggestion,' Harry says. 'I need an official photographer. Do you think he might be interested?'

Edie has no doubt Stan will jump at the chance. 'He's coming here later,' she tells Harry. 'You can ask him yourself.'

The journalist raises one silver eyebrow, and Edie blushes. 'Is there something you're not telling me, young lady?'

'Now, Harry, don't tease the poor girl,' Mary scolds.

Edie is unable to prevent the grin that spreads across her face.

'Well, well,' Harry laughs, 'you have been busy, little scribe.'

Epilogue

June 1916

The entire library is swathed in bunting, hundreds of cotton triangles in red, white and blue strung from corner to corner, hand-stitched by the patients. Bunches of flowers adorn the writing desks ranged along the edges of the room, with more blooms filling the shelves of the bookcases. In the centre of the space, the billiard table heaves with plates of sandwiches, towers of cakes, puddings and desserts.

Edie looks on in breathless wonder. Josie has gone to so much trouble. Where has all the food come from? She grips Stanley's hand tighter, as they are welcomed into the crowded room. So many staff and patients have come to celebrate her and Stanley's wedding, and the atmosphere in the library is electric. Quite a contrast with the marriage ceremony next door at St Nicholas Church.

The service had been brief, with only Stanley's parents, Dr Garland, Dr Maberry, the Levinsons, Susan, Josie and Mrs Stanten present. Harry had given Edie away, and Dr Garland had read out a short poem by Elizabeth Barrett Browning that had brought tears to everyone's eyes.

How do I love thee? Let me count the ways.

Mary had hand-sewn Edie's wedding dress, using some ivory silk she had stored away in the attic for her granddaughters. 'I can always get more,' she had assured Edie.

Mary had spent several evenings stitching tiny silk roses around the waist and over one hip of the dress, and lining the bodice with extra cotton for Edie's comfort. Alexandra had lent Edie a pretty lace shawl, and Abigail had donated a dainty pair of slippers that are just a tiny bit too big.

Edie's outfit today is a world away from her khaki army uniform. For a moment, she thinks of her mother, wishing she could be here to witness her daughter so happy. Tears spring to her eyes and she desperately blinks them away, as the room fills with applause and whistles, everyone looking at her and Stanley.

To be here in this library, surrounded by friends, married to the man she'd thought she'd lost forever is a miracle, Edie thinks. She's the luckiest woman alive.

'All right, Lawrence?' Stanley whispers in her ear.

Edie can only nod, yes, she is all right, but this whole thing is rather overwhelming. Stanley squeezes her hand, and then his parents appear before them. To Edie's surprise, Mrs Chay embraces her. 'You've made my son whole again,' she tells her. Edie swallows, unable to reply for fear she will cry.

Mr Chay shakes his son's hand, and before Edie can react she is separated from Stanley, as his parents lead him away to meet more friends and relatives who have arrived.

She feels a light touch on her elbow, and turns to find Josie, with a younger woman Edie hasn't met before.

'How are you feeling, Miss Mudlark?' Josie grins. 'Or should I say Mrs Stanley Chay?'

Edie can't help but laugh. 'The happiest I think I've ever been,' she confesses.

'This is Miss Khan,' Josie introduces the young woman with her. 'She's our new library assistant.'

'Pleased to meet you,' Edie shakes Miss Khan's hand. 'How are you finding working with our chief librarian?'

'Miss Everley's been so welcoming,' Miss Khan replies. 'There's so much to learn, but I hope I can be of some help . . .'

'You're a great help already,' Josie assures her.

Miss Khan's cheeks flush and she smiles at her feet.

'With Miss Khan's assistance, I can concentrate on my new project,' Josie tells Edie.

'Project?'

'I'm writing a book.'

'A novel? Like one of Miss Godson's?' Edie thinks of the late librarian's novels, all now published with Harry's help and gracing the library shelves.

Josie shakes her head. 'It's not a novel, no. It's about bibliotherapy.'

'I'm not sure I understand.' Edie hasn't heard the word before.

'The healing power of books,' Josie explains. 'It's what we do here, every day, but I wanted to formalize it somehow. Follow on from the work Miss Godson started.'

'I can't wait to read it,' Edie says.

'You'll be the first,' Josie promises. She leans closer. 'I'm honoured to give the reading today. Thank you for asking me.' She produces a little red book from her pocket – *Māori Myths*.

'Theo would be proud,' Edie manages.

Josie clasps the book to her heart. 'A book can't know who will read it,' she says, with a smile. 'Or how its story can change a life.'

At that moment, Mary and Susan appear, and Edie is engulfed by fussing women. Josie and Miss Khan melt away into the crowd, as Mary tucks and smoothes Edie's dress, and Susan straightens the lace shawl that has slipped down one shoulder.

'Now, don't be nervous, dear,' Mary says, tidying a wayward strand of hair behind Edie's ear.

'I'm fine, really,' Edie assures her. It's almost true. She's trying not to think about having to stand on the stage in front of all these people.

'Take deep breaths,' Mary says, as if Edie hasn't spoken. 'Think brave thoughts . . .'

She's interrupted by Dr Maberry calling for attention, and moments later Edie finds herself reunited with Stanley, as the two of them are led on to the stage to join Dr Garland, who addresses the gathering: 'Stanley and Edie have asked that I thank you all for coming today to celebrate their wedding. I'm sure you will join me in wishing this young couple a lifetime of happiness.'

The crowd erupts in clapping and cheering, and Edie grips Stanley's hand as they beam at one another. Edie makes her own, silent, vow: she would go to the ends of the earth for this man. And he would do the same for her, she knows.

'And now,' Dr Garland concludes, 'our wonderful librarian, Miss Josie Everley, will give a short reading.'

With a flash of a smile at Edie, Josie joins them on the stage. She opens Theo's book, and clears her throat.

'*There was once a shellfish,*' Josie begins, her voice soft but clear, '*that carried a message of love from East Cape to the Bay of Plenty.*' She swallows, catches Edie's eye, and they share another smile. '*A young man had fallen in love with a black-haired, blue-eyed girl who lived at Opape,*' Josie goes on. '*Every day, when he was in the forest hunting, or in his canoe fishing, he would think of her. He yearned for the woman so much, he decided to send her a message of love. He chose a shellfish from the beach, and whispered his love into it. Then he threw it into the sea, hoping it might one day reach his beloved.*'

Josie turns the page. Edie senses the air thrumming, the entire audience waiting with breath held, every soul in the room enthralled by the tale.

'*The little shellfish was tumbled about in the waves. It sank to the seabed, and rose again, over and over, borne on the currents. At last, it reached the warmer waters of the Bay of Plenty, and was washed up on the shores of Opape.*'

Stanley squeezes Edie's hand.

'*The young woman was collecting mussels on the beach,*' Josie reads on, '*and she picked up the shellfish. But it was too small, so she threw it back into the sea. Somehow, the shellfish kept getting washed up, and the young woman kept picking it up, and throwing it away again. At last, she began to recognize it by the markings on its shell. She realized there must be something special about the shellfish so she threaded it with flax and hung it round her neck. The shellfish sang to her, entering her heart and filling it with love. And she remembered the young man she'd met, so many moons before. She understood that she was in love with him, and couldn't live without him.*

'And so she went to him, at last.'

Author's Note

The Library of War and Peace is my love letter to libraries. I've been a librarian for over three decades, and during those years I've worked in all sorts of libraries – public libraries, private collections, primary and secondary school libraries, and once an eighteenth-century haunted library. (I only lasted a year there!)

Books are in my blood, ink runs in my veins, and when I discovered the true story of the Endell Street Military Hospital library, I knew I had to write this novel.

Endell Street Hospital was groundbreaking in so many ways. It was set up in 1915 by Dr Louisa Garrett Anderson and Dr Flora Murray, two pioneering doctors who defied an initially sceptical War Office to establish their own Women's Hospital Corps.

Having created an all-female-run military hospital in France (which was the inspiration behind my previous novel *Women of War*), the doctors and their team saved thousands of soldiers' lives, and the War Office then asked them to replicate their successful model back in Britain. This Dr Garrett Anderson and Dr Murray duly did, renovating and equipping a disused workhouse in Endell Street.

From the start, their new military hospital had its own library, which was run by two prominent members of the

Women Writers' Suffrage League. The WWSL had been founded in 1908 by Cicely Hamilton and Bessie Hatton, the aim to obtain the franchise on the same terms as men, and its members sought to do this through writing.

Elizabeth Robins, an American actress and writer, was one of the first members of the WWSL, and its first president. The British novelist Beatrice Harraden was another of the organization's members and she served as librarian at Endell Street from 1915 until the hospital closed, joined by Elizabeth Robins for the first year or so.

The philosophy of Endell Street library was a reader-led one. The librarians catered for the patients' requests when it came to their reading matter, rather than imposing their idea of what might be termed 'improving' books upon them. Many men feared having their lack of education or complete illiteracy exposed, so the librarians would take the time to sit at their bedsides, talking to the wounded soldiers to find out more about their interests and background. In this way, they could make informed recommendations, as well as meet specific requests, and this became a unique opportunity to experience care based on books and reading.

The library was a huge success, and in many ways broke the ground for our modern bibliotherapy today. The art of healing through reading books continues to be a powerful form of therapy, and libraries play a fundamental role in this.

What more fitting way to honour libraries than in a book?

Acknowledgements

First, my heartfelt thanks, as always, to my agent Alison Bonomi. Your support along this writing journey is invaluable.

A huge thank-you to the editorial team at Penguin Michael Joseph: Hannah Smith, Nick Lowndes, Hazel Orme, and everyone working tirelessly behind the scenes.

Thank you to the Society of Authors and their Authors' Foundation grant, for helping to fund my research.

To my beta readers, Marian Sweet and Scott Goldie, your early input and continued support is massively appreciated.

Thanks once again to the team of librarians and volunteers at Alton Library.

Julie Ma – my remote writing buddy, who's anything but remote: thanks for always saying the right thing at just the right time.

Goldfinch Books: so much more than a bookshop, you're virtually family to me now, and I hope you know how much you mean to me.

Thank you to my long-suffering family and friends (you know who you are); I'm beyond grateful for all your support.

Finally, the biggest thanks must go to Darren, my very own Stanley.

On a station platform, with nothing to read,
and a four-hour train journey stretching ahead of him...

That's where the story began for Penguin founder Allen Lane.
With only 'shabby reprints of shoddy novels' on offer,
he resolved to make better books for readers everywhere.

By the time his train pulled into London, the idea was formed.
He would bring the best writing, in stylish and affordable
formats, to everyone. His books would be sold in bookstores,
stationers and tobacconists, for no more than the price
of a ten-pack of cigarettes.

And on every book would be a Penguin, a bird with a certain
'dignified flippancy', and a friendly invitation to anyone who
wished to spend their time reading.

In 1935, the first ten Penguin paperbacks were published.
Just a year later, three million Penguins had made their
way onto our shelves.

Reading was changed forever.

—

A lot has changed since 1935, including Penguin, but in the
most important ways we're still the same. We still believe that
books and reading are for everyone. And we still believe that
whether you're seeking an afternoon's escape, a vigorous debate
or a soothing bedtime story, all possibilities open with a book.

Whoever you are, whatever you're looking for,
you can find it with Penguin.